McSWEENEY'S
ENCHANTED CHAMBER
of
ASTONISHING
STORIES

Also from McSWEENEY'S

McSWEENEY'S ENCHANTED CHAMBER
of
ASTONISHING STORIES

EDITED
by
MICHAEL CHABON

Illustrations by MIKE MIGNOLA

VINTAGE BOOKS

A Division of Random House, Inc. New York

A VINTAGE BOOKS ORIGINAL, NOVEMBER 2004

Copyright © 2004 by McSweeney's Publishing LLC

Illustrations copyright © 2004 by Mike Mignola

Library of Congress Cataloging-in-Publication Data
McSweeney's enchanted chamber of astonishing stories /
edited by Michael Chabon;
illustrations by Mike Mignola.—1st Vintage Books ed.
p.   cm.
ISBN 1-4000-7874-1
1. Short stories, American.   I. Chabon, Michael.
II. Mignola, Michael.
PS648.S5M38   2004
813'.0108—dc22
2004054617

www.vintagebooks.com

Printed in the United States of America
10 9 8 7 6 5 4 3 2 1

CONTENTS

INTRODUCTION

MICHAEL CHABON

SUPPOSE there is something appealing about a word that everyone uses with absolute confidence but on whose exact meaning no two people can agree. The word that I'm thinking of right now is *genre*, one of those French words, like *crêpe*, that no one can pronounce both correctly and without sounding pretentious.

Among those of us who use the term genre to label regions on a map (sf, fantasy, nurse romance) and not sections of an atlas (epic, tragedy, comedy), there is a deep and abiding confusion. To some of us, "science fiction" is any book sold in the section of the bookstore so designated. The typeface and imagery on the cover of the very attractive Vintage International edition of Nabokov's *Ada* would look distinctly out of place there, with the starships and the furry-faced aliens and the electron-starred vistas of cyberspace. *Ada*, therefore, is not science fiction. Accepting such an analysis sounds like the height of simplemindedness, and yet it is an analysis that you, and I, and both those who claim to love and those who claim to hate science fiction make, or at least accede to, every time we shop in a bookstore.

Genre, in other words, is—in a fundamental and perhaps ineradicable way—a marketing tool, a standard maintained most doggedly by publishers and booksellers. Though the costly studies and extensive research conducted by the publishing industry remain closely guarded secrets, apparently some kind of awful retailing disaster would entail if all the fiction, whether set on Mars or Manhattan, concerning a private eye or an eye doctor, were shelved together, from Asimov and Auster to Zelazny and Zweig. For even the finest writer of horror or sf or detective fiction, the bookstore, to paraphrase the LA funk band War, is a ghetto. From time to time some writer, through a canny shift in subject matter or focus, or through the coming to literary power of his or her lifelong fans, or through sheer, undeniable literary chops, manages to break out. New, subtler covers are placed on these writers' books, with elegant serif typefaces. In the public libraries, the little blue circle with the rocket ship or the atom is withheld from the spine. *This* book, the argument goes, has been widely praised by mainstream critics, adopted for discussion by book clubs, chosen by the *Today* show. Hence it cannot be science fiction.

At the same time, of course, there *is* a difference—right?—and sometimes an enormous difference, between, say, Raymond Chandler's "The King in Yellow," and F. Scott Fitzgerald's "Crazy Sunday," even though they are both set in and around Hollywood at roughly the same period. A difference that consists not merely of details of backdrop, diction, mores, costume, weather, etc., nor merely of literary style, nor of the enormously different outlook and concerns of the respective writers. If that were all there was to it, the distinction would be akin to that between *any* two books, chosen at random, from the shelves in the tony part of the bookstore: say Kathy Acker and William Trevor. (Keep that question in mind, though. Ask yourself just how damned *different* a book has to be, on the inside, from its neighbors, to get it consigned to the genre slums at the local Barnes & Noble. More different than *Moby-Dick* is from *Mrs. Dalloway*?)

No, there are the rules to be considered. These things—mystery, sf, horror—have *rules*. You can go to the How to Write section, away from the teeming ghettos, and find the rules for writing good mystery fiction carefully codified in any number of manuals and guides. Even among experienced, professional writers who have long since internalized or intuited the rules, and thus learned to ignore them, there are, at the very least, particular conventions—the shuttling of the private eye from high society to the lower depths, the function of a literary ghost as punishment for some act of hubris or evil—that are unique to and help to define their respective genres. Many of the finest "genre writers" working today derive their power and their entertainment value from a fruitful self-consciousness about the conventions of their chosen genre, a heightened awareness of its history, of the cycle of innovation, exhaustion and replenishment. When it comes to conventions, their central impulse is not to flout or to follow them but, flouting or following, to *play*. A great example of this is the British writer Terry Pratchett, whose giddy, encyclopedic, and ruthless knowledge of the history and conventions of sf and fantasy, in the service of a subversive wit and an elemental storytelling gift, has made him one of the UK's best and most widely beloved authors.

The genre known (more imprecisely than any other) as "literary fiction" has rules and conventions of its own: the primacy of a unified point of view; letters and their liability to being read or intercepted. And many of literary fiction's greatest practitioners, from Jane Austen to Angela Carter, Salman Rushdie to Steven Millhauser, display a parallel awareness of the genre's history and conventions, and derive equivalent power and capacity to delight from flouting, mocking, inverting, manhandling, from breaking or ignoring the rules.

Like most people who worry about whether it's better to be wrong or pretentious when pronouncing the word *genre*, I'm always on the lookout for a chance to drop the name of Walter Benjamin. I had planned to do so here. I intended to refer to Benjamin's bottomless essay "The Storyteller," and to try to employ the famous distinction he makes in it between the "trading seaman," the storyteller who fetches his miracle tales, legends, and tall stories from abroad, and the "resident tiller of the soil" in whose memory are stored up all the sharp-witted wisdom tales, homely lore, and useful stories of a community. Benjamin implies that the greatest storytellers are those who possess aspects, to some extent, of both characters, and I was thinking that it might be possible to argue that in the world of the contemporary short story the ""realistic"" (you just can't put enough quotation marks around that word) writers come from the tribe of the community-based lore retellers, while the writers of fantasy, horror, and sf are the sailors of distant seas, and that our finest and most consistently interesting contemporary writers are those whose work seems to originate from both traditions. But that claim felt a little shaky to me, and as, standing on the threshold of my thesis (by now probably obvious), I invoke the idea of playfulness, of mockery and inversion, the dazzling critic whose work I find myself thinking of most is Lewis Hyde, whose *Trickster Makes This World* rewards repeated reading every bit as endlessly as any work of Benjamin's.

Hyde's masterpiece concerns the trickster of mythology—Hermes among the Greeks, the Northmen's Loki, the Native Americans' Coyote and Raven and Rabbit, the Africans' Eshu and Legba and Anansi (who reappear in our own folklore in slave stories of High John de Conquer and Aunt Nancy), Krishna, the peach-stealing monkey of the Chinese, and our own friend Satan, shouting out, Who killed the Kennedys, when after all it was you and me. Trickster is the stealer of fire, the maker of mischief, teller of lies, bringer of trouble and upset and, above all, random change. And all around the world—think of Robert Johnson selling his soul—the trickster is always associated with borders, no-man's-lands, with crossroads and intersections. Trickster is the conveyer of souls across ultimate boundaries, the transgressor of heaven, the reconciler of opposites. He operates through inversion of laws and regulations, presiding over carnivals and feasts of fools. He is hermaphrodite; he is at once hero and villain, scourge and benefactor. "He is the spirit of the doorway leading out," as Hyde writes, "and of the crossroad at the edge of town (the one where a little market springs up)." For Trickster is also the god of the marketplace, of the city as intersection of converging roads and destinies, as transfer point, and perhaps that is why cities, Indianapolis excepted, have always been built at the places where incommensurates meet—sea and land, mountain and plain, coast and desert. Trickster goes where the action is, and the action is in the borders between things.

The word *genre* derives ultimately from a Greek and Latin root that can mean "people" or "nation" or "tribe" (whence also *genocide* and *gentile*). Maybe, as I suggested above, the most useful way to think of the various literary genres is not as discrete rooms in a house or red-lined sections in a bookstore, but as regions on a map, the map of fiction. I would put the country of romance at the center of this map, but as with all maps there is no real center, only a set of conventions. And as with the regions on a map, on the map of fiction there is overlap: sometimes it can be hard to say where science fiction shades unambiguously into fantasy, or horror into gothic romance, or mainstream literary fiction into any of its neighboring genres.

You could debate the configuration of this metaphorical map endlessly, I guess, but one thing that seems undebatable to me is that in spite of the continuing disdain or neglect in which most of the "nonliterary" genres are held, in particular by our writers of short stories, many if not most of the most interesting writers of the past seventy-five years or so have, like Trickster, found themselves drawn, inexorably, to the borderlands. From Borges to Calvino, drawing heavily on the tropes and conventions of science fiction and the mystery, to Anita Brookner and John Fowles with their sprung romance novels, from Millhauser and Thomas Pynchon to Kurt Vonnegut, John Crowley, Robert Aickman, A. S. Byatt, and

Cormac McCarthy, writers have plied their trade in the spaces between genres, in the no-man's-land. These great writers have not written science fiction, or fantasy, horror, or westerns—you can tell that by the book jackets. But they have drawn immense power and provided considerable pleasure for readers through play, through the peculiar commingling of mockery and tribute, invocation and analysis, considered rejection and passionate embrace, that are the hallmarks of our Trickster literature in this time of unending crossroads. Some of them have even found themselves straddling that most confounding and mysterious border of all: the one that lies between wild commercial success and unreserved critical acclaim.

It is telling that almost all of the writers cited above, with the notable exception of Borges, have worked primarily as novelists. This is not, I firmly believe, because the short story is somehow inimical to the Trickster spirit of genre bending and stylistic play. There are all kinds of reasons, many of which have to do with the general commercial decline of the short story and the overwhelming role, which I have only touched on lightly, that business decisions play in the evolution of literary form. But it strikes me—all right, it's the whole point of the exercise—that nearly every story in the collection you are about to read can be seen, in this sense, as a Trickster story. Some of them have been written by "popular" writers of "genre" fiction, others by "literary" writers with a feel, perhaps unexpressed before now, for "genre," and some by writers, like Jonathan Lethem or Steve Erickson, who have spent their whole careers at the boundary: "sometimes drawing the line," as Hyde writes of Trickster, "sometimes crossing it, sometimes erasing or moving it, but always there," in the borderlands among regions on the map of fiction. Because Trickster is looking to stir things up, to write serious, prizewinning, best-selling detective novels narrated by a sleuth with Tourette's syndrome, or an alternate history of Nazi Germany—that dusty sf trope—told by Hitler's private pornographer. Trickster haunts the boundary lines, the margins, the secret shelves between the sections in the bookstore. And that is where, if it wants to renew itself in the way that the novel has done so often in its long history, the short story must, inevitably, go.

McSWEENEY'S
ENCHANTED CHAMBER
of
ASTONISHING
STORIES

LUSUS NATURAE

by MARGARET ATWOOD

WHAT COULD BE DONE with me, what should be done with me? These were the same question. The possibilities were limited. The family discussed them all, lugubriously, endlessly, as they sat around the kitchen table at night, with the shutters closed, eating their dry whiskery sausages and their potato soup. If I was in one of my lucid phases I would sit with them, entering into the conversation as best I could while searching out the chunks of potato in my bowl. If not, I'd be off in the darkest corner, mewing to myself and listening to the twittering voices nobody else could hear.

"She was such a lovely baby," my mother would say. "There was nothing wrong with her." It saddened her to have given birth to an item such as myself: it was like a reproach, a judgment. What had she done wrong?

"Maybe it's a curse," said my grandmother. She was as dry and whiskery as the sausages, but in her it was natural because of her age.

"She was fine for years," said my father. "It was after that case of measles, when she was seven. After that."

3

"Who would curse us?" said my mother.

My grandmother scowled. She had a long list of candidates. Even so, there was no one she could single out. Our family had always been respected, and even liked, more or less. It still was. It still would be, if something could be done about me. Before I leaked out, so to say.

"The doctor says it's a disease," said my father. He liked to claim he was a rational man. He took the newspapers. It was he who insisted that I learn to read, and he'd persisted in his encouragement, despite everything. I no longer nestled into the crook of his arm, however. He sat me on the other side of the table. Though this enforced distance pained me, I could see his point.

"Then why didn't he give us some medicine?" said my mother. My grandmother snorted. She had her own ideas, which involved puffballs and stump water. Once she'd held my head under the water in which the dirty clothes were soaking, praying while she did it. That was to eject the demon she was convinced had flown in through my mouth and was lodged near my breastbone. My mother said she had the best of intentions, at heart.

Feed her bread, the doctor had said. *She'll want a lot of bread. That, and potatoes. She'll want to drink blood. Chicken blood will do, or the blood of a cow. Don't let her have too much.* He told us the name of the disease, which had some Ps and Rs in it and meant nothing to us. He'd only seen a case like me once before, he'd said, looking at my yellow eyes, my pink teeth, my red fingernails, the long dark hair that was sprouting on my chest and arms. He wanted to take me away to the city, so other doctors could look at me, but my family refused. "She's a lusus naturae," he'd said.

"What does that mean?" said my grandmother.

"Freak of nature," the doctor said. He was from far away: we'd summoned him. Our own doctor would have spread rumors. "It's Latin. Like a monster." He thought I couldn't hear, because I was mewing. "It's nobody's fault."

"She's a human being," said my father. He paid the doctor a lot of money to go away to his foreign parts and never come back.

4

"Why did God do this to us?" said my mother.

"Curse or disease, it doesn't matter," said my older sister. "Either way, no one will marry me if they find out." I nodded my head: true enough. She was a pretty girl, and we weren't poor, we were almost gentry. Without me, her coast would be clear.

In the daytimes I stayed shut up in my darkened room: I was getting beyond a joke. That was fine with me, because I couldn't stand sunlight. At night, sleepless, I would roam the house, listening to the snores of the others, their yelps of nightmare. The cat kept me company. He was the only living creature who wanted to be close to me. I smelled of blood, old dried-up blood: perhaps that was why he shadowed me, why he would climb up onto me and start licking.

They'd told the neighbors I had a wasting illness, a fever, a delirium. The neighbors sent eggs and cabbages; from time to time they visited, to scrounge for news, but they weren't eager to see me: whatever it was might be catching.

It was decided that I should die. That way I would not stand in the way of my sister, I would not loom over her like a fate. "Better one happy than both miserable," said my grandmother, who had taken to sticking garlic cloves around my door frame. I agreed to this plan, as I wanted to be helpful.

The priest was bribed; in addition to that, we appealed to his sense of compassion. Everyone likes to think they are doing good while at the same time pocketing a bag of cash, and our priest was no exception. He told me God had chosen me as a special girl, a sort of bride, you might say. He said I was called on to make sacrifices. He said my sufferings would purify my soul. He said I was lucky, because I would stay innocent all my life, no man would want to pollute me, and then I would go straight to Heaven.

He told the neighbors I had died in a saintly manner. I was put on display in a very deep coffin in a very dark room, in a white dress with a lot of white veiling over me, fitting for a virgin and useful in concealing my whiskers. I lay there for two days, though of course I could walk around at night. I held my breath when anyone entered. They tiptoed, they spoke in whispers, they didn't come close, they were still afraid of my disease. To my mother they said I looked just like an angel.

My mother sat in the kitchen and cried as if I really had died; even my sister managed to look glum. My father wore his black suit. My grandmother baked. Everyone stuffed themselves. On the third day they filled the coffin with damp straw and carted it off to the cemetery and buried it, with prayers and a modest headstone, and three months later my sister got married. She was driven to the church in a coach, a first in our family. My coffin was a rung on her ladder.

Now that I was dead, I was freer. No one but my mother was allowed into my room, my former room as they called it. They told the neighbors they were keeping it as a shrine to my memory. They hung a picture of me on the door, a picture made when I still looked human. I didn't know what I looked like now. I avoided mirrors.

In the dimness I read Pushkin, and Lord Byron, and the poetry of John Keats. I learned about blighted love, and defiance, and the sweetness of death. I found these thoughts comforting. My mother would bring me my potatoes and bread, and my cup of blood, and take away the chamber pot. Once she used to brush my hair, before it came out in handfuls; she'd been in the habit of hugging me and weeping; but she was past that now. She came and went as quickly as she could. However she tried to hide it, she resented me, of course. There's only so long you can feel sorry for a person before you come to feel that their affliction is an act of malice committed by them against you.

At night I had the run of the house, and then the run of the yard, and after that the run of the forest. I no longer had to worry about getting in the way of other people and their futures. As for me, I had no future. I had only a present, a present that changed—it seemed to me—along with the moon. If it weren't for the fits, and the hours of pain, and the twittering of the voices I couldn't understand, I might have said I was happy.

My grandmother died, then my father. The cat became elderly. My mother sank further into despair. "My poor girl," she would say, though I was no longer exactly a girl. "Who will take care of you when I'm gone?"

There was only one answer to that: it would have to be me. I began to explore the limits of my power. I found I had a great deal more of it when unseen than when seen, and most of all when partly seen. I frightened two children in the woods, on purpose: I showed them my pink teeth, my hairy face, my red fingernails, I mewed at them, and they ran away screaming. Soon people avoided our end of the forest. I peered into a window at night, and caused hysterics in a young woman. "A thing! I saw a thing!" she sobbed. I was a thing, then. I considered this. In what way is a thing not a person?

A stranger made an offer to buy our farm. My mother wanted to sell and move in with my sister and her gentry husband and her healthy growing family, whose portraits had just been painted; she could no longer manage; but how could she leave me?

"Do it," I told her. By now my voice was a sort of growl. "I'll vacate my room. There's a place I can stay." She was grateful, poor soul. She had an attachment to me, as if to a hangnail, a wart: I was hers. But she was glad to be rid of me. She'd done enough duty for a lifetime.

During the packing-up and the sale of our furniture I spent the days inside a hayrick. It was sufficient, but it would not do for winter. Once the new people had moved in, it was no trouble to get rid of them. I knew the house better than they did, its entrances, its exits. I could make my way around it in the dark. I became an apparition, then another one; I was a red-nailed hand touching a face in the moonlight; I was the sound of a rusted hinge that I made despite myself. They took to their heels, and branded our place as haunted. Then I had it to myself.

I lived on stolen potatoes dug by moonlight, on eggs filched from henhouses. Once in a while I'd purloin a hen—I'd drink the blood first. There were guard dogs, but though they howled at me, they never attacked: they didn't know what I was. Inside our house, I tried a mirror. They say dead people can't see their own reflections, and it was true; I could not see myself. I saw something, but that something was not myself: it looked nothing like the innocent, pretty girl I knew myself to be, at heart.

But now things are coming to an end. I've become too visible.

This is how it happened.

I was picking blackberries in the dusk, at the verge where the meadow met the trees, and I saw two people approaching, from opposite sides. One was a young man, the other a girl. His clothing was better than hers. He had shoes.

The two of them looked furtive. I knew that look—the glances over the shoulder, the stops and starts—as I was unusually furtive myself. I crouched in the brambles to watch. They met, they twined together, they fell to the ground. Mewing noises came from them, growls, little screams. Perhaps they were having fits, both of them at once. Perhaps they were—oh, at last!—beings like myself. I crept closer to see better. They did not look like me—they were not hairy, for instance, except on their heads, and I could tell this because they had shed most of their clothing—but then, it had taken me some time to grow into what I was. They must be in the preliminary stages, I thought. They know they are changing, they have sought out each other for the company, and to share their fits.

They appeared to derive pleasure from their flailings about, even if they occasionally bit each other. I knew how that could happen. What a consolation it would be to me if I, too, could join in! Through the years I had hardened myself to loneliness; now I found that hardness dissolving. Still, I was too timorous to approach them.

One evening the young man fell asleep. The girl covered him with his cast-off shirt and kissed him on the forehead. Then she walked carefully away.

I detached myself from the brambles and came softly toward him. There he was, asleep in an oval of crushed grass, as if laid out on a platter. I'm sorry to say I lost control. I laid my red-nailed hands on him. I bit him on the neck. Was it lust or hunger? How could I tell the difference? He woke up, he saw my pink teeth, my yellow eyes; he saw my black dress fluttering; he saw me running away. He saw where.

He told the others in the village, and they began to speculate. They dug up my coffin and found it empty, and feared the worst. Now they're marching toward this house, in the dusk, with long stakes, with torches. My sister is among them, and her husband, and the young man I kissed. I meant it to be a kiss.

What can I say to them, how can I explain myself? When demons are required someone will always be found to supply the part, and whether you step forward or are pushed is all the same in the end. "I am a human being," I could say. But what proof do I have of that? "I am a lusus naturae! Take me to the city! I should be studied!" No hope there. I'm afraid it's bad news for the cat. Whatever they do to me, they'll do to him as well.

I am of a forgiving temperament, I know they have the best of intentions at heart. I've put on my white burial dress, my white veil, as befits a virgin. One must have a sense of occasion. The twittering voices are very loud: it's time for me to take flight. I'll fall from the burning rooftop like a comet, I'll blaze like a bonfire. They'll have to say many charms over my ashes, to make sure I'm really dead this time. After a while I'll become an upside-down saint; my finger bones will be sold as dark relics. I'll be a legend, by then.

Perhaps in Heaven I'll look like an angel. Or perhaps the angels will look like me. What a surprise that will be, for everyone else! It's something to look forward to.

WHAT YOU DO NOT KNOW YOU WANT

by DAVID MITCHELL

MY THREE A.M. NIGHTMARE DISPERSED like a disappointed audience as I tried to find the Coke machine. A woman passed, in her fifties maybe, cuddling, saying, "All I want out of life is a good night's sleep." Too woozy to reply, I just smiled back. The second person I met at that sweltering hour was a barefoot girl of eighteen or nineteen, kneeling before the Coke machine, extracting a can from its cumbersome mouth. Pixie-nosed, Oriental, wearing surfer's clothes for pajamas, not an ounce of fat on her, bony as macaroni in fact. "You can't sleep either, huh?" I asked. Apparently she hadn't heard. I raised my voice. "So you can't go to sleep either, huh? We should throw us a party for insomniacs." The machine relinquished her 7UP but she still refused to acknowledge me. Her dead eyes bore through me. "Sure was a pleasure meeting you," I thanked her retreating figure. *Bitch.* But particles of the girl remained in the air. These I breathed in. Musk, salt, lime.

Back in room 404 my sheets were chewy with sweat. Jesus Molten Christ, where was the Hawaiian ocean breeze tonight? A double dose of aspirin downed with whiskey and Coke—revolting—helped my mind cut its tight moorings. Each lush leaf on the lime trees lining the Ganges at Varanasi, you once told me, houses a soul for forty-nine days before the soul is reincarnated. Did you make that up? Remember the crows on the floating carcasses, eating their rafts? I thought about the Oriental girl, lying on her bed, sipping her 7UP. Her blanking out of me belittled—erased—me more than any verbal insult. Oriental? Who knows? Anyone in Hawaii could be from anywhere, no matter how they look. Who was she thinking about now? Me? Doubted it, but. Hotel rooms store up erotic charge, and men sleeping alone are its copper wires. Once upon a time she would have smiled, stroked her midriff, struck up a conversation. One thing might have led to It. Was she sleep-walking? Or is my voltage weakening now I'm thirty-six? Mirrors are my friends no longer. Nightingale picks through my golden locks for gray hairs. I must laugh along.

"Not this way! *Not this way!*" Jesus Jackhammer Christ, who fell out of *that* nightmare? A minute passed, two, five, thirty, but I heard nothing more. Hush now, I told my wild pulse, hush, it's tomor-row morning already. I read *Confessions of a Mask* until Waikiki's tourists, elevators, juicers, chambermaids, toilets, showers, bellboys, lifeguards, deliverymen and waitresses resumed their appointed function in this three-square-mile vacation machine. My Marc Jacob shirt, I decided, should send the right signal to the police. On my way out through reception I was surprised to see not the miserable werewolf who had checked me in, but the Oriental girl from the Coke machine, reading a Chinese paperback with a demon doll on the cover. "Good book?" I asked. "Stephen King," she replied, glanc-ing up, but making no reference to the previous night. "Chinese?" I asked, indicating the book. "Me? The book? Breakfast?" As you know, my interpersonal skills include both patience and charm, so I learned that Wei is from Hong Kong and has helped her uncle in the running of Hotel Aloha since his wife killed herself one year ago. "Sleeping pills," Wei volunteered this detail. "Enough to kill an elephant." "How tragic," I responded. Uncle? If that hairy Caucasian belch really is her uncle then I really am Richard Nixon.

My attention drifted over the lost-property form like a balloonist surveying a strange city. Name, address, occupation. Occupation . . . how would "Dealer in esoteric memorabilia" sound? I nearly decided the form was a waste of time. Was that fat custodian of justice, picking his nose and wiping it under the seat of his chair, really going to get me nearer my holy grail? One Nozomu Eno at *Runaway Horses* and even Werewolf at Hotel Aloha were far likelier leads. In the end I wrote, "Trader," figuring officialdom may as well be on my side as not. Truth needed to be cut to size, however. The "missing item" I registered, therefore, was "an ivory-handled ornamental bread knife (approx. 40 cm) last housed in a flute case." That this knife was crafted by *the* Master Kakutani of Old Edo in 1868, I omitted to mention. That *the* Yukio Mishima had disemboweled himself with this very blade and attained his gory apotheosis on an otherwise nondescript November 25, 1970, I omitted to mention. That one month ago my business partner, Zachary Tanaka, was approached by one of the writer's ex-lovers, now an alcoholic dentist in Tokyo with debts up to his cancerous throat, for quick cash and no grief from the Mishima estate in return for this knife plus certificate of authenticity *sealed by Mishima himself*—verified by ourselves—I omitted to mention. That one week ago Zachary Tanaka had flown to Honolulu, phoned me in Yerbas Buenas to confirm he had receipt of the knife, then jumped to his death from the roof of Hotel Aloha here in Waikiki, I omitted to mention. That the dagger had not been found and that an ultranationalist emperor worshiper in Kyoto had upped his offer to ¥25 million—what, five years of police pay?—I damn well omitted to mention. "Ivory-handled ornamental bread knife, huh?" snorted the cop. "Is that for slicing ornamental bread?"

. . .

13

Wei studied her admirable reflection in two mirrors held in exact positions. "If you look at your face from different places," the girl explained, "you are reminded that we are not a Me, but an It who lives in a Me." I showed her your photograph, the one I took of you by your glider. "Never seen him." Wei shook her head. "Is he famous?" He is—was, I prompted—a Japanese-American named Zachary Tanaka who had stayed here two weeks ago. "So? Waikiki is Japan's national playground. Even we have *hundreds* stay here, every year, all shapes, all sizes," said Wei. Yeah, I said, but how many throw themselves from your roof? Wei did an *oh* face. "Uncle handled all of that. I slept through it, believe it or not. I sleep like a baby in this place. Ask Uncle about him." Disappointing. Werewolf was a last resort. Hotel owners are hustlers, and if "Uncle" scented how valuable this artifact might be, and if it *was* in his possession, well, it may as well be guarded by lasers. So I just asked Wei what happened to Zachary Tanaka's belongings. "The cops took everything," stated Wei. "It was just clothes and pilot magazines, I heard."

An hour in the creamy Hawaiian surf was an inviting prospect after a day of precinct offices. Were you on the bus to Koko Head, Vulture? Did you see that bullish ocean kicking up three-meter waves? Grace would say you were watching me lick up those spectacular rollers. For thirty pure minutes I achieved a state of grace with the sea. Everything I tried came off, but then, scanning the beach for admirers, I neglected a fundamental rule: Never rest idle with your back to the ocean. A godalmighty breaker crashed down on me, forcing me way under, where a churning riptide pulled me deeper. Stay calm, and normally the air in your lungs tells you which way is up, right? Not off Koko Head. No up, down, sound—save a dim roaring— and an inner voice lamenting, *Drowning, you're drowning,* and my lungs collapsing and ABBA, amazingly, singing *Supertrouper lights are gonna blind ya* to scenes flashing by. Not scenes of my life but of days after my death. Of my missing body, eaten by skipjack tuna. Of Wei or Werewolf reporting my absence to a nose-picking cop. Of Nightingale, assuming I'd bottled out of the wedding. I tell you of

my dip with death, Vulture, to illustrate my conviction that ninety-nine deaths in one hundred—accidents, disease, old age, you name it—are banal. There. My Big Thought. Only suicides can truly say, *Yes*, here *is my reason for dying, crafted by* my *hand according to* my *logic*.

A second breaker tumbled my puny ass farther up the sucking beach. Jesus Half-dead Christ, a gallon of Pacific or more I barfed up, then crawled to the high-water mark and lay prostrate and eyed the murderous surf. Funny, none of the other copper-skinned surfers had even noticed I'd almost died. A geriatric jogger passed at slower-than-walking speed, grinning at me without teeth or sanity. Finally I heaved myself over to my gear, then waited for the bus back to Waikiki. Another fundamental rule: Don't be caught on American soil without a car. My second reason for telling you all this is to explain the eat-now-for-tomorrow-we-die frame of mind of this week. If my cruelty to others is casual, I only follow the world's lead. And look, I'm paying for it now, aren't I? Oh, it's a fucking butcher's shop down here.

Nightingale called me from L.A., where she's spent the week modeling for a chain of cosmetic surgeons to check for the nth time about Not Having a Veil. Sure, honey, I crooned, veils are too Barbie doll. Nightingale went stony on me, so I agreed with whatever guff the bounteous moo spouted next, so of course that added condescension to my list of sins against womankind. Premenstrual sadism, I hope. The shinier the apples of attraction, Vulture, the wormier their maggots of repulsion. Afterward, I shaved, aftershaved with a Hugo Boss scent—an expensive mistake—put on my Paul Smith suit, waxed my hair and was leaving when I saw these words doodled on the phone pad:

long live the emperor i don't think they even heard me

You will recognize Yukio Mishima's final words, but I needed a minute to trace them to their source. That my unconscious mind

had not only digested his last utterance whole, but excreted it during an earwigging from Nightingale is further proof that our brains are dark globes lit by very distant stars.

Werewolf acted pissed that I'd assumed he'd know of Runaway Horses. "Bars spring up and die like weeds around here," he said. "Find it in a phone book." I asked him for a phone book. "Ain't got one. So sorry." All hail the service economy. Were his cracked eyeballs the last ones to see you? I was tempted to pluck them out to look for you, nickel-sized and inverted, impressed there. On Olohana Street I paid a Tin Man mime artist a dollar to direct me up to the intersection with Kunhio Avenue and down a flight of steps. Runaway Horses might have been any *gaijin*-friendly basement bar in Tokyo with a clientele three-quarters Japanese, one-quarter Western. I asked the barman if he had Sapporo beer. "Sure I do," he replied, opening one for me. I said, "Nozomu-*san*, I'm Vulture's associate." My clever opener shot my foot off. "That settles it!" growled the barman, "I'm changing the name *tomorrow*, new sign, everything, and *screw* 'Runaway Horses, Established 1998.' I am *not* Nozomu Eno. I am *Shingo Ogawa*, okay? *I* own this bar now. Eno skipped town a week ago. *Yes*, gambling debts. *No*, I don't know what stone he's hiding under. *No*, I'm not his friend, I don't know his friends, and *no*, his debts are nothing to do with me." The man went on in this vein at length, but I'd glazed over. That your last known lover disappears at the same time that this singular artifact vanishes into thin air pointed to an obvious conclusion. I persuaded Shingo Ogawa—just—to write down my details, in case Nozomu showed up. Then, casually, I mentioned an ivory-handled ornamental bread knife left here by another friend. Shingo Ogawa clenched his jaw. "Nothing like that here," he said, but I got a list of other Japanese bars you might have hung out at. One, I recognized from your last e-mail.

Bar Wardrobe, slotted above Waikiki Hula Karaoke Palace, was well named: cramped, dark, hot, varnished. Two inhabitants dwelt

within. One lay slumped in a pool of mahogany light, as if shot ten seconds ago. His companion was semiobscured by gloom. Was this Bar Wardrobe? I asked, just to ask something. Her nod said, *Stupid question.* When would the barman be back? She blew smoke over the snorer to indicate, *That's him.* Great. How could I get a drink? She shrugged. Well, how had she gotten hers? This time she deigned to answer verbally, "I have an arrangement with the management." So I clipped a $10 bill to the till and helped myself to a Kilmagoon and soda. No sign behind the bar of a battered flute case or a pre-Meiji-period knife. The woman lit a match whose flare-up lit a face younger than her voice. Hooked nose, defiant lips, Hawaiian blood or maybe Filipina, I guessed. Birthmark like a wine stain but my right hand brushed my left to confirm my engagement ring was in my soap bag at the hotel. Blemishes fasten memories. Don't *you* look at me that way, Vulture; when did you ever turn down a little entertainment? "You *are* a model," I began, "am I right? It takes one to—" She cut in. "Wanna hear funny joke?" Okay, I said. "Okay. Tall blond American marine walks into a bar in Manila, where he chooses a cute native girl. So lucky she feels! She, a trainee hairdresser in her first month in Manila, already on her way to luxury apartment in Beverly Hills or Honolulu. Not like cousins in sweatshops or worse. No way, not her. River of dollars, many drinks. You can't get pregnant your first few times, the marine laughs, later, on her back, then her front. A medical fact, he says. Sure, a warning goes off, but she's too drunk now to fight—stop me if you know this joke, okay?— and he *does* call her next weekend, and the next, and the next. 'My boyfriend this my boyfriend that,' she says to make the other hairdressers jealous. Three months the doctor gives her the news. You guess it yet? Pregnant as Queen Turtle. Funny, hey? Her boyfriend tells her their baby will be a beautiful Filipino-American son, okay, no problem, they move to California, okay. She weeps with joy. Good man, good father, not like her father, the fat sweaty incest pig. He promises to phone next night from base. Guess what? No call. Two weeks later an officer at the base tells her she isn't the first girl to be duped by an American saying, 'Hey, babe, I'm a marine, stick with me.' She has no one to discuss pregnancy to, so she begs and borrows and spends everything on a private clinic. Keep it secret. The operation is a five-star fuckup. Half her womb gets sucked out too. She can't stand for six months. Blood all the time. Well, this joke's over almost. Years later the same girl, she lives in Honolulu. She does hair for rich wives. Hears their chatter about husbands, about affairs, about babies. Some days she wants cut their wrists, some days hers, some days the wrists of this world. So. Whatever line you're to begin, don't. All of them I heard already, okay?"

"Do I *look* like a fucking marine?" I shut the door.

"What did you do to the *door?*" Monday night in room 404 was no more restful than Sunday. "What did you do to the *door?*" Hearing someone jibber at whatever stalks their dreams unnerves the lemon-yellow shit out of me. Wallpaper and paste is what separates our waking selves from those jibbering night stalkers. I padded down to the Coke machine at the end of the corridor, hoping to encounter Wei. All I met were black moths. Back in my room I took a round of aspirin, stripped, and watched my body in the mirror to see if I, too, was an It inhabiting a Me. The jury was out. I took the elevator up to the roof to try to see your last view, but the tiny access stairs were locked by the shiny new padlock. The replacement for the one you'd cut through. So I had to make do with sitting on the steps. Back in my room I read a story from *Death in Midsummer* called "Patriotism," where a military husband and wife commit seppuku together. Sex in death and death in sex. You loved it too; you'd underlined your favorite passages. I smoked a spliff but couldn't stop crying. Sadness is fertile and thorny and takes root in any soil.

Werewolf was all sympathy when I complained about my nightmare-prone neighbor. "The Holiday Inn's the eighty-floor fucker out by the lagoon. They insulate the walls there. Four hundred bucks a night. You'd like it. You'd sleep like a baby." Little wonder *your* wife checked out early, I *very* nearly told him. I walked to Shore Bird Beach Broiler for the breakfast buffet and the view of bikinis in the sun. Options *re:* Yukio Mishima's knife had dwindled to a pretty pathetic clutch. The police had not contacted me. In the *Hawaii Times* I saw that my personal ad—"Nozomu, contact me about Vulture"—had been misprinted as "Nozomi, contact me about vultures." Jesus Vegetable Christ. I caught a bus to Honolulu Center and spent the day making inquiries at various lost-property offices in museums, malls and the bus station, wherever I could think of; consulted the owners of antique shops; considered engaging a private detective, for ten seconds, before I realized how stupid I'd sound. Real-life *Maltese Falcon* quests are wastes of time. You do not find a lost object in a city unless you know *exactly* where to locate it, in which case it isn't really lost. The place itself got to me. Nightingale may love it here, models are paid to love Hawaii, but I wouldn't be sorry if Oahu sinks under a tsunami and soon. Palm trees are tarantula ugly. Honolulu is concrete ugly. Waikiki is glitzy ugly. Jetloads of Westerners microwaving themselves are pink ugly. Ala Moana Center, a monstrous cuboid vagina for Japanese tourists to ejaculate yen during seven-day orgies of spending, is unthinkably ugly. Mildewed side streets where syringes roll in weedy doorways of the Polynesian poor are just ugly, but fat vacationers paying fat prices for fat fat in fat seats in fat diners by fat parking lots of fat cars by fat freeways are ugly ugly ugly ugly. Wipe them out or wipe me out.

Nightingale called most evenings at nine. Matrimony, dear Vulture, is a political act. Don't look at me that way. Nightingale is attracted to my assets—depleted by the purchase of Yukio Mishima's knife— and I am aroused by hers. You Asians have always been pragmatic about this. Romantic marriage is a European fantasy, and Jesus Legal-aid Christ, we have the divorce rates to prove it. Fidelity is the smuggest elf of the love fantasy, so every evening by ten I was in Runaway Horses trying to get laid without lowering my standards too drastically. In L.A. Nightingale was shining up that Czech photographer's zoom lens, doubtless. Why should I mind as long as she is as discreet as I am? Marriage is a public act; sex is a private one. What I mind is that my forget-me-not eyes are not what they were. What I minded was Wei's mockery when I returned alone. What I minded is that Bar Wardrobe was locked by the time I scaled its stairs. Here's another Big Thought, one that most men do not know they know, although Mishima says it without spelling it out: Sex is not, as cliché claims, a little death—sex is man's *fuck you!* to death. When we are inside another body, death is not inside ours. Hence the absence of sex drives men to folly, lunacy or even worse.

Friday morning exposed a chink in my week's armored bad luck. Werewolf was perched on a hillock of angling equipment in reception, threading a fishing line. "Off fishing?" I asked, just as a galaxy-class SUV pulled up outside. Werewolf muttered, "No, it's my line-dancing morning," and left Wei at reception. Opportunity stuck its thumb up my ass. From a call box I got hold of Dwight Silverwind, telling him the hour of repayment was at hand, then sidled back to Hotel Aloha to watch where Wei put the key. When the call came her face went from complacency to worry in twenty seconds. Dwight can still work his magic, the fraudulent old prick. Five minutes later Wei went rushing out, carrying a document wallet and leaving reception guarded by Barney the dinosaur whose *Back at* . . . toy clock promised me a whole hour. One retrieved key and one deep metaphorical breath later I was in the back office, stashed with clutter from more prosperous days for Hotel Aloha. *Trespasser*, fretted Fear, *trespasser, trespasser*. Strung beads clatted as I passed into a lounge and kitchenette maintained with the minimum effort. The furnishings were bargain bin circa 1975. Fire escapes zigzagged the walls of the inner concrete courtyard. This rectangle of concrete must be where you fell. Here. Right here. Someone stepped over my grave. On the wall, a framed photograph held a poodle-cuddling woman in long-faded Hawaiian sunshine, perhaps at Lahaina. Mrs. Werewolf, deceased, I presume. No evidence of children, past or present. The bedroom housed an unmade bed and a dressing table hidden under bales of *Angler's Weekly* and *Playboy*. Well, Vulture, I searched in a cupboard of hammers, saws, chisels, power tools and screws in labeled boxes but no *seppuku* dagger or flute case; a bestiary of purple teddies, lime rabbits and lovey-eyed dalmatians; an empty fish tank, under mattresses, between folded towels, amid dead shoes and albums of fishing trips, inside an umbrella stand and casserole dishes. *Hurry*, nagged Fear, *hurry, hurry*. Possible footsteps from reception kept worrying me. How long had Wei been gone? How long before she smelled wild goose? Should I take every key I could find and search the entire hotel? Oh, impossible, a squad of spies would need a week. Then the reception bell chimed and a wheezy voice called through, "Frank? You at home?" I froze. The outer office door creaked. *Dildo!* shrieked Fear, *You left it ajar!*

"Frankie!"

I crouched down looking for a hiding place. "What you doing to yourself in there? It'll make you go blind. Ain't that why you bought Miss Slitty?" I scuttled under the table and beseeched the god of farce to do me this one favor but banged my head on a leg. "Frankie?" I heard heavy breathing. I saw his legs lumber by, close enough to touch. A bottle was opened, a glass filled. A magazine opened. A chuckle. "Thanks, Frankie, don't mind if I do." If he sat down now, he'd have a clear sight of me crouching here. My knee was killing me. Sixty seconds scraped by. Sixty more passed by before I suspected he might have gone.

Wei was in a royal bitch of a mood when I got back from lunch. "Those Immigration fatheads! Just after you left this morning, I get a call saying there's an inconsistency has been found with my green card extension, so present yourself immediately and ask for Olly Schmidt. No, no, it won't wait, immediately means *now*, so off I run and guess what happens when after *fifty* goddamn *minutes* my number finally flashes up? There *is* no Schmidt in Immigration! A Sampson, a Silvestri, a Stein, but no Schmidt. No one knows a *thing* about why I had to go there! Fatheads!" American bureaucracy for you, I sympathized, then steered the subject to the nocturnal disturbances on the fourth floor. Wei just frowned. "What shouting? I sleep like a baby in this place." Then what about her trip to the Coke machine the other night? Wei just gave me an *Are you crazy?* look. "I sleep like a baby in this place."

Nightingale called to check exactly when my plane got back to Yerbas Buenas, and to ask what I'd like for my welcome-back dinner. For an eternity of three or five seconds I contemplated telling her to marry someone who loves her back. "Peppered steak." I came to my senses, realizing there are several reasons why this information might be useful, one of whom might be Czech. "Your mozzarella salad, and you, my angel." *Jesus Gold-digging Christ*, I thought to myself climbing into the shower, *what a catch I am*. Brutal truth was, if Yukio Mishima's dagger failed to materialize, I have nowhere to fall but Nightingale's money. If she knew that, she'd call the wedding off. "I don't do cheap," she says. I can't afford to see her go. I don't do cheap, either. Fears of financial insecurity wrecked my shower. But what I saw on the bathroom mirror as I climbed out, finger-written in letters not yet steamed over, turned my warm skin cold:

<pre>
          d
        d   y
      d   y   i
    d   y   i   n
  d   y   i   n   g
  d   y   i   n   g   i
  d   y   i   n   g   i   n
  d   y   i   n   g   i   n   h
  d   y   i   n   g   i   n   h   e
  d   y   i   n   g   i   n   h   e   r
d   y   i   n   g   i   n   h   e   r   e
</pre>

Who? *When?* Dripping, I wrapped a towel around me, unlocked the door and looked down the buzzing corridor. *Who, me?* said the Coke machine. The elevator was climbing from 1F upward, not 4F down. Werewolf? Too subtle. Who else has a key? Wei? A joke? A threat? *Who?* A skeleton key? A cleaner? Another guest with a muddled-up key? The nocturnal shouter? But why that message? Back in the bathroom, the mirror letters were fading. Had they really been so clear? Isn't it more likely that room 404's previous occupant had drawn them on? Quarter-convinced by this, I dressed and wandered out for some air, for want of any other plan. Wei, far from hiding a triumphant smirk, was watching *Will and Grace* on a mini TV. Ten P.M. I wanted to speak to someone who knows me. Nightingale? Women attribute emotional calls to a guilty conscience. Jesus Null-and-void Christ, I miss you, Vulture. I found myself on a bridge over the Lunalilo Freeway, watching the lights in Pearl Harbor. Depression turns outdoors indoors. Dying in here.

Werewolf was at reception by the time I'd eaten and wandered back to Hotel Aloha. The scarlet carnation in the semen-cloudy vase had rotted to tampon maroon. My last-but-one night, so I had little to lose by getting out your photo and telling Werewolf I had a couple of questions. My hairy hotelier squinted. "So that Jap's why you're hanging around like a wedged turd. Well, ain't got nothing to say about *him*, 'cept I wish to sweet God he'd ended his misery in someone else's hotel. The paperwork he cost me! The favors I had to call in to hush it up." My request that Werewolf hand over those possessions which he'd "forgotten" to give to the police produced a row of browned fangs. "What're you saying?" Theft from a suicide is still theft is what I'm saying; that I knew about the knife; that I wanted it back. Werewolf chose a *lookey here, asshole* voice. "If I had *anything* belonging to that faggoty half-Jap"—he flicked your photo and I fought an urge to ram a pencil up his nostril and through his brain—"I'd probably drop it down the nearest sewer." I held his gaze but explained that your relatives would pay a reasonable sum for the knife's safe return. It has no monetary value, but it was a family heirloom. Werewolf went all *oh?* "A 'family heirloom'? Well, bless my bleeding heart, that changes everything. Then I'd *definitely* drop it down the nearest sewer. Will you tell Faggoty Jap's relatives that from me, during this dark and difficult time?"

The pyramid of mirror letters in 404 had faded away. Logic administered bromides: staying in a hotel where you died just two weeks ago, searching for another suicide's blade, wedding just around the corner . . . little wonder I was this wired up. I hadn't— haven't—gotten over what you did. Disbelief was my first reaction. You'd just closed a deal worth as much as Princess Diana's damaged diamond Rolex, second hand forever twitching on 8:17. More than the telegraph pole James Dean drove into. Mishima's knife would make us both wealthy for two or three years. You were the newest member of a balloonist's syndicate. *Please*, not a suicide. But the policewoman talked me through the coroner's verdict: the message on your mirror, *going down going down going down*, confirmed as yours by the state graphologist, to your prints on the wire cutter used to access the roof, ten other proofs, left little room for doubt. Nervous collapse? Compounded by your Mishima complex? But no. Doubt grows into counterfact in the tiniest crack.

"*Give it back!*" Percussive, savage, desperate. My limbs were sticky from sleeping in clothes. The shouter had been quiet for a few nights. I thought he'd left. "*Give it back!*" I called back, "Who *are* you? Are you okay?" No answer. I listened, I listened, I listened. I got up, crept outside and pressed my ear against 403. Silence. Against 405. Silence. Lights off in both rooms. On not quite a whim, I crept up to Wei's room and pressed my ear against her room. Her breathing? Or my own? Why did I feel that sense of being watched? Hotel Aloha has no CCTV. A black moth hinged its wings. Uneasy, I went back to my room and turned on the TV with the sound right down.

. . .

Saturday evening's Runaway Horses was fuggy with laughter, booming reggae and Asian-American youth in bloom. In my last clean Gucci shirt I took the very last seat at the bar and Shingo slid me my nearly last Sapporo in Waikiki. This time tomorrow, I'd be back in Yerbas Buenas with a business to try to rebuild. The Yukio Mishima Knife Book would be a bad passage in a disastrous chapter, but the main narrative would go on. A woman right by me cleared her throat and said, "I never thought you *were* marine. You're too stick-insect. They'd throw you out." Well, thank you very much, I smiled at the Filipina from Bar Wardrobe. She stepped over my irony. "I drank too many the other day, okay? Spoke too many too. What you learned, shush, is secret, please." Therapeutic to spill your guts occasionally, I assured her, and promised I'd never repeat a word. But my silence could be bought only by her name. Grace, she told me, and Grace took my Sapporo Black so I ordered another. Some loud Aussies across the bar shot me looks: rebuttees, I guessed. "So you live on Oahu?" asked Grace. "You a businessman or a tourist or what?" I surrendered to the seductive quasi-truth and told her I run a special business, one that never advertises, which obtains singular artifacts that are otherwise unobtainable. Grace was sharp. She asked how we got clients. Introduction only, I told her, unable to resist giving her a business card. She read, "'What You Do Not Know You Want.' That all?" I nodded, and told her I was on Oahu trying to locate a historic weapon for a wealthy client. Grace was fascinated. "Is all legal, your business?" I told her, "If we exercise discretion, the question doesn't apply." My codealer, I explained, had apparently entrusted this item to the ex-owner of Runaway Horses. . . . "Who," Grace filled in the blank, "is Runaway Barman now. Is hilarious joke, yes?" Hilarious, yes.

"Death isn't some faraway land, okay, at the end of time," Grace insisted several bottles later. I had no inkling how we got onto the subject. "Death is the white lines down the highway, okay, in your cutlery drawer, okay, in bottles in bathroom cabinets, inside cells of your body. Death, hey, we're made of the stuff. Death is the pond; we the living are the fish. So to answer your question, yes, of course, the dead are everywhere, and yes, they watch us. Like TV. When we interest them." Women love being asked if they are clairvoyant, so I did so. "Men *always* ask that," frowned Grace, "but intuition is just *seeing* and *listening*, is not being blind because it does not agree with culture or fashion or desires. Intuition is not mystical." Believing that the dead swarm around the living sounded pretty mystical to me, I suggested, if not morbid. "Buying and selling suicide weapons of your Japanese writer is not morbid?" Yes, Vulture, loose lips sink ships, but I haven't wanted a woman as much as I wanted Grace since you-know-when. "Such a knife will only attract devil's eye, no? Is obvious!" I said, Would she consider continuing our discussion in a less public venue? "Okay, sure, I consider." But when I got back from the bathroom, Jesus Mary Poppins Christ, her bar stool was straining under a German as big as a grizzly. *Gone*, shrugged Shingo. *Sorry.* I ordered a last beer to show those smirking Australians but dealt the bar a series of vicious toe pokes and hoped that Grace intuited each one.

Wei was drawing her self-portrait from a mirror and munching coffee-crusted macadamia nuts. "No, you can't have the picture," she said, handing me a piece of paper with a string of digits on it. "A woman called. Five minutes ago." The number was unfamiliar. "Not your Nightingale who sings every evening," Wei said, making me wonder if she listened in, "another." Hadn't the caller left a name? Wei shook her head. "Didn't you ask what she wanted?" Wei snorted like a sly pony and for one second I wanted to crack all her bony bones like biscuits in bags and see her sly smile *then*. Back outside, I tapped in the mystery number. Grace answered. She'd made me look pretty stupid in Runaway Horses, I told her. "You recover okay. Listen, I made one-two phone calls. If you still want that knife, I know someone can maybe help." Of course I still wanted that knife. Grace was coming to Hotel Aloha now. Through the glass, Wei watched me, fingers twizzling her braided hairband. I knew that look. Female jealousy is rich cream.

"Quicker to walk than to find cab." Grace led me at a brisk clip down poorly lit backstreets. She swatted away my requests for information, saying only that I was free to turn back anytime I wanted. None of the weak stars were familiar from my childhood astronomy. Was I being led into a trap like that time in Cambodia? Perhaps, perhaps. Through a doorway half-blocked with rusting junk we climbed five concrete flights, lit by lamps swarming with black moths. No view but other housing blocks and washing strung across balconies. Grace stopped before a nameless door. Monkey-wrench marks scarred the frame. To my astonishment she kissed me on the lips. Not erotically, not brashly, not shyly. Surely not pityingly? "What was that for?" Grace pressed the bell and ran back down the stairwell. Jesus Bodysnatched Christ—but before I could call out, a Japanese guy had stepped through into the milked moonlight, uttering my name, with your crucifix—it *had* to be, there's only one—on his hairless torso. Was I in room 404, dreaming this, or stuck in one of Dwight's fag-queen home movies? Certainly the youth was coffee-advert handsome, ponytailed, judo trousers, but he was stitched and patched from a very recent, pretty serious beating. "So you're here." His English was as American as it was Japanese. "Shingo told me you'd been into Runaway Horses. I, like . . . meant to call you"—he gingerly indicated his bruises—"but my creditors, like . . . changed the terms of repayment." His name came to me and I said it: Nozomu. Nozomu asked how I'd found him. Police sirens wailed from the dark mass under Diamond Head. Grace showed me here, I answered, gesturing at the stairwell, but even her footsteps had vanished. Nozomu frowned. "What Grace?" Grace the Filipina, Grace from Bar Wardrobe and Runaway Horses. Nozomu spat over the railing. "Shingo better not be giving my address to, like . . . no one. But you better come in, now you're here." I followed him into a poky apartment smelling of men, soy sauce and local marijuana. "I've only got, like . . . cold beer, but sit down anyway. I know what it is you come for. Don't worry. You're welcome to it."

Nozomu dug out a battered flute case from a closet of ratty towels, then shoved the moraine of surfing magazines and fast-food wreckage off the coffee table with his foot. "Vulture went to your seller's hotel, the Holiday Inn or somewhere. He brought it to my bar after closing. Never seen him so, like . . . high. Not even when he *was* high. When Vulture told me what it was, I was like . . . 'Yukio Mishima's suicide knife? Like, *sure*.' But Vulture showed me the Kakutani mark and I was like . . . '*Whaah! How* awesome!'" Nozomu unclipped the case and I assumed my professional calm. Twelve inches of gunmetal gray, blade tapering to a fang, shaft housed in an age-yellowed ivory handle. Just a piece of pre-Meiji ironmongery, but not. Events—grandiosely, "History"—imbue objects with a frequency just beyond the human ear, just. This frequency is our livelihood. The sunglasses shading Oppenheimer's eyes from the first H-bomb test in 1944; the shiny 3mm bullet that liberated Ernest Hemingway from Ernest Hemingway; and yes, Yukio Mishima's knife, radioactive with what it had done. I picked the weapon up—its lightness surprised me—and checked for the tiny characters "Kakutani" inscribed on its nub. There, the real thing, just as its certificate of authenticity promised. I very nearly laughed. "Vulture went back to his hotel to get some Big Island weed to, like . . . celebrate. But morning came and still no Vulture. I was like . . . 'He'll be back in day or two. For this little beaut at least.'" Nozomu meant the knife. "But I tell you, since he left it with me I got, like . . . an *evil* streak of luck. Every table I sat at, every game, every casino, hands of cards, good cards, strong cards, turned to shit. King Midas in reverse, right? My creditors cut my, like . . . lifeline, I lost my bar, oh, yeah, my motorbike got stolen the *day* after my insurance is finish. My fortune-teller, like, a guru really, told me today, like . . . 'an impure metal' in my life was, like, the source. Pretty, like . . . obvious, huh?" I grunted in sympathy. Your beautiful fool—still ignorant of *why* you never returned?—had no idea that he was about to hand me enough impure metal to buy his bar, everything in it and every*one* in it. "So it's no, like . . . bullshit? This dagger really killed Yukio Mishima?" The icy beer burned my fingers. "Well," I began, "Mishima *did* open up his abdomen with this blade, yes, but it takes hours to die from a single cut. To force one's innards out, a further cut is required, from crotch up to sternum. You'll appreciate, the subject rarely has the strength for this *jumonji-giri*, so tradition dictates that he—or she—appoint a *kaishakunin* to cut off the subject's head with a full-length samurai sword after the first cut. Mishima's appointee was a kid of twenty-five, Hissho Morita, a colonel in his private army of adoring boys. But with *jieitai* troops kicking down the door, helicopters thundering overhead and a tied-up general having a pulmonary seizure in the corner, Morita blew it and hacked at Mishima's shoulder blade instead. Morita missed *three* times, before a third compatriot, Furukoga, grabbed the sword and beheaded Mishima with one clean blow. So strictly," I finished up, "this knife is the shorter accomplice in Mishima's death, but the one with brains." TV laughter broke through the mosquito screen. I wanted to leave. There was no point giving Nozomu a sales pitch or the Mishima myth. "Why *did* Mishima do it? I heard it was, like . . . 'cos he didn't like how Japan was, like . . . Americanizing. But what difference could he make if he was, like . . . *dead*?" Millions of words have been shoveled into the grave of that very question, I replied, before parroting your theory: Yukio Mishima feared senility more than dying. By 1970 he felt his literary and physical prowess was sliding, so he exchanged his life for a piece of theater shocking enough, *entertaining* enough, to guarantee an immortality his literary canon could not. "Must have hurt like *fuck*," Nozomu muttered. "At least his death was *for* something," I said, replacing the knife in the flute case and getting to my feet. Nozomu asked where you are now. Werewolf *did* hush you up well. El Salvador, I lied to your last boyfriend. I'd seen you off from the airport here in Honolulu on

Sunday. Nozomu repeated, "El Salvador," like an orphan sighing, "When my father was alive . . ."

Is language erased, Vulture? Are quotations and word pyramids the last toys of literacy to go? You, who had a word—dozens, puns, similes—for everything, are you now struck dumb, Zachary Tanaka? Is this why you didn't warn me? Is this I heard only my own echoes? My key was in room 404 when I noticed, down the corridor, the PRIVATE door was ajar. Gone midnight. An invitation? You'll understand, I was jubilant with the promise of wealth. As you had been. Yukio Mishima's knife, in *this* flute case, under *my* arm, had sought *me* out, cutting me free of dependency on Nightingale, on orthodoxy. Come now, I assured myself, where's the harm in a little entertainment? One last time before a fling becomes adultery? Remembering the jealousy in Wei's face as Grace had led me to Nozomu's, I knocked on Wei's door. No answer, so I half peered in. Spray from a just-cut lime scented the air. Her room was identical to 404, even down to the print of the ukulele-strumming hula girl. "Wei?" Was she sulking? *Patter patter patter*—a poodle ran by, lead trailing from its collar. Rumors might scamper to Uncle if I dithered on the threshold, so in I slipped and closed the door. "Wei? It's me." A spine-cracked Chinese–English dictionary lay splayed. Clothes lay slumped on the armchair. Look. Wei's braided hairband. I picked it up and ran it between my nose and lip. "What do you think you're doing?" asked Wei. Jesus Cardiac Christ! The clothes on the chair *were* Wei, who now sat up like a big cat. "It says 'Private' on my door." Sex, or anything like it, was not going to happen. "Um, just making sure you're okay, Wei. You seemed upset earlier. But you're okay now. So. Off to bed. Early flight tomorrow. Ciao."

But the door was no longer there. You heard correctly. See for yourself. No door. Just wall. Where I came in. No door. No tricks. No *fucking* door. When I turned to Wei, unable to believe what my eyes and fingers swore was true, I knew my physical superiority counted for nothing. I got out the words, "How did you *do* that?" Wei watched me like a lecher in a strip bar. Fear choked me so I had to shout, *What did you do to the* door? Louder. *What did you do to the* door? Wei ran my seppuku knife between her nose and lip. But *I* was gripping the flute case. No. It lay open on Wei's lap. "How did you *do* that?" Wei pricked her tongue with the point. Testing. *Give it back! Give it back!* Wei proffered the ivory handle and my legs—mine yet no longer mine—walked me to her like an inexpertly deployed marionette. A muffled shout reached me from a nearby room: *"Who are you? Are you okay?"* but no reply was permitted. The It inside Wei is too strong for any battle of wills. You learned that, Vulture, when It made you scrawl on the mirror; cut the chain on the roof hatch; teeter on the lip; take one little step. It now made my fingers unbutton my shirt, buckled my knees, made my hand grip the ivory handle and aim the steel tip at my navel. Now I knew It knew what I feared most. *Not this way! Not this way!* It stilled my tongue. "Your hoax call from Immigration was entertaining." Wei's voice, not Wei's speech. "Did you find much in Uncle's room? Did you see Aunt? She still busies herself around Hotel Aloha." Wei leaned close enough to kiss me. "You're thinking, 'Why me?' Did those black moths you and Zachary used to dismember ever complain, 'Why me?' No, they blundered into the wrong room, at the wrong hour, lured by the wrong candle. That's all. You want cause? Effect? Logic? *Meaning? This* is the meaning, here. . . ." My right arm spasmed and the razor-sharp metal bored through my stomach wall. Left to right, *rip.* Severing cartilage, intestines, notching my spinal cord. Pain firecrackered, but the It in Wei kept my backbone erect and stopped the blackness swallowing the lights. It was feeding. My hand plucked the blade out and a jet of blood spattered like piss on the wall, I *heard* it, before the knife plunged back into my groin. My second juddering groan took a long time, hours, days, to burn out. Groin to sternum, *rip.* It arched me so my innards slithered out like a never-ending placenta, shittily, mushily. Now I was dead enough to glimpse you, Vulture. Wei's lips moved. *"This* is what you did not know you want."

VIVIAN RELF

by JONATHAN LETHEM

PAPER LANTERNS WITH CANDLES INSIDE, their flames capering in imperceptible breezes, marked the steps of the walkway. Shadow and laughter spilled from the house above, while music shorn of all but its pulse made its way like ground fog across the eucalyptus-strewn lawn. Doran and Top and Evie and Miranda drifted up the stair, into throngs smoking and kissing cheeks and elbowing one another on the porch and around the open front door. Doran saw the familiar girl there, just inside.

He squinted and smiled, to offer evidence he wasn't gawking. To convey what he felt: he recognized her. She blinked at him, and parted her mouth slightly, then nipped her lower lip. Top and Evie and Miranda pushed inside the kitchen, fighting their way to the drinks surely waiting on a counter or in the refrigerator, but Doran hung back. He pointed a finger at the familiar girl, and moved nearer to her. She turned from her friends.

The foyer was lit with strings of red plastic chili peppers. They drooped in waves from the molding, their glow blushing cheeks, foreheads, ears, teeth.

"I know you from somewhere," he said.

"I was just thinking the same thing."

"You one of Jorn's friends?"

"Jorn who?"

"Never mind," said Doran. "This is supposed to be Jorn's house, I thought. I don't know why I even mentioned it, since I don't know him. Or her."

"My friends brought me," said the girl. "I don't even know whose party this is. I don't know if *they* know."

"My friends brought me too," said Doran. "Wait, do you waitress at Elision, on Dunmarket?"

"I don't live here. I must know you from somewhere else."

"Definitely, you look really familiar."

They were yelling to be heard in the jostle of bodies inside the door. Doran gestured over their heads, outside. "Do you want to go where we can talk?"

They turned the corner, stopped in a glade just short of the deck, which was as full of revelers as the kitchen and foyer. They nestled in the darkness between pools of light and chatter. The girl had a drink, red wine in a plastic cup. Doran felt a little bare without anything.

"This'll drive me crazy until I figure it out," he said. "Where'd you go to college?"

"Sundstrom," she said.

"I went to Vagary." Doran swallowed the syllables, knowing it was a confession: *I'm one of those Vagary types*. "But I used to know a guy who went to Sundstrom. How old are you?"

"Twenty-six."

"I'm twenty-eight. You would have been there at the same time." This was hardly a promising avenue. But he persisted. "Gilly Noman, that ring a bell?"

"Sounds like a girl's name."

"I know, never mind. Where do you live?"

She mentioned a city, a place he'd never been.

"That's no help. How long you live there?"

"Since college. Five years, I guess."

"Where'd you grow up?"

The city she mentioned was another cipher, a destination never remotely considered.

"Your whole life?" he asked. Doran racked his brain, but he didn't know anyone from the place.

"Yeah," she said, a bit defensively. "What about you?"

"Right here, right around here. Wait, this is ridiculous. You look so familiar."

"So do you." She didn't sound too discouraged.

"Who are your friends here?"

"Ben and Malorie. You know them?"

"No, but do you maybe visit them often?"

"First time."

"You didn't, uh, go to Camp Drewsmore, did you?" Doran watched how his feelings about the girl changed, like light through a turned prism, as he tried to fit his bodily certainty of her familiarity into each proposed context. Summer camp, for instance, forced him to consider whether she'd witnessed ball-field humiliations, or kissed one of the older boys who were his idols then, he, in his innocence, not having yet kissed anyone.

"No."

"Drewsmore-in-the-Mist?"

"Didn't go to camp."

"Okay, wait, forget camp, it must be something more recent. What do you do?"

"Until just now I worked on Congressman Goshen's campaign. We, uh, lost. So I'm sort of between things. What do you do?"

"Totally unrelated in every way. I'm an artist's assistant. Heard of London Jerkins?"

"No."

"To describe it briefly there's this bright purple zigzag in all his paintings, kind of a signature shape. I paint it." He mimed the movements, the flourish at the end. "By now I do it better than him. You travel a lot for the congressman thing?"

"Not ever. I basically designed his pamphlets and door hangers."

"Ah, our jobs aren't so different after all."

"But I don't have one now." She aped his zigzag flourish, as punctuation.

"Hence you're crashing parties in distant cities which happen to be where I live."

"Hey, you didn't even know if Jorn was a guy or a girl. I at least was introduced, though I didn't catch his name."

He put up his hands: no slight intended. "But where do I know you from? I mean, no pressure, but this is mutual, right? You recognize me too."

"I was sure when you walked in. Now I'm not so sure."

"Yeah, maybe you look a little less familiar yourself."

In the grade of woods over the girl's shoulder Doran sighted two pale copper orbs, flat as coins. Fox? Bunny? Raccoon? He motioned for the girl to turn and see, when at that moment Top approached them from around the corner of the house. Doran's hand fell, words died on his lips. Tiny hands or feet scrabbled urgently in the underbrush, as though they were repairing a watch. The noise vanished.

Top had his own cup of wine, half-empty. Lipstick smudged his cheek. Doran moved to wipe it off, but Top bobbed, ducking Doran's reach. He glared. "Where'd you go?" he asked Doran, only nodding his chin at the familiar girl.

"We were trying to figure out where we knew each other from," said Doran. "This is my friend Top. I'm sorry, what's your name?"

"Vivian."

"Vivian, Top. And I'm Doran."

"Hello, Vivian," said Top curtly, raising his cup. To Doran: "You coming inside?"

"Sure, in a minute."

Top raised his eyebrows, said: "Sure. Anyway, we'll be there. Me and Evie and Miranda." To Vivian: "Nice to meet you." He slipped around the corner again.

"Friends waiting for you?" said Vivian.

"Sure, I guess. Yours?"

"It's not the same. They're a couple."

"Letting you mingle, I guess that's what you mean."

"Whereas yours are what—dates?"

"Good question. It's unclear, though. I'd have to admit they're maybe dates. But only maybe. Vivian what?"

"Relf."

"Vivian Relf. Totally unfamiliar. I'm Doran Close. In case that triggers any recall." Doran felt irritable, reluctant to let go of it, possibly humiliated, in need of a drink.

"It doesn't."

"Have we pretty much eliminated everything?"

"I can't think of anything else."

"We've never been in any of the same cities or schools or anything at the same time." It gave him a queasy, earth-shifty sensation. As though he'd come through the door of the party wrong, on the wrong foot. Planted a foot or flag on the wrong planet: one small step from the foyer, one giant plunge into the abyss.

"Nope, I don't think so."

"You're not on television?"

"Never."

"So what's the basis of all this howling familiarity?"

"I don't know if there really is any basis, and anyway I'm not feeling such howling familiarity anymore."

"Right, me neither." This was now a matter of pure vertigo, cliffside terror. He didn't hold it against Vivian Relf, though. She was his fellow sufferer. It was what they had in common, the sole thing.

"You want to go back to your friends?" she said.

"I guess so."

"Don't feel bad."

"I don't," lied Doran.

"Maybe I'll see you around."

"Very good then, Less-Than-Familiar-Girl. I'll look forward to that." Doran offered his hand to shake, mock-pompously. He felt garbed in awkwardness.

Vivian Relf accepted his hand, and they shook. She'd grown a little sulky herself, at the last minute.

Doran found Top and Evie and Miranda beyond the kitchen, in a room darkened and lit only by a string of Christmas lights, and cleared of all but two enormous speakers, as though for dancing. No one danced, no one inhabited the room apart from the three of them. There was something petulant in choosing to shout over the music, as they were doing.

"Who's your new friend?" said Miranda.

"Nobody. I thought she was an old friend, actually."

"Sure you weren't just attracted to her?"

"No, it was a shock of recognition, of seeing someone completely familiar. The weird thing is she had the same thing with me, I think." The language available to Doran for describing his cataclysm was cloddish and dead, the words a sequence of corpses laid head to toe.

"Yeah, it's always mutual."

"What's that supposed to mean?"

"Nothing, nothing."

"Look around this party," said Doran. "How many people could you say you've never been in a room together with before? That they didn't actually attend a lower grade in your high school, that you couldn't trace a link to their lives? That's what she and I just did. We're perfect strangers."

"Maybe you saw her on an airplane."

Doran had no answer for this. He fell silent.

Later that night he saw her again, across two rooms, through a doorway. The party had grown. She was talking to someone new, a man, not her friends. He felt he still recognized her, but the sensation hung uselessly in a middle distance, suspended, as in amber, in doubt so thick it was a form of certainty. She irked him, that was all he knew.

It was two years before he saw the familiar girl again, at another party, again in the hills. They recognized one another immediately.

"I know you," she said, brightening.

"Yes, I know you too, but from where?" The moment he said it he recalled their conversation. "Of course, how could I forget? You're that girl *I don't know*."

"Oh, yeah." She seemed to grow immensely sad.

They stood together contemplating the privileges of their special relationship, its utter and proven vacancy.

"It's like when you start a book and then you realize you read it before," he said. "You can't really remember anything ahead, only you know each line as it comes to you."

"No surprises to be found, you mean?" She pointed at herself.

"Just a weird kind of pre . . ." He searched for the word he meant. Pre*formatting*? Pre*cognition*? Pre*exhaustion*?

"More like a stopped car on the highway slowing down traffic," she said, seemingly uninterested in his ending the unfinished word. "Not a gaudy crash or anything. Just a cop waving you along, saying *nothing to see here*."

"Doran," he said.

"Vivian."

"I remember. You visiting your friends again?"

"Yup. And before you ask I have no idea whose party this is or what I'm doing here."

"Probably you were looking for me."

"I've got a boyfriend," she said. The line that was always awkward, in anyone's language. Then, before he could respond, she added: "I'm only joking."

"Oh."

"Just didn't want you thinking of me as Ben and Malorie's, oh, sort of *party accessory*. The extra girl, the floater."

"No, never the extra girl. The girl I don't know from anywhere, that's you."

"Funny to meet the girl you don't know, twice," she said. "When there are probably literally thousands of people you do know or anyway could establish a connection with who you never even meet once."

"I'm tempted to say small world."

"Either that or we're very large people."

"But maybe we're evidence of the opposite, I'm thinking now. Large *world*."

"We're not evidence of anything," said Vivian Relf. She shook his hand again. "Enjoy the party."

The next time *was* on an airplane, a coast-to-coast flight. Doran sat in first class. Vivian Relf trundled past him, headed deep into the tail, carry-on hugged to her chest. She didn't spot him.

He mused on sending back champagne with the stewardess, as in a cocktail lounge—*from the man in 3A*. There was probably a really solid reason they didn't allow that. A hundred solid reasons. He didn't dwell on Vivian Relf, watched a movie instead. Barbarian hordes were vanquished in waves of slaughter, twenty thousand feet above the plain.

They spoke at the baggage carousel. She didn't seem overly surprised to see him there.

"As unrelated baggage mysteriously commingles in the dark belly of an airplane only to be redistributed to its proper possessor in the glare of daylight on the whirring metal belt, so you repeatedly graze my awareness in shunting through the dimmed portals of my life," he said. "Doran Close."

"Vivian Relf," she said, shaking his hand. "But I suspect you knew that."

"Then you've gathered that I'm obsessed with you."

"No, it's that nobody ever forgets my name. It's one of those that sticks in your head."

"Ah."

She stared at him oddly, waiting. He spotted, beneath her sleeve, the unmistakable laminated wristlet of a hospital stay, imprinted *Relf, Vivian, Rm 315*.

"I'd propose we share a cab, but friends are waiting to pick me up in the white zone." He jerked his thumb at the curb.

"The odds are we're anyway pointed in incompatible directions."

"Ah, if I've learned anything at all in this life it's not to monkey with the odds."

There was a commotion. Some sort of clog at the mouth where baggage was disgorged. An impatient commuter clambered up to straddle the chugging belt. He rolled up suit sleeves and tugged the jammed suitcases out of the chute. The backlog tumbled loose, a miniature avalanche. Doran's suitcase was among those freed. Vivian Relf still waited, peering into the hole as though at a distant horizon. Doran left her there, feeling giddy.

All that week, between appointments with art collectors and gallerists, he spied for her in the museums and bistros of the vast metropolis, plagued by the ghost of certainty they'd come here, to this far place, this neutral site, *apart-but-together*, in order to forge some long-delayed truce or compact. The shrouded visages of the locals formed a kind of brick wall, an edifice which met his gaze everywhere: forehead, eyebrows, glasses, grim-drawn lips, cell phones, sandwiches. Against this background she'd have blazed like a sun. But never appeared.

> Oh Vivian Relf! Oh eclipse, oh pale penumbra of my
> yearning!
> Pink slip, eviction notice, deleted icon, oh!
> Stalked in alleys of my absent noons, there's nobody
> knows you better than I!
> Translucent voracious Relf-self, I vow here

Never again once to murk you
With pallid tropes of *familiarity* or *recognition*
You, pure apparition, onion—
Veil of veils only!

Doran Close, in his capacity as director of acquisitions in Draw-
ings and Prints, had several times had lunch with Vander Polymus, the editor of *Wall Art*. He'd heard Polymus mention that
he, Polymus, was married. He'd never met the man's wife, though,
and it was a surprise, as he stepped across Polymus's threshold for
the dinner party, bottle of cabernet franc in a scarf of tissue thrust
forward in greeting, to discover that the amiable ogre was married
to someone he recognized. Not from some previous museum fete
or gallery opening, but from another life, another frame of reference, years before. Really, from another postulated version of his
life, his sense, once, of who he'd be. He knew her despite the boy-
ishly short haircut, the jarring slash of lipstick and bruises of
eyeshadow, the freight of silver bracelets: Vander Polymus was
married to Vivian Relf.

Meeting her eyes, Doran unconsciously reached up and
brushed his fingertips to his shaved skull.

"Doran, Viv," said Polymus, grabbing Doran by the shoulder
and tugging him inside. "Throw your coat on the bed; I'll take
that. C'mon. Hope you like pernil and bacalao!"

"Hello," she said, and as Doran relinquished the bottle she
took his hand to shake.

"Vivian Relf," said Doran.

"Vivian Polymus," she confirmed.

"Shall we pry open your bottle?" said Vander Polymus. "Is it
something special? I've got a rioja I'm itching to sample. You know
each other?"

"We met, once," said Vivian. "Other side of the world."

Doran wanted to emend her *once*, but couldn't find his voice.

"Did you fucking fuck my wife?" chortled Polymus, fingers

combing his beard. "You'll have to tell me all about it, but save it for dinner. There's people I want you to meet."

So came the accustomed hurdles: the bottles opened and appreciated; the little dinner-party geometries—*No, but of course I know your name* or *If I'm not wrong your gallery represents my dear friend Zeus*; the hard and runny cheeses and the bowl of aggravatingly addictive salted nuts; the dawning apprehension that a single woman in the party of eight had been tipped his way by the scheming Polymus and another couple, who'd brought her along—much as, so long ago, Vivian Relf had been shopped at parties by the couple she'd been visiting. Hurdles? Really these were placed low as croquet wickets. Yet they had to be negotiated for a time, deftly, with a smile, before Doran could at last find himself seated. Beside the single woman, of course, but gratefully, as well, across from Polymus's wife. Vivian Relf.

He raised his glass to her, slightly, wishing to draw her nearer, wishing they could tip their heads together for murmuring.

"I used to think I'd keep running into you forever," he said.

She only smiled. Her husband intruded from the end of the table, his voice commanding. "What is it with you two?" Irrationally, Polymus's own impatience seemed to encompass the years since Doran and Vivian's first meeting, the otherwise forgettable, and forgotten, party. Doran wondered if anyone else on the planet had reason to recall that vanished archipelago of fume, conversation, and disco, tonight or ever. The ancient party was like a radio signal dopplering through outer space, it seemed to him now.

"You fuck him, Viv?" said Polymus. "Inquiring minds want to know."

"No," said Vivian Relf-Polymus. "No, but we were probably flirting. This was a long time ago."

Polymus and his wife had captured the attention of the whole table, with evident mutual pleasure.

"We had this funny thing," Doran felt compelled to explain.

"You remember? We didn't know anyone in common. You seemed really familiar, but we'd never met before."

This drew a handful of polite laughs, cued principally by the word *funny*, and perhaps by Doran's jocular tone. Beneath it he felt desperate. Vander Polymus only scowled, as for comic effect he might scowl at an awkwardly hung painting, or at a critical notice with which he violently disagreed.

"What I remember is you had these awful friends," said Vivian. "They didn't hesitate to show they found me a poor way for you to be spending your time. What was that tall moody boy's name?"

"Top," said Doran, only remembering as he blurted it. He hadn't thought of Top for years, had in fact forgotten Top was present at the Vivian Relf Party.

"Were you breaking up with some girl that night?"

"No," said Doran. "Nothing like that." He couldn't remember.

"If looks could kill."

Those people mean nothing to me, Doran wished to cry. *They barely did at the time.* And now, what was it, ten years later? It was Vivian Relf who mattered, couldn't she see?

"Do you remember the airport?" he asked.

"Ah, the *airport*," said Polymus, with a connoisseur's sarcasm. "Now we're getting somewhere. Tell us about the airport."

The table chuckled nervously, all in deference to their host.

"I haven't the faintest idea what he's talking about, my love."

"It's nothing," said Doran. "I saw you, ah, at an airport once." He suddenly wished to diminish it, in present company. He saw now that something precious was being taken from him in full view, a treasure he'd found in his possession only at the instant it was squandered. *I wrote a poem to you once, Vivian Relf*, he said silently, behind a sip of excellent rioja. Doran knew it was finer, much more interesting, than the wine he'd brought, the cabernet franc they'd sipped with their appetizers.

He might have known Vivian Relf better than anyone he actually knew, Doran thought now. Or anyway, he'd wanted to. It ought to mean the same thing. His soul creaked in irrelevant despair.

"This is boring," pronounced Vander Polymus.

The dinner party rose up and swallowed them, as it was meant to.

MINNOW

by AYELET WALDMAN

SHE WOULD DO HIM THE FAVOR, she thought, of letting him help her up the stairs. Matt held her around her waist, his arm stiff, his hand cool even through the fabric of her maternity shirt. Edie gazed along the narrow upstairs hallway, the walls hung with photographs all framed in matching gold leaf. Edie in her wedding gown, her eyes demurely fixed on the bouquet of tuberoses and orchids in her hands, a small smile playing on her lips, a gentle haze over the image as though the photographer had rubbed his lens with Vaseline. Matt in his hockey uniform, mugging for the camera, his gloved hand looped around the neck of a masked goalie. Matt in his long black cap and gown, holding his law school diploma up over his head in one hand and his young half sister upside down with the other, her shoe leaving a trail of gray mud along the smocked yoke of his gown. A magazine photograph of Edie and her two sisters from their modeling years: three little girls in matching seersucker dresses with bare feet and carefully tousled curls.

During the night, she saw, when Matt had come home to shower and change his clothes, he'd had the presence of mind to close the door to the small bedroom at the far end of the hall, and to take down the postcards from the lintel over the door. She had found the postcards in a shop on Fourth Street: pink-cheeked cherubs, each draped over and through a letter of the alphabet printed in elaborate Victorian typeface. Edie had bought four of them, brought them home, and spelled out the word "baby" over the door to the little bedroom. It had taken Matt two days to notice and another minute or two to realize what they meant.

He steered her into their bedroom with his cold, steady hand. "Get into bed, sweetheart. I'll bring you something to eat."

Edie knew that she ought be to be hungry. She had been hungry, it seemed, for the past twenty-three weeks, and she had eaten nothing at all since last night.

"I just want to take a shower."

In the bathroom, Edie tugged her pants down around her thighs and saw that the thick pad had slipped to one side, allowed a stream of stringy blood to soak the cotton of her panties and stain her leg. She pulled the pad loose and threw it away. She did not bother to rinse out her panties, just balled them up and threw them away too, covering the mess in the wicker trash can with a few wadded tissues.

"Everything all right?" Matt asked through the closed door.

"Fine," she said, and stepped into the shower.

She stayed in the shower a long time, washing her hair and scrubbing her blood-smeared thighs. When she was done she rubbed herself dry and smoothed lotion automatically onto her legs and feet, her elbows and hands. She avoided touching her belly. She rummaged through the medicine cabinet until she found Matt's stash of Ambien, swallowed one, and put the medicine bottle back, taking care to turn it so that the label was facing in the direction that it had been.

"You sure you don't want to eat something?" Matt said when she came out. He was sitting on the edge of the bed, pleating the duvet cover between his fingers.

"Maybe later," Edie said as she put on a clean pair of underwear and affixed in place one of the bulky pads the nurse had given her before they left the hospital. "I think I'll just try to sleep."

"Do you mind if I make myself some lunch? Or would you rather I stayed here until you fell asleep?"

"No, go eat something. I'm fine."

She put on her oldest, softest nightgown, slipped between the cool sheets of her bed, pulled the down comforter up to her nose, and inhaled the soft lavender scent of the rinse she had been using on their linens ever since her sister had sent her a bottle from London two years before. She sank deeply into the bed, wishing she could sink even deeper, that her bed could suck her into itself like a tar pit swallowing an animal. She flattened her body against the bed and disappeared into it as completely as she could.

She dreamed she heard a baby crying.

Every part of her resisted waking. Her body and mind clung to sleep, burrowed into it, fought the intrusion of sound and life and obligation. But the cry was ineluctable—high-pitched and insistent. It followed her into her hole and harried her like a ratting terrier. It yanked her up and out into the dim afternoon light of her bedroom.

Edie blinked, waking but not awake. The crying sounded loud in the stillness of the bedroom, but at the same time it was muffled, overlaid with a buzz of static, as if it were playing through a radio tuned just a point or two off the mark. She blinked again, the static of Ambien like rain inside her head, and she wondered if she was really awake, or if this was instead a false waking, a dream of consciousness rather than the real thing. She felt oddly cold and clammy and rolled over onto her side, telling herself sternly to wake up once and for all. A sharp pain stabbed through her breast and she touched something wet in the sheets. She sat up, her mind instantly clear. The sound of a baby crying had stopped, and she looked down at her chest. Her aching breasts were swollen, lumpy as bags of wet sand. She lifted her nightgown. Her nipples, which had grown dark and long over the course of her pregnancy, were each now as thick as a thumb. Pale yellow liquid beaded on the tips and dripped onto her soft and sagging belly. She crossed her arms against the surge of pain in her breasts.

One of the baby books prescribed cabbage leaves for engorgement, so the next morning Matt went to the supermarket. As soon as he left the house, as soon as the latch of the front door clicked into place, Edie heard the sound again: a baby crying. When it started up she was sitting at the kitchen table, savoring her first cup of real coffee in months, and she jumped, startled. She leaped up and went to the sink to run cold water over her burned wrist.

The baby wailed, and it was like a string connected its cry to Edie. She felt a tug start deep in each breast and travel through her belly down between her legs. She pressed her thighs together and looked at the front of the old sweatshirt of Matt's that she was wearing. There were two large, round dark spots over her breasts. Wondering to whom this baby belonged, who was the new mother whose good luck was so blithely inflicted on her neighbors, Edie opened the back door and went out onto the deck. The baby's cries faded. Nonetheless she peered over the fences into the adjoining yards. She knew that none of her immediate neighbors had babies. There was a three-year-old in the house directly behind them, but the cries were not those of a toddler. Edie went back into the house and walked through the family room. As she passed into the wainscoted dining room with the polished oval table and the high ladder-backed chairs they had inherited when Matt's mother had died, the cries began again, growing louder as she crossed into the living room, ever louder as she neared the stairs. She leaned the flat of her palm against the ivy-patterned wallpaper of the entryway, pulled open the front door, and went out onto the front porch. Once again, the cries were quieter outside than in. She walked back into the house and stood at the bottom of the stairs that led up to the hall that ended in a blank, closed door. She asked herself what it could mean that a woman who was responsible for the death of her baby heard bitter weeping reverberating through her empty house.

Edie put her hands over her ears and counted to ten. The hollow rush sounded so good that she stretched it to twenty. To thirty. The baby, a baby, some baby, cried and cried. The cotton of her sweatshirt grew soggy with her milk, fat and sweet and meant to feed a child who lived only in her guilty mind.

Suddenly, without thinking about it, Edie marched up the stairs. When she reached the top, she was breathing heavily, and she paused, staring at the closed door at the end of the hall. The baby's cries came much louder now, still muffled by static, but even more frantic, plaintive, as if he knew she was close by. She crept down the hallway toward the closed door, jelly legs, arms shaking, breasts spraying milk like blood from a nicked artery.

The room was filled with a pale, golden light. The sun shone through the striped yellow curtains and licked at the warm wooden furniture; the circular crib with the matching striped yellow canopy, bumpers and baby quilt; the baby dresser with the tiny yellow ducklings and pale green fish hand-painted along the bottom edge; the matching changing table; the half-finished mural along one wall. Ducks and fish again. All ducks and fish. Yellow, pale green, and white. Pale and pretty. Golden and yellow and happy and sunshine. Edie stood on the sage green carpet with the yellow border in the middle of the room and spun in a slow circle. She had chosen every single thing so carefully. She had spent weeks on her theme. Something gender-neutral, of course, because they were going to be surprised. Yellow. And green. Ducklings or dragons. Perhaps dinosaurs. Ducklings, finally. And then fish, little fishies because of what they called him, what Matt said the first time they saw him on the ultrasound. "He's like a little minnow, swimming inside you." So ducklings and fishies for their minnow. Duckling furniture. Cloth diapers with yellow and green fabric ticking. Layette. A glider rocker. A matching footstool. And the crib. A gorgeous, round crib, so expensive that even Matt had grumbled, had agreed only when she swore that she would never tell his father and stepmother how much they had paid for it.

Edie had chosen so carefully; her planning had been meticulous. But she did not plan to go into preterm labor. She did not expect to see her water break at twenty-three weeks. She did not plan to be confronted with the decision of whether to allow labor to proceed and death to come, or to fight off the inevitable for another week, two at the most. Her birth plan did not include a provision weighing the value of a life that might include brain bleeds and blindness, cerebral palsy and mental retardation. Or that might not. And so after months of decisions, ducks or fish, yellow or green, Edie had made one last, unexpected choice.

Edie closed the door behind her and walked back along the hallway, and as she moved the crying grew louder. She stopped in the doorway of her bedroom and looked in. On her dresser, its little row of five red lights and one green blinking with a furious intensity, sat the receiving end of the pale-blue plastic baby monitor she had bought and unpacked only a few days before. The transmitter she recalled setting up on the little scalloped wooden shelf over the baby's crib, but she had no memory of putting the receiver in her bedroom. Yet there it was, the cord snaking across the top of the bureau and down the side to the electrical outlet near the laundry hamper. The crying seemed to amplify with her gaze. She crossed to the dresser and switched it off: the red rows of lights went dark, and silence broke over the room.

Edie sat down on her bed and pressed her hands between her knees, her sweaty palms sticking together. As if her life weren't sufficiently awash in miserable irony, someone else in the neighborhood had to go and buy the same brand of baby monitor. The cries of that woman's living baby were being picked up by the monitor that Edie had purchased to keep her dead baby safe. She got up and rolled the dial, clicking it back on, and at once the baby's cries, wretched and hoarse, filled her bedroom. Who was this horrible mother in the house on the other end, and why didn't she go to her baby? Perhaps the baby had some kind of awful colic. What else could explain the constant anguish of his wails? No mother could be so neglectful, certainly no mother in this neighborhood, where the young women were like her, college-educated, professionals, all home for just a little while, while the children were small, so as not to miss this wonderful time in their lives.

Edie turned down the volume on the monitor but left it on. She stared at it for a while, listening to the quieted cries, and watching the row of angry lights as they climbed and subsided to mark the rise and fall of the unknown baby's screams. Then she heard the front door open and Matt call out.

"The cabbage man has returned," he said.

Matt stayed home from work for the rest of the week. Mostly they read the paper, all the papers, front to back, and watched television. Matt made a few excursions to the video store and the market, and each morning he went for a run. They spoke very little, except about what they should watch next, or what they should eat. Matt would ask her what she wanted, and Edie would say she didn't care, that he should decide. Whenever he left the house, Edie would turn on the baby monitor, and the baby would always be there, crying. It was almost, she thought, as if the baby were waiting for her to tune in. And no matter how many cabbage leaves she stuffed into her bra, no matter how sure she felt that lactation had finally ceased, whenever she heard the baby crying, her milk began to flow, steady and warm. After a while, the pain eased and it began to feel like pleasure, to feel sexy even. With the rush of milk from her nipples, Edie felt a corresponding tug between her thighs.

One night after they had turned off the light, Matt reached across the six inches of mattress that lay, an empty no-man's-land, between his side of the bed and hers. "Edie?" he said. "Come on over here."

"I'm not allowed."

"What?"

"For six weeks. I'm not allowed."

"Not that. I just want to hold you."

"Oh."

She rolled over in his direction. Clenched between her thighs and cradling her belly was the long body pillow he had brought home one day early in her pregnancy, when she'd begun complaining that her back hurt at night. Now it lay like an inert third body in the bed between them. He reached over the hump of pillow and caressed her hip.

"If you flip over, we can cuddle," he said.

She sighed and rolled onto her other side, taking the pillow with her, and he spooned his long body against her. She felt the brush of the hairs on his chest against her back and the insistent pressure of his thighs behind hers. His skin was hot, almost feverish, and she ached to move away to the cool comfort of her side of the bed. Finally, after what felt like hours, when his breathing was coming rhythmically, and he had thrown his arm over his face as he always did when he was deeply asleep, she slipped out of bed and went over to the dresser. She bent down and turned the monitor on to the very lowest setting. She pressed her ear against the speaker, feeling the lines of plastic against her soft cheek and the hard cartilage of her ear, and listened to the faint, echoing cry.

The next day Matt was due back at work. Edie lay on her side in bed while he took his shower. She watched steam billow from the bathroom door and disperse in the cool air of the bedroom. While he dressed, she stared at him critically, her hands tucked between her knees.

"You're in a good mood," she said.

"What are you talking about?" Matt said.

"You're happy."

Matt stopped, one arm in his suit jacket, the other pulling the pin-striped worsted across his chest. "I am *not* happy. How can you say that?"

She pointed to his tie. "You tied a Balthus."

Matt looked down at his chest. His grayish-purple silk tie was dotted with violets and was, it was true, expertly tied in a complicated knot. The nine-move Balthus was Matt's favorite knot, one that required an extremely long tie and one or two tries before it hung just right. He attempted a Balthus only when he had something to celebrate, or for luck. He'd worn a Balthus knot on his first day of work at the firm and to his first oral argument. He'd learned it for his law school graduation and, if she remembered correctly, he'd been wearing a Balthus knot in his tie on the evening he proposed.

Matt shrugged on his jacket. "I just felt like it," he said. "I don't know, maybe to cheer me up."

"You were whistling in the shower."

"I always whistle in the shower."

The ability to whistle underwater is an accomplishment underestimated by most people. Matt could not only whistle in the shower, but even while washing his hair. He also seemed to have some psychic pop music connection, and it was not infrequently that over breakfast they would find themselves listening on the radio to the very tune that Matt had been whistling in the shower, even when the song had been something as relatively out-of-date as Cheap Trick's "The Flame" or "Give It to Me Baby" by Rick James. Edie had, at first, been charmed by the shower whistling, then grown irritated by it. She was by now inured to it, which made its sudden absence after Minnow's birth and death shocking, even frightening. Still, when the whistling reappeared on Matt's first day of work, she was more angry than relieved. Matt had been so wonderfully solicitous to her these past two weeks. He had behaved precisely as a man whose wife has suffered a tragedy should behave. He had brought her tea, he had prepared her meals. He had even done the laundry. All the while, however, she had sensed a tentative fear underneath his solicitude, and now this tangible proof of his relief to be escaping her pissed her off.

"I have to go to work, Edie," Matt said. He leaned over the bed. "Are you going to be all right?"

"I'm fine," she said.

He sighed. He bent to kiss her but she turned away. His lips grazed her cheek and she held herself stiff to keep from shuddering.

"I'll call you from the office, okay?"

"Okay."

Once she was sure Matt was gone, she got out of bed and went to the monitor. Somehow the baby seemed sadder today. Less frantic, perhaps. His cry more monotonous, more hopeless. She left the monitor on and listened to the baby while she got dressed. She stuffed her bra with wads of toilet paper, regretting now that she had not bought breast pads, because she had never quite made up her mind that she was going to breast-feed.

"Where is your goddamned mother, you poor kid?" Edie said out loud. She unplugged the monitor, leaving herself in abrupt silence. She carried it downstairs, found two AA batteries in the kitchen junk drawer and fitted them into the monitor's battery compartment. She felt an odd sense of relief when the crying started up again as soon as the batteries were snapped into place.

She clipped the monitor to the waistband of her sweatpants and it hung, dragging the fabric down and slapping against her thigh while she walked. She turned the volume down until the baby's cries were just audible, and she put on her sneakers. The air was cool in the shade of the porch and she stepped quickly into the warm sun. Since returning from the hospital Edie had been no farther than the front and back porches of the house, and the brick of her front walk felt strange under her feet, hard and inflexible. She wrapped her arms around her body and set out down the walk along the flower beds and trimmed-back rosebushes. There were a few blooms on the apricot-colored rosebush, always the first to blossom, but the others—the red, the yellow, the purple and the many whites—were still in the bud stage.

Their neighborhood was full of young families, and Edie had always imagined that after she had the baby she would get to know the other young mothers. She would take Minnow—who would by then have graduated to a real name, perhaps Fiona or Finn after Matt's mother—to Mommy and Me, or to Gymboree classes at the Unitarian church on the corner. They would meet other babies and their mothers at the yoga studio in postnatal yoga classes, or at Starbucks. They would join the stroller crush at the café in Whole Foods. All those places that Edie now knew she would have to avoid.

She walked down the street listening to the baby monitor, her ears pricked for any change in volume or tone that would signify her proximity to the source of the cries. There was none. Still, one house, about six down from her own, caught her attention. The house had a very small front yard; it was set back from the sidewalk no more than six feet or so. A long porch ran along the front of the house, with broad steps on the left side and a huge picture window to the right of the door. On the porch was a Maclaren Techno XT, the very stroller she had put down on her registry. While Edie stared at the stroller that should have been her own, a cloud passed over the sun, darkening the sky. For a moment she could see into the front window of the house all the way through to the living room. Some kind of swing contraption was hanging in the wide archway between the front room and the one behind, and she thought she could see a baby bouncing in the swing, kicking off from the floor on its chubby legs.

The sky grew light and Edie's reflection stared back at her. She stood, one foot on the sidewalk, the other on the flagstone path leading to the house, and listened to the drone of the baby's cries through the monitor. They seemed no louder nor softer than they had since she'd left her own home, but she took a few tentative steps up the path anyway, listening to see if they changed. Although they did not, Edie continued, until she was standing on the front steps of the house, and then on the porch by the front door, her hand poised as if to ring the bell, her eyes fixed on the sight framed by the picture window.

There was indeed a baby in the bouncing swing. Edie stared at her, transfixed. She was blond, with thin, flyaway hair that hovered over her head as she rose and fell. Her fists were balled, one in her mouth, the other pushing at a pile of what looked like Cheerios on the tray of the bouncer. She was not crying, although the baby on the monitor maintained his constant wretched drone. Edie watched the baby girl fling herself up and down, jumping harder and harder. Then a small boy came running from out of Edie's field of vision, hit the back of the swing with his hand, and sent it spinning. He flung himself down on his belly on the floor, leaving the baby twirling in the bouncing swing, her face clenched in an angry, red fist, her screams audible through the window glass.

A woman rushed from the back of the house, a cordless telephone clutched between her raised shoulder and her ear. She tugged the baby free of her swing and hugged her to her hip. Then the woman bent over the small boy and shook his arm with her free hand, all the while continuing what appeared to Edie, through the window glass, to be an animated telephone discussion. Edie was overwhelmed by a sudden desire to grab the woman's arm and shake it, just as she was shaking the boy's. Edie could feel the soft white flesh beneath her fingers, could see the angry half-moon indentations her fingernails would leave. She staggered backward, afraid that the force of her rage would transmit itself through the glass and cause the woman to look up from her telephone conversation and her children.

Edie ran back down the path to the street. She unclipped the monitor from her waistband, pressed it to her ear, and listened to the baby's cries, comforted by their familiar monotony.

She kept walking, rounding the block and making a complete circuit, stopping to listen at every house where there was evidence of a child, but the sound came only through the monitor, distant and fuzzy. As she turned the corner to her street, the volume picked up and she quickened her pace. It grew louder and louder, clearer and clearer, until she was standing in front of her own house. Edie stood on the sidewalk in front of her house, staring up at the bay window hung with long, shiny curtains and swags, and listened to the baby's voice, clearer and louder than it had been at any time in her walk through the neighborhood.

She stumbled into the house and up the stairs to her bedroom, where she switched off the monitor, tossed it on her dresser, and crawled into bed. She fell immediately and thickly asleep and at once began to dream. She dreamed that her baby had been born, sick and needy, but alive. Undeniably alive. Minnow looked as he had in the hospital, when she had held him, wrapped in a pink-and-blue-striped blanket. His skin seemed translucent; she could see the red layer of muscle, the purple lines of his veins. His body felt limp, rubbery. But his face was frozen into a stiff, white mask. Only his feet were perfect. Small round toes, round heels. His foot rested in the palm of her hand, as delicate and flawless as an egg.

In her dream, Minnow cried for her all the time. He would not let her put him down, even for a moment. And she obliged. When he demanded to be nursed, she brought him close and closed her eyes, his mouth open wide on her breast, her nipple brushing the back of his throat. His suck was voracious and her contentment absolute.

Edie woke to a soaked bed and the sound of the baby's cries coming from the monitor.

She tugged her wet and sticky shirt away from her chest and then pulled it over her head. It was only when she was standing naked, dumping her wet clothing into the laundry basket, that she remembered turning off the baby monitor. She leaned over and picked it up, turning it over and over in her hand. It was on, although she was certain she had turned it off. As she spun the monitor, the baby's cries wobbled, as if they were undergoing a kind of Doppler effect. Edie spun it faster and faster, listening to the changing pitch of the baby's cries. Then she opened her hands and, fingers pointed wide, watched the monitor tumble onto the carpet. The baby kept up his droning cry. Edie picked up the monitor. On the back, next to the on/off dial, was a second small switch, marked with an A and a B. Edie flipped it, changing the channel to B. For a moment there was no sound from the monitor at all; she could hear nothing but her own breathing. Then there was a crackle of static, and the cries began again. Edie gently set the monitor back in its place on the dresser, and with the light touch of a single finger, turned the dial off.

Edie burrowed into the soft cocoon of her bed. "I have gone crazy," she said aloud. She waited to cry, to be overcome with fear at the thought at having succumbed to the septic psychosis of grief. While she was waiting, she fell asleep.

After Matt left for work, Edie took the receiving end of the monitor with her into Minnow's room. She set it down on the dresser, pulled open the top drawer and took out a small cardboard box with a brand-new nursing bra inside it. She slipped her bathrobe over her shoulders, strapped on the nursing bra, and opened up the flaps, adjusting her breasts so that her long, dark nipples protruded evenly from the holes cut in the fabric. She pulled two cloth diapers out of the stack on the shelf under the changing table, picked up the monitor, and sat down in the glider rocker. After she had shifted the footstool a few inches so that it was aligned comfortably with her lower legs, she splayed her feet out on the padding. She folded the cloth diapers into fat squares and placed one under each of her breasts. She centered the monitor on her lap and began rocking back and forth in the glider. Then she turned on the dial.

The baby cried, Edie rocked, and soon her milk began to flow. As the diapers grew wet with sweet, warm milk, the baby's cries softened. He hiccuped once, and then again. Soon no cries came through the baby monitor, only the sound of sucking and the click of the baby's swallow. And then the flutter of his breath as he slept.

Only the weekends were hard. Matt was gone all day during the week, and he worked late, often coming home as late as eight or nine. Edie could spend all day with the baby, rocking in the glider, nursing him, or just listening to him breathe. On weekends, Matt might work one day, but never both. He would never leave her alone on Saturday *and* Sunday. So on weekends she would have to steal her time with the baby, creep away in the middle of the night, or when Matt went out for a run. Otherwise her breasts would start to ache, and she would begin to grow frantic, knowing the baby was hungry. She would lie in bed next to Matt while he read his book or paged through the Sunday paper and she would stare at the monitor, knowing that if she turned it on she would hear her baby crying, knowing that he needed her and that he couldn't understand where she was and why she didn't come.

"What the fuck are you doing?"

Edie opened her eyes. Matt was standing in the doorway of the baby's room, staring at her. She looked down at her chest. Her sweatshirt was hitched up over her breasts and they hung, heavy and blue-veined, resting on the wadded cloth diapers.

"I'm just taking a nap," she said hoarsely. She cleared her throat and looked over at the monitor. The row of lights blinked merrily, indicating visually what she could not believe Matt didn't hear, the baby's soft snoring, audible under the static hum of the monitor.

"In here?"

"I like it in here."

"Why is your shirt up?"

Edie looked down at her naked chest and then up at Matt. She blinked. "My breasts hurt. Because of all the hormones. It helps if I keep them out in the air."

"Still?"

"Yeah."

"Is that a nursing bra?"

"What's with the third degree?" Edie yanked the flaps of her bra closed, silently begging the baby to stay asleep, not to wake up, not to cry. She did not know how she would explain the baby's cries to Matt or, worse, what it would mean if Matt could not hear him.

"Edie," Matt said.

She looked down, away from his flushed face, and as she did she caught sight of the tented fabric at the crotch of his mesh running shorts.

"Edie," he said again.

He crossed the room and pushed the footstool away, kneeling between her legs. While Edie clutched the armrests of the rocker, Matt unsnapped the flaps of her nursing bra and pulled them down. Over the monitor, the baby's breathing caught for a moment, and then settled again, bringing with it a corresponding tightening in Edie's breasts, tingling out to her exposed nipples. While she and Matt watched, a bead of thick white gathered at the tip of each nipple.

Matt bent over and licked the drop off first her right nipple, then her left. His tongue sent a shock through Edie's body, down through her stomach, to her groin. She made a low noise in her throat, quiet enough not to wake the baby. Matt bent over again, and began to suck, drawing her nipple, her areola, almost half her breast into his mouth. Her letdown came. He wrapped one of his arms around her waist and massaged her breast with his other hand, squeezing more and more of the liquid into his mouth. The other breast sprayed, soaking through the diaper to her lap, drenching Matt's shoulder, running down his neck to the collar of his shirt.

Edie twisted under Matt's grip, not trying to pull herself away but rather to push herself farther inside of him, to push more and more of her breast into his mouth, to press her groin against his thigh, to drown him.

Matt lifted his face. It was slick with fat. They stared at each other for a moment, and then she opened her mouth to his, pushing her tongue inside him, tasting the sweetness of her milk.

. . .

Matt brought Edie flowers. Tuberoses and sweet pea, fragrant and easily bruised. Edie held the cone of pale-pink tissue paper in her hands and stared vaguely at the bouquet, one ear cocked for the baby. Usually she turned the monitor off when she heard Matt open the front door. Today he had surprised her by arriving earlier than usual, and had caught her downstairs, eating a peanut butter sandwich—she was so hungry nowadays, especially late in the afternoon, when the baby seemed to need to linger on the breast.

"Don't you want to put them in water?" he said.

Edie plucked at the twist of raffia knotted tight around the blossoms. The stems squeaked in protest as she pulled at the cord, and while she reached across the kitchen counter for a knife she felt Matt slip his arms around her waist. She froze, one arm extended, a serrated blade trembling in her hand.

"I love you so much, Edie."

From the baby's room she heard a faint mewing sound. He was waking up.

Matt pressed against her. She could feel his erection, hard and unyielding against her back. He rubbed his face in her hair, inhaling with a congested snuffle. "You smell so good."

"It's the flowers."

"No, it's you."

Edie slid the knife under the raffia and jerked upward. The blade was dull and the cord more resilient than a pretty bow should be, so the edges of the blade caught and tugged, fraying and tearing but not slicing through.

"God damn it."

"Last night was so great," Matt said into her hair. "Weird, but great."

"God *damn* it!" She sawed the blade back and forth a few times and then wrenched it up. With a squeak, it tore through the raffia and, propelled by the force of her angry jerk, smacked Matt in the forehead. The flowers dropped out of the paper cone, scattering across the counter.

"Jesus!" he yelled, leaping back, his palm against the wound.

Edie turned to face Matt, the knife clenched in her fist. His mouth hung open, loose and flaccid. He lowered his hand and stared at the smear of red dirtying his palm. "Oh, no," he said weakly. Edie looked at the cut; ruby dots in a neat line from his hairline to his brow.

"How bad is it?" he said.

"I don't know."

"Do you think I need stitches?"

"Maybe."

"Shit. All right. Can you drive?"

She listened for a moment. She could just barely hear the baby stirring, beginning to cry. She pressed her hand against the side of one of her breasts; it was swollen and sore, full.

"No," she said.

"What?"

"I can't."

"What do you mean, you can't?"

"I can't go to the hospital now."

Matt picked up a dishtowel and pressed it against his forehead. A ragged red oblong immediately wicked through to mar the pristine white terry cloth. "I don't really want to go back there either, but I have to get this sewed up. Come on."

"No."

"Edie!"

"I can't."

Matt slammed his fist on the counter, making the flowers jump. "What is *wrong* with you? I'm hurt. Do you understand? I'm *hurt*. I need to go to the hospital and get stitches. Are you actually telling me that you won't drive me there?"

Edie stared at the spray of blooms. She wished she could explain why she couldn't leave. She wished she could tell Matt that as much as she wanted to take care of him, there was someone else who needed her more.

"Edie. *Edie!* You need to stop this. It's enough."

"What's enough?" she said, speaking to the flowers.

"You have to get over this already."

"Get over it?"

"You know what I mean. You think I'm not sad about Minnow? I'm sad! I lost my baby, too. But we have to move on, Edie."

"Why?"

"Why? Because Minnow is dead, and we don't have any other choice."

Edie laid the knife gently down on the counter and began picking up the strewn flowers.

"Please, Edie," he said.

With her index finger, she dabbed at the knife blade, wiping away a tiny droplet of his blood.

Three hours and four stitches later, Matt returned from the emergency room to an empty house. The tuberoses and sweet pea were carefully arranged in a cobalt-blue vase on the kitchen table, their stems freshly cut, two tablets of aspirin dissolving in the bottom of the vase. The house was neat, Edie's purse sat on its shelf next to the front door, her keys dangled from their hook on the kitchen wall, her cell phone rested in its charger, and none of her shoes were missing.

All this Matt noticed within minutes of his return. He wandered through the house taking inventory of Edie's absence and of the presence of her possessions, panic slowly twisting his bowels and causing the blood to pound in his aching forehead. He knew from the first moment that she was gone, that she was not on a walk or visiting a friend. He was, however, too sensible to allow himself to accept his own miserable certainty and so he waited, first in the kitchen, then on the front porch, then in their bedroom. His voice, when he called Edie's mother, was falsely jovial, the alarm all too audible beneath the lighthearted lack of concern. It was she who told him to call the police, she who gave him permission to give voice to his dread. The police, though, were less willing to give credence to his fears, and Matt spent a long night drifting from room to room in his house, alternately crying with worry for Edie's welfare, and cursing her for abandoning him. In the blackest part of the night, when the moon had set and the dawn not yet begun to lighten the sky, he stood in the doorway of Minnow's bedroom. The room was so dark that the furniture was nothing more than hulking shapes in the corners of the room. Matt gazed into the dark. Out of the corner of his eye he noticed a row of flickering red lights on the floor. He blinked and stared more closely. After a moment he realized that what he was looking at was the baby monitor. He sighed, turned around, and closed the bedroom door behind him.

Five months after Edie disappeared, Matt decided, finally, to pack up Minnow's room. Edie, he was not yet ready to let go of. Her clothes and shoes, the drawer full of lipsticks and moisturizer, hair elastics and tubes of sunscreen, those he left exactly as they were. But one Sunday he decided the baby's things could go. He disassembled the crib, packed the baby clothes away in two of the plastic bins Edie kept stacked in the garage, and took down the curtains. He wrapped the pictures in bubble wrap and put them in the front hall. A beer crate served well for the odds and ends in the room, and Matt filled it with diapers and baby wipes, the miniature manicure set, the soft-bristled brush with matching comb. He tossed in the transmitting end of the baby monitor and looked around the room for the receiver. It was on the floor next to the glider rocker, plugged into the wall socket. Matt knelt down and pulled the plug out of the wall. As he was getting to his feet, he stumbled over the leg of the rocker. He reached out to steady himself, knocking the baby monitor receiver against the floor, freeing the cord and activating the battery power. There was a burst of static and then a woman's soft humming filled the room.

Matt rocked back on his heels and listened. The tune was one he thought he recognized; it hovered just out of reach of his memory. The baby cooed, and a painful smile played over Matt's lips at the sweet sound and the mother's soothing hum.

Then the woman spoke and Matt's smile faded.

"It's all right, sweetie," Edie said. "Mommy's here."

ZEROVILLE

by STEVE ERICKSON

WHEN HE WAKES in the early hours before dawn, one morning near the end of summer, he knows he's almost reached the door. Lining the stairway of his house are the enlarged celluloid images of a thousand doors, although really they're all the same door, moving from one location to another, each growing closer to him or, more exactly, he grows closer to each.

It's the first or second summer of the new millennium, depending how you count one or zero. By now Monk's dreams have enough precision that a part of him would like to know, How do you count one or zero, and is it the first summer, or the second? He dreams very *efficiently*. Over the past two decades, the scenes in his dreams have become almost exact replicas of those from the movies that inspired the dreams. Lately when Monk wakes, he knows right away which reel to pull from the wall of shelves around him; he's taken to sleeping on the floor of the library so that when he has such a dream, immediately the film is at his fingertips. Up until now he's known the films well enough that he could put them in the projector and go to the very scene he's looking for, and then begin searching frame by painstaking frame on his editing table.

In the beginning, he barely realized what he was dreaming. Only from his years as a film editor had he developed an affinity for the subconscious of montage, for the id of the film that even the filmmaker doesn't know is there; and in the beginning almost twenty years before, when he had the first dream, night after night he tossed restlessly in a sleep mottled by glimpses, flashes, messages, echoes of one film in particular he had recently seen on videotape—until finally he tracked down a print, paying good money for it. "Boy you must love this picture, huh?" the guy in the Valley had said to him. It was a porn movie called *Nightdreams* about a woman in a psychiatric ward having a series of carnal hallucinations: in one she's a slave on her knees in the Arab desert, being taken by two men at each end of her; in another she's in Hell being fucked by the Devil . . . but while these images slithered into Monk's sleep as visual ephemera, what became clearer with each passing night and each passing dream was the door in the far background. In this particular case the door, just slightly ajar, stood alone on a distant barren veldt, although as far as Monk could tell there was no such image in the film at all.

For some weeks Monk watched the videotape over and over, freezing every new scene trying to find that door that beckoned him every night in his sleep. After a while he gave up and the dreams began to fade and he went back to watching other movies, at home on TV or sometimes—if something he wanted badly enough to see was being shown—going out to a theater or one of the nearby campuses; he hated going out. One night, four months after first seeing the porn picture, he began having another dream, following a screening at UCLA of an old silent Danish film: there among the stark black-and-white images of forbidding robed inquisitors and a young girl burning at the stake was the door again, this time a little bit closer than it had been before, a little more ajar than before, standing on the edge of a dark woods. The next day Monk returned to the school. "I can't let you take the print," the film department's curator told him.

"What if I use one of your editing rooms here on campus?" Monk asked.

"What are you looking for anyway?"

"I'm not going to hurt the print," Monk said.

"You're not William Jerome the film editor, are you?" No one called Monk that; anyone who still called him anything called him Monk. Something more than a reputation and less than a legend preceded him, built largely around the first picture Polanski made after the murders and then the Friedkin picture and *Your Pale Blue Eyes*; he had received Oscar nominations for the last two. Enough people knew about the troubled production of *Your Pale Blue Eyes* that it may have singularly inspired one of Hollywood's most perennial urban myths: that of the film that's "saved" in the editing room—except that Monk hadn't merely saved the film but transformed it. At Cannes that year, for the only time in the festival's history the jury invented a new award, the Prix Sergei, presented to *Pale Blue Eyes* for "the art of montage at its most revelatory." In the mid- to late seventies Monk had run with that Malibu crowd out at the beach for a while, Marty and Brian and Milius and Schrader and Ashby, and that crazy chick with the tits who played Lois Lane in the *Superman* movies. "What are you doing these days?" the UCLA film curator asked. "I heard you were directing something of your own."

By then it already had been, what, almost three years since Monk had worked on anything, since *Pale Blue Eyes* and the whole business with Zazi. "I'm . . . between projects," he answered, not wanting to even get into the Huysmans adaptation that he couldn't yet admit to himself was never going to happen. The curator sighed. "You understand it's on loan," he said, shrugging at a canister on the table next to them that, with a start, Monk realized was the very movie they were talking about, "from the Cinematheque. You have to be very careful."

"I promise."

"But . . . *what are you looking for?*" And it was almost a week before Monk found it, poring over the film exhaustively: there it was; and then, going back to the porn flick, as with the Joan of Arc picture he went through frame by frame until he found it—and what could such a thing mean? That buried in both a 1928 silent classic made eight thousand miles away and a 1982 porn movie was, in a single frame that no one could see when the films were run, in a single frame that revealed itself in the sort of clandestine bulletins only Monk received, was the same single door, on the edge of a woods in one picture, on an open desolate veldt in the other. From both movies Monk extracted the frames and enlarged them, so that above his bed where he slept, the two doors loomed side by side.

Over the weeks before he wakes near the end of the first or second summer of the new millennium, he sees her on the hillside that cascades below his house. The first time she's near the bottom, where the road that eventually leads to him begins to wind its way upward. He sees her standing there looking up at him, and the next moment she's gone; the next time he sees her, one dusk several days later, she's moved up the hill but stands motionless as before, like *Last Year at Marienbad*, where people are as statues on a vast terrace, except this woman plays all the statues, posed against the chaparral. Each time Monk sees her, she moves closer up the hill.

At some point in his long-ago career editing movies, he discovered that by cutting to a character's right or left profile, he could expose something about her. He could expose the side that was true and the side that was false, he could expose the side that was good and the side that was evil, he could expose the side that punished and the side that received, the side that dominated and the side that submitted. It was different with each person and each profile: what was represented by one actor's right might be represented by someone else's left. But once Monk deciphered which was which, a new visual vocabulary of meaning became available. "I would never betray you," one lover might say to another in a given scene; but by choosing one take over the other, one profile over the other,

Monk could bare credibility or mendacity, irrespective of the actor's intention, or the director's or the writer's.

This provided a modus operandi for all of Monk's work. It provided the prevailing logic by which all other decisions were made. As people had right profiles and lefts, places and moments had them as well; in a film, every shot was a profile, and by cutting from rights to other rights, or from rights to lefts or lefts to lefts, he could subliminally reinforce or sabotage the audience's perceptions. In Monk's mind this was the key that would unlock the secret of adapting Joris-Karl Huysmans' nineteenth-century decadent French novel *La Bas* that was to be Monk's directorial debut, before two things happened that aborted the project altogether. The first and less important was the change in the movie business in the late seventies and early eighties that consigned to exile the renegade film movement out of which Monk had originally emerged—a disruption in the very sensibility of moviemaking profound enough to render the later technological changes irrelevant. It's just as well, Monk would muse much later, staring out the windows of the house, that my career was over before I ever had to deal with digital: computers and all that? No, I was born to *cut* film, not move around ones and zeros.

The second, more important thing happened one morning when Monk stood before the mirror shaving. With his razor he was negotiating a mole on one side of his chin when it occurred to him that what he always thought of as his left side was in fact his right, that his perception of his own right and left was based on the same reflective reversal by which an entire species, staring into mirrors or glass or lakes over the millennia, had always confused rights and lefts. This realization could only confound Monk's aesthetic, which was to say that what he always thought of as his good side was in fact his evil, that what he always thought of as his true side was in fact his false. By the time Monk's blade had flicked the final streak of shaving cream, both his aspirations as a director and his career as a film editor were over, not to mention his relationship with Zazi. "I would never betray you," she had told him in a hushed turn to her left that she believed was her right—or in fact had she not said it to him at all, but rather he said it to her, in a reversal of the right and left of speaker and spoken-to?

By the time Monk moved into the house in the Hollywood Hills, he had been living on the edge awhile. Money from his film career finally running out after years of austere living, he vacated his loft in the industrial section of L.A.; the truth was he was slumming in the Hollywood Hills house, it wasn't his at all. It belonged to an old friend Monk hadn't seen since their school days at Emerson D, and he had dropped by one day to find the door open as though someone ran out to the local convenience store for beer and would return any moment. But no one came back and Monk just stayed on, waiting for inevitable eviction. The house was stacked in three levels against a hillside, the top floor being street level. On the third and bottom floor of the house Monk found the room that now served as his film library; lining the walls had been a sprawling, massive blue calendar that marked time according to the chronology of apocalypse. Monk moved in his reels of film and put up the enlarged stills of the door he had extorted from thousands of miles and a century of celluloid. If the time had long since passed when he really expected anyone to return, he still thought of the house as anyone's but his.

It's from the windows of this house where Monk watches the woman advance up the hill in frozen *Marienbad* poses that he also surveys the city in a panorama that almost justifies it. In the distance to the southeast is the cityscape of what might ironically be called a downtown—to the extent L.A. ever has had such a thing— that desperately scrambled skyward in anticipation of the Olympics back in the eighties. Directly below, occasionally blurting into Monk's view between the hills' knolls and gullies, is Sunset Boulevard, an asphalted urban timeline with not simply geographical addresses but temporal ones, from the utopian sixties in the west where hippies rampaged the gutters to the anarchic late seventies at the boulevard's far eastern end, where could be found Madame Wong's and the Chinatown punk scene. Back then Zanzibar Paladin had begun as bass player for the band the Rubicons before another singer's overdose bequeathed to her the mic and punk stardom, which was never the oxymoron punk culture liked to pretend.

The Rubicons played both Madame Wong's and, before it closed, the Starwood at Santa Monica Boulevard and Crescent Heights— and what was that club down on Pico, just west of the 405? By the time the Rubicons' *Tick Tock* EP was released, Zazi with her Soledad Miranda face already had been cast in *Your Pale Blue Eyes*, which Monk was brought onto after the studio replaced the director. Even in her first picture Zazi was canny enough to understand the advantages of befriending the editor who was going to choose which takes of her to use in the final film. As it happened, Monk had seen Zazi play at one of the local clubs not long before and perhaps could be excused for believing some sort of fate at work, not having even been in a club since Ciro's closed a decade before. "What's this?" Zazi said the first night she came to Monk's loft; she held in her hand the small model of a church that sat on a bookshelf. Standing in his small kitchen uncorking a bottle of red, Monk stared at Zazi holding the model a long time as he contemplated an answer. When was the moment in a relationship for such illicit biography, assuming this was to be a relationship at all? When was the moment for any sort of biography, illicit or not? "It's a church," he finally answered, knowing there was no way that could be enough.

"A church?"

"Uh, I designed it," he mumbled, "when I was a graduate student in architecture, at Emerson Divinity." Raised in northeastern Pennsylvania in a strict fundamentalist faith, Monk nonetheless had found the main advantage of divinity college was the small theater in the next town over, where he could see all the movies that had been prohibited to him as a child and adolescent.

"There is," Zazi said, cat eyes narrowing as she peered closely at the model's tiny solid walls, "no way in."

"Yes," Monk said, "the review committee was struck by that as well." It never occurred to them that it might rather be a church with no way out. Passing from one set of righteous hands to the other, the model had been appraised, scrutinized, scoured for an entrance. "Mr. Jerome," the chairman finally intoned, "is this some sort of joke?" I don't see, the student had answered, what's so funny, to which the chairman said, "Neither do we." He seemed so angry that for a moment Monk thought he might hurl the model to the floor like Moses hurling tablets, or Jesus a box of merchant's gold in the temple—at which point the committee would have seen the true sacrilege of Monk's thesis: that sealed inside, in the place where an altar might be presumed, was a tiny movie screen, white and blank because Monk had racked his brain to no avail trying to think of a single perfect image. L.A., on the other hand, is the cathedral of no walls, of nothing *but* ways in, built upon the dream of a species when and where the world has run out of space and time to dream. In his loft that night Monk and Zazi had the most demented sex of his life. "Through sensuality," she purred in his ear in the dark, tightening the collar around his neck and giving the chain a yank, "we make death not a lonely individual experience but an ecstatic collective one," and then another yank, "don't we, Mister Church Builder?"

When their romance went badly, was it worse that Zazi had left a woman for him? In her first physical relationship with a man, was there that much more at stake for her, had it been that much more a leap of faith for her, so that when they wouldn't take their attraction to a fatal end, it was that much more a betrayal? Not to mention the rumors, after the split, of Zazi's pregnancy and abortion, which sent a pang through the heart Monk no longer believed he had. Then Zazi's movie career nova'ed, imploding into nothingness, and she disappeared: "I would never betray you," but the more Monk thought about it, the harder it was to remember which of them had said it. Maybe it didn't matter. He left only so that she couldn't leave first. Now he watches a woman advance up the hillside in *Marienbad* freeze-frames, in sight one moment and invisible the next, as though someone is excising frames of her from the film of his life.

"So what do you think?" Monk asked one afternoon years later, returning to UCLA to show the film department's curator what he had found. Over the months that followed his discovery of the common door in the porn and Joan of Arc films, Monk began having more dreams and finding more doors in movies old and new, near and far-flung, foreign and domestic, celebrated and obscure. At the top of a Himalayan monastery when Kathleen Byron's jealous, lust-mad nun tries to push Deborah Kerr into the abyss and flings herself off instead, what seemed to an audience like attempted murder was a leap for the door that hovered in space just beyond the porticos, the same door that was in the adobe hut just above Marlon Brando's shredded and bloody right shoulder as Karl Malden lashes him with a whip. The same door that was there on the lake, not in the boathouse on the far shoreline but floating above the water itself, where lush Gene Tierney in dark glasses and bloodred lipstick coolly watches drown her husband's meddlesome brother as he frantically cries to her to save him. Monk excavated methodically, turning off the films' sound completely and replacing it with the music of a new L.A. noir on the CD player—Ornette Coleman's *Virgin Beauty*, X's *Unheard Music*, Japanese film scores—and from each and every one of these movies he would excise its single secret frame until, put together, the frames formed an altogether different film, a film that slowly closed in on a door that swung ever more open into a black void behind it. The curator shrugged, looking at a dozen of the frames laid out on the light table before him. "It's . . . a door." The two men stood staring at the light table for some time. "Is it supposed to mean something?"

Monk bit his lip. For a moment he was tempted to try to explain.

Then he decided against it. "It means," he finally said, "that someone else sees it too. It means," he said, "that someone else sees
what I see." Maybe it even means, he wondered, that I haven't lost
my mind.

Ten days before the end of the first (or second) summer of the new
millennium, Monk awakes in the early morning hours before dawn
to find the door nearer than ever, just within reach. In a pink wall,
it stands clearly open.

A month ago, he had his new and final dream. It was of a
movie he had never seen before, but so clear that he could describe
it in detail: a young Japanese model arrives one day at an art gallery
showing an exhibition of bondage photos for which she's posed.
There she sees a man running his hands over a sculpture of her; feeling as though his hands are on her own body, she flees the gallery.
Later that night in her apartment, distressed from her traumatic
day, she makes an appointment for a massage. The masseur who
arrives is blind, and the woman is startled to find she recognizes
his touch: "I have eyes in my fingers," he announces, and just as
he's chloroforming her into unconsciousness, she rips the dark
glasses from his face to recognize him as the man from the gallery.
When she comes to, she's in a strange warehouse, cavernous as a
cathedral. On the walls are the sculptures of eyes, noses, mouths,
torsos, arms and legs, and as she scurries among the shadows trying to elude her abductor, who can smell her scent and hear her
panicked breath, she scrambles over the monumental replications
of reclining female bodies, lurking in the valley of monumental
breasts, darting in the ravine of monumental thighs.

"It's called *Moju*," explained the film school curator to Monk
over the telephone. "In the States it's been released variously as
Warehouse and *Blind Beast*. Director's name is Masumura, a former
law student who drifted into movies after the war—not respectable
enough to receive the sort of attention Ozu or Kurasawa get, but
Antonioni among others championed him. Where did you say you

saw it?" It took a week for the curator to run down on the Internet a print that had made its way from Tokyo to East L.A. to London to Paris back to a small collectibles shop at Vesey and Church in lower west Manhattan. Driving out on Sunset Boulevard to UCLA to buy the film with practically every cent he had left, Monk felt a strange sense of urgency.

Whereas before some instinct had led Monk to the precise place where the hidden image was to be located, now he found himself searching the entire film. From its beginning to its end Monk prowled each scene as the young woman, imprisoned in the blind man's strange studio where he sculpts a statue of her, eventually becomes blinded herself by the endless darkness. Soon she seduces her captor, scheming to escape, only to submit willingly, becoming not just the model of his art but the art itself, the blind sculptor lopping off real arms, real limbs. Days passed as Monk searched. In his house the film unspooled from one floor to the next, loops of film hanging from the rafters like webs. As Monk felt time slipping away, as he felt himself racing to meet some deadline he neither knew nor understood, music without latitudes or hours that had been playing on the CD player—Duke Ellington's "Transbluency," Joy Division's "Decades," strange female chants satellite-broadcasted from Tuva—finally lapsed into silence. Yards of film unwound from the library to the screening room up to the living room as Monk went over every frame. In small handwritten signs fixed to the walls and draped with film strips, he charted the celluloid's narrative topography, psychic territories: Obsession. Seduction. Submission.

The days turned into weeks. Monk stalked the film's secret door on foot, sleeping less and then not at all. He grew more delirious with fatigue as he also grew more frantic; some irrevocable moment was at hand. Racking his brain to no avail, he sought a single perfect image of the door amid the walls of the movie's warehouse, among the bodies of the movie's characters. Soon he was chopping up the film viciously, as though the frame he was looking for was hidden not only from him but from the film itself, as though it might only be found somewhere within the film's flesh. Little pieces of black celluloid littered the floor like the ash and granite of toppled towers, up and down the stairs beneath a thousand stills of the door from a thousand other films, each growing closer. Isn't this dream mine to edit as I choose? Monk wondered. To cut as I choose? To flop right profiles with lefts and left profiles with rights, to reverse the utopian and anarchic ends of the boulevard as I choose? Outside he was certain he heard approach a Monumentalist Age, somewhere within the collision between an age of reckoning and an age of chaos. Mere blockbusterism! he howled to himself: what is it before the true monuments of the epoch come? Stumbling through the dark of his house, he ran his hands along the walls to follow up the stairs the trail of enlarged stills—*I have eyes in my fingers*—only to feel bare walls instead, and to find all the stills of the door gone. The door at the base of the spiraling steeple where James Stewart's eyes glint with rage at Kim Novak. The door

in the Hollywood cottage where a stormy Bogart loves and loses a terrified Gloria Grahame. The door

in a far medieval corridor as Vincent Price's depraved masquerade ball swirls by and Plague laps at the outer palace walls. The door

beneath the stone bridge that crosses a château moat where Brigitte Lahaie, nude beneath a black cloak, holds a bloody scythe. The door

in the Venice archway just beyond Janet Leigh's window, as Orson Welles leers over her in her sleep, pulling gloves onto fat hands. The door

that is anonymous among all the doors of a labyrinthine complex where Eddie Constantine pursues Anna Karina into the future. The door

in the corner of a balcony where, taking refuge from a party, Elizabeth Taylor and Montgomery Clift in each other's embrace are made of nothing but light and shards of the Void, the most beautiful couple in the history of movies, he the male version of her, she the female version of him. Down through the history of the movies, Monk will ponder at the end, what Wanderer has left these clues for him, in the form of the Movie of the Future, hidden one frame at a time in every movie ever made? Who has invaded every movie ever made in order to leave a single image among the twenty-four frames every second? What does it mean that there are the same number of frames per second as there are hours in a day? What does it mean that every second of a film is a day in the life of a secret film that someone has been waiting for Monk to find? In the final hours before dawn, Monk startles himself out of sleep, sits up from the library floor to the vision in his eyes, and stumbles to his feet to find all the images of the door on his walls gone except the last, now finally revealed itself to him, at the top of the stair within his reach. It is there, in a wall that is the color of a woman's body.

Or did whoever made this secret film of the future mean to show him a way out, or a way in? Outside, something in the hills casts a shadow. In his entryway, he still sees just well enough to make out someone's silhouette. "Zazi?" But he can't even be sure he has said it out loud.

Monk takes the knob in his hand. The door swings into a black gust. He's disconcerted to note that what in all the movies has always swung from left to right now swings from right to left. Momentarily he hesitates—somewhere nearby, at the foot of the hills and the coordinates of chaos, there seeps up from the ground a deluge—then steps through.

LISEY and THE MADMAN

by STEPHEN KING

For Nan Graham

I

THE SPOUSES OF WELL-KNOWN WRITERS are almost invisible; no one knows better than Lisey Landon, who has given only one actual interview in her life. This was for the well-known women's magazine that publishes the column "Yes, I'm Married to *Him*!" She spent roughly half of its five-hundred-word length explaining that her name (actually short for Lisa) rhymes with "CeeCee." Most of the other half had to do with her recipe for slow-cooked roast beef. Her sister Amanda, who can be mean, said that the accompanying photograph made Lisey look fat.

There was another photograph, one that first appeared in the *Nashville American* and then in newspapers around the world, mostly under the headline HEROIC GRADUATE STUDENT SAVES FAMOUS WRITER, or variations thereof. This one shows a man in his early twenties holding the handle of a shovel that looks almost small enough to be a toy. The young fellow is peering at it, and by his foozled expression the viewer might infer he has no idea at all of what he's looking at. It could be an artillery shell, a bonsai tree, a radiation detector, or a china pig with a slot in its back for nickels. It could be a whang-dang-doodle, a cloche hat made out of coyote fur, or a phylactery testifying to the pompatus of love. A man in what looks like a faux highway patrolman's uniform (no gun, but you got your Sam Browne belt running across the chest and a good-sized badge, as well) is shaking the dazed young man's free hand. The cop—he *has* to be a cop of some kind, gun or not—has a huge oh-thank-God grin on his kisser, the kind that says, *Son, you will never have to buy yourself another drink in a bar where I am, as long as we both shall live, so help me God, amen.* In the background, mostly out of focus, are staring people with dismayed what-the-hell-just-happened expressions on their faces.

And although thousands, perhaps even millions, of people have seen this photo, which has over the years become almost as famous as the one of the mortally wounded Lee Harvey Oswald clutching his belly, no one has ever noticed that the writer's wife is also in it.

Yes. Indeed she is. A part of her, anyway.

On the far right-hand side. Not quite halfway up.

If you look closely (a magnifying glass helps in this regard), you'll see half a shoe. Half a brown loafer. Half a *cordovan* loafer, to be exact, with a quarter-heel. Eighteen years later Lisey Landon can still remember how comfortable those shoes were, and how fast she moved in them that day. Faster than the award-winning photographer, certainly, and she'd not seen the dazed campus cop or the dazed young man—Tony, his name had been—at all. Not then, she hadn't. But she had earlier, and certainly later, in this picture, and how it had made her laugh. How it makes her laugh still. Because the spouses of well-known writers are almost always invisible.

But I got a shoe in there, she sometimes thinks. *I poked in a loafer. I did that much. Didn't I, Scott?*

Her position was always behind him at those ceremonial things;

behind him and slightly to the right, with her hands demurely clasped before her. She remembers that very well.

She remembers it all very well, probably better than the rest of them. Probably better than any of them.

II

Lisey stands behind and slightly to Scott's right with her hands clasped demurely before her, watching her husband balance on one foot, the other on the silly little shovel which is half-buried in loose dirt that has clearly been brought in for the occasion. The day is hot, maddeningly humid, almost sickeningly muggy, and the considerable crowd that has gathered only makes matters worse. Unlike the dignitaries in attendance for the groundbreaking, the lookie-loo-come-'n'-see folk are not dressed in anything approaching their best, and while their jeans and shorts and pedal pushers may not exactly make them comfortable in the wet-blanket air, Lisey envies them just the same as she stands here at the crowd's forefront in the suck-oven heat of the Tennessee afternoon. Just standing pat, dolled up in her hot-weather best, is stressful: worrying that she'll soon be sweating big dark circles in the light-brown linen top she's wearing over the blue rayon shell blouse. She's got on a great bra for hot weather and still it's biting into the undersides of her boobs. Happy days, babyluv.

Scott, meanwhile, continues balancing on one foot while his hair, too long in back—he needs it cut badly, she knows that he looks in the mirror and sees a rock star but she looks at him and sees a dolled-up hobo out of a Woody Guthrie song—blows in the occasional hot puff of breeze. He's being a good sport while the photographer circles. *Damn* good sport. He's flanked on the left by a fellow named Tony Eddington, who is going to write up all this happy crappy for the something-or-other (campus newspaper? surely the campus newspaper goes on hiatus at least during the month of August, if not for the entire summer?), and on the right by their stand-in host, an English department stalwart named

Roger Dashmiel, one of those men who seem older than they are not only because they have lost so much hair and gained so much belly so soon but because they insist upon drawing an almost stifling gravitas around themselves. Even their witticisms felt like oral readings of insurance policy clauses to Lisey.

Making matters worse in this case is the fact that Roger Dashmiel does not like her husband. Lisey has sensed this at once (it's easy, because most men do like him), and it's given her something upon which to focus her unease. For she *is* uneasy—profoundly so. She has tried to tell herself that it is no more than the humidity and the gathering clouds in the west presaging strong afternoon thunderstorms or maybe even tornadoes: a low-barometer thing, only that and nothing more. But the barometer wasn't low in Maine when she got out of bed this morning at quarter to seven; it had been a beautiful summer morning already, with the newly risen sun sparkling on a trillion points of dew in the field between the house and the barn which housed Scott's study. What her father, old Dandy Debusher, would have called "a real ham 'n' egger of a day." Yet the instant her feet touched the oak on her side of the bed and her thoughts turned to the trip to Nashville—leave for the Portland Jetport at eight, fly out on Delta at nine thirty—her heart dipped with dread and her morning-empty stomach, usually sweet, foamed with unmotivated fear. She'd greeted these sensations with surprised dismay, because she ordinarily *liked* to travel, especially with Scott: the two of them sitting companionably side by side, he with his book open, she with hers. Sometimes he'd read her a bit of his and sometimes she'd vice him a little versa. Sometimes she'd feel him and look up and find his eyes—his solemn regard. As though she were a mystery to him still. Yes, and sometimes there would be turbulence, and she liked that, too. It was like the rides at the Topsham Fair when she and her sisters had been young. Scott never minded the turbulence, either. She remembered one particularly crazy approach into Denver—strong winds, thunderheads, little prop-job commuter-plane all over the sky—

and how she'd looked over to see him actually pogo-ing up and down in his seat like a little kid who needs to go to the bathroom, with this crazy grin on his face. No, the rides that scared Scott were the smooth downbound ones he took in the middle of his wakeful nights. Sometimes he talked (lucidly—smiling, even) about things you could see only if you looked through the fingerprints on a water glass. It scared her to hear him talk like that. Because it was crazy, and because she sort of knew what he meant and didn't want to.

So it wasn't low barometer that had been bothering her—not then—and it certainly hadn't been the prospect of getting on one more airplane or eating one more airline snack (these days she brought their own, anyway, usually homemade trail mix). And then, in the bathroom, reaching for the light over the sink—something she had done without incident or accident day in and out for the entire eight years they'd lived here, which came to approximately three thousand days, less time spent on the road—she smacked the toothglass with the back of her hand and sent it tumbling to the floor, where it shattered into approximately one million stupid pieces.

"Shit *fire*, save your smuckin' matches!" she cried, lips drawn back from her teeth, frightened and irritated to find herself so: for she did not believe in omens, not she, not Lisey Landon the writer's wife; not little Lisey Debusher, either. Omens were for the shanty Irish.

Scott, who had just come back into the bedroom with two cups of coffee and a plate of buttered toast on a tray, stopped dead. "Whadja break, babyluv?"

"Nothing that came out of the dog's ass," Lisey said savagely, and was then sort of astounded with herself. That was one of Granny Debusher's sayings, and Granny D certainly *had* believed in omens, but that old Irish highpockets had gone on the cooling board when Lisey was only four. Was it even possible Lisey could remember her? It seemed so, for as she stood there, looking down at the stupid shards of toothglass, the actual *articulation* of the omen came to her, came in Granny D's tobacco-strapped voice . . . and comes back now, as she stands watching her husband be a good sport in his lightest-weight summer sport coat (which he will soon be sweating through under the arms nevertheless): *Broken glass in the morning, broken hearts at night.* That was Granny D's scripture, all right, handed down and remembered by at least one little girl before Granny D pitched down dead in the chicken yard with an apronful of feed and a sack of Bull Durham tied up inside her sleeve.

It isn't the heat, it isn't the trip, and it isn't Dashmiel, who ended up doing the meet 'n' greet job only because the head of the English department, with whom Scott had corresponded, is in the hospital following an emergency gall-bladder removal the day before. It is a broken . . . smucking . . . *toothglass* at ten minutes to seven in the morning combined with the saying of a long-dead Irish granny. And the joke of it is, Scott will later point out, it's just enough to put her on edge, just enough to get her either strapped or at least semistrapped.

Sometimes, he will tell her not long hence, speaking from a hospital bed (ah, but he could so easily have been on the cooling board himself, all his wakeful, too-thoughtful nights over) in his new high whistling and effortful voice, *sometimes just enough is just enough. As the saying is.*

And she knew exactly what he meant.

III

Roger Dashmiel has his share of headaches today, Lisey knows that. It doesn't make her like him any better, but sure, she knows. If there was ever an actual script for the ceremony, Professor Hegstrom (he of the emergency gall-bladder attack) has been too muddled to tell Dashmiel what or where it is. Dashmiel has consequently been left with little more than a time of day and a cast of characters featuring a writer to whom he has taken an instant dislike. When the little party of dignitaries left Inman Hall, temporary home of the library sciences staff, for the short but exceedingly warm walk to the site of the forthcoming Shipman Library, Dashmiel told Scott they'd have to more or less play it by ear. Scott shrugged good-naturedly and nodded. He was absolutely comfortable with that. For Scott Landon, ear was a way of life.

"Ah'll introduce you," Dashmiel said as they walked toward the baked and shimmering plot of land where the new library would stand. The photographer in charge of immortalizing all of this danced restlessly back and forth, hither and yon, snapping and snapping, busy as a gnat. Lisey could see a rectangle of fresh brown earth not far ahead, about nine feet by five, she judged, and pickup-trucked in that morning by the just-starting-to-fade look of it. No one had thought to put up an awning, and already the surface of the fresh dirt had acquired a grayish glaze.

"*Somebody* better do it," Scott said.

Dashmiel had frowned as if wounded by some undeserved canard. Then, with a sigh, he pressed on. "Applause follows introduction—"

"As day follows night," Scott murmured.

"—and then yew'll say a woid or tew," Dashmiel finished. Beyond the baked tract of land awaiting the library, a freshly paved parking lot shimmered in the sunlight, all smooth tar and staring yellow lines. Lisey saw fantastic ripples of nonexistent water on its far side.

"My pleasure," Scott said.

The unvarying good nature of his responses seemed to worry Dashmiel rather than reassure him. "Ah hope yew won't want to say *tew* much at the groundbreakin'," he told Scott rather severely as they approached the roped-off area. This had been kept clear, but there was a crowd big enough to stretch almost to the parking lot waiting beyond it. An even larger one had trailed Dashmiel and the Landons from Inman Hall. Soon the two would merge, and Lisey—who ordinarily did not mind crowds any more than she minded turbulence at twenty thousand feet—didn't like this, either. It occurred to her that so many people on a day this hot might suck all the air out of the air. Totally dopey idea, but—

"It's mahty hot, even for Naishveel in August, wouldn't you say so, Toneh?"

Tony Eddington—who would be *rahtin' all this up* for something called the U-Tenn *Review*—nodded obligingly but said nothing. His only comment so far had been to identify the tirelessly dancing photographer as Stefan Queensland, U-Tenn Nashville, class of '83, currently of the *Nashville American.* "Hope y'all will h'ep him out if y'can," Tony Eddington had said softly to Scott as they began their walk over here. Eddington was carrying a little wire notebook in which he had so far written absolutely nothing, so far as Lisey could see.

"Yew'll finish yoah remarks," Dashmiel said, "and there'll be anothuh round of applause. Then, Mistuh Landon—"

"Scott."

Dashmiel had flashed a rictus grin, there for just a moment, then gone. "Then, *Scott*, yew'll go on and toin that all-impawtant foist shovelful of oith." *Toin? Foist? Oith?* Lisey mused, and then it came to her that Dashmiel was saying *turn that all-important first shovelful of earth* in his only semibelievable Louisiana drawl. "Followin' that, we'll proceed on across yonduh parkin' lot to Nelson Hall—which is mercifully air-conditioned, Ah might add."

"All sounds fine to me," Scott replied, and that was all he had time for, because they had arrived.

IV

Perhaps it's a holdover from the broken toothglass—that *omenish* feeling—but the plot of trucked-in dirt looks like a grave to Lisey: XL size, as if for a giant. The two crowds collapse in around it in a circle, becoming one and creating that breathless suck-oven feel at the center. A campus security guard now stands at each corner of the ornamental velvet-rope barrier, beneath which Dashmiel, Scott, and "Toneh" Eddington have ducked. Queensland, the photographer, dances relentlessly, his old-fashioned Speed Graphic held up in front of his face. There are big patches of darkness under his arms and a sweat-tree growing up the back of his shirt. *Paging Weegee*, Lisey thinks, and realizes she envies him. He is so free, flitting gnatlike in the heat; he is twenty-five and all his shit still works. Dashmiel, however, is looking at him with growing impatience which Stefan Queensland affects not to see until he has exactly the shot he wants. Lisey has an idea it's one of Scott alone, his foot on the silly silver spade, his hair blowing back in the breeze. In any case, Weegee Junior at last lowers his big old box of a camera and steps back to the edge of the crowd's far curve. And here, following him with her somewhat wistful regard, Lisey first sees the madman, a graduate student with long blond hair named Gerd Allen Cole. He has the look, one local reporter will later write, "of John Lennon recovering from his romance with heroin—hollow eyes at odd and disquieting contrast to his puffy child's cheeks."

At that moment, beyond noting all that tumbled blond hair, Lisey thinks nothing of Gerd Allen Cole, *omens* or no *omens*. She just wants this to be over so she can find a bathroom stall in the bowels of the English department across the way and pull her rebellious underwear out of the crack of her ass. She has to make water, too, but right now that's pretty much secondary.

"Ladies and gentlemen!" Dashmiel says in the carrying but somehow artificial voice of a carnival barker. "It is mah distinct pleasure to introduce Mr. Scott Landon, authuh of the Pulitzuh prize–winnin' *Relics* and the National Book Award–winnin' *The Coster's Daughter.* He's come all the way from Maine with his loveleh wife to inauguarate construction—yes, at long last—on our vereh own Shipman Lah-brey! Scott Landon, folks! Let's hear it!"

The crowd applauds at once, and enthusiastically. The loveleh wife joins in, patting her palms together automatically, looking at Dashmiel and thinking, *He won the NBA for* The Coaster's Daughter. *That's* Coaster, *not* Coster. *And I sort of think you knew it. Why don't you like him, you petty man?*

Then she happens to glance beyond him and this time she really *does* notice Gerd Allen Cole. He is just standing there with all that fabulous blond hair tumbled down to his eyebrows and the sleeves of a white shirt far too big for him—he's all but floating in it—rolled up to his biceps. The tails of this shirt are out and dangle almost to the whitened knees of the old jeans he wears. Instead of applauding Blondie has got his hands clasped rather prissily together in front of him and there's a spooky-sweet smile on his face and his lips are moving, as if he's saying a prayer . . . but he's looking straight at Scott. As the wife of a public man (some of the time, at least), Lisey at once pegs Blondie as a potential problem. She thinks of guys like this as "deep-space fans," although she'd never say so out loud and has never even told Scott this. Deep-space fans always have a lot to say. They want to grab Scott by the arm and tell him that that they understand the secret messages in his books; deep-space fans know the books are really secret guides to God, Satan, or possibly the Coptic Gospels. They might be on about Scientology or numerology. Sometimes they want to talk about other worlds— secret worlds. Two years ago a deep-space fan hitchhiked all the way from Texas to Maine to talk to Scott about Bigfoot. That guy made Lisey a little nervous—there was a certain walleyed look of *absence* about him, and a knife (sheathed, thank Christ) in one of the loops of his backpack—but Scott talked to him a little, gave him a beer, took a couple of his pamphlets, signed the kid a paperback copy of *Instructions to be Left in Earth*, clapped him on the back, and sent him on his way, happy. Sometimes—when he's got it strapped on nice and tight—Scott is amazing. No other word will do.

The thought of actual violence does not now occur to Lisey— certainly not the idea that Blondie means to pull a Mark David Chapman on her husband. *My mind just doesn't run that way*, she might have said.

Scott acknowledges the applause—and a few raucous rebel yells—with the Scott Landon grin which has been caricatured in the *Wall Street Journal* (it will later appear on any number of Barnes & Noble shopping bags), all the time continuing to balance on one foot while the other holds its place on the shoulder of the silly shovel.

He lets the applause run for ten or fifteen seconds, whatever his intuition tells him is right (and his intuition is rarely wrong), then raises one hand, waving it off. And it goes. When he speaks, his voice seems nowhere near as loud as Dashmiel's, but Lisey knows that even with no mike or battery-powered bullhorn—and the lack of either here this afternoon is probably someone's oversight—it will carry to the very back rows of the crowd. And the crowd helps out. It's gone absolutely silent, straining to hear him: every golden word. A Famous Man has come among them. A Thinker and a Writer. He will now scatter pearls of wisdom before them.

Pearls before swine, Lisey thinks. *Sweaty swine, at that.* But didn't her father once tell her that pigs don't sweat? She can't exactly remember, and it's sort of an odd train of thought anyway, isn't it?

Across from her, Blondie carefully pushes his tumbled hair back from a fine white brow with his left hand. Then he clasps the left with his right again. His hands are as white as his brow and Lisey thinks: *There's one piggy who stays inside a lot. A stay-at-home swine, and why not? He looks like he's got all sorts of strange deep-space ideas to catch up on.*

She shifts from one foot to the other, and the silk of her underwear all but *squeaks* in the crack of her ass. Oh, maddening! She forgets Blondie again in trying to calculate if she might not . . . while Scott's making his remarks...very surreptitiously, mind you . . .

Her dead mother speaks up. Dour. Three words. Brooking no argument. *No, Lisey. Wait.*

"Ain't gonna sermonize, me," Scott says, and she recognizes the patois of Gully Foyle, the main character in his all-time favorite novel, Alfred Bester's *The Stars My Destination*. "Too hot for sermons."

"Beam us up, Scotty!" someone in the fifth or sixth row on the parking-lot side of the crowd yells exuberantly. The crowd laughs and cheers.

"Can't do it, brother," Scott says, "transporters are broken and we're all out of lithium crystals."

The crowd, being new to the riposte as well as the sally (Lisey has heard both at least fifty times; maybe as many as a hundred), roars its approval and applauds. Across the way, Blondie smiles thinly, sweatlessly, and continues to grip his left hand with his right. And now Scott does take his foot off the spade, not as if he's grown impatient with it but as if he has, for the moment, found another use for the tool. She watches, not without fascination, for this is Scott at his best, not reading scripture but strutting showtime.

"It's nineteen-eighty-six and the world has grown dark," he says. He slips the three feet or so of the little spade's wooden handle easily through his cupped hand, so that his fingers rest near the thing's business end. The scoop winks sun in Lisey's eyes once, and then it is mostly hidden by the sleeve of Scott's lightweight jacket. With the scoop and the blade hidden, he uses the slim wooden handle as a pointer, ticking off trouble and tragedy in the air in front of him.

"In January, the *Challenger* shuttle explodes, killing all seven on board. Bad call on a cold morning, folks. They never should have tried to launch.

"In February, at least thirty die on Election Day in the Philippines. Ferdinand and Imelda Marcos, meanwhile, responsible for the deaths of a hundred times that number—maybe four hundred times that number—leave for Guam and, eventually, Hawaii. No one knows how many pairs of shoes babyluv takes with her."

There's a ripple of laughter from the crowd. Not much. Tony Eddington is finally taking notes. Roger Dashmiel looks hot and put out with this unexpected current-events lesson.

"The nuclear reactor accident at Chernobyl kills thousands, sickens tens of thousands.

"The AIDS epidemic kills thousands, sickens tens of thousands.

"The world grows dark. Discordia rises. Mr. Yeats's blood-tide is still undimmed."

He looks down, looks fixedly at nil but graying earth, and Lisey is suddenly terrified that he is seeing it, his private monster, the thing with the endless patchy piebald side, that he is going to go off, perhaps even come to the break she knows he is afraid of (in truth she is as afraid of it as he is) in front of all these people. Then, before her heart can do more than begin to speed up, he raises his head, grins like a boy at the county fair, and shoots the handle of the spade through his fist to the halfway point. It's a showy move, a pool shark's move, and the folks at the front of the crowd go *ooooh*. But Scott's not done. Holding the spade out before him, he rotates the handle nimbly in his fingers, accelerating it into an unlikely spin. It's a baton twirler's move, as dazzling—because of the silver scoop swinging in the sun, mostly—as it is unexpected. She's been married to him since 1977—almost nine years now—and had no *idea* he had such a sublimely cool move in his repertoire. (How many years does it take, she'll wonder later, lying in bed alone in her substandard motel room and listening to dogs bark beneath a hot orange Nashville moon, before the simple stupid weight of time finally sucks all the wow out of a marriage?) The silver bowl of the rapidly swinging spade sends a *Wake up! Wake up!* sunflash running across the heat-dazed, sweat-sticky surface of the crowd. Lisey's husband is suddenly Scott the Pitchman, grinning, and she has never been so relieved to see that totally untrustworthy *honey, I'm hip* huckster's grin on her husband's face. He has bummed them out; now he will sell them the doubtful good cheer with which he hopes to send them home. And she thinks they will buy, hot August afternoon or not. When he's like this, Scott could sell Frigidaires to Inuits, as the saying is . . . and God bless the language pool where we all go first to drink our fill and then to strap on our business.

"But if every book is a little light in that darkness—and so I believe, so I believe, so I must believe, for I write the goddamn things, don't I?—then every library is a grand bonfire around which ten thousand people come to stand and warm themselves each cold day and night. We celebrate the laying of such a fire this afternoon, and I'm honored to be a part of it. Here is where we spit in the eye of chaos and kick murder right in his wrinkled old *cojones. Hey, photographer!*"

Stefan Queensland snaps to, but smiling.

Scott, also smiling, says: "Now—get one of this. The powers that be may not want to use it, but you'll like it in your portfolio, I'll bet."

Scott holds the ornamental tool out as if he intends to twirl it again, and the crowd gives a little hopeful gasp, but he's only teasing them. He slides his left hand back down to the spade's collar, his right to a position on the handle about a foot from the top. Then he bends, digs in, and drives the spade-blade deep, dousing its hot glitter in earth. He brings it up, tosses its dark load aside, and cries: "*I declare the Shipman Library construction site open!*"

The applause that greets this makes the previous rounds sound like the sort of polite patter you might hear at a prep-school tennis match. Lisey doesn't know if young Mr. Queensland caught the ceremonial first scoop, not for sure (she wasn't looking), but when Scott pumps the silly little silver spade at the sky like an Olympic hero, Queensland catches that one for sure, laughing as he snaps it. Scott holds the pose for a moment (Lisey happens to glance at Dashmiel and catches that gentleman in the act of rolling his eyes at Mr. Eddington—Toneh). Then he lowers the spade to port arms and holds it that way, grinning. Sweat has popped on his cheeks and brow in fine beads. The applause begins to taper off. The crowd thinks he's done. Lisey, who can read him like a book (as the saying is), knows better.

When they can hear him again, Scott bends down for an encore scoop. "This one's for Yeats!" he calls. Another scoop. "This one's for Poe!" Yet another scoop. "This one's for Alfred Bester, and if you haven't read him, you ought to be ashamed!" He's starting to sound out of breath, and Lisey, although mostly still amused, is starting to feel a bit alarmed, as well. It's *so* hot. She's trying to remember what he ate for lunch—was it heavy or light?

"And this one . . ." He dives the spade into what is now a fairly respectable little divot (Queensland documenting each fresh foray) one last time and holds up the final dip of earth. The front of his

shirt has darkened with sweat. "Well, why don't you think of whoever wrote your favorite book? The one that, in a perfect world, you'd
check out first when the Shipman Library finally opens its doors to
you? Got it? Okay—this one's for him, or her, or them." He tosses
the dirt aside, gives the spade a final valedictory shake, then turns
to Dashmiel . . . who should be pleased with Scott's showmanship,
Lisey thinks—asked to play by ear, Scott has played brilliantly—
and who instead only looks hot and pissed off. "I think we're done
here," he says, and makes as if to hand Dashmiel the spade.

"No, that's yoahs," Dashmiel says. "As a keepsake, and a token
of ouah thanks. Along with yoah check, of co'se." His smile—the
rictus, not the real one—comes and goes in a fitful cramp. "Shall
we go and grab ow'sefs a little air-conditionin'?"

"By all means," Scott says, looking bemused, and then hands
the spade to Lisey—as he has handed her so many other mostly
unwanted mementos over the past twelve years of his celebrity:
everything from ceremonial oars and Boston Red Sox hats encased
in Lucite cubes to the masks of comedy and tragedy . . . but mainly
pen-and-pencil sets. So many pen-and-pencil sets. Waterman,
Scripto, Schaeffer, Montblanc, you name it. She looks at the spade's
glittering silver scoop, as bemused as her beloved (he is still her
beloved, and she's come to believe he always will be). Every last
speck of dirt has slid off, it seems; even the blade is clean. There
are a few flecks in the incised letters reading COMMENCEMENT,
SHIPMAN LIBRARY, and Lisey blows them off. Then she looks at this
unlikely prize again. Where will such an artifact end up? She'd say
Scott's study over the barn, but in this summer of 1986 the study
is still under construction and probably won't be ready for occu-
pancy until October . . . although the address works and he has
already begun to store stuff in the musty stalls of the barn below.
Across many of the cardboard boxes he had scrawled SCOTT! THE
EARLY YEARS! Most likely the silver spade will wind up with this
stuff, wasting its gleams in the gloom. The one depressing surety
is that it'll wind up in a place where one of them will stumble

across it twenty years from now and try to remember just *what* in the blue *smuck*—

Meanwhile, Dashmiel is on the move. Without another word—as if he's disgusted with this whole business and determined to put it behind him as soon as possible—he starts across the rectangle of fresh earth, detouring around the divot which Scott's last big shovelful of earth has almost succeeded in promoting to a hole. The heels of Dashmiel's shiny black I'm-an-assistant-professor-on-my-way-up-and-you're-not shoes sink deep into the earth with every step. Dashmiel has to fight for balance, and Lisey guesses this does nothing to improve his mood. Tony Eddington falls in beside him. Scott pauses a moment, as if not quite sure what's going on, and then also starts to move, slipping himself in between Dashmiel and Eddington. He delighted her into forgetting her *omenish* feeling

(*broken glass in the morning*)

for a little while, but now it's back

(*broken hearts at night*)

and with a vengeance. She thinks it must be why all these details look so *big* to her. She is sure the world will come back into more normal focus once she has, in Dashmiel's words, grabbed herself a little air-conditioning. And once she's gotten that pesty swatch of cloth out of her butt.

This really is almost over, she reminds herself, and—how funny life can be—it is at this precise moment that the day begins to derail.

A campus security cop who is older than the others on this detail (she will later identify him from Stefan Queensland's news photo as Captain S. Heffernan) holds up the rope barrier on the far side of the ceremonial rectangle of earth. All she notices about him is that he's wearing what her husband might have called *a puffickly huh-yooge batch of orifice* on his khaki shirt. Her husband and his two flanking escorts—Dashmiel on Scott's left, C. Anthony Eddington on Scott's right—duck beneath the rope in a move so synchronized it almost could have been choreographed.

The crowd is moving toward the parking lot with the principals . . . with one exception. *Blondie* is not heading toward the parking lot. Blondie is still standing on the parking-lot side of the commencement patch. A few people bump him, and he's forced a few steps backward after all, onto the baked dead earth where the Shipman Library will stand come 1989 (if the chief contractor's promises can be believed, that is). Then he's actually stepping forward against the tide, his hands coming unclasped so he can push first a girl out of his way to his left and then a guy out of his way on his right. His mouth is moving. At first Lisey again thinks he's mouthing a silent prayer, and then she hears the broken gibberish— like something a bad James Joyce imitator might write—and for the first time she becomes actively alarmed. Blondie's somehow weird blue eyes are fixed on her husband, but Lisey understands that he does not want to discuss Bigfoot or the hidden religious subtexts of Scott's novels. This is no mere deep-space boy.

"The church bells came down Angel Street thick as falling oak trees," says Blondie—says Gerd Allen Cole—who, it will turn out, spent most of his seventeenth year in an expensive Virginia mental institution and was released as cured and good to go, thanks very much, and these words Lisey gets in the clear. They cut through the rising chatter of the crowd, that hum of conversation, like a knife through some light, sweet cake. "That rungut sound, ar! Like rain on a tin roof! Dirty flowers! Ya, dirty and sweet! This is how the church bells sound in the basement!"

A right hand that seems made entirely of long pale fingers goes to the tails of the white shirt, and Lisey suddenly understands

(*George Wallace oh Christ Wallace and Bremmer*)

exactly what's going on here, although it comes to her in a series of shorthand TV images from her childhood. She looks at Scott and sees Scott is speaking to Dashmiel. Dashmiel is looking at Stefan Queensland, the irritated frown on Dashmiel's face saying he's had *Quite! Enough! Photographs! For one day! Thank! You!* Queensland himself is looking down at his camera, making some adjustment, and C. Anthony "Toneh" Eddington is making a note on his pad.

She even spies the older campus security cop, he of the khaki uniform and the puffickly *huh-yooge* batch of orifice; this worthy is looking at the crowd, but it is *the wrong part* of the crowd. It's impossible that she can see all these folks and Blondie too, but she can, she does; she can even see Scott's lips forming the words *think that went pretty well*, which is a testing comment he often makes after events like this . . . and oh Jesus Mary and JoJo the Carpenter, she tries to scream out Scott's name and warn him but *her throat locks up*, dry and spitless, she can't say anything, and Blondie's got the tails of that lolloping big white shirt all the way up, and underneath are empty belt loops and a flat hairless belly and lying against his white skin is the butt of a gun which he now lays hold of and she hears him say, closing in on Scott a little from the right, "If it closes the lips of the bells, it will have done the job. I'm sorry, Papa."

I'm sorry, Papa.

She's running forward, or trying to, but oh God she's got such a puffickly *huh-yooge* case of gluefoot and someone shoulders in front of her, a coed with her hair tied up in a wide white silk ribbon with NASHVILLE printed on it in blue (see how she sees everything?), and Lisey pushes her with one hand, the hand not holding the silver spade, and the coed caws "*Hey!*" except it sounds slower and draggier than that, like the word *hey* recorded at 45 RPM and then played back at 33⅓ or maybe even 16 RPM. The whole world has gone to hot tar and for an eternity Scott and Dashmiel are blocked from her view; she can see only Tony Eddington, making more of his idiotic notes—a slow starter, but once he gets going . . . whooo! Boy takes notes like a house afire! Then the coed with the NASHVILLE ribbon stumbles clear of Lisey's field of vision—*finally!*—and as Dashmiel and her husband come into view again, Lisey sees Dashmiel's body language go from a drone to a startled cry of fear. It happens in the space of an instant.

Lisey sees what Dashmiel sees. She sees Blondie now with the gun (it will prove to be a Ladysmith .22, made in Korea and bought at a pawn-and-loan in South Nashville for thirty-seven dollars) pointed at her husband, who has at last seen his danger and stopped. In Lisey-time, all of this happens very, very slowly. She doesn't actually see the bullet fly out of the .22's muzzle—not quite—but she hears Scott say, very mildly, seeming to drawl the words over the course of ten or even fifteen seconds: "Let's talk about it, son, right?" And then she sees fire bloom from the gun's nickel-plated muzzle in a yellow-white corsage. She hears a pop—stupid, insignificant: the sound of someone breaking a paper lunch sack with the palm of his hand. She sees Dashmiel, that chickenshit southern-fried asshole, turn and plunge away to his immediate left. She sees Scott buck backward on his heels. At the same time his chin thrusts forward. The combination is weirdly graceful, like a dance-floor move. A black hole opens in the right side of his summer sport coat. "Son, you honest-to-God don't want to do that," he says, and even in Lisey-time she hears the way his voice thins a little more on every word until he sounds like a test pilot in a high-altitude chamber. Yet Lisey is almost positive he doesn't know he has been shot. His sport coat swings open as he puts his hand out in a commanding stop-this-shit gesture, and she realizes two things simultaneously: that she can see gouts of blood soaking into the front of his shirt and that she has at last—oh thank God for small favors—broken into some semblance of a run.

"I got to end all this ding-dong for the freesias," says Gerd Allen Cole with perfect fretful clarity, and Lisey is suddenly sure that once Scott is dead, once the damage is done, Blondie will either kill himself or pretend to try. For the time being, however, he has this first business to finish. The business of the author. Blondie turns his wrist slightly so that the smoking and somehow cuntish muzzle of the Ladysmith .22 points at the left side of Scott's chest; in Lisey-time the move is smooth and slow. Blondie has done the lung; his second bullet will be a heart shot, she thinks, and knows she can't allow that to happen. If her husband is to have any chance at all, this loony tune must not be allowed to put any more lead into him.

As if hearing her, repudiating her, Gerd Allen Cole says, "It never ends until you are. You're responsible for all these repetitions, old boy. You are hell, and you are a monkey, and now you are *my* monkey!"

This speech is the closest he comes to making sense, and making it gives Lisey just enough time to first wind up with the silver spade—her hands, somehow knowing their business in their own way, have already found their position near the top of the thing's forty-inch handle—and then swing it. Still, it's close. If it had been a horse race, the tote board would undoubtedly have flashed the HOLD TICKETS WAIT FOR PHOTO message. But when the race is between a man with a gun and a woman with a shovel, you don't need a photo. And in slowed-down Lisey-time there's no chance of a missed perception, anyway. She sees it all. She sees the spade's silver scoop strike the gun, driving it upward, just as that corsage blooms again (she can see only part of the flame and none of the muzzle; the muzzle is hidden by the blade of the spade). She sees the spade carry on forward and upward as the second shot goes harmlessly into the hot August sky. She sees the gun fly loose, and there is time to think, *Holy smuck! I really put a charge into this one!* before the commemorative spade connects with the blond fruitcake's face. His hand is still in there (three of those slim long fingers will be broken and Lisey could give Shit One about Monsieur Deep-Space Fruitcake Cole's fingers), but all the hand ends up protecting is his forehead. The spade's silver bowl connects solidly with the lower part of the would-be assassin's face, breaking his nose, shattering his right cheekbone and the bony orbit around his staring right eye, mashing his lips back against his teeth (and pretty well exploding the upper lip), breaking nine teeth, as well—the four in front will prove to be shattered right down to the gum line. All in all, it's quite a job. A Mafia goon with a set of brass knucks couldn't have done better.

Now—still slow, still in Lisey-time—the elements of Stefan Queensland's award-winning photograph are assembling themselves.

Captain S. Heffernan has seen what's happening only a second or two after Lisey, but he has also had to deal with the bystander problem, in his case a fat bepimpled fella wearing baggy Bermuda shorts and a T-shirt with Scott Landon's smiling face on the front. Captain Heffernan first grapples with this young fella and then shunts him aside with one muscular shoulder. The young fella goes flying with a dismayed what-the-fuck? expression on the speckled moon face beneath his crew cut.

By then Lisey has administered the silver spade to the would-be assassin. Gerd Allen Cole, aka Blondie, is sinking to the ground (and out of the photo's field) with a dazed expression in one eye and blood pouring from the other one. Blood is also gushing from the hole that was his mouth. Heffernan completely misses the actual hit.

Roger Dashmiel, suddenly remembering that he is supposed to be the master of ceremonies and not a jackrabbit, turns back toward Eddington, his protégé, and Landon, his troublesome guest of honor, just in time to take his place as a staring, slightly blurred face in the photo's background.

Scott Landon, meanwhile, shock-walks right out of the award-winning photo. He walks as though unmindful of the heat, striding toward the parking lot and Nelson Hall beyond, Nelson Hall which is home of the English department, and air-conditioned. He walks with surprising briskness, at least to begin with, and a goodly part of the crowd moves with him. The crowd seems for the most part unaware that anything has happened. Lisey is both infuriated and unsurprised. After all, how many of them actually saw Blondie with that cuntish little pistol in his hand? How many of them recognized the burst-paper-bag sounds as gunshots? The hole in Scott's coat could be a smudge of dirt from his shoveling chore, and the blood which has soaked his shirt is as yet invisible to the outside world. He's now making a strange and horrible whistling noise each time he inhales, but how many of them hear that? No, it's *her* they're looking at—some of them, anyway—the daffy dame who has just inexplicably hauled off and smacked some guy in the face with the ceremonial silver spade. A lot of them are grinning about it, actually *grinning*, as if they believe it's all part of a show being put on for their benefit; the Scott Landon Road Show. Probably they believe *exactly* that. Well, fuck them, and fuck Dashmiel, and fuck the day-late-and-dollar-short campus cop with his Sam Browne belt and oversize badge. All she cares about now is Scott. She thrusts the shovel out not quite blindly to her right and Eddington, their Boswell-for-a-day, takes it. It's either that or get smacked in the nose with it. Then, still in that dreadful slow-time, Lisey runs after her husband, whose briskness evaporates as soon as he reaches the suck-oven heat of the parking lot. He begins to stagger and weave; his upper body begins to curl into a shrimp shape. She sees this and tries to run faster and still it feels like she's running in glue. Behind her, Tony Eddington is peering at the silver spade like a man who has no idea what he's gotten hold of; it might be an artillery shell, a radiation detector, or the Great Lost Whang-Dang-Doodle of the Egyptian pharaohs. To him comes Captain S. Heffernan, and although Captain Heffernan will later in his secret heart *doubt* that it was really Eddington who laid the gun-toting nutjob low, the captain is not (even at one in the morning, even to himself, over bourbon and branch water), able to *swear* it was not Eddington but the wife who stopped the nutjob's clock before said nutjob could fire a second shot—the kill shot, most likely—into the writer. The mind is a monkey; the mind is a monster. The mind is sort of a madman, actually. Captain S. Heffernan knows these things, knows it's why so-called "eyeball witnesses" are never to be trusted, and that includes so-called professionals like himself. *Besides*, he tells himself, *that fat kid with the zitzes and the crew cut was in my way.*

In any case, the nutjob is down, the nutjob is puling through the hole that used to be his mouth, the nutjob is toast, and Stan Heffernan seizes the Eddington kid's free left hand and pumps it, feeling a large relieved grin spread across his face as he realizes he may just get out of this mess with his skin on and his job intact.

Lisey runs toward her husband, who has just gone down on his hands and knees in the parking lot. And Queensland snaps his picture as she goes, catching just half of one shoe on the far right-hand side of the frame . . . something not even he will realize, then or ever.

V

He goes down, the Pulitzer prize winner goes down, Scott Landon goes down, and Lisey makes the supreme effort to break out of that slow and terrible Lisey-time. She must succeed because she has heard the cry of alarm from the part of the crowd that's been moving with Scott and now she hears—in the maddening slow-speak of Lisey-time—someone saying *Heeeeee's hurrrrt!* She must break free because if she doesn't get to him before the crowd surrounds him and shuts her out, they will very likely kill him with their concern. With smotherlove.

She screams at herself in her own head

(*strap it on RIGHT NOW!*)

and that does it. Suddenly she is *knifing* forward; all the world is noise and heat and sweat, but she blesses the speedy reality of it even as she uses her left hand to grab the left cheek of her ass and *pull*, raking the goddamn underwear out of the crack of her ass, there, at least one thing about this wrong and broken day is now mended.

A coed in a shell top, the kind of top where the straps tie on the shoulders in big floppy bows, threatens to block her narrowing path to Scott, but Lisey ducks beneath her and hits the hot-top. She will not be aware of her scraped and blistered knees until much later—until the hospital, in fact, where a kindly paramedic will notice and put lotion on them, something so cool and soothing it will make her cry with relief. But that is for later. Now it might as well be just her and Scott alone here on the edge of this hot parking lot, this terrible black-and-yellow ballroom floor which must be a hundred and thirty degrees at least, maybe a hundred and fifty. Maybe more. Her mind tries to present her with the image of an egg frying sunny-side up in her Ma's old black iron spider and she thrusts it away. Scott looks up at her and now his face is waxy pale except for the black triangles forming beneath his eyes and the blood which has begun running from the right side of his mouth and down his chin in a scarlet stream.

"Lisey!" His voice is thin, whooping. "Did he . . . shoot me?"

"Don't try to talk," she tells him, and puts a hand on his chest. His shirt, oh dear God, it is not wet with blood but *soaked* with blood, and beneath it she can feel his heart running along so fast and light; it is not the heartbeat of a human being, she thinks, but that of a bird. *Pigeon-pulse,* she thinks, and that is when the girl with the floppy bows tied on her shoulders falls on top of her. She would land on Scott but Lisey instinctively shields him, taking the brunt of the girl's weight (*"Hey, shit! FUCK!"* the startled girl cries out) with her back . . . it is there for a moment and then gone. Lisey sees the girl shoot her hands out to break her fall—*oh, the divine reflexes of the young,* she thinks—and the girl is successful . . . but then she is crying, *"Ow! Ow! OW!"* This makes Lisey look at her own hands. They aren't blistered, not yet, but they *have* gone the deep red of a perfectly cooked Maine lobster.

"Lisey," Scott whispers, and oh Christ how his breath *screams* when he pulls it in.

"Who pushed me?" the girl with the bows on her shoulders is demanding. She is a-hunker, hair from a busted ponytail in her eyes, crying with surprise, pain, and embarrassment.

Lisey leans close to Scott. The heat of him terrifies her and fills her with pity deeper than any she has ever felt, deeper than she thought it was possible to feel. He is actually *shivering* with the heat. Awkwardly, using only one arm, she strips off her jacket. "Scott, don't try to talk. You're right, you've been sh—"

"I'm so hot," he says, and begins to shiver harder. What comes next—convulsions? His hazel eyes stare up into her blue ones. Blood runs from the corner of his mouth. She can smell it. It stinks. Now the collar of his shirt is filling in red. "I'm so hot, please give me ice."

"I will," she says, and puts her jacket under his head and neck.

"I will, Scott." *Thank God for his sport coat,* she thinks, not quite incoherent, and then has an idea. She grabs the hunkering, crying girl by the arm. "What's your name?"

The girl stares at her as if she were mad, but answers the question. "Lisa Lemke."

Same as mine, small world, Lisey thinks, but does not say. What she says is, "My husband has been shot, Lisa. Can you go over there to"—she cannot remember the name of the building, only its function—"to the English department and call an ambulance? Dial 911—"

"Ma'am? Mrs. Landon, is it?" This is the campus security cop, making his way through the crowd with a lot of help from his meaty elbows. He squats beside her and his knees pop loudly. *His knees are louder than Blondie's pistol,* Lisey marvels. He's holding his walkie-talkie, which was previously clipped to his Sam Browne belt in the place where a regular cop would wear his gun. When he speaks, he does so slowly and carefully, as though to a distressed child. "Mrs. Landon, I have called the campus infirmary. They are rolling their ambulance, which will take your husband to Nashville Memorial. Nashville . . . Memorial . . . Hospital. Do you understand me?"

She does, and her gratitude to this man is almost as deep as the pity she feels for her husband, lying on the simmering pavement and bleeding from his chest and mouth, shuddering in the heat like a distempered dog. She nods, weeping the first of what will be many tears before she gets Scott back to Maine—not on a Delta flight but on a private jet, and with a private nurse, and with another ambulance and another private nurse to meet them at the Portland Jetport's Civil Air Terminal. And all that is later. Now she turns back to the Lemke girl and says, "Lisey, he's burning up—is there ice, honey? Can you think of anywhere there might be ice?"

She says this without much hope, and is therefore amazed when Lisa Lemke nods at once. "There's a soda machine and two snack machines over there." She points in the direction of Nelson Hall, which Lisey can't see. All she can see is a crowding forest of bare legs, some hairy, some smooth, some tanned, some sunburned. She realizes they are completely hemmed in, that she's tending her fallen husband in a slot the shape of a large vitamin pill or cold capsule, and feels a touch of crowd-panic. Is the word for that *agoraphobia?* Scott would know.

"If you can get him some ice, please do," Lisey says. "And hurry." She looks at the campus security cop, who has gone to one knee on Scott's other side and appears to be taking his pulse—a completely useless activity, in Lisey's opinion. "Can't you make them move back?" she almost pleads. "It's so *hot*—"

He doesn't give her time to finish, but is up like Jack from his box, yelling, "Move it back! Let this girl through! Move it back! Let this girl through! Let him breathe, folks, let him breathe, all right, what do you say?"

The crowd shuffles back . . . very reluctantly, Lisey thinks. They want to see all the blood, it seems to her.

The heat bakes relentlessly up from the pavement. She has half expected to get used to it, the way you get used to a hot shower, but that isn't happening. She listens for the approaching howl of the promised ambulance and hears nothing. Then she hears Scott, croaking her name. At the same time he twitches weakly at the side of the sweat-soaked shell top she's wearing (her bra now stands out against the silk as stark as a swollen tattoo). She looks down at him and sees something she does not like: Scott is smiling. The blood has coated his lips a rich candy red, top to bottom, side to side, and consequently the smile looks like the grin of a clown. *No one loves a clown at midnight,* she thinks, and wonders where *that* came from. It will only be much later that night—that long and mostly sleepless night, listening to the August dogs howl at the hot moon—that she'll realize it was Lon Chaney. She knows because the line was the epigram of Scott's third novel, the only one she has hated, *Empty Devils*. The one that's sort of a riff on Romero's *Living Dead* movies.

"Lisey."

"Scott, don't try to talk—"

But he is relentless, twitching at her blue silk top, his eyes—dear God, they are so deep in their sockets now, but still so brilliant and fevery. He has something to say. And as always when he has something to say, he will find an audience if he can. This time he has her.

Reluctantly, she leans down.

For a moment he says nothing, but she can hear him getting ready to. He pulls air in a little at a time, in half gasps. The smell of blood is even stronger up close. A mineral smell. Or maybe it's detergent. Or—

It's death, Lisey, that's all. Just the smell of death.

As if he needs to ratify this, Scott says: "It's very close, honey. I can't see it, but I . . ." Another long, screaming intake of breath. "I hear it taking its meal. And grunting." Smiling as he says it.

"Scott, I don't know what you're tal—"

The hand which has been tugging at her top now pinches her side, and cruelly—when she takes the top off much later, in the motel room, she'll see the bruise: a true lover's knot.

"You . . ." Screamy breath. "*Know* . . ." Screamy breath, deeper. And still grinning, as if they share some horrible secret. Do they? "So . . . don't . . . insult my . . . intelligence. Or . . . your own."

Yes. She knows. *It*. The long boy, he calls it. Or just the thing. Or sometimes the thing with the endless piebald side. Once she meant to look up *piebald* in the dictionary—she is not bright about words, not like Scott is—she really did, but then she got sidetracked. And actually, it's more than just a few times he's spoken of that thing. Especially just lately. He says you can see it if you look through dirty water glasses. If you look through them just the right way, and in the hours after midnight.

He lets go of her, or maybe just loses the strength to hold on. Lisey pulls back a little—not far. His eyes regard her from their deep and blackened sockets. They are as brilliant as ever—as aware, as full of pain—but she sees they are also full of terror and (this is what frightens her the most) some wretched amusement. As if what's happened to him is in some way *funny*.

Still speaking low—perhaps so only she can hear, maybe because it's the best he can manage, probably both—Scott says, "Listen. Listen, Lisey. I'll make how it sounds when it looks around."

"Scott, no—you have to stop."

He pays no attention. He draws in another of those screaming lung-shot breaths, then purses his wet red lips in a tight O, as if to whistle. Instead of whistling he makes a low, indescribably nasty *chuffing* noise that drives a spray of blood up his clenched throat, through his lips, and into the sweltering air. A girl sees this gusher of fine ruby droplets and cries out in revulsion. This time the crowd doesn't need the voice of authority to tell them to move back; they do so on their own, leaving the three of them—Lisey, Scott, and the cop—a perimeter of at least four feet all the way around.

The sound—dear God, it *is* a kind of grunting—is mercifully short. Scott coughs, his chest heaving, the wound spilling more blood in rhythmic pulses, then beckons her back down with one finger. She comes, leaning on her burning hands. His socketed eyes compel her; his mortal grin compels her.

He turns his head to the side, spits a wad of blood onto the hot tar. Then he turns back to her. "I . . . could . . . call it that way," he whispers. "It would come. You'd . . . be . . . rid of me. My everlasting . . . quack."

She understands he means it, and for a moment (surely it is the power of his eyes) she believes it's true. He will make the sound again, only a little louder this time, and somewhere the long boy—that lord of sleepless nights—will turn its unspeakable hungry head. A moment later, in this world, Scott Landon will simply shiver on the pavement and die. The death certificate will say something sane, but she will know. His dark thing finally saw him and came for him and ate him alive.

So now come the things they will never speak of later, not to others nor between themselves. Too awful. Each long marriage has two hearts, one light and one dark. This is the dark heart of theirs, the one mad true secret. She will ponder it that night in the terrible moonlight while the dogs bark. Now she leans close to him on the baking pavement, sure he is dying, nonetheless determined to hold on to him if she can. If it means fighting the long boy for him—with nothing but her fingernails, come it to that—she will.

"Well . . . Lisey? What . . . do . . . you . . . say?"

Leaning even closer. Leaning into the shivering heat of him, the sweat- and blood-stink of him. Leaning in until she can smell the last palest ghost of the Foamy he shaved with that morning and the Prell he shampooed with. Leaning in until her lips touch his ear. She whispers: "Be quiet, Scott. Just be quiet." She pauses, then adds, louder—loud enough to make him jerk his head on the pavement: *"Leave that fucking thing alone and it will go away."*

When she looks at him again, his eyes are different—saner, somehow, but also weaker. "Have . . . you seen . . . ? Do . . . you know . . . ?"

"I know *you*," she says. "Don't you ever make that noise again."

He licks at his lips. She sees the blood on his tongue and it turns her stomach, but she doesn't pull away from him.

"I'm so hot," he says. "If only I had a piece of ice to suck . . ."

"Soon," Lisey says, not knowing if she's promising rashly and not caring. "I'm getting it for you." At last she can hear the ambulance howling its way toward them. That's something. Yet she is still in her heart convinced it will be too late. That sound he made, that *chuffing* sound, has almost shot her nerve.

And then, a kind of miracle. The girl with the bows on her shoulders and the new scrapes on her palms fights her way through to the front of the crowd. She is gasping like someone who has just run a race and sweat coats her cheeks and neck . . . but she's holding two big waxed paper cups in her hands. "I spilled half the shitting Cokes getting back here," she says, throwing a brief, baleful backward glance at the crowd, "but I got the ice okay. Ice is ni—" Then her eyes roll up almost to the whites and she reels backward, all loosey-goosey in her sneakers. The campus cop—bless him, oh bless him with many blessings, huh-yooge batch of orifice and all—

grabs her, steadies her, and takes one of the cups. He hands it down to Lisey, then urges the other Lisa, coed Lisa, to drink from the remaining cup. Lisey Landon pays no attention. Later, replaying all this, she'll be a little in awe of her own single-mindedness. Now she only thinks, *Just keep her from falling on top of me again if she faints,* and turns back to Scott.

He's shivering worse than ever, and his eyes are dulling out. And still he tries. "Lisey . . . so hot . . . ice . . ."

"I have it, Scott. Now will you for once just shut your everlasting mouth?"

And for a wonder, he does. A Scott Landon first. *Maybe,* she thinks, *he's just out of wind.*

Lisey drives her hand deep into the cup, sending Coke all the way to the top and splooshing over the edge. The cold is shocking and utterly wonderful. She clutches a good handful of ice chips, thinking how ironic this is: whenever she and Scott stop at a turnpike rest area and she uses a machine that dispenses cups of soda instead of cans or bottles, she always hammers on the NO ICE button, feeling righteous—others may allow the evil soft-drink companies to shortchange them by dispensing half a cup of ice and half a cup of soda, but not Lisa Landon! What was Good Ma Debusher's saying? *I didn't fall off a hay truck yesterday!*

His eyes are half-closed now, but he opens his mouth and when she first rubs his lips with her handful of ice and then pops one of the melting shards onto his bloody tongue, his shivering suddenly stops. God, it's magic. Emboldened, she rubs her freezing, leaking hand along his right cheek, his left cheek, and then across his forehead, where drops of Coke-colored water drip into his eyebrows.

"Oh, Lisey, that's heaven," he says, and although still screamy, his voice sounds more rational to her . . . more with-it, more *there.* The ambulance has pulled up on the left side of the crowd and she can hear an impatient male voice shouting, *"Paramedics! Let us through! Paramedics! C'mon, people, let us through!"*

"Lisey," he whispers.

"Scott, you need to be quiet."

But he means to have his say; as always, and until death closes his mouth sixteen years later, Scott Landon will have his say.

"Take . . . a motel room . . . close to . . . hospital."

"You don't need to tell me th—"

He gives her hand an impatient squeeze, stopping her. "It may . . . have heard you . . . *seen* you."

"Scott, I don't know what you're—"

The paramedics come shouldering through the crowd. She and Scott are down to only seconds now, and Scott knows it. He looks at her urgently.

"First thing . . . you do . . . water glasses . . ."

He can say no more. Luckily, he doesn't need to.

VI

After checking in at the Greenview Motel and before walking to the hospital half a mile away to visit her husband, Lisey Landon goes into the bathroom. There are two glasses on the shelf over the sink, and they are the real kind, not plastic. She puts both of them in her purse, careful not to look at either one as she does so. On her walk to the hospital she takes them out one at a time, still not looking at them, and throws them into the gutter. The sound of them breaking comforts her even more than the sound of the little shovel's scoop, connecting first with the pistol and then with Blondie's face.

[*The following story is the winner of the first August Van Zorn Prize for the Weird Short Story, awarded to the short story, by an emerging writer, that most faithfully and disturbingly embodies the august tradition of the weird short story as practiced by Edgar Allan Poe and his literary descendants, among them August Van Zorn. "7C," Mr. Roberts's first published fiction, was selected from over six hundred submissions, many of them of considerable literary merit, and disturbing indeed. The editors are grateful to everyone who participated in the contest.*]

7C

by JASON ROBERTS

I'M CLUMSY, I guess. Or self-oblivious. I suppose those are two ways of saying the same thing. Point is, damage just shows up on my body. Please, *please* don't struggle like that. We are exactly where we're going to be.

Thank you.

Damage just appears. My wife Eun-Ha had a routine. I shave in the shower, because the steam is good to soften up the stubble. They have special shower mirrors but they don't really work, so I'm just mostly shaving by touch. Which is not a problem—I know my face—but with all that warm water you don't feel the cuts so much, and anyway the blood gets washed right off. She gets the bathroom after me, and passing in the hallway she cups, would cup, my jaw to turn it for inspection. A slap slowed down to a caress. "You've sprung a leak," she'd tell me, if I had.

Since I was naked but for the towel she would, of course, notice other things going on with my skin. A deep beginning bruise, yellow like a spot of jaundice, just above the elbow. Fresh welts on my knuckles. Once a dark purple mass on the outside of my thigh, marbling and swirling like a weather system, big as a fist and spreading. Accident-class, assault-class bruise. You'd think I'd remember how I got it, but no.

She'd trace the outline, raise an eyebrow. "Yolanda's playing rough," she'd say. That was the running joke, that I had a Yolanda and she had an Orlando.

One morning she says, "How did I miss that one?" She guns out a finger to touch my temple.

I had to step back into the bathroom and angle the mirror toward the window light to see it clearly. It was slight and faint, just a line of paleness against pale. Once I saw it I could lightly draw my fingers across and feel it, the smallest of interruptions on my skin. It was thin like a blade slip or a paper cut, but those are straight lines. They don't rise from your left eyebrow to arc down your cheek, then swoop back up to terminate below the edge of the mouth, just a tremor's length from where the lips meet and end.

She stepped in close. In addition to her residency she does Life-Wing air escorts of critical patients, and this has given her a tendency to snap out assessments. "That's an old scar," she said. "Very old. You were little when you got it, and it healed almost perfectly but it's grown with you. A crescent like that means you probably ran into the edge of something round. I'm going to guess closet rod."

I didn't remember.

"Then it must be ancient. From before you can remember. Which is probably a good thing, considering it must have been a pretty traumatic smack. You're lucky it wrapped around your eye instead of putting it out. Your parents never mentioned it?"

I didn't remember. "Maybe it's not a happy story."

She was pulling my head down, closer to her, closer to the light. "Maybe they're a little bit ashamed. Some moment of neglect. You should tweak them on it. It's probably the oldest thing you have, and it probably always will be. Something you'll take to the grave. So what, did you do some sunbathing? Is that what brought it out?"

That was her tweak on me.

. . .

Did you know I'm an astronomer? I'm sorry, we should have gotten to know each other better. Maybe if we weren't next-door neighbors. If you were down the hall, or not on the seventh floor, we might have chatted up in the elevator. But there's something comforting, I guess insulating, about staying strangers with the people right on the other side of your walls. You hear a sound, you don't have to extrapolate based on personal knowledge what it's all about. I'm just realizing this myself.

I'm an astronomer. Which is why my wife joked about sunbathing, although it's no longer true that we stay up all night peering through telescopes. Our instruments hardly ever have eyepieces, just capture fields, and we don't look at the results until we run it through what's called data reduction, which is software designed to throw away everything except what we want to see. Our scopes aren't here, anyway—they're in Utah, and the talk is of Ecuador next. Light pollution keeps chasing them farther out. But the Astronomy department is still in the same building that was built for it in 1927, when they were poking refractors through the roof and speculating about canals on Mars. The very few windows are little art deco slits, and having one in your office is a perk of seniority. I will never have one.

My specialty is primordials, the mechanics of how our universe got underway. I always get one response to that: *Oh, you mean you study the Big Bang.* No, I don't study the Big Bang. Nobody does. The Bang is a point stabbed on a chalkboard. It doesn't really exist, or more accurately it is outside of existence. It doesn't exist in the way the rest of existence does. I'm sorry, I'm not much of a popularizer. Let's just say it's like ballistics—you can trace the path of the bullet, but only to the point where it emerges from the gun. You can't follow it back to the ammo box, or the mind of the bullet maker. I study distant and therefore early objects, because farther out in space is farther back in time—the longer it takes light to travel to us, the older that light is when it arrives. And the earliest objects are encapsulated in the oldest light.

. . .

Good, you're starting to settle down. I'll bet you can't even walk anymore, much less run. Here, I'll let you go. Try with all your might. Go ahead.

Thought so.

Something was up with the scar. Two days later it had stopped looking like a white thread, a flick of fishing line. It was starting to redden and bump out slightly, like a minor burn. By now even Harlan noticed, or rather everyone at work noticed but only Harlan was comfortable pointing it out. We were at lunch, and with his mouth full he reached across the table into the space between us and made a counterclockwise motion with his finger. I didn't understand, so he muffled out, "It's like you were looking into a coffee can."

I would say Harlan is like a brother to me, but I have a brother and it's nothing like that. My brother sells industrial safety supplies and seems to make a hobby out of indignation. Harlan and I were postdocs together, and we just got along, even when we weren't agreeing on something. Never spoke about it, but eventually it was understood that we were going to, I don't know, live companionable, alongside lives. That kind of friend. We've published some papers together. Eun-Ha always said she liked him well enough, which I think was supposed to mean she respected our closeness without particularly wishing to share it. It's a closeness of like minds, not personalities, though. He's Mutt to my Jeff, nervous-quick and smart-mouthed, whereas I have always been shambling and sparsely worded.

Here's the thing about looking at old light. It's like watching a young woman in one of those early silent movies. You see she's beautiful, laughing, so animated and vivid the screen barely contains her, and you think: Dead. Gone to dust, before I was born. I have spent the last three and a half years mapping spectrum variations in high-redshift quasars, the farthest objects we can see. They're also the brightest things we've ever seen, the energy of a thousand galaxies packed into a space as small as our solar system. We're pretty sure that their brilliance comes from a black hole at the center, drawing the stars together and swallowing them. And since the light I'm seeing left about ten billion years ago, that means the last star was swallowed long before the Earth was formed. Not even gone to dust or gone to dark matter, just gone. A negation.

What's strange is that quasars don't belong in the beginning. They should be signs of an old universe, one winding down. It takes vast amounts of time for a star to collapse into a black hole, then an even more immensely long time for the black hole to congregate whole galaxies into a mass dense enough to look like a single star. That's where the word comes from—it's short for quasi-star. So why is it when we capture the light from the young universe, they're already there? Every schema has to strain, if not backflip, to account for it. One theory is that everything happened faster back then. Another is that quasars are, somehow, just born old.

So I stop shaving in the shower. The scar is getting a little tender, and I'm going to the mirror first thing anyway. Eun-Ha comes off her shift at the clinic with a handful of the tiny free samples they give to physicians, little tubes of something called Dermex. I let her rub one in.

"It looks angry today," she says. "That's the term, right? An *angry* scar. I don't know why they call it that."

People are staring outright now. People I know do it pointedly. I'm expected to explain, like a guy hobbling into work on a fresh cast. "I was looking into a coffee can," I say.

I start coming in at night, ostensibly to oversee the new Utah captures but really to stay clear of that look I'm getting. Just until it passes. Harlan and I still eat together most days, but it's my breakfast and his dinner. Eun-Ha doesn't complain. Standard procedure for an astronomer's wife, and the residency and the LifeWing flights play enough havoc with her own schedule. The building has a good quiet late at night. It's never entirely empty—at least three or four people rattling around—so you don't get that creeped-out, alone-and-therefore-victim kind of quiet. I caught up on my work. I thought happy, pleasant, healing thoughts. I did not examine my scar, strange, sourceless and spreading, more than a dozen times a night.

Look, I'm really sorry that I had to stick you with that needle. But it didn't hurt a bit, did it? Shake your head, yes or no. What did I tell you? Not a bit.

I went to a specialist. I had a theory it was an allergic reaction or something environmental, some spin on Toxic Building Syndrome. But the dermatologist was adamant. "It's just an old scar," she said.

"But it's getting worse," I said.

"It's inflamed, not infected. My guess is it's getting worse because you don't stop touching it. Use the Dermex. Try not to scratch or rub."

"I'm not touching it, and it's not an old scar. It appeared out of nowhere. It's getting worse."

She was silent for a moment. She wore glasses with clear plastic frames, as if that would somehow make them disappear. When she spoke again, it was slower, with a quiet earnestness and lots of eye contact. "It's like the little pits in your car windshield," she said. "They're there all along, but you only see them when you get the idea to look for them. This is . . . maybe taking a little too firm a hold on your awareness. Are you familiar with the term *obsessive-compulsive disorder*? I have some pamphlets."

She was right: it's amazing what you notice only when you're keyed into seeing it. As we traded passing nods in the corridors, I saw for the first time that Tim Callien had an unmistakable jag across his throat, and Amy Holzer had a half dozen ragged-looking slivers on the undersides of both forearms. At some point, something had happened to Guresh Subrahamian's right ear.

Those weren't the only small things I was beginning to notice. At my next breakfast-slash-dinner with Harlan, I noticed how he shifted uncomfortably in his seat, and how he could hardly look me in the face. I noticed that when he was paying the bill at the register he reached into his pocket and pulled out not just change, but a little tube of Dermex. The physician-only sample size.

I'm not a jealous man. I'm not a paranoid man. But I was all caught up on my work, and time on your hands late at night turns your head into an echo chamber. By now the crescent on my face had bloomed to the thickness and pinkness of a pencil's eraser tip, with darkening scarlet-tinged edges. I thought of how repellent it made me, how even my best friend won't look at me straight. I thought of Eun-Ha's hands, gently rubbing in the medicine. I thought of the tube in Harlan's pocket.

I was getting back at dawn, and I'd do my best to not wake Eun-Ha. I'd walk slowly into our bedroom, spend some time looking at her asleep, assess her sprawl so I could enter the bed without disturbing her. One morning she was on her side, one arm flung out, the other pushing down the sheet. She usually wears an old T-shirt of mine but it must have been a warm night. She was just in panties.

Sunlight from the break of the drapes was shafting on the rise of her breast, and for the first time I could see her own faint white-thread scars. Six vertical lines, exactly parallel, about half an inch apart.

I crawled in beside her. I never mentioned what I saw. I reached out to stroke them, but in her sleep she turned away. When I awoke I started wearing a bandage on my face.

Obsessive-compulsive. Kind of an awkward term, isn't it? Two big words handcuffed together, one meaning *can't stop thinking*, the other *can't stop doing*. I did some reading, especially about a subset called dermatitis artefacta, "self-induced or self-aggravated bizarre lesions without an obvious cause." Clearly, I wasn't going to get the help I needed until I disproved this ridiculous, this *specious* diagnosis. I wasn't touching, couldn't bear to touch, during my waking hours, but who knew what happened while I slept? The bandage kept rubbing off against my pillow.

I wore gloves to bed, wrapped my face in gauze, even asked Eun-Ha once to bind my wrists, a request that brought only a stare and her quick exit from the room. By then it was moot, because I was hardly sleeping at all. I started coming home later and later, until I was getting back long after she'd already left for the clinic. That made it easier, some nights, to not come back at all. I stopped showing up for breakfast-slash-dinner as well, and it was telling that Harlan didn't press the matter beyond a thirty-second phone call.

In the gaping hours of solitude I turned to make-work tasks. Correlated infrareds and radios by spectrum spikes, just to see what might pop out. Toyed with the math on every approach to the quasar-creation mystery. Thought a lot about old light in new time.

You're trembling. Are you cold, or trying to cry? It's okay. It'll all be over soon. I promise.

Amy Holzer's arms became my revelation. She was pushing a floor button when I noticed how her little shrapnel-like marks had changed. At first I thought it was just the low fluorescents of the elevator, but I stepped in and saw clearly the red coruscations, felt the hard ridge of scabbing. She yelped and jumped back, and before I could apologize for my abruptness the doors had opened and there was Tim Gallien, his throat-jag glaring like a second smile. Also gone to scab. He gave a confused shout but I was already pushing past him, heading for one office in particular.

Guresh Subrahamian opened his door wearing a bandage on his ear.

It was pointless to explain. They were the wrong specialty, them and everyone else in the building. Only another primordial-ist might understand, and there was only one I truly wanted to understand. I was halfway to Harlan's when I pulled to the curb, took a deep breath and let the long-suppressed thoughts come flooding in: *You know he's not there. You know where he is.*

I headed back here, to our apartment building. In the car I tore off my own bandage, and reached up to touch where I had been forbidden to touch. I could only catch quick glimpses of my face in the rearview mirror, in the flashes of streetlight, but they were enough to serve as a final confirmation. By the time I parked in my slot alongside Eun-Ha's I was crying, breath-gasping voiceless sobs.

I found the spare key she'd given me and opened up the trunk of her car. Air transport doctors need to be ready at a moment's notice, so Eun-Ha drives around with a dedicated bag just for LifeWing calls. I shouldered it, and as I walked I shuffled through its depths to find the K-Sticks. I couldn't find a scalpel, so some trauma shears would have to do.

I've gotten used to entering my bedroom quietly, to navigating the almost-darkness. They were sleeping. Side by side and skin to skin, flat on their backs, his hand resting on the juncture of her hip and thigh. I tugged the drapes a little ways apart, just enough for a strong spill of moonlight across their bodies. Enough to reveal the thin rubying of their scar lines. There was a whir and hum as the air-conditioning kicked in; it was another warm night. I looked straight up and saw the familiar grille of the ceiling air vent, right above our bed.

Dropsticks are single-use syringes of Droperidol. They're used when a patient starts thrashing around on a LifeWing flight, and needs to be immediately immobilized for everyone's safety. That much Droperidol is not a tranquilizer; it's a paralytic. You're awake, able to look around and understand what's happening to you, just temporarily disconnected from voluntary control of your body. Eun-Ha calls it "cutting the strings," because the patient collapses like a marionette. It was, she said, an unsettling thing to do to someone. She didn't like their eyes while it was happening to them.

If administered patiently, through the desensitized pads of the foot, a Dropstick does not awaken a full-grown man deep in post-coital sleep. It is almost a pinprick, a stingless bite of some nocturnal insect.

After a while I knelt, and gently prodded Harlan with the trauma shears. His lids fluttered and opened, and I understood what

Eun-Ha meant about the eyes of the suddenly paralyzed. Before he could try to speak I put a hand on his lips, leaned in close and whispered, "Please don't wake her up. I don't know if I can be strong if she wakes up, and I don't want her to suffer."

Like I say, he's Mutt to my Jeff. It was no trouble to carry him into the tiled quiet of the bathroom. I sat him on the floor of the shower, propped him up as best I could.

"Look, I'm really, really sorry about this. But I knew that if I came barging in you'd think it was about your sleeping with my wife, and it would be unpleasant. What I need is for you to listen, okay?"

His eyes were getting to me. You're looking at me the same way. Can you possibly stop, or even just turn away? No, of course not.

"Thought experiment, Harlan. Let's say the independent-causality theories are roughly correct. Quasars aren't part of the Big Bang; they're little bangs, bullets from a different gun firing through time in a different direction. They're born backward, born old, at least that's how it reads to us. It's like languages—some read from left to right, some from right to left."

He shivered a bit, still staring. The shower stall was damp and cold, and he was naked.

"So. With that as a given, let's assume that a new quasar was coming into existence. How would it manifest itself? No, don't try to speak just yet. You'll just exhaust yourself. Let me run with it. How would such a quasar makes its debut?"

I splayed and cupped my fingers, mimed an expanding ball. *Kaboom.*

"Explosively, yes? Of course. But there's more to be considered, because now we're not just talking matter hitting antimatter, but timelines colliding. One arrow hitting another arrow in mid-flight. Okay. Now, how would that impact manifest itself? I'll give you one hint. I'll give you two."

I pointed to the scars on his bare chest. Angry scars, as Eun-Ha would describe them. Then I ran my finger along the counterclockwise half circle on my face. It was no longer a scar but a fullfledged wound.

"Collisions send out shock waves. There would be damage, maybe even annihilation, but it would creep up on us. Remember, we're reading backward. The injury that kills you would show up as an unhealing scar, one that goes on unhealing until it's a fresh trauma, until the moment when it's actually inflicted. I don't remember getting this, because I haven't yet. But I will. Soon."

He could only speak by exhaling in the shape of words, and only with great effort. I took his face in my hands and turned it closer to my ear.

we were/just getting/it out of/our system

"Of course. That was my assumption."

please/you need help/please/delusional

God*damn* it. I was crying again. "It's going to hurt, Harlan. I just want to be with Eun-Ha when it happens. I was hoping you would understand."

But he was unconscious now. I found a towel to wrap him in, and laid him on the floor in what I hoped was a comfortable position. I looked at his prone form and thought, *I'm sorry, I really am. But one of us has to die alone.*

I was getting ready to flick out the light when the towel rustled and twitched, and Harlan lurched his torso upright. His eyes were still closed. His head lolled slack on his shoulders, as if the neck were just a sheaf of skin. In a roil of blind motion, betraying no awareness whatsoever, he simply propelled his body toward the door. His hand was on the knob before I flung him down.

His head hit the tiles with an audible crack, but it was just a moment before he was moving again. Eyes still shut, thankfully, still utterly limp but with a strange momentum just the same. A marionette struggling to draw himself forward despite the cut strings.

Half in panic, half in rage, I emptied another Dropstick into him, then another. It slowed him down some, but still he moved. I bear-hugged into a collapse, throwing my weight on him until I heard the snap of bones.

Still he moved.

I grabbed syringes randomly from Eun-Ha's bag, stabbed and plungered them in without bothering to read what drugs they were. The fourth needle broke off in his chest. He got the door open anyway.

I couldn't tackle him again without waking Eun-Ha. I could only watch as he made his nerveless disarticulated way back to my bed, to my wife's side. He climbed back in, assuming the same easy position I'd found him in, draping his hand over her exactly as before. She wriggled slightly, moving into his touch. With the opened bathroom door spilling soft light down the hallway, I could see them both more clearly. I could see how their scars fit together.

On her, in the pale expanse below her breast: six vertical lines, exactly parallel. On him, bisecting the sternum and pectorals: five more. I didn't place the pattern until another whir and hum led my eyes upward. The ceiling air vent grille.

I loved them both, but I couldn't let it happen. I was *not* going to be the one to die alone. I waited until he was absolutely still, then summoned all my strength and plucked him straight up, right off of her and the bed. I slung him over one shoulder, held tight to the LifeWing bag and kept closing doors behind me until we were here. Outside the apartment, in the seventh-floor common corridor, just shy of the elevator landing.

Trauma shears are designed to cut the clothing off an accident victim's body. They're nicknamed pennycutters, because they're strong enough and sharp enough to do exactly that. Jeans, leather jackets—they just slice right through. The skin above an artery hardly taxes them at all.

I don't know why I went to the trouble. If he could quietly, ceaselessly clamber his way back on broken ankles and half a pharmacy in his veins, I don't know why I thought a slit throat was going to stop him. It didn't. I rummaged around the bag, and found what I was looking for still packaged in its sterile plastic, never used. An amputation saw.

That's when you heard the commotion, isn't it? My neighbor of how many months? Anonymous until now. I suppose it was the muffled thumps outside your door. You were curious. You investigated. I suppose I must have looked a fright.

Boy, I'm full of apologies tonight! But I'll say it again: I'm sorry. I had just finished up with Harlan and there you were, with your face inflamed with a scar of your own. I took one look at the door behind you and I knew that it was meant to be. This is where it'll happen. It took a Dropstick and some explanation to convince you. But you're convinced, right?

You're giving me that look again. That trying-to-wake-up look.

I tried to do my own waking up. I tried to convince myself that Harlan was right, that I was sick, a seriously deluded man spinning jealousy into fantasies of a starburst apocalypse. I would rather be blithely insulated by insanity. That would be a better thing to bear than this.

But there he goes. Harlan—I'd rather just call it Harlan's body by now—collecting himself. Piling and sliding the pieces into a semblance of a man. There: he's found both hands. Now no doors can keep him, not from the fate that draws him like a sideways gravity. The ceiling vent will kill them. Nothing else can.

It's my last profound hope that Eun-Ha doesn't wake up beforehand, doesn't discover the approximation lying by her side.

We don't die alone, either. That's some consolation. See the door numbers, the numbers for apartment 7C? See how the pointed slash on your face exactly matches the 7, and how my curve-cut, my half-circle, will be created by the C? It won't be long now. Our wounds will tell us when.

Oh, good. We're finally starting to bleed.

THE MINIATURIST

by HEIDI JULAVITS

For Lois Duncan

AS THE TIRE CHAINS CONTINUED their maddening irregular clinking and the steeply pitched road disappeared for a third time beneath a snowdrift, Jennifer reminded herself: it was Helen's idea to spend the weekend in the creepy Cascades in mid-February, mere miles from the cabin where, just last year, a man had killed his entire family in a fit of winter melancholy.

"What's the odometer say?" Maureen asked. She held Helen's handwritten directions to the window to catch what little light eked between the frantic white particles, zooming this way and that like a flock of crazed, speck-sized pigeons.

"We've gone four-point-five miles," Jennifer said.

"I think we missed the Davis Creek turnoff," Maureen said. "It was supposed to be four miles after the general store."

"We didn't miss the turnoff," Jennifer said. "There hasn't been a turnoff. There hasn't even been a house."

Maureen shrugged. Clearly she thought Jennifer had missed the turnoff.

Jennifer white-knuckled the steering wheel and seethed. This whole trip was idiotic—three sort-of sisters spending a "relaxing" weekend before the fire, pretending to be excited about Helen's upcoming wedding to Maureen's ex-boyfriend.

Ever since Helen asked the two of them to be her only brides-maids, Maureen had decided that Helen was *actually not so bad* when, in Jennifer's opinion, Helen was a manipulative and fake-cheerful pain in the ass. Jennifer and Maureen first met Helen in the lawyer's waiting room before the reading of their father's will, eight days after their father had drowned while fly-fishing on the Penatoqua River. A freak accident, that had yet to sink in—as had the fact that their father had a family before their family, and now they had a half sister named Helen who wore a straw hat with a daisy on it and was, as Jennifer later put it, *effervescently* flipping through a beauty magazine in the antechambers of Murray, Plumb and Murray. Helen the effervescent mourner, who left that afternoon quite a bit richer than either Maureen or Jennifer, had effervescently become their best friend in the past five years, getting drunk on blackberry schnapps and repetitively confiding in them how she'd also lost her mother when she was seven (she died in a fire), subjecting them to dull stories of the "dear, dear woman"—Aunt Margaret, actually her mother's best friend—who had raised her in the suburbs of Louisville. But Aunt Margaret lived far away, and her friends from UCLA were well-meaning flakes. That explained why she was so immediately fond of her half sisters, with whom she shared nothing in common save a dead father. *Dependable*, she called them. *Stalwart*, which Jennifer took to mean she thought they were fat. *My real family*. The best thing Jennifer could say about Helen was that she was a passionate collector of dollhouses. This made Helen remarkably fun to mock, and mocking Helen helped Jennifer and Maureen continue to feel like members of the same family, now that they didn't have parents to bind them together with commonly shared annoyances.

Recently, however, this dynamic had changed. Jennifer would start to complain about Helen's wedding invitation (hand-painted on an antique lace handkerchief) or her insistence that the father in her Victorian dollhouse "looks just like *our* dad!" and Maureen, typically an eager Helen-basher, would vacantly demur, *She's actually not so bad.*

This did not prevent Jennifer from trying to enlist Maureen's dormant mean side.

"Helen's directions suck," she said.

"There's a blizzard," Maureen pointed out.

"There's a blizzard, and Helen's directions suck," Jennifer said.

Maureen didn't respond.

Finally, a turnoff. Unmarked, as best Jennifer could tell.

"Take this," Maureen said.

Jennifer didn't ask why. Jennifer took the turnoff. She was happy to make it Maureen's fault if it turned out to be a stupid decision.

"What next?" she asked.

"Keep an eye out for the mailbox that looks like a mini log cabin."

"How cute," Jennifer said. She started to say something about Scott's parents' terrible taste—their home in suburban Seattle featured metallic wallpaper in the bathrooms—but stopped herself. Scott-bashing was also off-limits these days. Did it matter that he and Maureen had scarcely split before he fell in love with Helen? Hardly. Did it matter that he approached both Jennifer and Maureen with a glassine smile so bogus and vacant that it made them speculate he'd been turned into a pod person? Apparently not.

Maureen, in Jennifer's opinion, was far too forgiving. It verged on unethical. It meant she was capable of betrayal, in a purely passive sense, simply because she was too understanding to get appropriately angry with people who deserved it.

If the main road was treacherous, this road was doubly so. From the dull, crunching sounds the chains made, they weren't on a paved road. They were on dirt.

"Do Helen's directions say anything about a dirt road?" Jennifer asked.

Maureen shook her head.

There was a new sound, too. A high-pitched grinding that wasn't coming from the tires.

"I think we should turn around," Jennifer said. "This is a logging road or something."

She looked at Maureen, peering tensely through the windshield at the snow. It was starting to get dark; the snow was a gray color, not even pretty and new-seeming as it fell.

The road was growing more and more narrow and soon turning around would be impossible, unless they found a driveway, which seemed unlikely. Where the fuck were they? They should return to the general store and ask directions. Never mind that the parking lot was full of trucks with gun racks and whale-sized plow attachments (the interior metal scoops strangely gilled, they looked like beached Pleistocene fossils to Jennifer, abandoned at this high altitude by the receding ocean some trillion-odd years ago), and that she and Maureen had as good a chance of getting gang-raped in the restroom as receiving directional assistance of any sort. It was all Helen's fault, and she would make sure that Helen knew it. It almost made her *want* to get raped, so that she had more reason to be mad at Helen.

It was this attitude—cavalier, pissed off, vaguely self-destructive—that made her a bit uncareful. Normally, she was skepticism personified—her skepticism intensified by a wild imagination that could seek out the dark possibilities in even the most banal situation. Normally, she knew better than to drive onto the presumed shoulder of a road that was obscured beneath a layer of snow and could have been anything—could have been air.

Jennifer swung the car perpendicular to the road. The chains restricted her turning radius, and she had to back up, then forward, then back, then forward. Each time she put the car into gear she heard the whining sound, the hysterical pitch of the wind that a person might mistake for human screams, if a person were so inclined. Jennifer was not so inclined at this moment. She jolted the transmission into drive a final time, nudging the right wheels onto the shoulder that wasn't a shoulder, which was in fact, she was soon to learn, a deep, if narrow, ditch. She felt the wheels start to slide, and she corrected, swinging the wheel hard to the left. The chains clawed at the slope and the car hung there for two or three seconds as the wheels spun, long enough for her to catch Maureen's expression, which struck her as strangely, passively *sad*, given the circumstances. Or disappointed, but really it was a look of sadness, as if Jennifer had, one final foolish time, fallen prey to her own infrequent impetuosity, and screwed them both for good.

The sound of the chains breaking off the right front tire was unmistakable, a muffled, metal-bone twang. The tire slipped, and the car dropped thuggishly onto its own chassis; Jennifer felt her spine compress.

She and Maureen sat without speaking and stared through the windshield at the darkening woods, now tilted at a thirty-degree angle.

Jennifer's first impulse, a defensive one, was to blame Maureen. But Maureen didn't seem to fault Jennifer for their current predicament; she seemed weirdly detached, or at peace with their newly befucked circumstances.

Maureen smiled. "I guess we're walking," she said.

Where was the question. They were at least five miles from the gang-bang store. They'd passed no houses. *Where* was on the tip of Jennifer's tongue, still unspoken, when, in the rearview mirror, a light flashed. Jennifer turned to see where the light was coming from, but she couldn't see it. There was nothing in the woods but blackness and snow. She turned back to the rearview mirror. She saw it again. The light, unmistakable.

"Look," Maureen said, pointing at the mirror.

The light disappeared again but they walked uproad anyway, assuming they would find a driveway, and hopefully a house. After a half hour of trudging through the six inches of snow (which quickly became eight inches, nine inches, ten) Jennifer wanted to turn back. In the car there was wine, and corn chips and limited heat. They had a half tank of gas, which would probably last them a few hours. They had lots of clothes plus both their bridesmaid dresses, each zipped in its own individual thick plastic bag that might even work as a tent or windbreaker. Helen had wanted them to bring the bridesmaid dresses to the Cascades because, she'd said coyly, *I have a fun idea*. The bridesmaid dresses were white, which Jennifer thought peculiar, but Helen assured her it was very au courant in the hipper bridal circles.

But they should return to the car. They wouldn't freeze. Probably, at least, they wouldn't freeze. And they wouldn't have to spend the night with some isolation-loony local, who might or might not decide to kill his family and whomever else was available for killing that night.

Jennifer was about to suggest that they return to the car, when Maureen pointed to the left and quickened her pace.

Jennifer squinted. She couldn't see anything but Maureen, hopping up and down beside something.

It was a waist-high pole. Atop it—a tiny log cabin.

"We found it!" Maureen said.

Maureen practically ran up the driveway, energized by their incredible luck. Jennifer tromped behind her. She did not feel lucky or saved; she felt strangely endangered by their accidental discovery. She had never been a lucky person, for one. And she mistrusted easy solutions to problems. This miraculously easy solution seemed worthy of scrutiny. But her sense of unease was quashed by a new wave of irritation toward Helen, inspired by the twee, snow-smothered log cabin. Though most of Helen's collection was in storage, she kept a five-story Victorian dollhouse (mauve clapboards, plum gingerbread trim, truly hideous, in Jennifer's opinion) on the dining room table in her small Seattle apartment, the back glassed-off, the dolls within engaged for cryogenic eternity in moronic dollhouse tasks: Sweeping. Sleeping.

Staring at a fake bowl of soup. Jennifer fantasized about removing the glass backs and putting the mother naked on the toilet, forcing the father into a missionary sex position with the daughter on the dining room table. Helen would catch Jennifer staring at the dollhouses malevolently, and she would pinch her arm and say to her, *You're so adorable! I just want to squash you up and put you in one of my dollhouses!*

By the time Jennifer reached the top of the driveway, Maureen was already knocking on the door of an old log cabin. *Old.* No way was this Scott's family's new ski house. This made her feel both better and worse. It was a coincidence about the mini log cabin, a bizarre coincidence, nothing more.

"This isn't Scott's place," Jennifer said.

She saw a movement out of the corner of her eye. *What the fuck?* She looked. Nothing. But in her peripheral vision she saw a woman in a white dress, running. Again she turned her head. Again, nothing, just gusts of snow threading between the birches.

"Did you see that?"

"What?"

Jennifer scrutinized Maureen.

"Nothing," she said finally. "This house isn't Scott's house. It's old."

"So? Scott's place is old," Maureen said.

"It's not old. It's new."

"It's new to *them.*"

"If this is Scott's place, where's Helen's car?"

There were no cars in the driveway. Not Helen's or anyone's.

"She's probably out looking for us," Maureen said.

Jennifer was too tired to point out the obvious—there were no tire tracks on the driveway, no tire tracks on the road. There was no mattress-sized indentation in the snow where the car might have been parked.

She was about to suggest they go back to the car—she was suddenly overtaken with a trembly, manic twang that might have been nothing more ominous than the innocent beginnings of hypothermia—when the door to the cabin opened. An older woman, hunched and small and harmless-seeming, at least from a distance. She pulled Maureen inside by the wrist, as if she already knew her.

Jennifer stood in the snow, shivering. Then her heart jumped. In her peripheral vision she saw the woman in white dash into the woods, but when she turned her head, again, the woman had disappeared. Though she felt wrong in the bones, and drained, and paranoid to the point of nausea, she had no choice but to follow her sister inside.

The house's interior smelled of camphor and stale dresser sachets and wool. A few oil lamps and a pair of ugly purple candles threw their paltry light over the shapeless, afghan-strewn furniture, the chaotic, knickknacky shelves. It was the sort of interior that usually featured many, many cats, cats like throw pillows on the couch, cats like andirons in the fireplace, cats like cookie jars on the counters. There were no cats, and this bothered Jennifer, who wanted something predictable to latch onto at this moment, a way to make generic sense of this woman—"Meg"—and who the hell she was, aside from a suspiciously sweet ex-hippie and possible serial killer. Jennifer guessed from her slightly hobbled gait and her tree root hands she was about seventy, though her face—round and freakishly lineless—introduced a level of doubt to her estimations. She seemed pleasant enough, if a bit unskilled socially. She smiled a lot in lieu of talking; she didn't nod, but her look implied that she was nodding constantly as if to say *yes* or *of course, I already knew that.*

Meg made tea and served it to them in ancient cups with tobaccoed fissures traversing the insides. Maureen explained their situation: the directions, the car, the ditch.

"Is this Davis Creek Road?" Jennifer asked.

Meg smiled. "Pardon?"

"Davis Creek Road. Is this it?"

Meg fiddled with her white hair, catching a lock by her chin between two fingers and sweeping them upward, encouraging the ends to curl. This was a familiar and intensely grating gesture to Jennifer; Helen, who'd recently had her hair bobbed, started doing it with an obsessiveness Jennifer couldn't help but point out to her. Helen had stopped for five minutes, before absently resuming.

"I don't know of a Davis Creek Road," Meg said.

"Have you lived here long?" Jennifer asked, perhaps more sharply than she intended. Maureen tossed her a *rein it in* look.

"About twenty-five years," Meg said.

"You said it's a new house, right, Jennifer?" Maureen interjected. "Maybe it's a new road, too."

"No new houses around here," Meg said. "I'd know about a new house."

"Well," Jennifer said, "Helen gave us shitty directions. We're probably not even in the right town."

Meg smiled. Maureen smiled. They sat in silence and listened to the hard snow pelting like rice against the windows. Meg kept smiling long past the reasonable fade point for polite smiles and Jennifer began to wonder if she'd been lobotomized thirty years ago, then dumped on the mountain by some relative to live out her years in emptily grinning solitude, conversing with finches and beavers.

"Do you have a phone?" Jennifer asked. Suddenly, she wanted out of here. She'd prefer even Helen's company to this woman's bland eeriness. Jennifer asked Maureen for the directions to Scott's house.

"There's no phone number on the directions," Maureen said.

Jennifer rolled her eyes. Typical Helen. "Do you have a phone book?"

Meg said yes, she had a phone book, but she doubted that a new house would be listed. She told Jennifer to call Information, and pointed her toward a bedroom. The phone was on the nightstand between two twin beds, each with a white coverlet sewn with tiny white pompons. Jennifer heard something rustle under the bed—a cat!—and she made kissing noises at the coverlet hem as she waited on the line for the directory assistance operator. No cat appeared, so she reached under the bed to feel for it. Instead she found a flat, padded book. She slid it from under the coverlet. A photo album, or a scrapbook, an old one, the leather cracked, the gold-leaf border flaked away.

The phone rang and rang. She hung up and dialed again. Absently, she flipped through the leather album. It didn't seem like snooping; it felt like a way to legitimately pass time while waiting for the operator. She opened to a page of newspaper clippings from February 1936. In one clipping: a photo of a bride with a bobbed haircut, who bore an uncanny resemblance to Helen, if Helen were a brunette. *Helen Helen Helen.* She felt polluted by her. Jennifer clapped the book shut and slid it hastily under the bed. Ever since that day in the lawyer's waiting room, Helen had been insinuating herself into Jennifer's life with increasing coziness, until Jennifer couldn't go two minutes without hearing Helen's name. She had become friends with Jennifer's friends, she had lassoed Scott, and now she'd won Maureen's affections. Why couldn't people see her for the inexpert manipulator she was? How could all these people allow themselves to be seduced by her? The question was: What did Helen want? Jennifer didn't know the answer to this question, and this unnerved her more than knowing might.

The operator came on the line.

When she returned to the living room, Maureen and Meg were still sitting on the couch.

"There's no listing," Jennifer reported. "In fact, there's no Davis Creek Road."

Maureen appeared puzzled, but not puzzled enough. Jennifer was moving past puzzled to completely pissed off and vaguely scared. It occurred to her that Helen had sent them on a wild goose chase to the Cascades. It made sense—much more sense than her asking Maureen and Jennifer to be her only bridesmaids, especially when she supposedly had such a devoted cadre of cap-toothed (if flaky) sorority confidantes to fill the slots. She'd always secretly suspected that Helen hated them as much as they hated her—and who could blame her? She and Maureen had been their father's daughters, while Helen spent her childhood as an abandoned, dirty mystery he'd kept hidden from everyone but his lawyer. Her niceness was a ruse. It had always been a ruse, and this weekend she'd planned to expose it as a ruse—just before she married Maureen's ex-boyfriend at a spectacularly expensive wedding (where all of Jennifer's and Maureen's friends would be in attendance) paid for with money that might have been theirs, if only she hadn't existed.

Meg said something about *of course you'll be spending the night* and *I have food enough for a week if this storm lasts as long as they're predicting*. Jennifer started to protest—no, they'd simply call a tow truck, they'd be out of her hair in a matter of hours—but then she started to like the idea of staying on the mountain, maybe even for a few days until the blizzard petered out. Give Helen a good scare. Make her think they'd met some terrible end in a snowbank, via wolves or avalanche. It would serve her right to worry a little, and cast an unexpected pall over her claustrophobically orchestrated wedding week.

"We'd love to stay," Jennifer said.

After dinner the three sat around the fire and drank a cloying blackberry-tasting liqueur that was nonetheless quite addictive. Jennifer had begun to warm to Meg, who told them about her son, a driftwood artist in Mendocino, her dead husband, a former appliance dealer, her grandchildren, relocated to the East. Maureen asked how Meg could live in a log cabin, so far away from other people.

"Don't you get scared?" she asked.

Meg's manner grew vaguely chilly. "Why do you ask?"

"You're here all alone; it's so isolated and spooky. . . ."

Meg stood from the couch and put her gnarled hands on her hips.

"If you girls are reporters, I'll call the police right now." She pointed an unsteady finger toward the bedroom.

Maureen giggled nervously. "Are you serious?"

"Perfectly," Meg said.

"We're not reporters," Jennifer said. "Really we're not."

Meg didn't seem ready to believe them.

"I've told every reporter I will not talk about this cabin to them. I will not feed people's terrible need to think the worst of innocent dead folks."

Jennifer experienced a stabbing ice pick of a thought—*this was the cabin where that man killed his family.*

"Maybe it's best if we just call a tow truck and be on our way," Jennifer said, wanting anew to get out of the cabin and far away from Meg, whose eyes had developed a shifty, tweaked cant.

This calmed Meg down.

"I'm just tired of fending off rumors. I've been doing it my entire life, and I'm tired of it. I just want to be left in peace."

"Of course," Jennifer said. "But I still think we should call the tow truck."

"*No,*" Meg said sharply.

She smiled.

"No," she repeated. "I won't allow it. I'm not that much of a monster."

She refilled their liqueur glasses and the three of them experienced a newly discomforted level of silence.

"I suppose now I've piqued your interest, haven't I?" Meg said. "I suppose after my outburst it would be inhospitable not to tell you."

"You don't have to tell us anything," Jennifer said. Someone had killed himself in this cabin, someone had made a meal of his wife and kids, someone had been dismembered and used for firewood. "I for one would like to get a good night's sleep."

Meg regarded her queerly. "There's very little chance of that."

"How comforting," Jennifer said. Maureen giggled.

"It's not so bad," Meg said. "It happened a very long time ago."

What happened so very long ago, according to Meg, was this. Meg's great-aunt—a woman named Sarah—was considered a bit of a strange, and possibly cursed, girl. Her entire family had been killed in a fire that she, miraculously, survived. Sarah claimed she escaped from her room in the attic, while her parents and sisters died in their beds on the second floor. She claimed that their rooms were already ablaze, that she'd been led by a voice that guided her through the smoky halls and stairways to the front door and safety.

An orphan, Sarah was sent to live with a religious aunt in Smithville. Her aunt suspected Sarah of being possessed by an evil spirit, and had her exorcized by a priest, who died of a heart attack days after. A ballet teacher who disliked Sarah was crippled in a train accident. A rival for the affections of a man Sarah loved was facially disfigured by a neighbor's otherwise mild German shepherd. At the age of twenty-one, Sarah became engaged to a local banker's son, who was a known ladies' man, and Sarah was convinced that he was already carrying on a few side affairs. Sarah befriended four of the prettiest girls in town, women with whom her fiancé was known to flirt on his lunch breaks from the bank. She asked them to be her bridesmaids, and the five of them came to this cabin for a weekend before the wedding.

"According to one of the surviving girls, the five of them got very drunk and ran around in the snow. Then Sarah asked the girls to try on their bridesmaid dresses and stand in front of a mirror so she could see how they looked. The first girl did so. Then the second girl, the third girl. Finally, the fourth girl tried on her dress and stood in front of the mirror. The dresses were high-necked, white. They looked like bridal gowns themselves, with a thin string of silver beads at the neck—*like a wire garrote*, one of the girls later said. At any rate, the last girl stood in front of the mirror and started to scream. Another girl claimed that her friend started bleeding from the neck, just beneath the silver beads. Soon the entire dress front was a creeping bloom of blood. But when she looked at her friend directly, the dress was white. The blood was visible only in the mirror. Even stranger, however, was this: the girl didn't seem to know she was bleeding. She thought her dress was on fire. She ran out of the house, clawing at the neckline. She was barefoot, and she disappeared into the woods. The girls looked for her. A search party looked for her, for days. She was never found."

Jennifer refilled her liqueur glass and didn't comment.

"Sarah sounds like a witch!" Maureen said, thrilled.

Meg took a long sip of her liqueur. "People will say that about the unlucky, the prescient, the superstitious. Sarah was very superstitious."

"Did she marry the banker's son?" Maureen asked.

Meg nodded. "She did. And apparently, the man *had* been having an affair with the girl who disappeared. The police figured the girl had gone crazy with jealousy or guilt and leaped off the bluff just beyond." Meg gestured toward the wall behind her. "It drops two hundred feet to the Penatoqua River. They assumed her body was swept downstream and out to the Pacific."

"Is Sarah still alive?" Jennifer asked.

"She died twenty-five years ago. She'd always been a dollhouse fanatic, and I think that hobby kept her alive after her husband died. Fly-fishing accident. She went to all the miniaturists' conventions, even had a store down in Smithville."

"Dollhouses," Jennifer said dully.

"Our half sister is a dollhouse collector," Maureen said dopily.

"She probably prefers the term *miniaturist*," Meg said.

"We actually don't know what she prefers. We don't know that much about her," Jennifer said. She realized that she was drunk, very drunk, in a heavy, syrupy, vaguely seasick way.

"What Jennifer means is that we didn't know she existed until recently," Maureen said. "But we're all as close as any family now, aren't we?"

Jennifer didn't answer.

"That was always the problem with Sarah," Meg said. "The poor girl just wanted a proper family. Tried everything in her power to get one. Every time she got close, however, something went wrong."

"Some things simply aren't meant to be," Maureen said.

"Indeed," Meg said. "Some might say there are those among us who are cursed. We destroy what we think we want once we're in danger of getting it. I think that's why Sarah was so fond of her dollhouses. It was the only family she could really control."

Meg stared at her liqueur glass, her eyes stunned and sad-seeming.

"Well," she said suddenly. "I've kept you awake telling you scary stories. It comes with the territory out here. And you girls are probably itching to get to bed." Meg led them to the side bedroom, where Jennifer had used the phone. She gave them towels and an oil lamp.

"I have some old nightshirts in here," she said, opening the closet. She shoved aside some hanging things wrapped in plastic and retrieved two folded plaid flannel nightshirts from a back shelf.

"Also," she said, pausing before the open closet, "I don't know if either of you are interested, but I have two of Sarah's bridesmaid dresses."

"You *do?*" Maureen shrieked.

"I'm not interested," Jennifer said.

"*I* am," Maureen said. "Can I see them?"

Jennifer grabbed a towel and a nightshirt and excused herself to the bathroom. The dark of the house closed in around her; the bathroom was lit by a single candle; all she could see was the black silhouette of her head in the mirror as she washed her face in the basin of water Meg had provided. Her heart felt like it was attacking her own insides, an enemy organ, a small ticking bomb. She'd never felt so uneasy, so certain that something was terribly, dreadfully *wrong.* It was too weird; there were too many spooky coincidences.

The dollhouses. The white bridesmaid dresses. The fly-fishing accident. The pictures in the photo album. *Meg*, whose name she presumed was Margaret. She started to think she'd been coaxed into a trap, unwittingly, like a stupid animal. It made her start to wonder: How much *did* they know about Helen's past? How did they even know that she was the person she claimed to be? Their father had certainly never told them about this other daughter, this former wife; they had accepted Helen's existence because the news had been delivered by a lawyer, and because the monstrous deceit it implied was so completely unlikely. Only a man whom you could never imagine doing such a thing had the potential to do such a thing. That was how she and Maureen and their few surviving relatives had rationalized it. It could never in a million years have happened. Thus, naturally, it had happened.

But what if it hadn't? What if Helen was a fake, some kind of resurrected witch, pretending to be their father's daughter? What if she'd even been involved in their father's death? His body had never been found; he'd been swept away by a current while fishing alone on a mild stretch of the Penatoqua. The rangers had found his rucksack, his coat, his uneaten lunch. Downstream, they'd found his pole.

Jennifer splashed some more water on her face, and pressed her shaking hands against her cheekbones. She was drunk, and she knew she was letting her imagination get the best of her. But she couldn't get Helen's smiling face out of her head, that innocent, high-voiced and mostly daft way she had of talking that now seemed malice-tinged and eerily sinister.

When she returned to the bedroom, Meg and Maureen were inspecting a dress spread over the bed's pompon coverlet.

"Jennifer, look at this," Maureen said. She was fingering the fabric of the neckline; the tiny silver beads had tarnished and stained the fabric beneath them a blackish gray.

"It's beautiful," Jennifer said. But she didn't think it was beautiful. The neck was so narrow it made it hard to swallow just looking at it. And the beads, now that they'd tarnished, looked even less like decoration and more like the blade of a straight-edged razor.

"Sarah said that these dresses were the best way to test a person's loyalty," Meg said. "Those who failed the test would, as she put it, *get their eternal deserts*."

"Superstition or witchcraft?" Maureen asked, clearly not expecting an answer.

"Can we put that away now?" Jennifer asked, hardly able to keep the panicked testiness from her voice.

Meg wrapped the dress back in the plastic zipper bag and returned it to the closet. She told the girls to help themselves to bread and jam if they woke early. She wished them a pleasant sleep, and withdrew. Jennifer heard her in the living room, blowing out lamps and candles. With each breath, the dark came closer and closer, a dense, impermeable substance. It made her feel like she was being buried alive.

"You okay?" Maureen asked.

"I'm . . . just a little freaked out," Jennifer admitted.

"You? Why?"

"What do you mean, *why*?"

"You actually believe that stuff about the blood on the dress? It's just a stupid ghost story."

Jennifer shrugged. "It's more than just that. It's . . . *everything*."

Just then she remembered the scrapbook album under the bed. She pulled it out and began flipping through it.

Maureen grew alarmed. "You don't have Meg's permission to look at that."

Jennifer put her finger to her lips. She turned the warped cardboard pages until she came to the picture of the bride. This time she clocked the name: Sarah Mills Herrick. She read the small squib of text accompanying the photo. It mentioned that the bride was given away by her aunt and ward, Peggy Dischinger.

She thrust the album into Maureen's lap.

"She looks just like Helen, don't you think?" Jennifer said.

Maureen squinted. "Well . . ."

"Stop it! She looks exactly like Helen!"

"Okay, maybe a little bit. Don't get *mad* just because I don't agree with you."

Jennifer caught her reflection in the mirror above the dresser: again, nothing but a black silhouette. She was becoming a stranger to herself, a blank of negative space.

"I think you're drunk," Maureen said. "And I think you're overreacting."

"I'm not overreacting," Jennifer said. She turned back a page in the album, to a jaundiced newspaper clipping. The headline read BRIDESMAID VANISHES ON DAVIS CREEK ROAD. There was a photo of a large-lipped, narrow-eyed woman. She appeared feline, self-satisfied, confident. Tragically so, given what happened to her.

"Maureen!" Jennifer pointed to the article.

"So?"

"Meg said she'd never heard of Davis Creek Road."

Maureen studied the headline.

"I'm sure there's an explanation."

"Such as?"

"Maybe it hasn't been called that for decades," she said. "Even the operator had never heard of it."

Maureen continued flipping backward through the album. Thirty years earlier—1906—another wedding announcement. Another Helen look-alike, her hair curled and dark, but the face was unmistakably Helen's face. This woman—named Vera Herrick Dow—was also, according to the accompanying article, "given away by her aunt and ward, *Margaret* Dischinger."

Jennifer bit her lip, wondering how much she wanted to reveal her own paranoia to her sister.

"Helen was raised by her aunt Margaret," she said quietly.

Maureen rolled her eyes. "*Please.* Helen has nothing to do with this."

"I can't believe you're not more freaked out," Jennifer said. "The coincidences are too great. You're making me feel like I'm crazy."

Maureen smiled. "That's what sisters are for."

Maureen got up from the bed and walked toward the closet. She started to take off her clothes—her sweater, her jeans.

"What are you doing?" Jennifer asked.

Maureen didn't answer. She opened the closet door. Jennifer heard the high-pitched whine of a zipper.

"*Maureen!*"

Maureen held the bridesmaid's dress against her chest. Then she lowered it and stepped into the skirt, pulling it up over her waist, threading her arms through the sleeves.

She turned around. "Button me up, will you?"

Jennifer stood numbly. The dress didn't have buttons; it had many tiny metal hooks running the length of Maureen's spine, from her waist to just under her hairline.

The hooks were painstaking.

"Get the oil lamp," Maureen said, once Jennifer had finished. "I want to test my loyalty."

Maureen walked over toward the mirror. Jennifer approached her from behind.

"Give it to me," Maureen said. She grabbed the lamp from Jennifer. The oil sloshed inside the hollow stand, the flame stretched high, blackening the inside of the glass chimney.

"See?" she said, placing the lamp on the dresser so that it illuminated her front and she was visible, finally. "No blood."

Jennifer looked at her sister's reflection in the mirror. Her plainish features appeared unusually bewitching, in an anemic sort of way.

"Great. That proves a lot. What does that prove?"

Maureen didn't answer her. She appeared stricken, suddenly. Or surprised. She gestured frantically at her neck.

"Maureen?"

Maureen reached behind her head and flailed at the buttons. Jennifer realized her sister wasn't breathing.

"Maureen!"

Maureen fell onto the floor and started laughing.

"You *suck*," Jennifer said. But she laughed too. It was a relief, actually, the low-level adrenaline having peaked and now, finally, subsiding entirely, her heart shrinking back into its cage. She realized she was tired. She was drunk and she was, in fact, behaving like a nut.

Jennifer feigned a kick at Maureen's middle.

"That's supposed to make me feel better?" she asked.

"No," Maureen said. "After you try the dress on, then you'll feel better."

"Forget it."

"Humor me," Maureen said.

"Nope."

"Come on. Then you'll know you're just imagining shit."

Jennifer agreed. Her body, postpanic, felt rubbery and liquid, both weightless and susceptible to the slightest gravitational pull. She helped Maureen unbutton the dress, she removed her own nightshirt, she stepped into the dress's barbed, crinoline-lined skirt. The sleeves were tight around her arms; the seams, with their disintegrating strips of flashing, prickled. Most offensive was the smell—old lavender and, to her nose, closet dust with a gamey undertone of urine.

Jennifer turned and looked out the window as Maureen hooked her in—each hook winching tighter the circumference of her ribs, compacting her organs. Beyond her own half-visible reflection, the snow continued to fall. And fall. And fall and fall and fall. It was mesmerizing, like watching the night sky come undone, every fixed point of light shifting in tandem and collecting at the bottom, one large crash site of stars. She felt herself drifting to sleep to the rhythm of all those plummeting ex-planets, her lids lowering just enough to make a scored, lashy muddle of the world.

The woman came out of nowhere. She slammed against the window, her two palms pressed against the pane, blue. Her face was blue, almost black, lips pulled back to reveal a gaping, toothless mouth. She wore the same dress that Jennifer wore.

Jennifer screamed and pushed herself away from the window.

"Jesus!" Maureen looked at her like she was crazy. "What the *hell?*"

"Didn't you see the woman?"

"What woman?"

"She was wearing . . . oh God, she was wearing this dress!"

Jennifer began to sob dryly. She reached behind her neck and scrabbled, frantically, to release the hooks. Her breath felt thinned down to the finest threads.

"Calm down. *Jennifer.*" Maureen yanked Jennifer's arms downward.

"Maureen, take this thing off of me."

"Of course," Maureen said. "But first look in the mirror."

"I don't want to look in the mirror!" Jennifer hissed. "*Unhook me.*"

"First you need to look in the mirror," Maureen said. "You'll still be scared if you don't."

Jennifer was shaking, almost hyperventilating. Normally she was the one in control—no, *always* she was the one in control—but now Maureen had the upper hand. It was the slightest shift of power, but it unnerved Jennifer; it signaled to her that something between them had irreversibly changed.

Maureen nodded toward the mirror. Jennifer turned, slowly, one eye on the window, feeling that woman was watching them. The window remained empty, save for the snow that the wind whisked into a looming, transparent shape and flung against the window. Jennifer laughed.

"Why are you laughing?" Maureen asked.

"Nothing. I'm just . . . I thought the snow was a ghost."

"You're really wound up," Maureen said. "I've never seen you so wound up."

"You have no idea." Jennifer told Maureen her, admittedly, insane suspicions about Helen—that she was involved with their father's death, that she was an impostor, that she'd sent them on this wild goose chase and possibly wanted them dead. As she spoke, she noticed Maureen growing more and more remote, her face drifting into shadow; she threw repeated glances at the closet, at the window, as though perhaps they were being eavesdropped upon.

"Crazy, right?" Jennifer concluded. "I told you, you had no idea."

Maureen smiled nervously. "Let's get you out of this dress and into bed," she suggested.

"But I haven't looked in the mirror," Jennifer said.

"Forget about that," Maureen said sharply. "You just need to get some sleep."

Maureen started to unbutton the hooks of the dress. Jennifer could feel her hands shaking against her shoulder blades.

"No," Jennifer said, pulling away. "No, let me look."

Jennifer walked over to the mirror. The flame on the lamp chattered weakly along the tip of the blackened wick. Still, it threw a pallid light, enough to see her reflection, if she leaned over the dresser, close to the mirror. A mixed message: her eyes were stricken, oblong, her skin a muted gauzy gold. She appeared both more ethereally attractive and more crimped and neurotic than she'd possibly ever appeared; the effect was foreign, pleasing.

She was so transfixed by her reflection that at first she didn't hear Maureen moaning in the background.

"No, oh, no . . ."

She caught Maureen's eye in the mirror, and followed it downward to her neck, clamped beneath the satin and the string of beads, her chest.

Blackness spread. In the available light, it looked like an avid shadow, a creeping void made visible.

Jennifer peered down at the dress. Nothing. It was white, stainless.

"Maureen?"

Jennifer stood in the middle of the room. A noise. She snapped her neck in the direction of the window. That woman, that cat-eyed woman. She scratched at the window as her face, fading in and out of the faint light thrown by the oil lamps, shifted and changed, bones moving under the skin, mouth lengthening, until she was no longer the cat-eyed woman; she was the spitting image of the one live person Jennifer had only ever seen in mirrors—herself.

It was then that the dress began to burn. The sleeves cinched in tight, the waist, the neck, making her gag. The seams, already prickly, intensified their irritation until she felt like her arms were being torn open by a serrated knife. The woman in the window was scratching and scratching—no, in fact, she was beckoning. *Come here. Come here.*

She ran in her bare feet through the dark living room and out the door. The snow was as cold as the burning sensation inside her dress; impossible to determine which was more painful, or differently painful. It was too much of one thing, too much of another. Still snow fell from the sky and whipped around her in bundles that looked like bodies and then people—a hovering parade of women in white dresses, closing in on her from both peripheries and moaning like a chant, an incantation, an expression of antique, weary misery. The women whisked her up the hill, up and up behind the house through an empty zone in the trees, and her feet were so cold, so senseless, that the air felt no different from the frozen ground. She was running through space now but the women stayed with her, they spiraled around her like twisting bedsheets as she dropped and dropped and dropped.

She awoke in an attic. She knew it was an attic because of the unfinished ceiling, the rafters, the steeply pitched roof. The wall to her left was all brightness, a huge window. It hurt to look at it.

Jennifer was achy; she was surprised to find herself wearing a plaid kilt and a green sweater, a pair of hard brown shoes that numbed her feet. She descended the stairs into a gaudily wallpapered hallway, empty save for a table and a black phone. *I'll call Maureen*, she thought, but the phone receiver wouldn't come free of the cradle; the two were fused together, one piece of metal, clumsily painted. There were no numbers on the dial.

She walked down the main staircase into a living room, where a fake fire, made of sharp bits of orange construction paper, "burned" in the fireplace.

"Hello?" Jennifer called out.

No answer. She walked through a study, lined with books that were also fake—the shelf was a single strip of painted spines. She called out a second time. The house appeared deserted. At least, she thought it was deserted, until she entered the kitchen. A man sat at the table, reading a paper. There was a grapefruit on a plate, a cup and saucer. A woman stood by the stove wearing an apron, a dress with a flared skirt, ugly brown shoes similar to Jennifer's. She was frozen in place, stirring a pot. There was no smell of food.

"Excuse me," Jennifer said. No one said anything. Nobody moved. She crept closer to the woman by the stove. Her hair fell over her face. Jennifer moved closer, put a hand under her hair, lifted it free—and screamed.

The cat-eyed woman stared at her pot blankly, her lips frozen in a half smile. Jennifer backed away, shaking. She backed right into the breakfast table, knocking it over. The wooden grapefruit spun away; the coffee cup, glued to its saucer, lay on its side, its coffee contents perfectly intact.

Oh, God, Jennifer said to herself, *Oh, my God . . .*

Her father stared at the space where his paper had previously been. Beyond him, a wall of glass stretched from floor to ceiling. Jennifer ran to the glass, pressed her hands against it. The view was wavy, uncertain, distorted as though through a magnifying lens. She was looking into another house, a giant house, a house that struck her as vaguely familiar, but she couldn't be certain because her brain was overcome by a fossilized feeling of rictus, as were her arms and hands. She righted the table, retrieved the wooden grapefruit, the cup and saucer, returned the paper so that it was again directly beneath her father's gaze. Tired now, scarcely able to move, she dropped beside her father and waited, for eternity, to be served breakfast.

THE CHILD

by RODDY DOYLE

HE HADN'T SLEPT IN DAYS. He hadn't slept in weeks. He was never aware of waking up. He was just there. Awake. Lying there.

All night.

There was no safe time.

He tried a hotel. In his own town. He thought it might work. Just one night away. But it didn't. He didn't sleep. It was day at the curtains; he gave up.

He hadn't yawned in days. He hadn't stretched. He never closed his eyes. They'd stopped being sore.

There was no safe time.

He was past tiredness. It was in his breath, though. In his chest. The catch, the warning. The exhaustion; more.

Sometimes he came at night. The child. He'd hear the breath, the silence. Sometimes twice, three times. He'd be there. Sometimes not for days. But he was always there.

Always. And not just at night. Not just when he was alone. There was no time when he wasn't there. When he didn't feel him.

He didn't go out now. Go to the cinema, or just out—a few drinks, a walk. He didn't do that. He went home and stayed there.

But that was no good. Home wasn't safe. Home was nothing now. The walls, the books—nothing.

The first time, he'd looked up—he'd been reading the paper— and the child was there. Staring at him. From a seat on the other side of the carriage. He'd stared back for a few seconds, and looked back down at the paper. And he wouldn't have remembered, except for the second time. Another day. A few days later, the end of the week. He was standing this time. The carriage was full. He tried to get his book from his pocket, and the child was there beside him. Looking up at him. Small, tucked in against his hip. But he hadn't felt him. And he couldn't feel him now.

He got off a station early. He pushed his way off. He looked around as the platform emptied. The child was gone.

But he wasn't.

A boy. A small one. He didn't know ages; he didn't know children. He didn't know people with children.

It wasn't the train the next time, and the next time wasn't for weeks. It was in a café that he sometimes went to on his way home. He was about to push the door open. The child was standing in there. Facing him, looking out.

He stopped; he didn't go in. He didn't know why not. He couldn't. He walked away, felt foolish. He turned and went back. He got to the door. The child was there, alone. No mother at a table or at the counter. He couldn't go in—he couldn't lift his hand to the door. He couldn't do it.

That was the first night he didn't sleep at all. He got up, walked around, tried to read, got back into the bed, held his penis, got back out, tried to read—exhausted at half-five, awake and amused, laughing privately at himself by the time he got to work. He walked past the café on his way home. It was raining; there was steam on the windows and door glass. He didn't stop.

He wrote it down. "Boy. eight or nine." Eye color, hair color—

he didn't know. "Thin." He put these words in a jotter he'd taken from work. He left it on the table beside the bed, with a pen. In case he woke up with something to add. He'd seen it in a film, the jotter beside the bed, ready for the dreams.

He didn't dream. He never remembered dreams. He lay on the bed. He listened to the rain and the fridge. He slept. He woke. He looked at the clock. Half-five. He was tired but pleased. He'd slept.

It rained for days then. Steam on the train windows, steam on the office windows, on the café windows and door. He decided to go in. His hand went to the door. Water ran from the sleeve of his raincoat, down his arm. He pushed the door. He saw the word on the glass. "DAD." Written with a finger. He stopped as he pushed. He saw the child.

"Gray shirt." He wrote it later, in the jotter.

Hair and eye color? He still didn't know, although he'd stared at the child for a long time. Until a woman behind him had wanted to enter, and he'd stepped back, and the door closed slowly in front of him. "DAD."

The child looked back at him.

"No expression," he wrote. "Expressionless."

He wanted to speak, to say something. To get him to speak, to hear. "What do you want?" It was too aggressive—he couldn't think. The woman behind him; he'd stepped back. The door closed. The letters weren't clear on the glass; streams of water ran through them.

He went.

He didn't sleep.

He thought about the child. He heard the clock, the fridge. He didn't sleep. He put on his glasses. He leaned across, turned on the light. He saw the word on the notebook. "DAD."

And then he was really scared.

He searched the flat. It was small; there was nowhere to hide. But he looked everywhere. He went back to the jotter beside the bed. He picked it up. The pencil had gone down hard on the paper. The word was cut into the next page, and the next, the next. DAD. DAD. DAD. DAD. A real hand had done it. He listened: he was alone. He brushed his teeth. He got under the shower. He thought he heard—he turned off the water. He listened. A house alarm, streets away. Tires on the wet road.

He changed carriages on the train. He got out and pushed along crowded platforms. He got into different carriages— he began to see himself doing it. He felt stupid, self-important. He wanted it over with. He wanted to grab him, to feel the bony fact. "What do you want?" He wanted to hear a voice. While he was awake, dressed, in charge of the situation. "Who are you?"

But the child wasn't on the train and he wasn't in the café. He hadn't seen him at work; he didn't see him now.

He had to wait.

He woke in the night and felt something in the room— breath, something, an echo of what had woken him. He leaned over to the light, and knew it was hopeless. He turned the light on. Nothing there. He lay awake. He turned off the light. He held his penis. He lay still.

He stopped eating. Food made him feel sick. He could feel it turn. DAD. He had no children.

He got into bed. He closed his eyes. He waited.

He was sure he had no children. There was his ex-girlfriend. Two years together. There were women before that. He remembered them all. He wrote their names in the jotter. "Marion, Brenda." Down the page. "Frances, Karen." In reverse order. Down the years. "Hazel." He stopped at the first one. "Tina."

He tore out the page—there was a faint "DAD" on the new page—and wrote the names again, more space between them. Three lines each. "Brunette." He wrote that beside Tina. He looked at it. He put a line through it. "Brown hair," he wrote. "Sixteen. Nice. Too nice."

He felt the fingers on his hand.

"Blond. V. red when embarrassed. Angry."

At the counter.

"Hair color? Not sure Karen is right. Sharon?"

He was buying a paper. Going to work. He went for money in his pocket—fingers, he felt them, suddenly.

"Dyed green. Different colors."

He felt the fingers let go—he felt. He looked.

"Laughed a lot. Too much."

Beside him, against him. Looking up at—staring at him. The hand still there, in the air, half-open. Right against him—

He got away from the counter. The child was against him, right there. He got out to the street.

He stepped back.

"Eyes?" he wrote later.

There was space between them. People passed. They went around the child, made sure they didn't knock against him. He was there.

"Who are you?"

The child looked at him. The look on his face—he didn't know children—was painful, begging, trying to smile, win.

He put his hand out.

People went around them.

He stretched out his arm, brought his hand closer to the child. He moved his fingers—they brushed against nothing. A woman smiled down at the child.

He ran.

"Why?" he wrote later.

He was sick, appalled. He'd felt the hand on his, in the shop. But his fingers couldn't touch what he could see. He'd touched the shoulder—it wasn't there.

"Ghost?" he wrote.

He ran across the street. He changed his mind as he ran, but it was two more streets before he stopped. He leaned against a post office wall. He waited for the sweat to turn cold. People passed. He didn't look. He waited. He stopped gasping. He looked.

No child.

"Colorless."

He looked in the door of the post office. He went to the next corner, stood so he could see down two streets, turn slightly and see down another.

He didn't go to work.

He sat on the bed. He picked up the jotter. He flicked open a new page. He heard breath. He didn't look.

He wrote.

Block letters.

"I DO NOT BELIEVE IN GHOSTS."

He'd held the fingers; he'd felt them.

He read the names of the women, down the page.

Marion

Brenda

Frances

Karen

Hazel

Tina

He flicked to a new page.

"Child." He underlined the word. What did he look like? Who did he look like? What was happening?

He flicked back to the women. He needed surnames. He was keeping it real. The child was real; the child had a mother.

He didn't look.

"Marion Murphy."

Three years since he'd seen her. She'd met someone else. "We'll still be friends." It had surprised him how little he'd cared. But even if she'd been pregnant when she'd left, that child would be much too young.

"Brenda Wilson."

He got up. He looked in the kitchen, the toilet. He came back. He sat on the bed.

"Brenda Wilson."

He could hear it. The breathing.

He stood up. He couldn't hear it.

He sat back on the bed.

"Brenda Wilson."

He hadn't liked her. He'd never liked her. But they'd met because she was at the desk beside him at work. His previous job. "Blond. V. red when embarrassed. Angry. Good-looking." That was true. "The best-looking." They hadn't lived together; it had lasted a couple of months. He'd left for a new job—the one he had now. He'd applied for it before they'd met, but she hadn't believed him. A year before Marion. A bit more. Not enough for her to be the mother.

The mother of what?

What was he doing?

He'd never slept with her—slept.

He listened.

He'd never gone to sleep beside her. She'd been an aggressive sleeper; she took it to bed with her—punching out, kicking, snoring like she was doing it on purpose. She'd frightened him, a bit.

"Candidate?"

What was he doing? "Candidate?" The child wasn't his. No child was his.

She was still out there. Maybe at the same desk. A phone call would tell him.

What?

What was he doing?

Was it some sort of trick, a revenge thing or something? Maybe not Brenda Wilson. Some other woman.

"Who?" he wrote.

"Why?"

He wasn't a wild man, or cruel. He'd never been violent or very unpleasant. He was shy. They'd all said it.

"Frances."

Frances what? What was he doing?

"Frances Crooked Tooth." He put a line through that. He was not a cruel man.

He heard something. A press being shut slowly, air being dislodged. The kitchen. He put down the jotter. He stood up.

He looked in the presses. He looked in the sink. He listened.

He went back to the bed. He picked up the jotter. He knew before he looked, the thickness of the jotter in his fingers—the page was different.

He looked.

"I DO NOT BELIEVE IN GHOSTS."

He stood up. He sat down.

His words.

Not his writing.

He got down on the floor. He looked under the bed. He left all the doors open, the press doors, the room doors. He moved things away from the walls. He took everything out of the presses, put everything on the table. He went to the bed and the jotter. "I DO NOT BELIEVE IN GHOSTS." He took the duvet off the bed. He folded it small, put it back. He put the pillows on top of it. That was everything. There were no closed doors, no hiding places.

He waited. He walked. He looked in the corners. He went back to the bed. The pen was where he'd left it. He picked it up. He picked up the jotter. He listened.

"Frances."

He tried to get at her surname. "Kind of brown hair—crooked tooth." He put a line through "kind of." He put two lines through "crooked."

"Brown hair—tooth."

It hadn't lasted. A few weeks. He didn't know what she'd done for a living. A teacher. Something with children. Retarded children. Something like that. And he'd broken her bra. He remembered that. Trying to get it off, and her annoyance.

She'd sent the child after him, revenge for the bra. He didn't smile. He knew he couldn't.

"Nice."

She had been. Nice. He'd liked her. It just hadn't worked out.

"Incompatible."

He left "Nice," put a line through "Incompatible." He just hadn't wanted the effort. Getting to know each other.

"Too nice."

He'd offered to buy her a new bra. Not actually buy it—pay for it. She wouldn't let him.

"Loser. Not great."

He had it. The name.

"Costello."

Frances Costello.

The kitchen. Something rubbed against something.

He got down on his knees. He crept. He stood up. He didn't want to be too low down.

He looked—he knew. Nothing.

He slept sitting up. He held the jotter. He tried to sleep.

He slept.

He didn't.

The child was there. At the jotter. Pulling it from his hand.

He woke. His neck was sore. He stood up, stretched, pulled off his socks.

The jotter was gone.

He went around; he charged. Empty shelves, open doors. It was gone. Back to the bed. Gone.

It was on the table beside the bed.

Where he'd left it.

No.

There was no more sleep. That night. Any night. He waited.

"Karen or Sharon."

He didn't know.

"Green hair. Different colors."

He didn't know how long ago. Six years, seven. He tied thread to the jotter, to his finger. He closed his eyes. He waited. He met her twice. Both of them drunk. They did it once, the green hair time.

He didn't sleep. He knew he didn't.

The second time her hair was blue and they were both embarrassed. They'd met by accident, in front of a cinema. She went to the toilet and didn't come back.

"Good riddance."

The thread pulled—he opened his eyes. He checked it, brought his finger closer to his face. The jotter slid toward him. It fell off the table. He picked it up. It wasn't the jotter. It was a different—

He ran. Around the rooms. Kitchen. Noise behind him—he roared, he turned. The jotter. He was dragging it behind him. He tore at the thread. It wouldn't break. It dug into his finger.

"Who are you!"

He didn't touch the jotter. Black cover. Not his. His was green. He sat on the floor, against the wall. He lifted his finger. The jotter slid at him. He flipped open the cover. "Boy. Eight or nine." He pulled the jotter closer to him. He turned another page—the list of women. It was his jotter. Except the cover. His was green.

"Green!"

He tried the hotel.

He was past tiredness. It was in his breath, in his chest. The catch, the warning. He hadn't yawned in days.

The hotel. He thought it might work. He walked there. He walked close to the street, away from doors and gateways. Three miles. It was raining. The money was wet in his pocket. He looked before he entered. He put his face to a window. He couldn't see properly. Running water, condensation. He went to the entrance. He could see. People, adults. No families, children—child. He entered. He tried to dry himself with his coat. The foyer wasn't busy. He checked behind a pillar.

The receptionist didn't like him.

"Sign. Here."

The lift was empty. The doors were slow. No one else entered.

"Naomi."

The fourth floor. The corridor. Empty. He checked the numbers on the wall; his room was to the right. He followed the arrow.

"Tall."

The key was a card. It worked the first time. He pushed the door shut; it was slow across thick carpet.

Under the bed. Behind the curtains. He searched the room. He left the light on. He turned it off. The bedside light. He turned that off. He didn't sleep. He held his penis. He heard something—the child. He charged through the room. He threw something. Something broke. Someone knocked. He didn't answer. He stayed still. The knock again. Silence. He lay on the bed. He sat up. It was day at the curtains; he was sweating.

He left. He didn't eat. He hadn't eaten. In days, weeks—he wasn't sure. He wasn't hungry. He was never hungry.

"Naomi."

Who was that? He didn't know her. "Gorgeous." He kept writing. "Tall. Great. Bit of a bitch." He didn't know what he was doing.

The name on the receptionist's tag. Naomi.

Was he going mad?

No.

He walked. People looked; he saw that. They were looking. He looked at himself. Up at a window. A shoe shop. He stared, tried to see himself in the glass. He took off his glasses; he could see better up close without them. He could see. He looked fine. He pushed down his hair. Fine. He put his glasses back on. He looked fine. He was fine.

He saw him. In the glass. He turned.

There was nothing. Cars, adults.

He turned again. To the window. The child was still there. Behind, right behind him. He turned again, and fell. He got up. Before hands could grab him. He was fine. A bit wet. The child was inside—that was it. In the shoe shop. Looking out at him. He was in there.

Ghosts didn't have reflections.

He wasn't a ghost.

He had him.

He ran at the door. He had him. He could see him now, clearly. Standing in there. Waiting.

He hit the door. He was fine. He pushed the glass, felt the heat—in.

Gone. The child—

There were boxes, piled. A wall of them—shoe boxes. That was where—he pulled at them, no weight, they fell away. He pulled them down, he climbed over them. He dropped his bag, got at them with both hands. Screams behind him. He didn't look. He had him now.

"Gotcha."

"Sir?"

"Gotcha, gotcha!"

He stood on boxes, broke boxes, climbed across them. He fell, he slipped. On boxes—he was fine. The wall was gone. The child—gone. No child.

The changing rooms. He looked around; he tried to stand. None—a shoe shop; no need for rooms. He crawled over boxes. People over him. Hands on his clothes.

"Come on."

"Where are you!?"

Hand in his hair—he was off the ground. His glasses fell off. He was carried out. His leg hit the door. Out to the street. A hand put the glasses back on his face. Shoved them; they were crooked. Bent. He couldn't see. He couldn't hear properly. Off the ground. Being held up—three men. They stopped moving. He heard a car door, car doors. More shadows—he was surrounded. He could see blue—uniforms. They moved again. They dropped him—he fell. Against a car. A hand pushed, the back of his head. A police car. His cheek hit the roof. It was wet—the roof was wet. He couldn't think of . . . They were putting handcuffs on him. He could feel the cuffs against his skin, the cold, pain—they twisted his wrists. They held his arms. It was raining.

"The child," he said.

"What child? Get in."

A hard hand on his head. Pushed down, into the car. His hands behind his back—difficult, sore. Squashed between two cops. They were moving—the car was moving. He had to say something. He needed to start. A hand in front of his eyes. It straightened his glasses. He could see, through finger marks, drops of water. The car braked. An arm stopped him from falling forward. He couldn't turn his head much; there wasn't space. They were moving again. He saw his bag. On a cop's knees. He saw big hands coming out of the bag. He saw his jotter.

"What's this?"

He didn't answer.

"Jesus."

"What?" The other cop.

"Who are these people? Marion, Brenda, Frances. They're all women."

"What?"

"What women?" The driver.

"Jesus."

He heard the pages being flicked.

"'Blonde. V. red when embarrassed. Angry. Good-looking. The best-looking. Candidate?'"

The cop to his left moved. Trying to put space between them.

"Candidate for what?"

He was going to explain.

Somewhere calm. Not in the car.

"For what? Hey."

Not in the car. He'd start at the beginning. He'd try to.

"Oh, Jesus."

"What?"

"Naomi. Gorgeous. Tall. Great. Bit of a bitch."

"Jesus."

"Sick."

"Isn't there a Naomi on that list?"

"What list?"

"The missing women."

"Oh, Christ."

"I think you're right. And a Frances."

He'd explain.

"What about this one? 'Green hair. Different colors. Good riddance.'"

"Oh, Jesus."

The car stopped.

His list was a different list. He didn't know what they were talking about.

Doors opened. The cops got out; he could feel the car lift. He could feel the space, air. A hand at his sleeve.

"Come on."

He was pulled out. Shoulders. Legs were caught—his face hit the ground.

The ground was gone—he was standing. Pushed.

"The child."

"Go on."

Pushed. He could taste blood. He could feel it. His eyes, glasses gone—he couldn't see.

"The child."

They couldn't hear. He was pushed.

DELMONICO

by DANIEL HANDLER

"**W**HAT'S A DELMONICO?"

The two gentlemen had scarcely entered the place. From where I was sitting they were only silhouettes in the shiny doorway, blaring with rude sun. It was after six but dead summer, so the sun hadn't set. I don't drink in the daytime, but if it's after six you'll probably find me at the Slow Night. It's been remarked to me that my regular spot at the bar isn't the best one, as I have to whirl around whenever somebody walks in, just to see who it is. I suppose that's true, that I could choose a better bar stool if I wanted a better view of the outside world. But that's not what I like to look at when I come in.

Davis was at the cash register, her back to the door, holding two or three dollars in her palm. She was about to give them to a guy, as change for the drinks she made for him and his girlfriend. Then the guy was going to hand them back to Davis. This is how it went with Davis as long as I'd ever seen it. Davis was gorgeous, is what she was, gorgeous not in the way she looked but in the way she was. When she mixed you a drink and handed back your change you'd hand it over to her no matter what you paid and what you ordered. It wouldn't matter if you had your girl with you, waiting at one of the tables with a high-heeled foot tapping on the carpet. You'd give it back, all your puny dollars, and still you'd feel like you hadn't forked it over fast enough. "Delmonico?" Davis said, and looked back at the gentlemen. She cocked her head, but not like she was thinking, more like she was considering whether these guys deserved the real answer. They didn't move. I tried to look at them myself but the sunlight still made them nothing but shadows. All I could notice was that one was taller than the other. Davis had probably noticed six or seven things more, and she'd just that second turned around from the register. "Delmonico," she said again. "Gin, vermouth, brandy. A dash of bitters."

The shorter gentleman gave his friend a little tap with his hand. "I told you she was smart," he said, and then the two of them stepped inside and let the door shut behind them. Davis put her hands on her hips like this offhand compliment wasn't nearly enough. The guy slid his money back to Davis and took his seat.

Time and time I want to tell Davis that I love her, but she's so smart there's no way she hasn't figured it out already.

The Slow Night is on a fairly main drag, more or less half a block away from two other bars and just about across the street from another. These bars are called Mary's, and O'Malley's, and The something. I've never been inside them and never intend to. One of them—Mary's, I think—has those little flags all over the ceiling, fluttering like a used-car lot. You can see it from the street because they prop the door open. All of them have the neon in the window and even on a quick walk-by you can hear the roar of music and laughing and the little earthquakes of bottle caps falling to the floor. The bars are full in the evenings, because I guess there are lots of people in the world who like to have a pitcher of something, and sit underneath a TV yelling at each other. In the daytime they're dead like anyplace, with just a few puttering around. One of them has a pool table and people gather for that, with the chattering of the balls like teeth on a chilly day. I don't wish any of these people any harm and am grateful that these other bars take them away. The Slow Night looks closed from the outside, with heavy draperies on the windows and no real sign, just the name fading away over the entrance. The doors are closed except when someone is walking through them. From the doorway are two steps down into the bar—mostly for show, I think, because it's not a basement place. Inside, all the furniture's real—real bar stools, real tables and chairs, and a real jukebox giving the world the music of the lonely, with Julie London and Hank Williams, and some quieter jazz things I never can determine. They don't serve food although sometimes a bowl of nuts might appear from someplace, and the only thing one might call entertainment is a few sections of the day's paper stacked up at the very end of the bar, in case one needs to check on something outside. Nowhere is there any advertisement of any sort, except the clock which says Quill, right in the middle of the face. Davis doesn't know what that is. It came with the place.

The bar has something of a reputation, in guidebooks fools buy and read. "Don't let the exterior fool you," is the sort of thing that passes as praise, "the Slow Night is the real deal—the sort of place in which your parents might have met, with real leather booths and a lady behind the counter who will mix you any poison you can dream up." But these lazy lies—no booths, you don't dream up cocktails—aren't really the thing. Below the surface of the city, murmured between I don't know who, is the story that Davis is very smart. Not smart like a bartender who knows his World Series, but *smart*, like if you have a problem you can bring it up after you've ordered a drink and she will likely solve it for you. I've seen this in action—actually seen it happen. Divorce lawyers. Grad students. Geological survey men. She fixes their puzzles, although they're no less puzzled, really, when they leave. The gentlemen must have known this too, although the tall one had to ask his quiz master question before he believed it. They took off their hats and sat down.

"Holy—" the guy said from the table, but his girlfriend shushed him. The tall gentleman gave the guy a real angry look, and the guy lowered his eyes and took a long, long sip from his drink. Martinis, both of them, the guy and the girl both. That's the kind of couple that stays together.

"My friend here," said the short gentleman, "was hoping not to be recognized."

"You wander around hoping not to be recognized," Davis said, "then you ought not to let everybody know."

"Do you know who I am?" the tall gentleman asked.

"A customer, I'm guessing," Davis said. "I recognize everyone who comes in that way. I ask them what they want to drink and they tell me and we go from there. So far it's worked okay. Do you gentlemen really want Delmonicos? It's no drink for beginners."

"Scotch," said the shorter one. "For both of us, please," at the same time as his friend said, "I'm not sure I like your attitude."

Davis just kept her hands on her hips. I looked down at the rest of my bourbon. Davis has offered to make me something nicer, time and time again, but just a little bourbon on ice is what I get, and what she gives me. The shorter one coughed a little into his hand, and looked at his friend. "You'll have to excuse him," he said to Davis. "He's going through a lot."

Davis wasn't sure this was enough, but she nodded. "What kind of Scotch?"

"What kind is there?" the tall one said.

"There's cheap," she said, "there's good, and there's pretentious."

"I usually drink Banquo Gold," he said. "Eight-year-old, if you have it."

"Pretentious it is," she said, and his friend smiled. "Ice? Lemon?"

"I don't have to take this," growled the taller one. "It's a stu-pid idea, anyway. Bruno, let's get out of here. I should get out of here. I should have my *head* examined. I have a lawyer taking my money fast enough. I don't have to chase after some legendary bar skirt."

Bruno, a short name if there ever was one, tried to grab his friend again. "Relax, okay?" he said. "So she jokes around, so what?"

"I've had enough of women *joking around*," the taller one said. "Let's go."

"Look, why don't we have a drink?" Bruno said. "You want one anyway, right?"

"We can go across the street," the taller one said.

"You think they won't know you across the street?" Bruno said.

"Sure," Davis said. "Everybody across the street'll want to buy a drink for the guy who killed his wife."

The girlfriend gasped at her table. The two gentlemen flicked her a look of annoyance. "So you do know me," the taller one said. "You recognize me, what, from the papers?"

"Papers, TV," Davis said, shrugging. "You think that hat makes you invisible? Callahan Jeffers. That's who you are."

"I didn't kill my wife," the man snarled. "But I suppose you won't believe that unless it's in the papers, too."

"Don't you want it in the papers?" Davis asked. "I believe that's known as clearing your name."

"Let's go," Callahan Jeffers said to Bruno. "She's not going to help me if she thinks I did it."

"I don't think you did it," Davis said. "But I still don't help people who get rude in my bar."

"What have I done that's rude?" Jeffers asked. "You've been mocking me since I sat down."

"You haven't sat down," Davis said.

"You know what I mean."

"What I mean," Davis said, "is why don't you sit down, drink some good Scotch, and ask me what you want to ask me?"

Callahan Jeffers looked at her for a second or two, and put his hat down on the bar. "Ice," he said, "and lemon."

"For two," Bruno said.

Davis poured, and the gentlemen took their drinks—like you might take a hike if a very dangerous person suggested it. Bruno laid a bill on the table Davis couldn't see, but from her bored glance it must have been enormous. She turned around and rang out change, placing her hard-earned cash on the bar before she even picked up the bill. The men let it stand. They were going to tip her later. I hated those guys. They weren't gentlemen after all.

Jeffers took a seat and took a sip and nodded. "So," he said, "there's no invisibility potion in a Delmonico, right? Or the gin, brandy, and whatever don't turn into an invisibility potion?"

"When your mother told you that there was no such thing as a stupid question," Davis said, "you didn't believe her, did you?"

"He's not used to women like you is all," Bruno said. "Since I've known him he goes for a different type."

"I don't want to hear about the type," Davis said. "I want to hear about the girl."

"She's no girl," Jeffers said. "She's my wife. Or was. Or *is*. She's gone."

"So you say," Davis said. "Do me a favor and don't tell me things I know already. You're Callahan Jeffers. You're very rich. You've never worked a day in your life, and neither did your father. You were sent to Europe for what rich people call 'schooling' and what everybody else calls 'school.' When you returned you made a big splash as an eligible bachelor. You invested in things for what we might call a living. You beat up a room-service waiter during a seventy-two-hour birthday party in an enormous suite, and you gave him a lot of money and two years later the mayor had you on some special citizens' commission on crime."

"I was drunk," Jeffers said. "That night in the hotel. I was very drunk and it was wrong. I've said it a thousand times. I had a drinking problem, and I worked it out."

"There are many people who come into my bar and order Scotch," Davis said. "None of them are reformed alcoholics."

"I just said I worked it out," Jeffers said. "That's what I believe.

What you say about paying off the waiter was true. He was a fag and I bought him what fags want, which is a condo on the beach and a handsome face. I don't think that's a crime. People who resent me for money would do the same thing if they had it."

"And yet," Davis said, "with these statements, the police nevertheless suspect you of some sort of crime."

Callahan Jeffers stood up, although not without first taking another gulp of his drink. If you spend time in a bar you hear a number of men snarl. I don't know if they snarl more in bars or if that's just where I hear them snarl, but they snarl, like some animal you find messing around in the trash, or out in the angry woods where stupid people camp. "*I didn't kill my wife!*" he said. "I don't know how she did it, but she set me up. She's a bitch, a bitch someplace laughing at me. And she'll keep laughing until I'm all locked up."

"They're not going to lock you up," Bruno said.

"Says you." Callahan didn't sit down but he finished his drink. It made him look weak, the grab for the glass but still standing like he might leave.

"Says everyone, including the lawyer," Bruno said. "There's no body, so there's no crime. You haven't even been arrested."

"Arrested," Jeffers said. "Everything's gone now even if the police never touch me. I killed her is what everyone thinks. Mayor's special commission. I was going to be *mayor*."

"He was weighing the odds of running, yes," Bruno said. "Those odds have changed."

"My whole odds have changed with this," Jeffers said. He looked around like he was going to spit on the floor and then looked at Davis again. What would have happened if this guy had spat on the floor? I think of that sometimes on sleepless nights, when the sugar from the bourbon wakes me up and makes me look at life. "I'm not the mayor now. I'm just a man who killed his wife. I'm gone and she's laughing. She's not dead any more than I'm Santa Claus. She fucked me somehow. I don't get it. No one gets it. Bruno said maybe you might."

"No," Davis said. "I certainly don't get why anyone would fuck you. You want another Scotch?"

"Take mine," Bruno said quickly, and handed over his drink. Where do they get guys like him? All the way back in his family tree maybe there were whipping boys.

"Tell me the thing," Davis said, "while I get everybody another round. Mr. Jones, you okay back there?"

I stay quiet when the bar's got customers, so I just nodded into my bourbon. It was half-gone. Maybe six months before it was a man with stolen eels. He was a marine something—you know, not like he'd actually ever been in the marines. The eels were valuable and shipped across the ocean from a faraway sea, or maybe it was the other way around. When the man opened the tanks there was nothing but grime and seaweed. The eels were valuable but only if they were alive, and it was hard enough keeping them alive if you were a specialist with a government grant, let alone some black-market eel thug. Davis found them. She drew a little map on a cocktail napkin with the words "Slow Night" written on it, the address below, because the man was from out of town and didn't know where the warehouse district was. You'd think a man who spent too much time with eels would have lost some social skills, but he was gorgeously grateful.

"I'll tell you the thing," Bruno said. "Mr. Jeffers met Nathalie at a club."

"The circus was in town," Jeffers said.

"It's true," Bruno said. "This girl was trash, I told him. Her parents were from different countries and ate fire for a living. She spun around on one of those things they dangle from the top of the tent."

"Trapeze," Davis said. "I remember the wedding pictures."

"I told him she'd never clean up," Bruno said. "Girls like that, from a circus? No. He made me go to her last show. She leaped through a hoop; I don't know what else she did. She takes a bow with the clowns and the Chinamen and he wants to marry her?"

"She was a beautiful woman," Davis said. "I remember the pictures."

Callahan Jeffers looked at her and almost smiled. "She was," he said. "She hit me like a ton of bricks."

Davis put two fresh Scotches down on the counter. Behind her the guy and his girlfriend were listening, their martinis forgotten. "And what'd you hit her like?" Davis said.

"It was just some fights," Jeffers said. "She had a temperament, you know? I guess it was wrecked from the start. I bought us a beautiful house, furnished it up, but she just couldn't sit still."

"A Wesson, wasn't it?" Davis asked. "One of the last untouched Wessons in this town."

"You know architecture?" Bruno asked.

"Why is it," Davis asked, "that people think a girl sitting around a deserted bar all day is *less* likely to be well-read?"

"It's completely restored," Jeffers said, with what would have passed for pride among the very dim. "The staircases, the banisters, the window dressings, the whole bit. I paid a flouncy faggot to track down as much of the pricey crap as he could dig up. Two benches in the front hall. The dining table and twelve chairs. You know, black and square—all that German minimal stuff he did. Nathalie was crazy about it. She said it calmed her down—*no*. What was the word? Whittled her down. The whole place was whittled down. The living room had one couch and a mirror balanced in the corner. The bedroom had just two huge black bureaus with square drawers. My study had one of Wesson's only rugs, a big black thing with one gray stripe, and a chandelier from his personal collection, all spidery on the ceiling. And a desk that looked like a fucking altar. It was enormous. It cost everything. But I bought it to show her I cared."

"The study," Davis said, "where you last saw her?"

"We were fighting," Callahan Jeffers said.

"What else is new?" Bruno said.

"She got home late," Jeffers said. "I don't know how it started. Bruno and I went to the fights. She'd never do that with me. We got home around ten but she still wasn't home. An hour later she walks in with Timothy Speed."

DANIEL HANDLER · DELMONICO

"The designer," Davis said.

"The *fag*," Callahan Jeffers said. He put one fist down, very gently, on the bar, like a man showing his gun. "The fag I paid a fortune to spend my fortune on furniture to whittle down my wife. I threw him out."

"Mr. Jeffers'd had a drink or two," Bruno said with a very small shrug.

"She yelled at me, I yelled at her, she pushed me around a little. . . ." Callahan stopped talking. "I know what you're going to say. I shouldn't hit women."

"You shouldn't hit women," Davis said.

"I know that," Jeffers said. "But it was fighting. It was a fight. We were always getting worse. She thought I was catting around, which I was a little. But she drove me there! As soon as I married her she went a little crazy."

"She couldn't take it, with the swells," Bruno said. "A circus performer, Mr. Jeffers. She was climbing the walls because she climbed walls for a living. You can't dress that up."

"She dressed up fine," Jeffers said, "but nothing made her happy. I couldn't take it forever, you know? You want to make someone happy, but if the first fucking fifteen thousand tries don't do it, you get tired of an unhappy person and her yelling."

"So she locked herself in the study," Bruno said. "It locks from the inside. She wouldn't come out."

"What did you do?" Davis asked.

Callahan Jeffers looked at her like a horse I saw once. Some kids were making fun of it. The horse's eyes said, *Someday I will not be pulling this flatbed hayride. I will come to your room when you are sleeping and I will stomp on you, you damn kids.* The rich man lifted both fists and pounded in slow, heavy beats. Everybody's drinks bounced. "Come out!" he yelled. "Come out! Come out! *Come out! Come out!*"

He stopped and sat down. The jukebox finished a song—"And here I am, facing tomorrow, alone in my sorrow, down in the depths

180

of the ninetieth floor"—and stopped, out of money, like much of this town. The guy and his girl shared one quick glance and skedaddled. When the door swung open and shut it was much darker outside. For a moment I couldn't remember anything I'd done before Callahan Jeffers entered the Slow Night and started yelling. The rich man, once an eligible bachelor and probably one again, drew a handkerchief out of his pocket and wiped his face. I took a sip, mostly melted ice.

"It's true," Bruno muttered. "That's what he did."

"She didn't come out," Jeffers said. "We waited all night, Bruno and I."

"Bruno and you," Davis said. "Where did you wait?"

"Outside," Jeffers said. "Just outside that locked door. There's a little space with two chairs that hurt to sit in. We sat in them."

"Could you hear anything?"

"She made a crying phone call," Jeffers said. "It was Timothy Speed. He told me. I practically had to beat it out of him. He said she called and went through the whole blow by blow, and cried. She said I was going to kill her. That's what he told the police. He said she said. Why they would believe that of me—"

"You, a known drunk who beats people up," Davis said.

"*I didn't kill her!*" Jeffers said. "She cried to the fag and she hung up. She hung up and ordered a drink."

"What?" Davis asked.

"She said she wanted a drink," Jeffers said. "A Delmonico. She always liked the fancy things. When I met her she was asking for a Singapore Sling."

"Gin again," Davis said. "Gin, cherry brandy, bitters, lime, ginger beer. There are some who say you can't trust a gin woman. How did you make her a Delmonico if you didn't know what it was?"

"I don't make the drinks in my home," Jeffers said. "I have a man."

"He woke up Gregor," Bruno said. "It was late."

"Gregor loved it," Jeffers said. "Gregor loves Nathalie and he loves . . . I don't know. *Drama*. The trick with the mixing and the right glass for a lady who asks. He made one and brought it on a tray with a shaker and everything. He knocked on the door and she made him swear we were at least fifteen feet away."

"Which we were," Bruno said.

"He handed her the tray and she slammed the door again and locked it. We heard the cocktail shaker pour and then we heard nothing."

"Nothing?" Davis said.

"For two hours," Jeffers said. "It was morning, almost morning. Gregor went back to bed. Bruno fell asleep in the ugly chair. I paced outside and pounded some more. Bruno woke up."

"I did," Bruno said. "I woke up and made the point that perhaps you should go to bed rather than pounding on a door that incidentally cost a fortune. You were making marks."

"And then we heard a shattering of glass," Jeffers said. "Give me another Scotch."

"I'll think about it," Davis said. "You're making enough noise without another round. You scared two customers away before the martinis were over."

"Not my problem," Jeffers said.

"No," Davis agreed, and walked out of the bar to collect the glasses the kids had left behind. "Mine. If the study is the rounded room on the ground floor, then there are three enormous windows—"

"Painted shut," Jeffers said. "We were going to redo them. They hadn't been touched."

"And a small one in the far corner," Davis finished.

"That's the one that broke," Bruno said. "But the window doesn't go anywhere. It's a what's-it. A *lightwell*. Even if she could have fit through that window, which she couldn't—"

"She might," Jeffers said. "She was wasting away. I know she looked fine in the picture but she was starving herself. She wasn't doing well. She was making herself skinny to make me angry."

"That's not usually how it goes," Davis said.

"She was depressed, she said." Jeffers shook his head. "What's that thing where girls make themselves skinny for attention?"

"Marriage," Davis said.

Jeffers gave her one curt laugh. "I heard the window, I didn't know what to think. One day we were fighting and she found a nail on the ground. A nail! And scratched herself across the arm. With broken glass, I didn't want her to—"

"We used one of the chairs to break the door down," Bruno said. "Gregor heard us and came upstairs. The chair was broken too."

"Now what else is really in this room?" Davis said. "Rug and desk, you said. Curtains?"

"Heavy dark things," Jeffers said. "Like in here. Just like in this place. Timothy Speed made her get them. That's the first place we looked. We thought she'd thrown herself out one of the big windows, although she was so light they might not have broken. Who knows. But she wasn't there. And don't think behind the door because I looked there and kicked the goddamn wall. I'm telling you she wasn't hiding. She must have gone out the other one."

"It's a *lightwell*," Bruno said. "It goes up to a skylight made of marble you can shine light through. The light is yellowy. I don't like it. But that's where it goes."

"Up to a skylight," Davis said, "and down to where?"

"To another window, in the basement," Bruno said. "Painted shut. Not messed with. The police used what I have read was a fine-tooth comb."

"She was gone," Jeffers said. "When we saw the window we ran downstairs to the basement. There were four cases of wine stacked up against that window. They were dusty. She wasn't there. We ran all the way up to the roof. The sun was coming up over the park, I'm telling you, the goddamn birds were singing but my wife was not on the roof and there's no way she was ever on the roof."

Davis stopped wiping the table. "Afraid of heights?"

"No," Jeffers said. "You can't open that marble thing. It's old. Wesson didn't build it to be opened."

"Who went up on the roof?" Davis said. "All of you? Gregor too?"

"Gregor's old," Jeffers said. "He dozed in the other chair."

"The police have been with him a million times," Bruno said. "That's why they haven't arrested Mr. Jeffers, I think. They believe that I'd help him murder somebody and hide a body, but not Gregor. They thought maybe they couldn't shake me, but two hours with the cops and Gregor would cry like a baby."

"He lost his mom young," Jeffers said. "That's why he's such a fucking baby."

"I really don't like you," Davis said. She walked back to the bar and ran a thoughtful hand down the wood, close to where I was sitting. I couldn't help watching her even though it must have looked schoolboy. "A girl," she said, "goes into a room with nothing in it but antique furniture and closed windows. Someone brings her a drink. Glass breaks. A tiny window that goes nowhere is broken. The other ones aren't, and you're sure, right? Because they're tall. You might have missed a small break at the top."

"When we got back from the roof I ripped those drapes down myself," Jeffers said.

"Which hasn't helped your case," Bruno said. "He trashed that whole room and then had to tell the cops that nothing had been broken but the window. We got an Italian guy doing the wiring and an old man with a shop in his garage. He's the only man who can fix a Wesson chair, so he says."

"Yes," Jeffers said. "I threw the chair."

"The chair that broke the door?" Davis asked.

"No," Jeffers said. "Another chair. The chair by the desk. It was like a throne but I lifted it and I snapped it over the desk."

"So there was another chair in the room," Davis said. "What else?"

"Papers in the desk," Jeffers said. "I don't know. Nothing. A letter opener, maybe? When I tipped it over I didn't notice anything missing."

"The drink," Bruno said.

"What?" Davis asked.

"The Delmonico," Bruno said. "The tray was there and the little shaker full of melting ice. But the glass and the drink were gone. Gin, vermouth, brandy, dash of bitters."

"An invisibility potion," Jeffers said. "Like I said. Gone like her."

"Mr. Jones," Davis said, "put something on the jukebox."

She handed me two of Callahan's unearned dollars. He glared at me. I walked to the jukebox and chose Chet Baker, which is what I do often.

"What was she wearing?" Davis asked.

"A necklace," Jeffers said. "A lot of money around her neck. Diamonds and I think sapphires, I don't know. A vintage thing somebody found for me. A present after a fight. And a silk dress I ripped. And her shoes, but her shoes were sitting on the desk, right next to the phone which I ripped out of the wall. Just tell me where the fuck she is or stop with the stupid questions. I'm so tired of this. The cops ask all the same things, what was she wearing, like I would have forgot to mention jet-pack."

"I'm going to pour you one more Scotch," Davis said. "And you'll drink it and I'll tell you something and you'll leave. And you'll pay for another bourbon for Mr. Jones."

"Who the hell is Mr. Jones?" Jeffers asked.

"A customer who doesn't give me any trouble," Davis said, her back to the bottles. She poured, and then she reached up and coaxed two martini glasses from a rack above her head. I always forget about that. The gentlemen sipped and I sipped and she filled the two glasses with ice and left them on the bar, while she busied herself with a shaker. Gin. Brandy. You know where this is going. She trembled the bitters bottle over the shaker, stirred, and shut the lid. The ice shifted in the glass. The jukebox played.

There's something about this I'm not telling right. How nasty Jeffers was, maybe, or the sheer implausible mess of a circus wife, a thuggish friend, a tale of an old butler and a locked-up room. The gorgeous shadow of the Slow Night while outside the sun sank, and the quiet of an early drink you didn't deserve. You do not meet people very often like Davis, with a smile from nowhere and a wavering frown, thinking things over so beautifully just to watch her was beauty enough, like the lilt in a good jazz singer, the curve of a good lyric like a secret closing in on itself. This suspense is killing me. I can't stand uncertainty. Tell me now. I've got to know whether you want me to stay or go. Love me, or leave me and let me be lonely. You won't believe me. I love you only. I'd rather be lonely than happy with somebody else. You might find the nighttime the right time for kissing, but nighttime is my time for just reminiscing, regretting instead of forgetting with somebody else. There'll be no one unless that someone is you. I intend to be independently blue. I want your love, but I don't want to borrow—to have it today, to give back tomorrow. For my love is your love. There's no love for nobody else.

When the song ended Jeffers lifted his glass to drain it. It finished, and the sliver of lemon hit his grimacing mouth. "Well?" he said, and pointed to the icy glasses. "What're those?"

"Delmonicos," Davis said. "Like the one that vanished. But it didn't vanish. She threw the glass at the window. Both broke. You couldn't tell one from the other."

Jeffers turned his glass over. This wasn't polite. The Scotch was on the rocks, and the bar got wet with the slop of his ice. The puddle stopped before the two glasses, the ice ghosting into water, that Davis had ready for I couldn't imagine who. "And my wife?"

"That I can't tell you," Davis admitted. She opened her palm and brushed the pile of money, very slowly, into the puddle of Callahan's drink. "Time to go, fellas."

"She's not smart," Jeffers said to Bruno, pointing at him and sneering. "She doesn't know."

"I'm smart enough," Davis said. "If you don't stand up and leave I will walk out of this bar myself. Across the street is a roomful of drunk cops. I'll tell them that Callahan Jeffers, a man finished in this town, is harassing me."

It was true. Funny thing: Davis lets cops drink for free, but hardly anybody ever takes her up. Across the way, O'Malley's lets them drink for half price, and by closing there's a whole platoon staggering outside. Bruno grabbed Callahan's shoulder. Callahan put on his hat. When the door swung open the light was almost gone, and when it swung shut Davis poured the ice out of the glasses and drained the cocktails from the shaker. "Join me," she said. "I haven't had one of these in years."

I put my bourbon aside. "It's not a drink for beginners," I said.

"You're not a beginner," she said. She'd overmeasured, or maybe some of the ice had melted—the glasses were brimming full. Carefully, carefully, she walked them both over, nearly teetering. "All those fishbowls I had to carry in Miss Brimley's class," she said. "Finally coming in handy. To us, Mr. Jones. To our good health."

I didn't drink. "Where is she?" I said.

Davis shrugged, which was a sight to see, each shoulder rising and falling like a sheet in the wind. "I don't know. Probably in some summer cottage of Timothy Speed's. Dyeing her hair or however that goes. Everybody wants to join the circus when they run away from home, but that might be too easy. He'd look for her there, maybe. But a dead girl'll need money."

"Speed could help her sell the necklace," I said.

"That'd be a start," she said, and sighed. "When did you figure it?"

"When you reached for those glasses," I said. "Nobody ever remembers to look up. The drink broke the window and made them look the wrong way. Just the time she needed. They took a trip to the basement, they took a trip to the room, and by the time they got back from the roof she was out the front door like a person. Speed left a car maybe."

"And Gregor? Really dozing, you think?"

"Really dozing, I think," I said. "Without shoes she could tiptoe past him. Or maybe he could lie to the cops after all. Maybe he watched her swing down from that chandelier, as skinny as she was, and let her go after all the fights he saw. She must have been very scared."

"Scared?" Davis said. "She hatched a plan to ruin her husband. It's like he said. They'll never charge him but he'll never be mayor, either. He'll just be a rich guy who got away with murder."

"That's what he is anyway," I said. "That's why she was scared. Scared to fall. If she fell it'd be the end of her—maybe from hitting the floor, or maybe from her husband hitting her. It was a risk. Even an acrobat. Even someone who'd whittled herself away to almost nothing."

"Then she had almost nothing to lose," Davis said. She took a sip and pursed her lips. It's a bitter drink, or maybe bitter's not what I mean. It's sharp and sour. It's complicated. It's difficult to get down unless that's the sort of thing you like. "I feel that way myself sometimes," she said. "Almost nothing, or maybe that's just Chet Baker nudging me to say that. You think I was wrong not to tell him."

"You told him where the drink went," I said. "That's enough for someone like that. Without a body they won't charge him. He'll never know for sure. Maybe Timothy Speed will even blackmail him."

"Or just keep overcharging him for furniture," Davis said. "Wesson never made any rugs. The whole point of a Wesson is the sheer lines of the place. The floors are bare so you can see the wood."

"Callahan Jeffers," I said, "would never see the wood."

"Not for the trees," Davis agreed. She put her drink down and walked to the jukebox with one of Jeffers's damp bills. She punched a number in and her hair just slayed me in the red lights shining inside the machine that sits in the Slow Night waiting for people to ask it to sing. I tried the drink myself but didn't like it, but I liked watching the tilt of the surface of the drink as I moved the glass, like water too cold to swim in. When we're alone like this the room sinks in a bit, like we're locked away from all the people. There are some who can't stand to stay in a room like that but this is my regular spot, right here at the bar where I can see her. Time and time I want to tell Davis that I love her, but of course she's so smart—of course she is—there's no way she hasn't figured it out already.

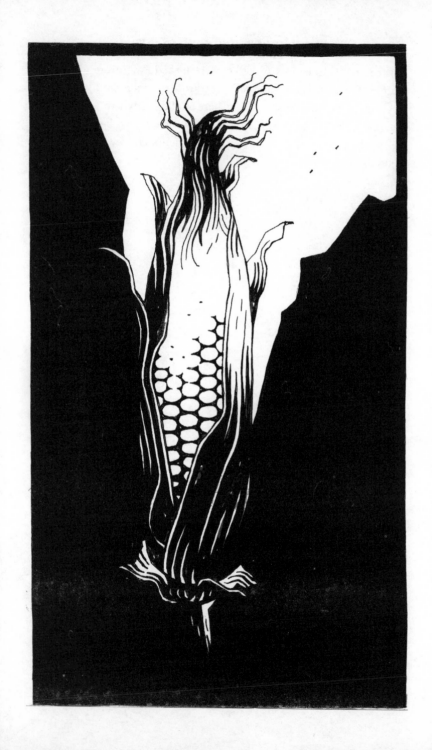

THE SCHEME *of* THINGS

by CHARLES D'AMBROSIO

LANCE VANISHED behind the white door of the men's room, and when he came out a few minutes later he was utterly changed. Gone was the tangled nest of thinning black hair, gone was the shadow of beard, gone, too, was the grime on his hands, the crescents of black beneath his blunt, chewed nails. Shaving had sharpened the lines of his jaw and revealed the face of a younger man. His shirt was tucked neatly into his trousers and buttoned up to his throat. He looked as clean and bland as an evangelist. He bowed to Kirsten with a stagy sweep of his hand and entered the station. All business, anxious over yet another delay, he returned immediately with the attendant in tow, a kid of sixteen, seventeen.

"This here's my wife, Kirsten," Lance said.

Kirsten smiled.

"Pleased," the kid said. He crawled under the chassis of the car and inspected the tailpipe.

"Your whole underside's rusted to hell," he said, standing up, wiping his hands clean of red dust. "I'm surprised you haven't fallen through."

"I don't know much about cars," Lance said.

"Well," the kid said, his face bright with expertise, "you should replace everything, right up to the manifold. It's a big job. It'll take a day and it'll cost you."

"You can do it?" Kirsten asked.

"Sure," the kid said. "No problem."

Lance squinted at the oval patch above the boy's shirt pocket. "Randy," he said, "what's the least we can do?"

"My name's Bill," the kid said. "Randy's a guy used to work here."

"So Bill, what's the least we can get away with?"

"Strap it up, I suppose. It'll probably hold until you get where you're going. Loud as hell, though."

The kid looked at Kirsten. His clear blue eyes lingered on her chest.

"Let's get it fixed," she said, feeling transparent.

"We'll have to make do," Lance said. He ran his tongue into the gap between his teeth. "We represent a charity." Lance handed the kid one of the printed pamphlets, watching his eyes skim back and forth as he took in the information. "Outside of immediate and necessary expenses, we don't have much money."

"Things are sure going to hell," the kid said. He shook his head, returning the pamphlet to Lance.

"Seems that way," Lance said.

The kid hurried into the station and brought back a coil of pipe strap. While he was under the car, Lance sat on the warm hood, listening to the wind rustle in the corn. Brown clouds of soil rose from the fields and gave the air a sepia tint. Harvest dust settled over the leaves of a few dying elms, over the windows of a cinder-block building, over the trailers in the courtyard across the street. One of the trailer doors swung open. Two Indians and a cowgirl climbed down the wooden steps.

"You got a phone?" Lance asked.

"Inside," the kid said.

Lance looked down and saw the soles of the kid's work boots

beneath the car, a patch of dirty sock visible through the hole widening in one of them. He walked away, into the station.

The kid hadn't charged them a cent and they now sat at an intersection, trying to decide on a direction. The idle was rough. The car detonated like a bomb.

"Here's your gum," Lance said.

He emptied his front and back pockets and pulled the cuff of his pants up his leg and reached under the elastic band of his gym socks. Pink and green and blue and red packages of gum piled up in Kirsten's lap. He pulled a candy bar from his shirt pocket and began sucking away at the chocolate coating.

"One pack would've been fine," Kirsten said. "A gumball would have been fine."

"Land of plenty, sweetheart," he said.

Kirsten softened up a piece of pink gum and blew a large round bubble until it burst and the gum hung like flesh from her nose.

"Without money, we're just trying to open a can of beans with a cucumber," Lance said. "It doesn't matter how hungry we are, how desirous of those beans we are—without the right tools, those beans might as well be on the moon." Lance laughed to himself. "Moon beans," he said.

Kirsten got out of the car. The day was turning cold, turning to night. She leaned through the open window, smelling the warm air, wafting unpleasantly with the mixed scent of chocolate and diesel.

"What's your gut feel?" Lance asked.

"I don't know anymore, Lance."

She walked toward the intersection. Ghosts and witches crossed from house to house, holding paper sacks and pillowcases. The streetlights sputtered nervously in the fading twilight. With the cold wind cutting through her T-shirt, Kirsten felt her nipples harden. She was small-breasted and sensitive and the clasp on her only bra had broken. She untucked the shirt and hunched her shoulders forward so the nipples wouldn't show but still the dark circles pressed against the white cotton. The casual clothes Lance had bought her in

Key Biscayne, Florida, had come to seem a costume and were now especially flimsy and idle and ridiculous in Tiffin, Iowa.

A young girl crossed the road, and Kirsten followed her. She thought she might befriend the girl and bring her home, a gambit, playing on the gratitude of the worried parents Kirsten always imagined when she saw a child alone, parents whose concern she conjured out of a lifetime of indifference and neglect. The pavement gave way to gravel and the gravel to dirt and finally a narrow dusty path in the weeds dipped through a dragline ditch and vanished into a cornfield. The girl was gone. Kirsten waited at the edge of the field, listening to the wind, until she caught a glimpse of the little girl again, far down one of the rows, sitting and secretly eating candy from her sack.

"You'll spoil your dinner," Kirsten said.

The girl clutched the neck of her sack and shook her head. Entering the field felt to Kirsten like wading from shore and finding herself, with one fatal step, out to sea, each row was so identical, angling away to infinity. She sat in the dirt, facing the girl. The corn rose over their heads and blew in waves, bending with the wind, giving off a swollen sigh.

"Aren't you cold?" Kirsten said. "I'm cold."

"Are you a stranger?" the girl asked.

"What's a stranger?"

"Somebody that kills you."

"No, then, I'm not a stranger."

Kirsten picked a strand of silk tassel that hung in the little girl's hair.

"I'm your friend," she said. "Why are you hiding?"

"I'm not hiding. I'm going home."

"Through this field?" Kirsten said.

"I know my way," the little girl said.

The girl was dressed in bibbed overalls and dirty pink thongs but Kirsten wasn't quite sure it was a costume. A rim of red lipstick distorted the girl's mouth grotesquely, and blue moons of mascara gave her eyes an unseeing vagueness.

"What are you supposed to be?" Kirsten asked.

The girl squeezed a caramel from its cellophane wrapper, and said, "A grown-up."

"It's getting dark," Kirsten said. "You aren't scared?"

The little girl shrugged and chewed the caramel slowly. Juice dribbled down her chin.

"Let me take you back home."

"No," the girl said.

"You can't stay out here all by yourself."

The girl recoiled when Kirsten grabbed her hand, fighting back in a tantrum of kicking feet and twisting arms, her thin body jolting away in fear. "Let me go," she screamed. "Let me go!" The fury in her voice shocked Kirsten into letting go of the hand. The girl ran off through the corn. Kirsten chased after her, but again very quickly the girl was gone, the sound of the wind swallowing the last of her screams. Kirsten stared down the long dark rows but in every direction the stalks swayed and the dry leaves turned as if the little girl, passing by, had just brushed against them.

When Kirsten finally found her way out of the field she was in another part of town. She walked the length of the street, looking for signs, deciding at last on a two-story house in the middle of the block. A trike lay tipped over in the rutted grass and a plastic pool of water held a scum of dead leaves and twigs. Clay pots with dead marigolds—wooly brown swabs on bent, withered stalks—lined the steps. A family of carved pumpkins sat on the porch rail, smiling toothy candlelit grins that flickered to black, guttering in laughter with every gust of wind. On the porch, wet newspapers curled beside a milk crate. Warm yellow light lit the downstairs, and a woman's shadow flitted across a steam-clouded kitchen window. The upper story was dark.

Kirsten heard a radio playing. She knocked on the door.

A haggard woman in her mid-forties answered. Her hair was knotted up on her head with a blue rubber band, a few fugitive strands dangling down over her ears, one graying wisp curling around her eye. A smudge of flour dusted the side of her nose.

"Yes?" the woman said.

"Evening, ma'am." Kirsten handed the woman a flyer. "I'm with B.A.D," she said. "Babies Addicted to Drugs. Are you busy?"

The woman switched on the porch light and held the printed flyer close to her face. Closing one eye, she studied the bold red statistics on the front of the flyer and then flipped it over and looked into the face of the dark shriveled baby on back.

"Doesn't hardly look human, does it?" Kirsten said.

"No, I can't say it does," the woman said.

"That's what's happening out there, ma'am. That, and worse." Kirsten looked off down the road, east to where the pavement went from black to gray and the town ended abruptly and the world opened up to cornfields and darkening sky. She thought of the little girl. About a mile distant a lighted combine moved slowly over a knoll.

"Smells nice inside," Kirsten said.

"Cookies," the woman said.

"You mind if I come in?"

The woman looked quickly down the road and, seeing nothing there, said, "Sure. For a minute."

Kirsten sat in a Naugahyde recliner that had been angled to face the television. Across from her was a couch covered with a clear plastic sheet. The woman returned with a plate of cookies. She set them in front of Kirsten and slipped a coaster under a coffee cup full of milk.

"I work for B.A.D.," Kirsten said. "My partner and me have been assigned to the Midwest territory. I got into this when I was living in New Jersey and saw all this with my own eyes and couldn't stand by and do nothing. Those babies were just calling out to me for help."

"I've got three children myself," the woman said.

"That's what the cookies are for," Kirsten said. She bit into one of the cookies; the warm chocolate melted over her tongue.

"Homemade," the woman said. "But the kids like store-bought. They're embarrassed."

"Homemade is better."

"Well, all they want is Wing-Dings and what have you."

"They'll appreciate it later, ma'am. I know they will. They'll remember it and love you."

In the low light, Kirsten again saw the spectral smudge of flour on the woman's cheek—she had reached to touch herself in a still, private moment as she thought of something she couldn't quite recall, a doubt too weak to claim a place in the clamor of her busy day.

"That baby on the flyer isn't getting any homemade cookies. That baby was born addicted to drugs. There's women I've person-ally met who would do anything to get their drugs and don't care what all happens to their kids. There's babies getting pitched out windows and dumped in trash cans and born in public lavatories."

"Things are terrible, I'm sure, but I can't give you any money. I worked all day making the kids Halloween costumes—they want store-bought, of course, but they can't have them, not this year."

"What're they going to be?"

"Janie's a farmer, Randall's a ghost. Kenny's costume was the hardest. He's a devil with a cape and hood and a tail."

If she could coax five dollars out of this woman, Kirsten thought, she could buy a cheap bra out of a bin at the dimestore. Her breasts ached with swelling. When she'd seen the trikes tipped over on the lawn out front she'd assumed this woman would reach imme-diately for her pocketbook.

"With a ten-dollar donation, you get your choice of two mag-azine subscriptions, free of charge for a year."

Kirsten showed the woman the list of magazines. "*Cosmo*," she said. "*Vogue, Redbook*, all them."

"I'm sorry," the woman said.

The front window washed with white light.

"You had better go." The woman stood up. "I don't have any use for your magazines."

On the porch they met a man, his face darkened with the same brown dirt and dust that had rolled through and clouded the sky and eclipsed the sun that day. Golden spikes of straw stabbed his hair and the pale gray molt of a barn swallow clung to his plaid shirt. A silent look passed between the man and the woman, and Kirsten hurried away without a word, down the steps.

"I thought she was trick-or-treating," the woman said as she shut the door.

"Nothing?" Lance said. "Nothing?

Kirsten tore the wrapping from another piece of gum. They had driven to the outskirts of town, where the light ended and the pavement gave way to gravel and the road, rutted like a washboard, snaked off toward a defile choked with cottonwoods. Every street out of town seemed to dead-end in farmland, and now a combine swept back and forth over the field, rising and falling like a ship rolling over high seas. A wake of dust rose behind it, swirling in the gold light of the floodlamps. The engine roared as the combine moved passed them, crushing a path through the dry corn.

"A man came home," Kirsten said.

"So?"

"So the lady got all nervous and said I had to go."

"Should've worked the man," Lance said. He ran his finger along the outline of her breasts, as if he were drawing a cartoon bust. "We've talked about that. A man'll give money just to be a man about things."

"I'm too skinny," Kirsten said.

"You're filling out, I've noticed. You're getting some shape to you."

Lance smiled his smile, a wide, white grin with a hole in the middle of it. Two of his teeth had fallen out, owing to his weakness for sweets. He worried his tongue in the empty space, slithering it in and out along the bare gum.

"I wish I had a fix right now," Kirsten said. She hugged herself to stop a chill radiating from her spine. The ghost of her habit trailed after her.

Again the voracious growling of the combine came near, mowing down cornstalks, cutting a swath through the field. Kirsten watched the golden kernels spray into the holding bin. A man sat up front in a glass booth, smoking a pipe, a yellow cap tilted back on his head.

"My cowboy brain's about dead," Lance said. "What do you think?"

Kirsten had died once, and made the mistake, before she understood how superstitious he was, of telling Lance. Her heart had stopped and she had drifted toward a white light that rose away like a windblown sheet, hovering over what she recognized as her cluttered living room. She was placid and smiling into the faces of people she had never seen before, people she realized instantly were relatives, aunts and uncles, cousins, the mother she had never known. Kirsten was adopted, but now this mother reached toward her from within the source of light. Her pale pink hands were fluttering like the wings of a bird. A calm told Kirsten that this was the afterlife, where brand-new rules obtained. She woke in a Key Biscayne hospital, her foster mother in a metal chair beside the bed, two uniformed cops standing at the door, ready to read Kirsten her rights.

"Don't always ask me," Kirsten said.

"Just close your eyes, honey. Close 'em and tell me the first thing you see."

With her eyes closed, she saw a child, alone, running, lost in the corn.

"Let's get out of here," she said.

"That's what you saw?"

"Start the car, okay? I can't explain everything I see."

She had met him in Florida, in her second year of detention. Her special problem was heroin; his was methamphetamine. They lived in a compound of low pink cinder-block buildings situated maddeningly close to a thoroughfare with a strip of shops, out beyond the chain-link fence, out beyond a greenbelt. At night, neon lights lit up the swaying palm fronds and banana plants, fringing the tangled jungle with exotic highlights of pink and blue. They'd climbed the fence together, running through the greenbelt, vanishing into the fantastic jungle. A year passed in a blur of stupid jobs, stints driving a cab, delivering flowers, and, for Kirsten, tearing movie tickets in half as a stream of happy dreamers clicked through the turnstiles, afterward sweeping debris from the floors in the dead-still hours when the decent world slept. Lance worked a second job deep-frying doughnuts in blackened vats of oil, dressed in a white suit.

But this, Lance had said, this would allow them to turn their backs on that year, on everything they'd done for living and survival. A regular at the doughnut shop set them up with their kit—the picture ID, the magazine subscriptions, the pamphlets. Although the deal worked like a pyramid scheme, it wasn't entirely a scam; a thin layer of legality existed, and 10 percent of the money collected actually went to the babies. Another 10 percent was skimmed by collectors in the field, and the remainder was mailed to a P.O. box in Key Biscayne. Of that the recruiters took a percentage, and the recruiters of the recruiters took an even bigger cut. That's the way it was supposed to work, but upon leaving Florida the tenuous sense of obligation weakened and finally vanished, and Lance was no longer sending any money to the P.O. box. They were renegade now; they kept everything.

The trail of dust caught up to them and enveloped the car and settled back to the ground. Lance got out of the car. He tried to break the dragging tailpipe free, but it wouldn't budge. He wiped his hands. He looked at Kirsten.

"I don't know," she said. Down the road the yellow lights of a farmhouse glowed like portals. A dog barked and the wind soughing through the corn called hoarsely. "I'm cold," Kirsten said.

"The worst they can do is say no," Lance said.

"They won't," Kirsten said.

Lance grabbed his ledger and a sheaf of pamphlets and his ID. They left the car and walked down the road in the milky light of a gibbous moon that lit the feathery edges of a high, isolated cloud. The house was white, and seemed illuminated, as did the ghostly white fence and the silver silo. When they opened the gate, the dog barked wildly and charged them, quickly using up its length of chain; its neck snapped and the barking stopped and when it regained its feet the dog followed them in a semicircle, as if tracing a path drawn by a compass.

On the porch was a pumpkin, not carved. The white door was coated with dust, and the handprints of an impatient, pounding child were pressed into it, faintly, down low. Before they could knock, an old woman answered with a bowl of candy. Her hair was thin and white, more the memory or suggestion of hair than the thing itself. Her eyes were blue and the lines of her creased face were topographic, holding the image of the land around her, worn and furrowed, dry, finished. She was a small woman, slight in build, like Kirsten. Her housedress drifted vaguely around her body like a fog.

"Evening, ma'am," Lance said.

When Lance was done delivering his introduction, he turned to Kirsten for her part, but she said nothing, letting the silence become a burden. The whole of the night—the last crickets chirring in the cold, the brown moths beating against the yellow light, the moon shadows and the quiet that came, faintly humming, from the land itself—pressed in close, weighing on the woman.

Finally Kirsten said, "If you could give us a place to stay for the night, we'd be grateful."

Lance had only meant to use a phone. He said, "Now, honey, we can't impose."

"I'm tired and I'm cold," Kirsten said.

Again the silence accumulated around them like a world filling with water, and now the only sound that would break it would be an echo of the old woman's doubt or guilt.

"My husband's gone up to bed. I hate to wake Effie."

"No need," Kirsten said. "If we could just sleep tonight in your girl's room, we'll be gone in the morning."

"My girl?"

"That's a lovely picture she drew," Kirsten said, "and it's wonderful that you hang it in the living room. You must have loved her very much."

A quelling hand went to the woman's lips, keeping quiet the quiet within the house. She backed away from the door—not so much a welcome as a surrender, a ceding of the space—and Kirsten and Lance entered. Years of sunlight had slowly paled the wallpaper in the living room and drained the red from the plastic roses on the sill. A familiar path was padded into the carpet, and a pair of suede leather slippers waited at their place by the sofa. The air in the house was warm, warm and still and faintly stale like a held breath.

Kirsten woke feeling queasy and sat up on the cramped child's mattress. She massaged her breasts and pulled aside the curtain. The old couple were in the backyard. The wife was hanging a load of wash on a line, socks, a bra, underwear, linens that unfurled like flags in the wind. The husband hoed weeds from a thinning garden of gaunt cornstalks, black-stemmed tomato plants and a few last, lopsided pumpkins that sat sad-faced on the ground, saved from rot by a bedding of straw. A cane swung from a belt loop in his dungarees.

"Any dreams?" Lance said. He reached for Kirsten, squeezing her thigh.

"Who needs dreams," Kirsten said, letting the curtain fall back.

"Bitter, bitter," Lance said. "Don't be bitter."

"I'm not bitter."

"You sound bitter."

He picked his slacks off the floor and shook out the pockets, unfolding the crumpled bills and arranging the coins in separate stacks on his stomach.

"Let's see where we're at," he said.

Lance grabbed his notebook from the floor and thumbed the foxed, dirty pages in which he kept a meticulous tally of their finances.

"You don't need a pencil and paper," Kirsten said.

"Discipline is important," he said. "When we strike it rich we don't want to be all overwhelmed and clueless. Can you see them old folks out there?"

"They're out there."

"It must be something to live in a place like this," Lance said. He put down the notebook and peered out the window. "Just go out and get yourself some corn when you're hungry." He pressed his hand flat against the glass. The fields to the east had been harvested and were brown and stubbled, heaving in waves to the horizon, where a combine crawled over a hill like a giant green bug. "It looks weird out there."

Kirsten had noticed it also. "It looks too late," she said.

"That's the whole problem with the seventies."

"It's 1989, Lance."

"High time we do something about it then." He pulled the curtain closed. "I'm sick and tired of washing my crotch in sinks."

"I'll go out and talk to them," Kirsten said.

"Where'd you go last night?" Lance said.

She didn't want to say, and said, "Nowhere."

"Get a look at yourself in that mirror there," he said.

Kirsten sat in a small child's chair, looking at herself in the mirror of a vanity that had also, apparently, served as a desk at one time—beside the perfume bottles and a hairbrush and a box of costume jewelry were cups of crayons and pens and pencils and a yellowed writing tablet. Kirsten leaned her head to the side and began to brush her hair, combing the leaves and dirt out of it.

"Lance," she said.

"Yeah?"

"Don't take anything from these people."

"You can't hide anything from me," he said, with an assured, tolerant smile.

Kirsten set down the brush and walked out into the yard, where the old woman was stretched on her toes, struggling to hang a last billowing sheet.

"Lend me a hand here," she said. "The wind's blowing so—"

Kirsten held an end and helped fasten the sheet. Wind combing through the standing corn raised a hollow rattle, a dry burr that encircled the yard and carried with it a cloud of dust and chaff that blew and clung to the wet cotton.

"I probably shouldn't even bother hanging out the wash this time of year," the old woman said. She pronounced it "warsh."

The combine's swallowing mouth opened a path along the fence. The old woman shuddered and turned away. Soon the hills would be completely harvested and laid bare.

"You have a beautiful place," she said. "All this land yours?"

"We got two sections. Daddy's too old to work it now, so we lease everything to a commercial outfit in Kalona."

"You must eat a lot of corn."

"Oh, hon, that's not sweet corn. That corn's for hogs. It's feed."

"Oh," she said.

"That blue Rabbit up the road yours?" The old man walked with an injured stoop, punting himself forward with the cane. He introduced himself—Effie Bowen, Effie and his wife, Gen Bowen. He was short of breath and gritted his teeth as if biting the difficult air. A rime of salt stained the brim of his red cap.

"That's us, I'm sorry to say."

He tipped the hat back, bringing his eyes out of the shade.

"Momma thinks I can tow you with the tractor," he said. "I say she's right. I went and looked at it this morning."

"I'm not sure we can afford any major repairs," Kirsten said.

"You work for a children's charity," the old woman said.

"That's right."

"We'll get you going," Mr. Bowen said. "Up to the Mennonites, right, Momma?"

The old woman—Gen—nodded. "I put towels out. You kids help yourselves to a hot shower, and meanwhile Daddy and me'll tow your car up to the plain people and then we'll just see."

"We'd like to go into town," Kirsten said, "if that's okay."

"Sure," the old woman said. She looked at her husband. "Yeah?"

"Of course, yes. Yes."

Fresh oil shone like obsidian at their feet, the blackened road like a liquid flowing over the fields until, turning to gravel, it sank down into a dusty basin that held town. Main Street was wide and empty, the storefronts colorless in the flat light. A traffic signal swaying over the only intersection ticked like a clock in the quiet. Feeling faint, her stomach cramping, Kirsten sat on the curb. A hand-lettered sign on a sheet of unpainted plywood leaned against a low stucco building, advertising: FRESH EGGS, MILK, BROCCOLI, CHERRIES, BREAD, POTATOES, WATERMELON, STRAWBERRIES, ROOT BEER, ANTIQUES.

"No corn," Lance observed, pitching a rock at the sign. "You gonna tell me?"

She shook her head. "I just went for a walk, Lance. Nowhere," she said, pressing a print of her hand in the dust. She was wary of Lance, knowing that if she let him, he would tap her every mood, make of a bad morning a change in the map, turn the car south if she so much as frowned. He treated her like an oracle or divine, believing a rich and deserved life ran parallel to theirs, a life she alone could see, and so he would probe her dreams for directions and tease her premonitions for meanings, as if her nightmares and moods gave her access to a world of utter certainty, when in fact Kirsten knew the truth, that every dream was a reservoir of doubt. She had spent most of her life revolving through institutions— foster care, detox, hospitals, detention. Even the woman she called Mother was an institution, a fumbling scheme. Her brothers were boys with pallors like warm cheese, sweating and impotent as they sat out another day, pinching at the knees of their pajamas; and her sisters were girls like herself who'd passed through some door in back of love where they were beaten or whored or drugged and left yearning and clueless; her mothers had come to nothing but the bafflement of hospital life in a bathrobe, and her fathers were stripped of strength and dressed like dolls in paper gowns, their hairless legs faintly embarrassing even in frank life inside institutions. This improvised family of shifting faces sat together in common rooms furnished with donated sofas and burned and torn lampshades and ashtrays of cut green glass, in lounges that were more home to her than home ever was, the inmates more family than she'd ever known.

It was in those lounges, in mornings that never began, in afternoons that lasted forever, in nights that wouldn't end, charged with the vast assignment of swallowing all the horror of those idled hours, that Kirsten elaborated her sense of the other world. She stripped her diet of the staples of institutional life—the starches, the endless urns of coffee and the sugar cubes and creamers, the cigarettes. She cropped her hair short. She stopped wearing jewelry, and one afternoon, while the janitor mopped the hallway, she slipped the watch from her wrist and dumped it into his dingy bucket of water. She cleaned her room and kept it spare, and was considered a model inmate, neat and quiet and nearly invisible. By experimenting she discovered that the only deeply quiet time on the ward was in the dark hour before dawn, and so she began to wake at four A.M., first with an alarm clock, then automatically, easing from sleep into a stillness that was spacious and as close to freedom as anything inside detention could be, when she would pull a candle from her dresser drawer, melt it to her bedpost, sit in her chair, and stare at the mirror bolted to her wall. For days she waited for something to appear in the clear depth, looking into the glass as if into a great distance, and saw nothing. An instinct told her she was trying too hard, but giving up was a conscious effort too, and she saw only herself, day after day, week after week, until one one morning her arms lost life and went leaden, her fingers curled, and the mirror turned cloudy, her face fading as if it had sunk below the surface of the glass. The next morning she learned again that guiding the images made them go away and she spent another disconsolate hour staring at herself. Eventually she was able to sit without panic as her image sank and vanished into the murky gray of the mirror.

She worked on the mirror gazing and she believed and word got around. Lance's fascination was fast, and it frightened and attracted her. Early in her detention, a social worker had advised Kirsten that the only thing better than heroin was a future, and that was Lance's gift, a restlessness that seemed about tomorrow, a desire that made the days seem available. She'd snorted once, banged once, and that was it; she'd found her answer—heroin had given her love, acceptance, security, and so had death, and now crying too—a feeling would come over her—a perfection better than the absence of pain—and she would see the pink fluttering hands—never anything more—just the hands reaching out, pressed flat against the glass. Often she emerged from her trances with her hand stretched to meet the hand in the mirror. In league with Lance, she felt her visions might stay, might last beyond the morning, but he was impatient, and his sense of her gift was profane and depleting, with every half thought and reverie expected to strike pay dirt.

"Okay, fine," Lance said. "Let's hit the trailer court."

"I'm tired of those smelly trailers."

"We've talked about this I don't know how many times."

"I want the nice houses. Those people have the money."

"They have the money," he said, "because they don't fall for bullshit like ours."

Kirsten started up the steps of the biggest and nicest house on the street. With its wide and deep veranda it seemed to have been built with a different prospect in mind, a more expansive view. She knocked and wiped her feet on the welcome mat and shuffled through her pamphlets and forms. Dressed in overalls and stuffed with straw, a scarecrow slumped on a porch swing, its head a forlorn sack knotted at the neck with a red kerchief. Kirsten knocked again, and then once more, but no one answered.

"See," Lance said.

"See nothing," Kirsten said. She marched across the lawn to the neighbor's door. Lance remained sitting on the curb, picking apart a leaf. No one answered her knock. She shuffled through her materials, stalling.

"Time to hit the trailer trash," Lance said.

Kirsten ran to the next house. A ghost hung from the awning, and the family name, Strand, was engraved on a wood plaque above the door. She drew a deep breath and knocked. For some time now she'd done things Lance's way. She would only solicit homes where she found signs of a shoddy slide—a car on blocks, a windowpane repaired with tape, some vague loss of contour in the slouching house itself—fissures in somebody else's hope where she and Lance could crawl through. But what had happened? They'd become sad little children, they were petty thieves and liars, swiping things no one would miss—five dollars here, ten dollars there—and laying siege to it with large plans, intricate calculations. Lance had his theories but lately it occurred to Kirsten that he was conducting his life with folklore. He had a knack for discovering the reverse of everything—the good were bad, the rich were poor, the great were low and mean—and it was no surprise they were now living lives that were upside down.

A little girl pulled the door open a crack, peering shyly up at Kirsten.

"Is your momma home?"

"Momma!"

The woman who came to the door, wiping her hands on a dishtowel, was a fuller version of the little girl, with the same blond hair and blue eyes. Kirsten told the woman she was from B.A.D. and offered her one of the brochures.

The little girl clung to her mother's leg. She wore one yellow sock, one green, orange dance tights, a purple skirt, a red turtleneck.

Kirsten said, "Did you get dressed all by yourself this morning?"

The little girl nodded and buried her face in the folds of her mother's skirt.

The mother smiled. "Cuts down on the fighting, right, April? We have a deal. She dresses herself; then she has to eat all her breakfast." She handed Kirsten the pamphlet. "I just made some coffee," she said. "Do you like Pop-Tarts?"

Kirsten leaned forward in a faded green chair by the window and watched Lance aimlessly tossing rocks and sticks in the street.

The woman brought two cups of coffee and a plate with Pop-Tarts, toasted and cut in thirds, fanned around the edges.

"You'd be surprised how many around here get into drugs," she said.

"I'm not sure it would surprise me, ma'am," Kirsten said. "Everywhere I go I hear stories from people who have been touched by this thing." She sipped her coffee. "This tragedy."

"I worry about this little one," the woman said.

Kirsten bit a corner of a Pop-Tart, feeling the hot cinnamon glaze melt on the roof of her mouth. On the mantel above the fireplace was a collection of ceramic owls. They stared steadily into the room with eyes so wide-open and unblinking they looked blind.

"My owls," the woman said. "I don't know how it is you start collecting. It just happens innocently; you think one is cute, then all of a sudden"—she waved her hand in the air—"you've got dumb owls all over the place."

"Keep them busy," Kirsten said.

"What's that?"

"April here—and all kids—if they have something to do they won't have time for drugs."

"That makes sense."

"People think of addicts as these lazy do-nothing sort of people, but really it's a full-time job. Most of them work at it harder than these farmers I seen in these cornfields. It takes their entire life."

The woman cupped her hands over her knees, then clasped them together. Her wedding band was either on the sill above the kitchen sink, left there after some chore, or she was divorced. Kirsten felt a rush of new words rise in her throat.

"You know what it's like to be pregnant, so I don't have to tell you what it means to have that life in you—and then just imagine feeding your baby poison all day. A baby like that one on the pamphlet, if they're born at all, they just cry all the time. You can't get them quiet."

It was a chaotic purse, and the woman had to burrow down through wadded Kleenex, key rings and doll clothes before she pulled out a checkbook.

"I never knew my own mother."

The woman's pen was poised above the check, but she set it down to look at Kirsten. Then she filled in an amount and signed her name.

"I myself was put out for adoption," she told a young couple next door, carrying forward the same conversation. They nodded and offered in unison looks that were sympathetic and uncomprehending. It was a look she'd lived with all her life and felt vaguely ashamed of, seeing something so small and frail and helpless at the heart of other people's understanding. They meant well and it meant nothing. Sympathy exposed a blank that had confused her as a child before she learned to keep quiet and go without.

"And I never really get away from this feeling. Sadness, you could call it. My mother, my real mother, I mean, is out there, but I'll never know her. I sometimes get a feeling like she's watching me in the dark, but that's about it. You know that spooky sense you get, where you think something's there and you turn around and, you know, there's nothing there?"

They did, they did with nods of encouragement.

"When I think about it, though, I'm better off than these babies. Just look at that little one's dark face, his shrunken head. He looks drowned."

The couple leaned together and examined the pamphlet. The picture was still ghoulish, no matter how many times Kirsten showed it to people. Its eyes were crimped shut and its mouth was open in a violent wail so that when you stared at the black oval the baby's purple flesh was like a loose envelope of skin closed over nothing. There was nothing inside that child.

"Mostly they just want their mothers for the methadone or what have you in the milk. That's what they're crying about. They want their fix."

Although the couple studied the picture, lingering to show their concern, Kirsten knew she hadn't convinced them of the horror. Sitting on the sofa with their knees angled in and their heads nearly touching, she saw how closely they resembled each other in quiet, subtle ways. They had the same color lips, they shared a clear line in the jaw and an identical wideness in the forehead. Meeting each other for the first time, they must have felt mysteriously moved, as if they'd discovered a profound secret. A weight must have gone out of their lives. Looking at them, Kirsten knew what would happen, and then that's what happened: they rejected the dark malformed baby on the pamphlet by giving her fifteen dollars.

She shook off a slight doubt as she waited at the next house. For now the words that came out of her were the right ones. She believed what she was saying. A man answered, and immediately Kirsten smelled the sour odor of settledness through the screen door. A television played in the cramped, cluttered front room. A spider plant sat on a stereo speaker, still in its plastic pot, the soil dry and hard yet with a pale shoot thriving, growing down to the shag, as if it might find a way to root in the fibers. Pans in the sink he scrubbed as needed, coffee grinds and macaroni on the floor, pennies and dimes caught in clots of dog hair. A somber, unmoving light in rooms where the windows were never opened, the curtains always closed.

"Some got to be addicted," the man said, after Kirsten explained herself. "They never go away."

"That may be so," Kirsten admitted. "I've thought the same myself."

He went to the kitchen and opened the fridge.

"You want a beer?"

"No, thanks."

The blue air around the television was its own atmosphere, and when the man sank back in his chair it was like he'd gone there to breathe. He looked at Kirsten's breasts, then down at her feet, and finally at his own hands, which were clumsy and large, curling tightly around the bottle.

"Where you staying?"

"About a mile out of town," she said. She handed the man a pamphlet. "I've had that same despair you're talking about. Nothing's going to change enough to wipe out all the problem."

"Bunch of niggers, mostly."

"Did you look at the one there?"

"Tar baby."

"That kid's white," Kirsten said. She had no idea if this was true. He didn't say anything.

Kirsten nodded at the television. "Who's winning?"

"Who's playing?" the man said, shrugging indifferently. He was using a coat hanger for an aerial. "The blue ones, I guess."

"But a little—isn't that enough? If you can save one baby from this life of hell, isn't that okay?"

"Doesn't matter much," he said. "In the scheme of things."

"It would mean everything," Kirsten said, "if it was you."

"But," he said, "it's not me."

The vague blur of the television interested him more. "Where?"

"Where what?"

"Where'd you say you were staying?"

"With Effie Bowen, Effie and his wife, Gen."

She wanted to tell him more about the baby but he dropped the pamphlet on the floor.

"It's a small place," he said. "Everybody knows everybody. Everybody's related to everybody else."

He pushed himself out of the chair. He swayed and stared dumbly into a wallet full of receipts.

"Well, tonight, you say hi to them for me. You tell Effie and Gen Johnny says hi." When he looked at Kirsten, his eyes had gone neutral. "You tell them I'm sorry, and you give them this," he said, leaning toward Kirsten. Then his lips were gone from her mouth, and he was handing her the last five from his billfold.

"I wish I was invisible," Lance said, palming his thin hair back in place. "I'd just walk into these houses and they wouldn't even know."

"And do what?"

"Right now I'd make some toast."

"Hungry?"

"A little."

"Wouldn't they see the bread floating around?"

"Invisible bread."

"You get that idea from your cowboy brain?"

"Don't make fun of the cowboy brain," Lance said. "It got us out of that goddamn detention. It got us over that fence."

"We are ghosts to these people, Lance. They already don't see us."

"I'd like to kill someone. That'd make them see. They'd believe then."

Kirsten cupped her left breast and lifted it, relieving the dull ache. "I think I'm getting my period," she said.

"Great," Lance said. "All we need."

"Fuck you," Kirsten said. "I haven't had a period in two years."

She turned over one of the pamphlets. Seeing the dark, inconsolable face reminded Kirsten of a song her mother would sing, but while the melody remained the lyrics died inside the memory, because the mere thought of this mother was collaborating in a lie and everything in it was somehow corrupted. Words to songs never returned to her readily—she had to think so hard just to recall a Christmas carol, trying to join in, once a year. It was like Mother—never in her life had she said or thought or read or heard the word without a twinge. Saying it aloud she felt like a mimic, an imitator in a world of authentic things. The word came to her with an echo, rising from a hollow she tried to fill with adjectives that would absorb and dampen the sound. Her real or true or birth or actual or genuine or biological mother . . . but in the end Mother was just something she felt in the dark sometimes.

"A little baby like that one," she said, "he'll scream all the time. Their little hands are jittery. They have terrible fits where they keep grabbing. They keep squeezing their hands real tight and grabbing the air. They can't stop shaking, but when you try to hold them they turn stiff as a board."

"To be perfectly honest," Lance said, "I don't really give a fuck about those babies."

"I know."

"I just don't care."

"I know."

When they returned to the farmhouse, the car was sitting in the drive and dinner was cooking. The kitchen windows were steamed, and the moist air, warm and fragrant, settled like a perfume on Kirsten's skin. She ran hot water and lathered her hands. The bar of soap was as smooth and worn as an old bone, a mosaic assembled from remnants, small pieces thriftily saved and then softened and clumped together. Everything in the house seemed to have that same thing, softened by the touch of hands—hands that had rubbed the brass plating from the doorknobs, hands that had worn the painted handles of spoons and ladles down to bare wood. Kirsten rinsed the soap away, and Gen offered her a towel.

"You don't have any other clothes, do you?" the old woman asked.

"No, ma'am," she said.

"Let's go pull some stuff out of the attic," Gen said. She drew a level line from the top of her head to the top of Kirsten's. "We're about the same size, I figure. You won't win any fashion awards—it's just old funny things, some wool pants, a jacket, a couple cardigan sweaters. But you aren't dressed for Iowa." She pronounced it "Ioway."

"I'd appreciate that, ma'am."

"Doing the kind of work you do I don't imagine you can afford the extras," she said as they climbed a set of steps off the upstairs hallway. "But in this country we don't consider a coat extra."

The old woman tugged a string, and a bare bulb lit the attic. In the sudden glare the room seemed at first to house nothing but a jumble of shadows. "I've held on to everything," she said.

"I met a man in town today," Kirsten said. "He said he knew you and Effie."

"Johnny?" the old woman said. She slit the tape on a box with her thumbnail and handed Kirsten a sweater that smelled faintly of dust and camphor.

Kirsten held the woman still and kissed her on the lips. "He said to give you that."

"What happens?" Gen asked, flatly, as if the years had worn wonder out of the question.

"It was a combine," Kirsten said.

Gen nodded.

"Your little girl doesn't know she's dead. She's still out there."

"How do I know you know all this?"

"I saw her," Kirsten said. "And when me and Lance come to the door last night, we never knocked."

From a rack against the wall, the old woman took down a heavy wool overcoat and handed it to Kirsten.

"You were waiting for her. You wait for her every year."

On the same rack was a wedding dress, draped in plastic, the veil floating loosely inside a pillowcase. Gen stepped in front of a cheval mirror and held the dress against her body, modeling it for a moment.

"You made this," Kirsten said, holding the silk to her skin.

"Every stitch except the veil. That belonged to my mother."

"It wasn't your husband's fault."

"He feels the guilt all the same," the old woman said.

"He had to," Kirsten said.

"Had to what?"

"Live," she said. "He had to live his life, just the same as me and you. Just the same as your little girl."

They set four places with the good plates and silver and flowery napkins in the dining room. There was a ham pricked with cloves and ringed around with pineapple and black olives and green beans and salad and bread. Effie fussed over his wife as if he'd never had dinner with her, passing dishes and offering extra helpings, which she refused each time, saying help yourself; Kirsten eventually caught on, seeing that this solicitude was the old man's sly way of offering a compliment and serving himself a little more at the same time. The food was good, and Kirsten would remember that it all glistened, the juices from the ham, the butter running off the beans, the oil on the salad. Gen's part of the dinner was chorelike—she spent most of the meal up on her feet, offering, spooning, heating, filling.

Effie's conversation made a wide, wandering tour of the land. Jesse James used to hide out in this country, he said. Then he was talking about no-till planting, soil that wasn't disked or plowed.

"You got corn in just about everything," he said. "In gasoline, spark plugs, crayons, toothpaste, disposable diapers—"

"No, really?" said Lance.

"You bet," the old man went on, "and paint, beer, whiskey. You name it."

He said one out of four hogs produced in this country came from Iowa—which he too pronounced "Ioway." Hogs till hell wouldn't have it, he said, thundering the words. The topic of hogs led to a story he'd read about Fidel Castro roasting a pig in a hotel room in New York, and then he told about their travels, a trip to Ireland and another to Hawaii, which he pronounced "Hoy."

After dinner, there was pumpkin pie—prizewinning, Effie announced, as the tin took center stage on the cleared table.

It was delicious, the filling warm with a buttery vanishing feel on Kirsten's tongue. "What's in it?" she asked.

"Oh," Gen said. "Cinnamon, ginger, nutmeg, allspice, vanilla—but real pumpkin's the key." Gen, satisfied with the satisfaction at her table, smiled at her husband, who gravely put down his fork.

"When you come," Effie said, "Momma said you mentioned our little girl."

"Our little girl," Gen said, looking at her husband.

They didn't speak directly, but checked, checked each other's eyes or the turn of the mouth, checked for subtle signs, looked for agreement. It was like they found what they needed somewhere in the space between them, and spoke aloud only to verify that it was there, that they'd both seen it.

"You knew about our girl," Effie started again.

The old man wouldn't say the word because it was a broken word. "Your daughter," Kirsten said.

"I guess," he said, then changed directions. "I wondered if you were an old friend. Maybe from school. Most of them have grown and gone away. I used to see—it would have been so long ago but . . ." He trailed off, his pale blue eyes wetly sparkling in the weak, splintered light of the chandelier.

Lance said, "Kirsten's been to the other side. She's seen it."

"I would believe you," Effie said. "Some around here don't credit dowsers but we always have. We never had reason not to. We always had plenty water." He cleared his throat. "I would pay you if you could tell us—where is she at?"

Kirsten was about to speak when she felt a hand slide over her knee, the fingers feeling their way until they rested warmly in her hand, holding it tight. She glanced at the old woman.

"It was only that picture on your wall," she said to Effie.

The picture was the one every child draws, the house, the leafy tree, the sun in one corner, the birds overhead, the winding walkway widening like a river flowing out from the front door, the family standing on the green grass, a mother with her triangle dress, the father twice as big as everybody, the stick fingers overlapped and linking.

It was the picture every child drew a hundred times and no one ever saved.

"It was just that picture," Kirsten said. "I wish I could say it was more, but it wasn't."

Effie pressed his fork against the crumbs of pie crust still on his plate, gathering them.

"She just drawn it at school," he said. "She put me and Gen in, her and her brother."

"Stephanie," Kirsten said, "and Johnny."

The old man glanced at his wife.

"She spelled all the names on the picture," Kirsten said.

Gen whispered yes but it was Effie who had to speak up. "I never breathed right or walked right after," he said. "Never farmed, neither."

In Kirsten's mind her mother was always the dark, a pressure inside a great sleeping volume. And now, tonight, at this table, the old woman wanted her daughter to be the picture. It was something she could give her husband.

"That was the best pie I ever had," Kirsten said.

"Show your ribbons, Momma," Effie said.

"Oh, no," Gen said, waving her hand, shooing away the approach, the temptation of something immodest.

"Well, that's right," Effie said. "The pie's right here, huh?" He looked around the table. "The pie's right here."

Kirsten hovered above the field and could hear the engine of the combine and the crushed stalks snapping under the header, a crackling noise that spread and came from everywhere at once, like fire. The stalks flailed and broke and dust and chaff flew up and then, ahead, she saw the little girl running down the rows, lost in the maze, unable to search out a safe direction. Suddenly the girl sat on the ground, her stillness an instinct, looking up through the dry dead leaves, waiting for the noise to pass. Kirsten saw her there—a little girl being good, quiet, obedient—but when the sound came closer, she flattened herself against the dirt, as if the moment might pass her by. When it was too late, she kicked her feet, trying to escape, and was swallowed up, and the noise faded, leaving a denuded strip behind, a scroll of dirt and stover that curved over the fields like handwriting. Then Kirsten saw her own reflection floating in the vague gray haze of the vanity.

"Lance," she said.

"What the fuck?"

"We're leaving," she said.

"Why, what?"

Kirsten gathered the old woman's clothes in a garbage sack and had Lance carry them to the car. She made the bed and fluffed the thin pillows. The house was quiet.

She sat again at the small painted vanity. She took a blue crayon from the cup and wrote a thank-you note. She wrote to the old woman that one second of love is all the love in the world, that one moment is all of them; she wrote that she really liked the pumpkin pie, and meant it when she said it was the best she'd ever had, adding that she never expected better taste and would remember it always; she thanked her for the hospitality and for fixing the car; and then she copied down the words to the song the woman she called Mother sang:

Where are you going, my little one, little one?
Where are you going, my baby, my own?
Turn around and you're two, turn around and you're four,
Turn around and you're a young girl going out of the door.

Lance was gone for a long time, and Kirsten, looking over the note, considered tearing it up each time she read it. As she sat and waited she felt a sudden release and reached under the elastic of her underpants. When Lance finally returned he was covered in dry leaves and strings of silk and tassel, as if he'd been out working in the fields. They went outside and pushed the car down the gravel drive, out to the road. It started up, beautifully quiet.

"Wait here," Kirsten said.

She walked back to the yard. It was cool and the damp night air released a rich smell of dung and soil and dust and straw, a smell Kirsten was sure belonged only to Iowa, and only at certain hours. She pulled her T-shirt over her head. She was reaching for the clothespin that held the old woman's bra when something made her look up. The old woman was standing at the upstairs window, her hand pressed flat against the glass. Kirsten took the bra from the line and slipped the straps over her shoulders. She fastened the clasp and leaned forward, settling her breasts in the small white cups. The women looked at each other for what seemed like an eternity, and then Kirsten pulled on her shirt and ran back to Lance.

Under the moonlight they drove down mazy roads cut through the fields.

"Goddamn, the Lord sure hath provideth the corn around here," Lance said. He imitated the old man compulsively, "I'll be plenty glad to get out of this Ioway. Ioway! And Hawaii—d'you hear the way that old guy said Hawaii? Hoy, it sounded like. Hoy, Christ Almighty. I'm sorry, but those people were corny. And yes, that's a pun, purely intended. And going on about Castro's fucking pigs in the bathtub. What'd he say, they cooked a hog in that hotel room? What the hell." Lance was taking charge again, his mind hard, forging iron connections. He was feeling good; he was feeling certain. "And goddamn, I hate ham! Smells like piss!" He rolled down the window and yelled, "Good-bye, fucking Ioway!" He brushed corn silk from his sleeve and shook bits of leaves from his hair.

"Here's something for you." He reached in his pocket and handed her a long heavy chain.

"Looks to me like gold and emeralds, with a couple rubies mixed in," he said.

"That's costume jewelry, Lance."

"It's real," he said, bullying the truth, hating its disadvantages, its need for verification, "and they won't miss it, Kirsten.

They're old, honey. They're gonna die and they got no heirs, so don't you worry." He grinned widely and said, "I got something out of the deal too." He waited. Kirsten just stared at the cheap, gaudy chain, pouring it like water from one hand to the other.

Lance said, "Look in back."

When she turned around, all she saw was dark countryside through the rear window, a trail of dust turning red in the taillights.

"See?"

"What?"

"Under the blanket," Lance said.

She turned around again and pulled away the blanket. The rear seat was overflowing with ears of corn. Lance had turned the whole back of the car into a crib.

"I picked a bunch of corn for the road."

"I got my period."

"Ioway corn," Lance said. "Makes me hungry just thinking about it."

THE DEVIL of
DELERY STREET

by POPPY Z. BRITE

MARY LOUISE STUBBS was thirteen the year the family troubles began. She was called Melly because four of her younger siblings could not say her full name, or hadn't been able to when they were younger. Her fifth sibling, Gary, was only a baby and couldn't say much of anything yet. Once that strange and dreadful year was over, her mother, Mary Rose, would not allow its events to be referred to in any more specific way than "our family troubles." That was how Melly always remembered them.

Her memories seemed to date from the afternoon of her cousin Grace's funeral. Grace, the younger child of Mary Rose's sister Teresa, had been carried away by a quick and virulent form of childhood leukemia. Now everyone was busy pretending that she had been a saint among nine-year-old girls. With the terrible unambiguous eye of an adolescent, Melly saw only hypocrisy in this. Grace hadn't been any saint; she was actually kind of a sneaky kid who liked to pinch smaller children when no grown-ups were looking. Melly had loved her, but didn't see the need to pretend she was now perched on the knee of the Blessed Virgin Mary.

The Stubbs family was gathered in their regular pew at Saints Peter and Paul, a dusty old brick church in downtown New Orleans, and Melly was having a hard time staying awake. She didn't usually sleep during regular Mass, let alone funerals, but a scratching in the wall of her bedroom had kept her up last night. She'd meant to ask her father if he would buy some rattraps, but the memory of wakefulness had left her as soon as she brushed her teeth and combed her long, coarse dark hair. She had the Sicilian coloring of her mother, a former Bonano, as did most of the other kids; only Gary was shaping up to be Irish-fair like their father.

Now, though, she began to nod off. Her brother Little Elmer, the next oldest after Melly, extended a finger and poked her in the ribs. "Father Mike ain't *that* boring," he whispered.

"Shhh," she replied. Father Mike was young, with soft dog eyes and a thick shock of wavy hair, and Melly had a little crush on him. Not a sexy crush—it would be almost a sin to think about a priest that way—but a little warm feeling in her chest whenever she saw him.

"You the one falling asleep, not me—"

"Y'all both hush," their father murmured from Melly's other side, barely audible, and they shut up. Elmer Stubbs was a mild-tempered man, but there'd be misery later if Mary Rose caught them talking during a funeral Mass. Fortunately she was at the far end of the pew, twisting a Kleenex in her small, expressive hands. It was warm for March, and occasionally she'd reach up to blot the sweat from her brow, though she always pretended she was patting her jet-black beehive hairdo. How Melly loached that beehive! "It's 1974, Momma," she said frequently, "time to comb it out." And Mary Rose always replied, "Nuh-uh, babe, I don't want to look like a hippie," as if a slightly more modern hairdo would transform her from a diminutive Italian housewife into a pot-smoking flower child.

Melly sat up straighter in the pew, stretched her eyes open, and hoped the rat would depart for more attractive horizons by tonight. They lived in a poor neighborhood, the Lower Ninth Ward, but their house on Delery Street was clean. Melly knew it was, because she had to do a lot of the cleaning. Some of their neighbors' yards were full of chicken bones and crawfish shells and Melly didn't know what-all else, scattered among rusty garbage cans and hulks of old cars. Surely a rat could fill his belly more easily at one of those houses.

Her wishes went unanswered for the time being; at home later, as she was changing the baby in the upstairs bedroom he shared with four-year-old Rosalie, she heard more scratching and a series of bangs behind the wall. "What you doing, Mr. Rat?" she muttered. "Building you a whole 'nother house back there?"

Gary laughed and showed her the clean pink palms of his hands, as he did when anybody spoke in his presence whether they were talking to him or not. He was the sweetest-natured baby she'd ever seen, and the only one of her siblings who made her think she might want kids of her own someday. He had a little fluff of sweet-smelling curly hair on the top of his head, and his eyes were the warm brown of pecan shells, not so black you couldn't tell the irises from the pupils like her own. She pinned his clean diaper shut and hoisted him onto her shoulder. "You gonna kill that old rat for me?" she asked him, and he laughed again.

Life went on as usual in the big old clapboard house, Little Elmer and Carl playing touch football after school, Henry with the other seven-year-olds in the decrepit playground down the street, Melly watching after Rosalie and the baby while Mary Rose went to Mass or fixed dinner. The house smelled of garlic and red gravy, of boys, of the sweet olive bushes that bloomed on either side of the stoop in March. They were nothing to look at the rest of the year, but every spring they turned even the poorest corners of the city luxurious with their scent.

The rat was gone for a week or two, and Melly figured her father must have put down some traps. Then suddenly it was there again, scratching behind the wall above her bed. This time the sound came deep in the night and didn't seem funny at all. She had shared her bedroom with Little Elmer until last year, when her mother said a growing girl needed her privacy and made Little Elmer bunk with the younger boys. And Melly had certainly been a growing girl: she'd gained five inches last year. She didn't like sleeping alone, though, had never done it in her life and wasn't used to the way shadows could mass around you when no one was breathing in the next bed. The creaky old house was no longer the well-known friend of her childhood, but a strange place that wanted to trap her somehow. What would happen when it caught her? Melly didn't know, but something deep in her gut seemed to liquefy when she thought of it.

She lay awake listening to the rat in the wall. Little Elmer had moved his toys into the boys' room, and Melly had put hers away in the attic, certain she would never need them again. Even Trina, the baby doll who'd been with her almost since her own babyhood, was stifling up there in a heavy garbage bag to keep out the dust. The room felt very empty. If a shadow should appear on the wall, she would know nothing was there to cast it.

The rat gnawed more loudly. Melly sat up, meaning to bang on the wall and scare it away. She did so one, two, three times. The rat banged back in perfect imitation.

She drew away, indrawn air hissing between her teeth. No rat could have made that sound, three sharp, deliberate knocks. She extended her fist toward the wall, hesitated, then knocked once more. A mocking flurry of raps answered her, coming from the spot her knuckles had touched, then six feet above that, all the way to the right corner, to the left corner, to the ceiling, and finally under the bed. The mattress quaked. She flung herself off it, crossed the room without seeming to touch the floor, and shot into the hall screaming.

The next day was Saturday, and Mary Rose had to go to Canal Street to start looking at suits for Henry's First Communion. Carl tagged along in hopes of getting something from the bakery at D. H. Holmes. In a display of sudden, perceptive kindness typical of Stubbs males, Little Elmer volunteered to watch Rosalie and Gary. "Why don't you go shopping with Momma?" he said to Melly. "I bet she lets you get a dress or something."

"She's not gonna let me get any dress. I got all my spring school clothes already, and you know the rent's due next week."

"Well, but you like to look at stuff. Go on—I'll watch the babies."

"I ain't no baby," protested Rosalie, who was listening.

"I'll believe that when you get big enough to quit saying *ain't*." Little Elmer lifted her onto his lap. "Go on, Mel."

Full well knowing that her brother had given up a Saturday afternoon of street football in order to let her have a few hours away from the house that had frightened her so badly last night, Melly tried to enjoy herself. The life of Canal Street whirled around them, car horns, billboards, pink and gold neon signs, old ladies in their best shopping clothes, hippies in tattered regalia, a trio of lithe young black men with Afro picks embedded in their fantastic poufs of hair. Every breath was a mélange of exhaust, fried seafood, perfume, and, on the French Quarter side of the street, some mysterious tang that Melly thought might be the smell of burning marijuana. She walked beside her mother and admired the displays in the windows of the big department stores. She didn't argue when Mary Rose *tsk*ed at how short the skirts had gotten. The boys danced behind her making devil horns with their fingers and singing: "'Takin' care of business . . . it's a crime . . . takin' care of business and workin' overtime!"

"They don't say 'it's a crime,'" said Melly, who spent just as much time listening to the radio as they did.

"Yeah?" said Carl truculently. "What they say, then?"

"'It's all mind,' I think."

"That don't make no sense!"

"*Doesn't* make *any* sense," said Mary Rose.

"But Momma, *you* say 'don't make no sense.'"

It was an old family game, and all three children chorused with their mother: "Do as I say, not as I do."

As they were riding up the escalator at Maison Blanche, Melly felt safe enough to say, "Momma, what happened in my bedroom last night?"

"A bad dream," said Mary Rose firmly and without hesitation, as if she had been waiting for this question. "You just had a bad dream."

"I wasn't asleep yet, Momma. I was wide-awake, and that's not any rat in my wall."

"You make an Act of Contrition tomorrow, babe. That rat ain't gonna bother you no more."

"An Act of Contrition?" Melly didn't know what she had expected her mother to say, but it wasn't that. "Why I gotta make an Act of Contrition? What'd I do wrong?"

"Nothing, Melly, nothing." They reached the top of the escalator. Mary Rose stumbled as she stepped off it, and Melly reached to steady her. "It's just to be safe."

Melly saw that her mother's eyes were frightened.

"Just to be safe," Mary Rose repeated. "It never hurts to be safe."

Saint Joseph's Day fell on a Tuesday that year, and Melly was allowed to miss school to join her mother on her altar-visiting rounds. They went to the altar at Saint Alphonsus and the one at Our Lady of Lourdes, then a tiny one belonging to a lady in their own neighborhood, and last to the altar of Mary Rose's sister Teresa. It was generally known in the Stubbs and Bonano families that Teresa was rich; her husband, Pete, was whispered to make more than $10,000 a year. They lived across the parish line in Chalmette, in a one-story brick house smaller than the Stubbs's but far newer. No one had expected Teresa to make an altar so soon after the death of her child, but Teresa said Saint Joseph had been helping her all these years and she wasn't going to turn her back on him now. "This year is more important than ever," she had told

Mary Rose, and while Melly wasn't certain what she meant, Mary Rose seemed to take comfort in the words.

The altar was set up in the carport, three long tables groaning with roasted fish, stuffed artichokes, anise cookies, devotional candles, a big gold crucifix, and a tall statue of Saint Joseph holding the baby Jesus. The statue was wreathed with Christmas lights that blinked on and off, creating an intermittent halo effect. Mary Rose tucked a few dollars into the brandy snifter that had been set on the altar for donations, took a lucky bean from a cut-glass bowl full of them, and grabbed herself a plate of food. "You want some spaghettis?" she asked Melly.

"No, Momma." Melly did, but she had vowed to go on a diet for Lent. She was already planning to make the Rosy Perfection Salad she'd found on a Weight Watchers card, even though the picture looked like a bad car wreck garnished with parsley. Instead she joined some other kids, mostly cousins and neighbors, to hear the music in the side yard.

Teresa had bragged about having a live band, but it was just an accordion player and an old man with a microphone. As was often the case at any Italian party, they were playing "Che La Luna." The kids began a circle dance as the old man sang, "'Mama dear come over here and see who's looking in my window . . . It's the baker boy and oh, he's got a cannoli in his hand . . .'" The circle parted to let Melly in. On her right was her cousin Angelina. On her left was a boy she didn't know, maybe her age, with big brown eyes and a Beatles haircut. In fact, he looked a little like Paul. She hoped her hand wasn't sweaty as he grasped it. "*In the middle!*" the old man cried. The kids screamed with laughter as they raised their arms and crowded toward the middle of the circle. The music went faster and faster, and the dance followed suit. Caught up in the moment, she squeezed the boy's hand, and she was almost certain that he squeezed back. A strange warm feeling welled up just under her rib cage, like a line of electricity being drawn out of her.

She thought the shrieks of the women behind her were part of the festivities, so she didn't know anything was wrong until something hit her in the back. It didn't fall away, but clung there, heavy and hard between her shoulder blades. A *bug* was her first thought, but reaching back, she could feel that it was bigger than even the largest New Orleans cockroach. Something cold, with four arms and a lumpy part in the middle. A crucifix—it felt like the big metal one that had been on the altar. Melly couldn't understand how it was stuck to her, and she couldn't pull it off.

"Get it off me!" she yelled. The band stopped playing with a squeal of accordion feedback. The other children backed away. The boy who looked like Paul wiped his hand on his pants as if cleansing himself of her touch. She knew the gesture was probably automatic, but that made it hurt all the worse.

"Please get it off me!"

Here came Mary Rose, pushing through the crowd of children, spinning her daughter around and yanking hard at the crucifix. It clung to Melly's back as if some immensely powerful magnet were buried deep inside her, perhaps where her heart should be. "Please, Momma," Melly sobbed, and Mary Rose yanked even harder, but the crucifix didn't budge.

Now here was Aunt Teresa with a little pitcher that had been sitting on the altar, a pitcher labeled HOLY WATER. She upended the pitcher over Melly's back. A couple of the kids giggled. "Pull on it again," said Teresa. Mary Rose did, and the image of Jesus came off in her hand, but the cross stayed stuck to Melly. Several women in the crowd crossed themselves and fumbled rosaries out of their pocketbooks.

Melly pushed away from her mother, out of the circle, out of the little fenced yard. She had never felt more alone and freakish than she did standing there in the sun-baked street, one small person with a big holy-water stain running down her back and at least thirty people staring at her from the other side of a fence. The warm electric feeling abruptly left her and the cross clattered to the asphalt.

Everybody was silent except for one old lady still praying: "Hail Mary, fulla grace, the Lord is with thee . . ."

"Grace?" Teresa whispered. "Grace?"

Melly turned her back on all the staring eyes. There was a soft collective intake of breath. Through her thin nylon blouse, it was easy to see the raw red cross-shape that had been printed in her flesh.

Melly had only disjointed flashes of the next few hours. She remembered repeating through tears, "I'm sorry, Aunt Teresa, I'm sorry," as Teresa stood holding the figure of Jesus and the denuded cross, looking from one to the other as if she couldn't quite understand how they went together. She heard people telling each other what had happened: "Did you see the way it jumped off the altar, just *flew?*" She didn't remember the ride home at all; the next thing she knew, she was in her own bed, half-asleep, rocked by some strange nausea that seemed to originate in her chest instead of her stomach. Over and over she nearly drifted off; over and over the bed jerked just as she slid over the edge of consciousness, yanking her back to wakefulness. "Please let me sleep," she moaned, and a voice answered her.

"You can sleep when you're dead, Mary Louise. . . ."

It was a harsh and guttural voice, a voice that might have last spoken a thousand years ago or never. The words seemed to result from an intake of breath rather than an outflow, as if the speaker were suffocating. It was the worst voice Melly had ever heard, and yet suddenly she wasn't scared so much as angry. If this thing had a voice, then it had a personality, and if it had a personality, then she could damn well tell it why it shouldn't be pounding on her walls and making holy objects stick to her back. "Who are you?" she said, sitting up.

"The Devil."

"No you're not. The Devil wouldn't waste his time scaring some poor girl from Delery Street. Who are you really?"

Silence.

"Are you Grace?"

Still nothing. She felt that she had offended it. And now she was frightened again; how had she dared to speak to such a thing, surely not the Devil but maybe some low minion? Even if it was only a ghost—she laughed at herself a little, thinking, "*only* a ghost"—she oughtn't to be talking to it.

Melly sighed, got her beads out of the nightstand drawer, and started saying the rosary. She got all the way to the second decade before the beads were snatched out of her hands and scattered across the room.

Mary Rose got Father Mike to come over and bless the house. He made clear that it wasn't an exorcism, that he wouldn't perform an exorcism if she asked, that furthermore he didn't believe the Stubbs house was haunted; he was doing it only to put her mind at rest and maybe calm Melly down a little. Melly thought that was ridiculous. Right now she was the calmest person in the house. She found that she no longer had the warm little crush on Father Mike.

One day when her parents thought she was upstairs, she overheard the tail end of a conversation between them. Though she knew her father was an uncommonly good man, she would never quite forgive him for asking Mary Rose, "Don't you think there's some chance she's doing all this to get attention?"

"No, I don't think so," Mary Rose had replied. "This isn't the first time crazy things happened in my family. You know that little end table my momma used to keep by her sofa?"

"I can't say I do."

"You know, Elmer, that little black table with the Italian patterns. It was hand-painted by my great-grandmother in Sicily. Lord, how that woman hated cursing and arguing—at least that's what Momma told me. Well, she passed away long before my grammaw brought the table to America, but whenever anybody in the house would start cursing or hollering at each other, the table would rise up and beat them!"

"Mary Rose, nuh-uh."

"I swear on my mother's sweet name. It happened to me a couple times, when I was real little and pitching a fit. I remember seeing that thing fly through the air toward my head—Jesus Lord! But when it hit you, it never hurt. It'd just tap you real soft, like it was saying, *You better behave*."

"What happened to it, then?"

"The effect just wore off, I guess. Teresa's got the table now, and you know how bad her kids cut up sometimes, but that table ain't moved in thirty years. At least not that I know of."

"Well, maybe this thing with Melly will kinda taper off."

"I hope so," said Mary Rose with a long-suffering sigh. "It's hard on her, and it's hard on me too."

It was not at all hard on the younger kids. They loved it, and got to the point where they would egg it on. "Bet you can't lift me up in this chair!" Henry would say, pulling his feet up in expectation of a ride. The spirit never gave him one, but sometimes it would tilt the chair and dump him onto the floor, reducing Rosalie and Gary to helpless giggles.

"Draw something in my book!" Rosalie would demand, leaving her scratch pad open with a crayon on top and hiding her eyes. When she looked again, often as not there would be a page full of meaningless scribbles.

"The baby done 'em," Melly said one time, trying to vacuum around them.

"He did not! He was right here by me the whole time, weren't you, Gary?"

"Lady draw," said Gary.

"Huh, you mean you can see it?" said Henry. "Aw, Melly, I wish he could tell us what it looks like! A lady, huh?"

"Shut up!" Melly told them. "Don't talk to it, don't ask it to do things, just leave it alone! You don't know how it makes me feel."

"It's not *yours*," Henry said unkindly.

"*Yes, it is!*" she screamed at him. The startled look in his eyes made her feel bad, but she couldn't stop. "It is too mine! Do whatever you want, but give me . . . give me . . . oh, I don't know what I'm saying!" She ran from the room, leaving Henry to get up and turn off the vacuum.

Little Elmer and Carl did not enjoy the spirit and stayed away from home a lot that year, immersing themselves in boy business. All in all, though, Melly thought it was amazing what people could get used to. When she heard scratching and raps in her wall, she rolled over and tried to go back to sleep. Sometimes it stopped there; sometimes things began flying around, toilet paper and jig-saw puzzles and sausages strewn around the living room, every flowerpot in the house turned upside down. Sometimes an object would hit her, but she was never hurt or (after the Saint Joseph's Day incident) even seriously humiliated. Once, when she was sit-ting in the kitchen watching Mary Rose make a lasagna, there was a popping sound near the refrigerator and an egg rose into the air. Mary Rose hadn't had any eggs on the counter, so it must have come from inside the fridge. It floated lazily toward Melly, then hovered over her head. *Great*, she thought, *it's gonna smash in my hair*. Instead it tapped her lightly on the forehead, then fell and splattered gaudily against the faded old linoleum. Melly got up to fetch the dustpan, no more upset than she would have been if a dog had piddled on the floor. Once it was clear that no one was going to be hurt, the incredible had come to seem almost normal.

She wondered if this had anything to do with being Catholic, with accepting as unquestioned fact the existence of saints watch-ing over you, helping and perhaps even hindering your enter-prises; with taking for granted that the wafer in your mouth would change into flesh, the wine into blood; with praying to a ghost. She did not ponder this very deeply, because she was not a deep girl and she knew no other way to be but Catholic. When she said her prayers, she sometimes added some extra ones for the spirit in case it was a soul in purgatory.

It never spoke to her again after the night it said it was the Devil. Melly thought it might be embarrassed to have made such a claim, or possibly embarrassed to have provoked her angry response, like an overtired child who doesn't realize he's being obnoxious until he goes a step too far and his mother yells at him. She did not feel that the spirit had ever been angry with her; in retrospect, even making the crucifix stick to her back seemed little more than a desperate way of getting attention. Why it had wanted her attention so badly she didn't know, nor did she wish to ponder the question.

The nights of rapping and banging came farther apart; there would be two in a week, then one, then none for two or three weeks. When they did come, the raps and flying objects seemed weaker somehow, as if the force behind them were winding down. No further scribbles appeared in Rosalie's drawing pad. Gary, though he was talking a blue streak now, said nothing more about a lady.

As Melly lay in bed one night, she felt something strange happening in her viscera. At first she thought she was bleeding, but there was no wetness, only a sensation of something warm draining from her. She put her hand on the concavity beneath her breasts, but it began to tingle unpleasantly and she took it away again. A few minutes later the sensation stopped. She felt wonderfully relaxed. It was as if she had been in pain for a long time, and had gotten so used to it that she no longer noticed the pain until it stopped.

After that night there were no more noises, no more strange happenings at all. For some time there was an undercurrent of tension in the house and among the family, as if they were bracing themselves for another assault. None came. "I miss the ghost," Henry said at the dinner table one night.

Mary Rose turned on him. "There was no ghost in this house, young man! Say anything like that again and I'll warm the seat of your pants for you!"

Henry's mouth fell open, affording everyone an unlovely view of half-chewed braciola. *Poor Henry,* Melly thought. *That was probably the most exciting year of his life, and Momma's never even gonna let him talk about it.*

She didn't want to talk about it either, though. Henry would have to sift through his memories alone.

Another year passed. Melly grew a couple more inches, but nothing like the rapid stretch she'd experienced just before the odd events began. Gradually she stopped fearing that she was going to be a circus freak, the Giant Lady. She'd probably gotten some extra height from Elmer, that was all. She joined the math club at school, went out on a few dates, got involved with Saints Peter and Paul's youth group. All she wanted in the world was to be a normal teenage girl; she wanted that so badly that she thought she could taste acceptance, sweet on her tongue, when other kids treated her as just one of them. Kids who had no idea that a crucifix had once clung to her back like it was a magnet and she was iron, kids who never suspected that something possibly dead had once knocked on her bedroom wall.

When the scratching started up again, so soft and sly that at first it might have been her imagination, she thought for one black moment of just putting a bullet in her head. Elmer didn't like guns, but crime in the neighborhood had begun to spiral upward, and he had one on the high shelf of the bedroom closet. Melly knew where the bullets were kept. But she didn't want to die, and she wasn't going to let this stupid mindless thing tempt her into it. She rolled over and went back to sleep.

At breakfast the next morning, the saltshaker rose off the table and floated across the kitchen. Henry's face lit up, and he began to say something. As Mary Rose's eye fell upon him, he shut his mouth with a snap. Everyone else ignored it, even Gary, who at three was exquisitely sensitive to the feelings and wants of his family. He got along with everybody, and wouldn't dare mention the floating saltshaker once he'd observed that the others didn't want to see it. Melly could see that Henry still wanted to say something, but she added her own glare to Mary Rose's, and he wilted.

There were a few more raps, a few more scratches. Then the sounds stopped again, and for a few days there was a distinctly injured air to the house, as if some unseen presence felt rejected. Then there was nothing except the usual vibrant atmosphere of a house full of children.

Melly had skipped Saint Joseph's Day last year, but this year Gary and Rosalie were going to be angels in Teresa's tupa-tupa, the ceremony in which the Holy Family entered the home and were fed from the altar. She couldn't stand to miss that, so she squared her shoulders, steeled her spine, and accompanied the family to Teresa's house.

Cousin Angelina was playing the Blessed Virgin Mary. As soon as they got there, Melly saw her standing near the altar, slightly pudgy in a white dress, a light blue headscarf, and her usual pink-framed glasses that made her eyes look a little like a white rabbit's. She stuck out her tongue at Melly. Melly held her nose and crossed her eyes. "Who's gonna be Saint Joseph?" she whispered to Mary Rose.

"Well, Teresa wanted Pete to do it, but he said that'd be incestuous since he's Angelina's father. So they got some boy from the neighborhood. I don't know his name." As she spoke, Mary Rose herded her pair of angels up the driveway toward the carport. They were dressed in white gowns with posterboard wings and tinsel halos. Flashbulbs started going off as if they were walking the red carpet at the Academy Awards. Gary looked a little scared. Rosalie looked smug, as if she'd always known she was destined for stardom.

Drawing closer to the altar, Melly caught sight of Saint Joseph, a tall, slim boy wearing a rough brown robe and carrying a crooked staff. He turned, and she saw that it was the boy who had held her hand in the circle dance two years ago, the boy who looked a little like Paul McCartney. The boy who had seen her crying in the street with the shape of a crucifix embedded in her flesh.

Just as she was about to look away, he gave her a smile so sweet it made her stomach flutter. "How you doing?" he said. "I looked for you last year, but you weren't here."

"I . . . I wasn't feeling too good last year."

"Well, nice to see you. Maybe you'll dance with me later, huh?"

"Sure." Then, before she knew what was going to come out of her mouth, she said, "But I'm staying out of the circle dance!"

For a moment he looked almost shocked, and she was sorry she'd said it. Then something else dawned on his face, a mixture of surprise and admiration. He hadn't thought she would have the guts to bring it up, she guessed. From the corner of her eye she saw Angelina watching them jealously.

"Yeah," he said. "I'd do that if I were you. This year the whole altar might just rise up and bash you on the head."

"You never know."

He turned away and headed for the house. Behind her, Melly heard Mary Rose urging the angels, "Follow Mr. Joe. Y'all gonna eat soon."

"I'll take 'em," said Melly. She coaxed Gary and Rosalie into the house, dropped them off with the ladies who were coordinating the tupa-tupa, and went into the kitchen to see if she could help with the food.

Aunt Teresa was at the stove fussing over a huge pot of red gravy. She turned and saw Melly, and for a moment fear flickered in her eyes, or maybe just sorrow. Melly wondered if she should have come after all. Then Teresa smiled, held out her arms, and drew Melly to her.

Later, as she was standing with Paul (whose real name turned out to be Tony, but she couldn't get that first impression out of her head, wasn't even particularly anxious to do so) looking at the altar, she saw the gold crucifix that had stuck to her back. She could tell it was the same one because there was a big blob of dried glue showing between the figure of Jesus and the cross. A rosary made of painted fava beans was looped over it, and there were oranges arranged around its base. Melly reached out a hand, hesitated, then gently touched the crucifix.

"Good-bye," she said under her breath, and was relieved when nothing answered her.

REPORTS *of* CERTAIN
EVENTS *in* LONDON

by CHINA MIÉVILLE

ON THE TWENTY-SEVENTH OF NOVEMBER 2000, a package was delivered to my house. This happens all the time—since becoming a professional writer the amount of mail I get has increased enormously. The flap of the envelope had been torn open a strip, allowing someone to look inside. This also isn't unusual: because, I think, of my political life (I am a varyingly active member of a left-wing group, and once stood in an election for the Socialist Alliance), I regularly find, to my continuing outrage, that my mail has been peered into.

I mention this to explain why it was that I opened something not addressed to me. I, China Miéville, live on ——ley Road. This package was addressed to a Charles Melville, of the same house number, ——ford Road. No postcode was given, and it had found its way, slowly, to me. Seeing a large packet torn half-open by some cavalier spy, I simply assumed it was mine and opened it.

It took me a good few minutes to realise my mistake: the covering note contained no greeting by name to alert me. I read it along with the first few of the enclosed papers with growing bewilderment, convinced (absurd as this must sound) that this was to do with some project or other I had got involved with and then forgotten. When finally I looked again at the name on the envelope, I was wholly surprised.

That was the point at which I was morally culpable, rather than simply foolish. By then I was too fascinated by what I had read to stop.

I've reproduced the content of the papers below, with explanatory notes. Unless otherwise stated they're photocopies, some stapled together, some attached with paper clips, many with pages missing. I've tried to keep them in the order they came in; they are not always chronological. Before I had a sense of what was in front of me, I was casual about how I put the papers down. I can't vouch that this was how they were originally organised.

{Cover note. This is written on a postcard, in a dark blue ink, a cursive hand. The photograph is of a wet kitten emerging from a sink full of water and suds. The kitten wears a comedic expression of anxiety.}

Where are you? Here as requested. What do you want this for anyway? I scribbled thoughts on some. Can't find half the stuff. I don't think anyone's noticed me rummaging through the archives, and I managed to get into your old place for the rest (thank God you file), but come to next meeting. You can get people on your side but box clever. In haste. Are you taking sides? Talk soon. Will you get this? *Come to next meeting.* More as I find it.

{This page was originally produced on an old manual typewriter.}

BWVF Meeting, 6 September 1976
Agenda.
    1. Minutes of the last meeting.
    2. Nomenclature.
    3. Funds.

4. Research notes.

5. Field reports.

6. AOB.

1. Last minutes:

Motion to approve JH, Second FR. Vote: unanimous.

2. Nomenclature:

FR proposes namechange. "BWVF" dated. CT reminds FR of tradition. FR insists "BWVF" exclusive, proposes "S (Society) WVF" or "G (Gathering) WVF." CT remonstrates. EN suggests "C (Coven) WVF," to laughter. Meeting growing impatient. FR moves to vote on change, DY seconds. Vote: 4 for, 13 against. Motion denied.

{Someone has added by hand "Again! Silly Cow."*}*

3. Funds/Treasury report.

EN reports this quarter several payments made, totalling £—*[The sum is effaced with black ink.]*. Agreed to keep this up-to-date to avoid repeat of Gouldy-Statten debacle. Subscriptions are mostly current and with

{This is the end of a page and the last I have of these minutes.}

{The next piece is a single sheet that looks word-processed.}

1 September 1992

MEMO

Members are kindly asked to show more care when handling items in the collection. Standards have become unacceptably lax. Despite their vigilant presence, curators have reported various soilings, including: fingerprints on recovered wood and glass; ink spots on cornices; caliper marks on guttering and ironwork; waxy residue on keys.

Of course, research necessitates handling, but if members cannot respect these unique items conditions of access may have to become even more stringent.

Before entering, remember:

CHINA MIÉVILLE · REPORTS of CERTAIN EVENTS in LONDON

- Be careful with your instruments.
- Always wash your hands.

{The next page is numbered "2" and begins halfway through a paragraph. Luckily it contains a header.}

BWVF PAPERS, NO. 223. JULY 1981.

uncertain, but there is little reason to doubt his veracity. Both specimens tested exactly as one would expect for VD, suggesting no difference between VD and VF at even a molecular level. Any distinction must presumably be at the level of gross morphology, which defies our attempts at comparison, or of a noncorporeal essence thus far beyond our capacity to measure.

Whatever the reality, the fact that the two specimens of VF mortar can be added to the BWVF collection is cause for celebration.

This research should be ready to present by the end of this year.

Report on Work in Progress: VF and Hermeneutics
by B. Bath

Problems of knowledge and the problematic of *knowing*. Considerations of VF as urban scripture. Kabbala considered as interpretive model. Investigation of VF as patterns of interference. Research currently ongoing, ETA of finished article uncertain.

Report on Work in Progress: Recent changes in VF Behaviour
by E. Nugen

Tracking the movements of VF is notoriously difficult. [*Inserted here is a scrawl—"No bloody kidding. What do you think we're all bloody doing here?"*] Reconstructing these patterns over the *longue durée* [*the accent is added by hand*] is perforce a matter of plumbing a historical record that is, by its nature and definitionally, partial, anecdotal and uncertain. As most of my readers know, it has long been my aim to extract from the annals of our society evidence for long-term cycles (see Working Paper 19, "Once More on the Statten Curve"), an aim on which I have not been entirely unsuccessful.

I have collated the evidence from the major verified London sightings of the last three decades (two of those sightings my own) and can conclusively state that the time between VF arrival at and departure from a locus has decreased by a factor of 0.7. VF are moving more quickly.

In addition, tracking their movements after each appearance has become more complicated and (even) less certain. In 1940, application of the Deschaine Matrix with regard to a given VF's arrival time and duration on-site would result in a 23 percent chance of predicting reappearance parameters (within two months and two miles): today that same process nets only a 16 percent chance. VF are less predictable than they have ever been (barring, perhaps, the Lost Decade of 1876–86).

The shift in this behaviour is not linear but punctuated, sudden bursts of change over the years: once between 1952 and '53, again in late 1961, again in '72 and '76. The causes and consequences are not yet known. Each of these pivotal moments has resulted in an increased pace of change. The anecdotal evidence we have all heard, that VF have recently become more skittish and agitated, appears to be correct.

I intend to present this work in full within eighteen months. I wish to thank CM for help with the research. [*This CM is presumably Charles Melville, to whom the package was addressed. Clipped to the BWVF papers is this handwritten note:* Yes, Edgar is a pompous arse but he is on to something big.]

{What is it Edgar N. is on to? Of course I wondered, and still wonder, though now I think perhaps I know.}

{Then there is a document unlike the others so far. It is a booklet a few pages long. It was when I started to read this that I stopped, frowned, looked again at the envelope, realised my inadvertent intrusion, and

decided almost instantly that I would not stop reading. "Decided" doesn't really get the sense of the urgency with which I continued, as if I had no choice. But then if I say that, I absolve myself of wrongdoing, which I won't do, so let's say I "decided," though I'm unsure that I did. In any case, I continued reading. This document is printed on both sides like a flyer. The first sentence below is in large red font, and constitutes the booklet's front cover.}

Urgent: Report of a Sighting.

Principal witness: FR. Secondary: EN.

On Thursday, 11 February, 1988, so far as it is possible to tell between 3:00 a.m. and 5:17 a.m., a little way south of Plumstead High Street SE18, Varmin Way occurred.

Even somewhat foreshortened from its last known appearance (Battersea 1983—see the VF Concordance), Varmin Way is in a buckled configuration due to the constraints of space. One end adjoins Purrett Road between numbers 44 and 46, approximately forty feet north of Saunders Road: Varmin Way then appears to describe a tight S-curve, emerging halfway up Rippolson Road between numbers 30 and 32 (see attached map). [*There is no map.*]

Two previously terraced dwellings on each of the intersected streets have now been separated by Varmin Way. One on Rippolson is deserted: surreptitious enquiries have been made to inhabitants of each of the others, but none have remarked with anything other than indifference to the newcomer. Eg: In response to FR's query of one man if he knew the name of "that alley," he glanced at the street now abutting his house, shrugged and told her he was "buggered" if he knew. This response is of course typical of VF occurrence environs (See B. Harman, "On the Nonnoticing," BWVF Working Papers no. 5.)

A partial exception is one thirty-five-year-old Purrett Road man, resident in the brick dwelling newly on Varmin Way's north bank. Observed on his way toward Saunders Road, crossing Varmin Way he tripped on the new curb. He looked down at the asphalt and up at brick corners of the junction, paced back and forward five times with a quizzical expression, peering down the street's length, without entering it, before continuing on his journey, looking back twice.

{This is the end of the middle page of the leaflet. Folded and inserted inside is a handwritten letter. I have therefore decided to reproduce it here in the middle of the leaflet text. It reads:

Charles,

In haste. So sorry I could not reach you sooner—obviously phone not an option. I told you I could work this out: Fiona was only on-site because of me, but I modestly listed her as principal for politics' sake. Charles, we're about to go in and I'm telling you even from where I'm standing I can see the evidence; this is the real thing. Next time, next time. Or get down here! I'm sending this first class (of course!) so when you get it rush down here. But you know Varmin Way's reputation—it's restless, will probably be gone. But come find me! I'll be here at least.

Edgar

{At the end of this note is appended, in the same handwriting as that of the package's introductory note: What a bastard! I take it this was when you and he stopped seeing eye-to-eye? Why did he cut you out like that, and why so coyly? *The leaflet then continues:}*

Initial investigation shows that the new Varmin Way–overlooking walls of the houses now separated on Purrett Road are flat concrete. Those of Rippolson Road, though, are of similar brick to their fronts, bearing the usual sigil of the VF's identity, and are broken by small windows at the very top, through the net curtains of which nothing can be seen. (See "On Neomural Variety," by H. Burke, WBVF Working Papers no. 8.)

Those innards of Varmin Way which can be seen from its adjoining streets bear all the usual signs of VF morphology (are, in other words, apparently unremarkable), and are in accordance with earlier documented descriptions of the subject. In this occurrence, it being short, FR and EN were able to conduct the Bowery Resonance Experiment, stationing themselves at either end of the VF and shouting to each other down its lengths (until forced to stop by externalities). [*Here in Edgar's hand has been inserted, "Some local thuggee threatening to do me in if I didn't shut up!"*] Each could clearly hear the other, past the kinks in this configuration of Varmin Way.

More experiments are to follow.

{When I reached this point I was trembling. I had to stop, leave the room, drink some water, force myself to breathe slowly. I'm tempted to add more about this, about the sudden and threatened speculations these documents raised in me, but I think I should stay out of it.

Immediately after the report of the sighting was another, similarly produced pamphlet.}

Urgent—Report of an Aborted Investigation.

Present: FR, EN, BH. [*Added here is another new comment in Charles's nameless contact's hand. It reads: "Dread to think how gutted you were to be replaced by Bryn as new favourite. What exactly did you do to get Edgar so pissed off?"*]

At 11:20 p.m. on Saturday, 13 February, 1988, from its end on Rippolson Road, an initial examination was made of Varmin Way. Photographs were taken establishing the VF's identity (figure 1). [*Figure 1 is a surprisingly good-quality reproduction of a shot showing a street sign by a wall, standing at leg height on two little metal or wooden posts. The image is at a peculiar angle, which I think is the result of the photograph not being taken straight on, but from Rippolson Road, beyond. In an unusual old serif font, the sign reads* varmin way.]

As the party prepared for the expedition, certain events took place or were insinuated which led to a postponement and quick regrouping at a late-night café on Plumstead High Street. [*What were those "certain events"? The pointed imprecision suggested to me something deliberately not com-*

mitted to paper, something that the readers of this report, or perhaps a subgroup of them, would understand. These writings are a strange mix of the scientifically exact and the imprecise—even the failure to specify the café is surprising. But it is the baleful vagueness of the certain events that will not stop worrying at me.]
When the group returned to Rippolson Road at 11:53 p.m., to their great frustration, Varmin Way had unoccurred.

{Two monochrome pictures end the piece. They have no explanatory notes or legend. They are both taken in daylight. On the left is a photograph of two houses, on either side of a small street of low century-old houses which curves sharply to the right, it looks like, quickly unclear with distance. The right-hand picture is the two façades again, but this time the houses—recognisably the same from a window's crack, from a smear of paint below a sash, from the scrawny front gardens and the distinct unkempt buddleia bush—are closed up together. They are no longer semi-detached. There is no street between them.}

{So.

I stopped for a bit. I had to stop. And then I had to read on again.}

{A single sheet of paper. Typewritten again apart from the name, now on an electronic machine.}

Could you see it, Charles? The damage, halfway down Varmin Way? It's there; it's visible in the picture in that report. [*This must mean the picture on the left. I stared at it hard, with the naked eye and through a magnifying glass. I couldn't make out anything.*] It's like the slates from Scry Pass, the ones I showed you in the collection. *You* could see it in the striae and the marks, even if none of the bloody curators did. Varmin Way wasn't just passing through; it was *resting*, it was *recovering*, it had been attacked. I am right.

Edgar

{I kept reading.}

{Though it's not signed, judging by the font, what follows are a couple of pages of another typed letter from Edgar.}

earliest occurrence I can find of it is in the early 1700s (you'll hear 1790 or '91 or something—nonsense, that's just the official position based on the archives—this one isn't verified, but believe me, it's correct). Only a handful of years after the Glorious Revolution we find Antonia Chesterfield referring in her diaries to "a right rat of a street, ascamper betwixt Waterloo and the Mall, a veritable Vermin, in name as well as kind. Beware—Touch a rat and he will bite, as others have found, of our own and of the Vermin's vagrant tribe." That's a reference to Varmin Way— Mrs. Chesterfield was in the brotherhood's precursor (and you'd not have heard her complaining about that name either—Fiona, take note!).

You see what she's getting at, and I think she was the first. I don't know, Charles, correlation is so terribly hard, but look at some of the other candidates. Shuck Road; Caul Street; Stang Street; Teratologue Avenue (this last I think is fairly voracious); et al. So far as I can work it out, Varmin Way and Stang Street were highly antagonistic at that stage, but now they're almost certainly noncombative. No surprise: Sole Den Road is the big enemy these days—remember 1987?

Incidentally, talking of that first Varmin occurrence, did you ever read all the early cryptolit I sent you?)

The Clerk entered into a Snickelway
That then was gone again by close of day

Fourteenth century, imagine. I'll bet you a pound there are letters from disgruntled Britannic procurators complaining about errant alleyways around the Temple of Mithras. But there's not much discussion of the hostilities until Mrs. Chesterfield.

Anyway, you see my point. It's the only way one can make sense of it all, of all this that I've been going on about for so long. The Viae are fighting, and I think they always have.

And there's no idiot nationalism here either, as

{And here is the end of the page. And there is another message added, clearly referring to this letter, from CM's nameless interlocutor. "I believe it," he says, or she says, but I think of it as a man's handwriting, though that's a problematic assumption. "It took me a while, but I believe Edgar's bellum theory. But I know you, Charles, 'pure research' be buggered as far as you're concerned. I know what Edgar's doing, but I cannot see where you are going with this."}

Urgent—Report of a Traveller
Wednesday, 17 June, 1992

We are receiving repeated reports, which we are attempting to verify, of an international visit. Somewhere between Willesden Green and Dollis Hill (details are unclear), Ulica Nerwowosc has arrived. This visitor from Krakow has been characterised by our comrades in the Kolektyw as a mercurial mediaeval alleyway, very difficult to predict. Though it has proved impossible to photograph, initial reports correlate with the Kolektyw's description of the Via. Efforts are ongoing to capture an image of this elusive newcomer, and even to plan a Walk, if the risks are not too great.

No London street has sojourned elsewhere for some time (perhaps not unfortunate—a visit from Bunker Crescent was, notoriously, responsible for the schism in the BWVF Chicago Chapter in 1956), but the last ten years have seen six other documented visitations to London from foreign Viae Ferae. *See table.*

DATES	VISITOR	USUAL RESIDENCE	NOTES
6/9/82–8/9/82	Rue de la Fascination	Paris	Spent three days in Neasden, motionless from arrival to departure, jutting south of Prout Grove NW10.
3/1/84–4/1/84	West Fifth Street	New York	Appeared restless, settling for only up to two hours at a time, moving among various locations in Camberwell and Highgate.
11/2/84	Heulstrasse	Berlin	A relatively wide thoroughfare, the empty shopfronts of Heulstrasse cut north of the East London Crematorium in Bow for half a day, relocating late that night to Sydenham, and moving for three hours in backstreets, always just evading investigators.
22/10/87–24/10/87	Unthinker Road	Glasgow	This tiny cobbled lane, seemingly only a chance gap between the backs of houses, occurred on the Thursday morning jutting off Old Compton Street W1, spent a day occurring with stealthy movements farther and farther into Soho, unoccurred on the Friday, recurring on Saturday, only to cut sharply south toward Piccadilly Circus and disappear.

15/4/90?	Boulevard de la Gare Intrinsèque	Paris	Uniquely, this Via Fera was not witnessed by an investigator, but by a rare noticing civilian whose enquiries about a French-named street of impressive dimensions and architecture in the heart of Catford came to the brotherhood's attention.
29/11/91– 1/12/91	Chup Shawpno Lane	Calcutta	The pale clay of C. S. Lane, its hard earth road cut by tram tracks, were exhaustively documented by TY and FD during its meanderings through Camden and Kentish Town.

{There is a thick card receipt, stamped with some obscure sign, its left-hand columns rendered in crude typeface, those on the right filled out in black ink.}

BWVF COLLECTION.

DATE: 7/8/1992
NAME: C. Melville
CURATOR PRESENT: G. Benedict
REQUESTED:

    Item 117: a half slate recovered from Scry Pass, 7/11/1958.

    Item 34: a splinter of glass recovered from Caul Street, 8/2/1986.

    Item 67: an iron ring and key recovered from Stang Street, 6/5/1936.

{This next letter is on headed paper, beautifully printed.}

Société pour l'étude des rues sauvages
20 June 1992

Dear Mr. Melville,

Thank you for your message and congratulations for have this visitor. We in Paris were fortunate to have this pretty Polish street rest with us in 1988 but I did not see it.

I confirm that you are correct. Boulevard de la Gare Intrinsèque and the Rue de la Fascination have both stories about them. We call him le jockey, a man who is supposed to live on streets like these and to make them move for him, but these are only stories for the children. There are no people on these *rues sauvages*, in Paris, and I think there are none in London too. No one knows why the streets have gone to London that time, like no one knows why your Importune Avenue moved around the Arc de la Défence twelve years ago.

Yours truly,
Claudette Santier

{There is a handwritten letter.}

My Dear Charles,

I'm quite aware that you feel ill-used. I apologise for that. There is no point, I think, rehearsing our disagreements, let alone the unpleasant contretemps they have led to. I cannot see that you are going anywhere with these investigations, though, and I simply do not have enough years left to indulge your ideas, nor enough courage (were I younger . . . Ah, but were I younger what would I *not* do?).

I have performed three Walks in my time, and have seen the evidence of the wounds the Viae leave on each other. I have tracked the combatants and shifting loyalties. Where, in contrast, is the evidence behind your claims? Why, on the basis of your intuition, should anyone discard the cautions that may have kept us *alive*? It is not as if what we do is safe, Charles. There are reasons for the strictures you are so keen to overturn.

Of course, yes, I have heard all the stories that you have: of the streets that occur with lights ashine and men at home! of the antique costermongers' cries still heard over the walls of Dandle Way! of the street riders! I do not say I don't believe them, any more than I don't— or do—believe the stories that Potash Street and Luckless Road courted and mated and that that's how Varmin Way was born, or the stories of where the Viae Ferae go when they unoccur. I have no way of judging. This mythic company of inhabitants and street tamers may be true, but so long as it is also a myth, you have nothing. I am content to observe, Charles, not to become involved.

Good God, who knows what the agenda of the streets might be? Would you really, would you *really*, Charles, risk attempting ingress? Even if you could? After everything you've read and heard? Would you risk taking sides?

Regretfully and fondly,

Edgar

{This is another handwritten note. I think it is in Edgar's hand, but it is hard to be sure.}

Saturday, 27 November, 1999
Varmin Way's back.

{We are near the end of the papers now. What came out of the package next looks like one of the pamphlet-style reports of sightings. It is marked with a black band in one corner of the front cover.}

Urgent—Report of a Walk
Walkers: FR, EN, BH (author)

At 11:20 p.m. on Sunday, 28 November, 1999, a walk was made the length of Varmin Way. As well as its tragic conclusion, most members will be aware of the extraordinary circumstances surrounding this investigation—since records began, there is no evidence in the archives of a Via Fera returning to the site of an earlier occurrence. Varmin Way's reappearance, then, at precisely the same location in Plumstead, between Purrett and Rippolson roads, as that it inhabited in February 1988, was profoundly shocking, and necessitated this perhaps too quickly planned Walk.

FR operated as base, remaining stationed on Rippolson Road (the front yard of the still-deserted number 32 acting as camp). Carrying toolbags and wearing council overalls over their harnesses and belay kits, BH and EN set out. Their safety rope was attached to a fence post close to FR. The walkers remained in contact with FR throughout their three-hour journey, by radio.

In this occurrence of Varmin Way, the street is a little more than a hundred metres long. [*An amendment here: "Can you imagine Edgar going metric? What kind of a homage is this?"*] We proceeded slowly. [*Here another insertion: "Ugh. Change of person." By now I was increasingly irritated with these interruptions. I never felt I could ignore them, but they broke the flow of my reading. There was something vaguely passive-aggressive in their cheer, and I felt as if Charles Melville would have been similarly angered by them. In an effort to retain the flow I'll start this sentence again.*]

We proceeded slowly. We walked along the unpainted tar in the middle of Varmin Way, equidistant between the street lamps. These lamps are indistinguishable from those in the neighbouring streets. There are houses to either side, all of them with all their windows unlit, looking like low workers' cottages of Victorian vintage (though the earliest documented reports of Varmin Way date from 1792—this apparent aging of form gives credence

{To my intense frustration, several pages are missing, and this is where the report therefore ends. There are, however, several photographs in an envelope, stuffed in among the pages. There are four. They are dreadful shots, taken with a flash too close or too far, so that their subject is either effaced by light or peering out from a cowl of dark. Nonetheless they can just be made out.

The first is a wall of crumbling brick, the mortar fallen away in

scabs. Askew across the print, taken from above, is a street sign. VARMIN WAY, it says, in an antiquated iron font. Written in Biro on the photograph's back is: "The Sigil."

The second is a shot along the length of the street. Almost nothing is visible in this, except perspective lines sketched in dark on dark. None of the houses has a front garden: their doors open directly onto the pavement. They are implacably closed, whether for centuries or only moments it is, of course, impossible to tell. The lack of a no-man's-land between house and walker makes the doors loom. Written on the back of this image is: "The Way."

The third is of the front of one of the houses. It is damaged. Its dark windows are broken, its brick stained, crumbling where the roof is fallen in. On the back is written: "The Wound."

The last picture is of an end of rope and a climbing buckle, held in a young man's hands. The rope is frayed and splayed: the metal clip bent in a strange corkscrew. On the back of the photograph is nothing.}

{And then comes the last piece in the envelope. It is undated. It is in a different hand from the others.}

> What did you do? How did you do it? What did you do, you bastard?
>
> I saw what happened. Edgar was right, I saw where Varmin Way had been hurt. But you know that, don't you?
>
> What did you do to Varmin Way to make it do that?
> What did you do to Edgar?
>
> Do you think you'll get away with it?

That was everything. When I'd finished, I was frantic to find Charles Melville.

I think the ban on telephone conversations must extend to e-mail and Web pages. I searched online, of course, for BWVF, "wild streets," "feral streets," "Viae Ferae," and so on. I got nothing. BWVF got references to cars or technical parts. I tried "Brotherhood of Witnesses to/Watchers of the Viae Ferae" without any luck. "Wild streets" of course got thousands: articles about New Orleans Mardi Gras, hard-boiled ramblings, references to an old computer game and an article about the Cold War. Nothing relevant.

I visited each of the sites described in the scraps of literature, the places where all the occurrences occurred. For several weekends I wandered in scraggy arse-end streets in north or south London, or sometimes in sedate avenues, even once (following Unthinker Road) walking through the centre of Soho. Inevitably, I suppose, I kept returning to Plumstead.

I would hold the before and after pictures up and look at the same houses of Rippolson Road, all closed up, an unbroken terrace.

Why did I not repackage all this stuff and send it on to Charles Melville, or take it to his house in person? The envelope wrongly sent to ——ley Road was addressed to ——ford Road. But there is no ——ford Road in London. I have no idea how to find Charles.

The other reason I hesitated was that Charles had begun to frighten me.

The first few times I went walking, took photos secretively, I still thought as if I were witnessing some Oedipal drama. Reading and rereading the material, though, I realised that what Charles had done to Edgar was not the most important thing here. What was important was how he had done it.

I have eaten and drunk at all the cafés on Plumstead High Street. Most are unremarkable, one or two are extremely bad, one or two very good. In each establishment I asked, after finishing my tea, whether the owner knew anyone called Charles Melville. I asked if they'd mind me putting up a little notice I'd written.

"Looking for CM," it read. "I've some documents you mislaid—maps of the area, etc. Complicated streets! Please contact:" and then an anonymous e-mail address I'd set up. I heard nothing.

I'm finding it hard to work. These days I am very conscious of corners. I fix my eyes on an edge of brick (or concrete or stone), where another road meets the one I'm walking, and I try to remember if I've ever noticed it before. I look up suddenly as I pass, to catch out anything hurriedly occurring. I keep seeing furtive motions and snapping up my head at only a tree in the wind or an opened window. My anxiety—perhaps I should honestly call it foreboding—remains.

And if I ever did see anything more, what could I do? Probably we're irrelevant to them. Most of us. Their motivations are unimaginable, as opaque as brickwork sphinxes'. If they consider us at all, I doubt they care what's in our interests: I think it's that indifference that breeds these fears I cannot calm, and makes me wonder what Charles has done.

I say I heard nothing, after I put up my posters. That's not quite accurate. In fact, on the fourth of April 2001, five months after that first package, a letter arrived for Charles Melville. Of course, I opened it immediately.

It was one page, handwritten, undated. I am looking at it now. It reads:

Dear Charles,

Where are you, Charles?

I don't know if you know by now—I suspect you do—that you've been excommunicated. No one's saying that you're responsible for what happened to Edgar—no one can say that; it would be to admit far too much about what you've been doing—so they've got you on nonpayment of subscriptions. Ridiculous, I know.

I believe you've done it. I never thought you could—I never thought anyone could. Are there others there? Are you alone?

Please, if ever you can, tell me. I want to know.

Your friend.

It was not the content of this letter but the envelope that so upset me. The letter, stamped and postmarked and delivered to my house, was addressed to "Charles Melville, Varmin Way."

This time, it's hard to pretend the delivery is coincidence. Either the Royal Mail is showing unprecedented consistency in misdirection, or I am being targeted. And if the latter, I do not know by whom or what: by pranksters, the witnesses, their rene-gade or their subjects. I am at the mercy of the senders, whether the letter came to me hand-delivered or by stranger ways.

That is why I have published this material. I have no idea what my correspondents want from me. Maybe this is a test, and I've failed: maybe I was about to get a tap on the shoulder and a whis-pered invitation to join, maybe all this is the newcomer's manual, but I don't think so. I don't know why I've been shown these things, what part I am of another's plan, and that makes me afraid. So as an unwilling party to secrets, I want to disseminate them as widely as I can. I want to protect myself, and this is the only way I can think to do so. (The other possibility, that this was what I was required to do, hasn't passed me by.)

I can't say he owes me an explanation for all this, but I'd like a chance to persuade Charles Melville that I deserve one. I have his documents—if there is anyone reading this who knows how I can reach him, to return them, please let me know. You can contact me through the publisher of this book.

As I say, there is no ——ford Road in London. I have visited all the other alternatives. I have knocked at the relevant number in ——fast and ——land and ——nail Streets, and ——ner and ——hold Roads, and ——den Close, and a few even less likely. No one has heard of Charles Melville. In fact, number such-and-such ——fast Street isn't there anymore: it's been demol-ished; the street is being reshaped. That got me thinking. You can believe that got me thinking.

"What's happening to ——fast Street?" I wondered. "Where's it going?"

I can't know whether Charles Melville has broken Varmin Way, has tamed it, is riding it like a bronco through the city and beyond. I can't know if he's taken sides, is intervening in the unending savage war between the wild streets of London. Perhaps he and Edgar were wrong, perhaps there's no such fight, and the

Viae Ferae are peaceful nomads, and Charles has just got tired and gone away. Perhaps there are no such untamed roads.

There's no way of knowing. Nonetheless I find myself thinking, wondering what's happening round that corner, and that one. At the bottom of my street, of ——ley Road, there are some works going on. Men in hard hats and scaffolding are finishing the job time started of removing tumbledown walls, of sprucing up some little lane so small as to be nameless, nothing but a cat's run full of rubbish and the smell of piss. They're reshaping it, is what it looks like. I think they're going to demolish an abandoned house and widen the alleyway.

We are in new times. Perhaps the Viae Ferae have grown clever, and stealthy. Maybe this is how they will occur now, sneaking in plain sight, arriving not suddenly but so slowly, ushered in by us, armoured in girders, pelted in new cement and paving. I think on the idea that Charles Melville is sending Varmin Way to come for me, and that it will creep up on me with a growl of mixers and drills. I think on another idea that this is not an occurrence but an unoccurrence, that Charles has woken ——ley Road, my home, out of its domesticity, and that it is yawning, and that soon it will shake itself off like a fox and sniff the air and go wherever the feral streets go when they are not resting, I and my neighbours tossed on its back like fleas, and that in some months' time the main street it abuts will suddenly be seamless between the Irish bookie and the funeral parlour, and that ——ley Road will be savaged by and savaging Sole Den Road, breaking its windows and walls and being broken in turn and coming back sometimes to rest.

THE FABLED LIGHT-HOUSE
at VIÑA DEL MAR

by JOYCE CAROL OATES

2 *NOVEMBER 1848.* This day—my first on the fabled Light-House at Viña del Mar—I am thrilled to make my first entry into my Diary as agreed upon with my patron Dr. Bertram Shaw. As regularly as I can keep the Diary, I will—that is my vow made to Dr. Shaw, as to myself—tho' there is no predicting what may happen to a man so entirely alone as I—one must be clear-minded about this—I may become ill, or worse. . . .

So far I am in very good spirits, & eager to begin my duties. My soul, long depressed by a multitude of factors, has wonderfully revived in this bracing *spring* air at latitude 33° S, longitude 11° W in the South Pacific Ocean, some two hundred miles west of the rockbound coast of Chile, north of Valparaiso; at the realization of being—at last, after the smotherings of Philadelphia society— thoroughly *alone.*

(Though I am accompanied by my loyal fox terrier Mercury, an exuberant & agreeable companion ever at my heels, I cannot consider him *society.*)

(Ah! I will admit, quite frankly in this Diary for any who wish to read it at a later date, my pride was deeply wounded, to learn, obliquely, of Dr. Shaw's initial doubts as to my ability to manage the light, owing to the fact that my reputation is that of a purely *literary sensibility*; & secondly of his difficulty in securing the backing of the Philadelphia Society of Naturalists to offer me the position, & what it entails of participation in an experiment in pure science; what these specific doubts were, on the Society's part, I cannot imagine. . . . Apart from my admitted melancholia of these past two years, since the tragic & unexpected death of my wife, V., that has had no effect upon my rational judgment; as all who know me can confirm.)

This fine day, I have much to rejoice in, having climbed to the pinnacle of the tower, with good-hearted Mercury leaping & panting before me; gazing out to sea, shading my dazzled eyes; all but overcome by the majesty of these great spaces, not only the ever-shifting lavalike waters of the great Pacific, but the yet more wondrous sky above, that seems not a singular sky but numerous skies, of numerous astonishing cloud formations stitched together like skins! Sky, sea, earth: ah, vibrant life! The lantern (to be lit just before dusk) is of a wondrous size quite unlike any mere domestic lantern I have seen, weighing perhaps fifty pounds. Seeing it, & drawing reverent fingers across it, I am filled with a strange sort of zest, & eager for my duties to begin. "How could any of you have doubted me," I protest, to the prim-browed gentlemen of the Philadelphia Society, "I will prove you mistaken. Posterity be my judge!"

One man has managed the Light-House at Viña del Mar from time to time in its history, tho' two is the preferred number, & I am certainly capable of such simple operations & responsibilities as Keeper of the Light entails, I would hope! Thanks to the generosity of Dr. Shaw, I am well outfitted with supplies to last through the upcoming six months, as the Light-House is an impressively sturdy bulwark to withstand virtually all onslaughts of weather in this *temperate zone* not unlike the waters of the Atlantic east of Cape

Hatteras. "So long as you return to 'rescue' me, before the southern winter begins," I joked with the captain of the *Ariel*; a burly dark-browed Spaniard who laughed heartily at my wit, replying in heavily accented English he would sail into the waters of Hades itself if the recompense was deemed sufficient; as, given Dr. Shaw's fortune, it would appear to be.

With this, any phantom doubts I might have entertained of being abandoned to the elements were put immediately to rest; for I acknowledge, I am one of those individuals of a somewhat fantastical & nervous disposition, who entertains worries where there are none, as my late beloved V. observed of me, yet who does not sufficiently worry of what *is*. "In this, you are not unlike all men, from our esteemed 'leaders' downward," V. gently chided. (V. took but fond note of my character, never criticizing it; between us, who were related by cousinly blood as by matrimony, & by a like predilection for the great Gothic works of E. T. A. Hoffmann, Heinrich Von Kleist, & Jean Paul Richter, there fluidly passed at all times as if we shared an identical bloodstream a kindred humor & wryness of sympathy undetectable to the crass individuals who surrounded us.)

But—why dwell upon these distracting thoughts, since I am here, & in good health & spirits, eager to begin what posterity will perhaps come to call *The Diary of the Fabled Light-House at Viña del Mar*, a document to set beside such celebrated investigations into the human psyche as the *Meditations* of René Descartes, the *Pensées* of Blaise Pascal, *Les reveries du promeneur solitaire* of Jean-Jacques Rousseau, & the sixty-five volumes of Jean Paul Richter.

Except: the *Diary* will provoke universal curiosity, for its author will be *Anonymous*.

4 November 1848. This day—my second upon the Light-House— I make my second entry into the Diary with yet more resolution & certainty of purpose than the first. Yesterday evening, promptly in the waning hours of day, Mercury & I climbed to the great lantern,

& dealt with it as required; ah! There is indeed wind at this height, that tore at our breaths like invisible harpies, but we withstood the assault; I took great pleasure in striking the first match in an imagined procession, & bringing it to the tonguelike wick so soaked in a flammable liquid, it seemed virtually to *breathe in* the flame from my fingers. "Now, that is done. I declare myself Keeper of the Light at Viña del Mar: that all ships be warned of the treacherous rocks of the coast." Laughing then aloud, for sheer happiness, as Mercury barked excitedly, in confirmation.

Now, in an attitude of satisfied repose, I have broken off from my morning's routine of Plotinus & Jeremias Gotthelf, the one purely investigative, the other for purposes of translation (for the Swiss-born Gothic master Gotthelf is all but unknown in my native country, & who is more capable of rendering his vision into English, than I?) to record these thoughts in the Diary; that never would be thought, in Philadelphia:

Unexpectedly, in my forty-first year, how delighted I am, to at last being "helpful" to my fellows, however they are strangers to me, & utterly unaware of me except as the Keeper of the Light-House at Viña del Mar; not only to be helpful in this practical way, in aiding the princes of commerce, but to participate in Dr. Shaw's experiment, in that way providing a helpfulness to scientific knowledge, & simultaneously to fulfill my great yearning, since V.'s death, to be *alone.* Ah, what pleasure! Plotinus & Gotthelf; no companion but Mercury; a task so simple, a ten-year-old might execute it; vast sea & sky to peruse as figures of *the most fantastical art.* To live immersed in society was a terrible error for one of my temperament. Especially as I have been, since the age of fifteen, susceptible to cards, & drink, & riotous company. (By my agreement with Dr. Shaw, my debts of some of $3,500 were erased as by the flourish of a magician's wand!) Yet now I am privileged to be *alone,* in a place of such solitude I have passed hours merely staring out at the ocean, its boundless waters quivering and rippling as with restive thoughts; here indeed is the true *kingdom by the sea*, I have long yearned for. "Dr. Shaw, I am indebted to you, & will not disappoint you, I vow!"

5 *November 1848.* This day—my third upon the Light-House—I make my third entry into the Diary in somewhat mixed spirits. For in the night, which was a night of rowdy winds keeping both master & terrier uneasily awake, there came hauntingly to me, as it were mockingly, an echo of *alone*: strange how I never observed, until now, how ominous a sound that word has—*alone.* In my lumpy bed I'd half fancied there was some perversity in the stony composition of these funnel-like walls—but no!—this is all nonsense. I refuse to become nervous about the very isolation I had so wished for, since V.'s piteous death; and that will never do, for I have given Dr. Shaw my promise, & could not disappoint that good man.

Alone I will hear as music, in the way of the legended *Ulalume*: that melancholy so sweetly piercing, its effect is that of pain exquisite as ecstasy. *Alone* I consign to mere shadows, as my perky Mercury has done; & take pleasure in observing the vast domain of the sky, so much more pronounced at sea than on land. *Alone* I observe the curiosity, remarked upon by the Gothic masters, that nature seems but a *willed phenomenon*, of the imagination: the sun ascending in the eastern sky; a vision of such beauty, even the crudest of cumulus clouds is transformed. Yet without the Keeper of the Light, which is to say "I" ("eye"), could such beauty be revealed, let alone articulated?

I will rejoice in this, the supremacy of "I"; though the more languid breeze of afternoon smells of brine & somewhat rotted things, from a pebbly shore of the island, I have yet to explore.

7 *November 1848.* Exploring the Light-House, with my faithful Mercury. Aboard the *Ariel*, I was told conflicting tales of its history, & am uncertain what to believe. The claim is that the Light-House at Viña del Mar is of unknown origin: discovered on the small rockbound island as a tower of about half its present size,

constructed of rough-hewn rock and mortar, *before the era of Spanish dominance*. Some believe that the tower is centuries old; others, more reasonably, that it must have been constructed by a tribe of Chilean Indians now extinct, who had a knowledge of seafaring.

It is true, the primitive tower yet remains, at the base of the Light-House; beyond twenty feet, the tower is clearly "new"— tho' we are talking still of at least a century. This most hazardous stretch of waters west of the coast of Chile, looking as if the treacherous Andes had intruded into the sea, has long been notorious to sailors, I have been told; the need for a light-house is obvious. And yet, such a lofty structure!—you might almost call *godly*.

(Yet I could wish that such godliness had been tempered by restraint: these circular winding stairs are interminable! Nearly as exhausting, & yet more vertiginous, descending as ascending! Within these few days at Viña del Mar, my leg calves and thighs are aching, & my neck is stiff from craning to see where I am stepping. Indeed, I have slipped once or twice, & would have fallen to crack my skull if I had not reached out immediately, to seize the railing. Even frisky Mercury pants on these stairs! Initially my count of the stairs was 190, my second was 187, my third, 191; my fourth, I have put off. The tower would appear to be about two hundred feet, from the low-water mark to the roof above the great lantern. From the bottom *inside* the shaft, however, the distance to the summit is beyond two hundred feet—for the floor is twenty feet below the surface of the sea, even at low tide. It seems to me the hollow interior at the base should have been filled in with solid masonry, of a keeping with the rest of the sturdy tower. Undoubtedly the whole would have been thus rendered more *safe*—but what am I thinking? No mere sea, no hurricane, could defeat this solid iron-riveted wall—which, at fifty feet from the high-water mark, is four feet thick at least. The base on which the structure exists appears to be chalk: a curious substance, indeed!)

Well! I take a curious pride in the Light-House, of which I am sole Keeper. I did not linger belowground, for I have a morbid fear of such dank, confining places, but prefer to tramp about in the open air at the base of the tower. Gazing upward I declared, as if Posterity might be listening: "Here is a construction of surpassing ingenuity yet devoid of mystery: for a light-house is but a structure designed by men for purely commercial, hardly romantic or esoteric purposes." At my heels, Mercury barked excitedly, in a frolicsome sort of echo!

And now, the restless terrier is larking about in the boulders, & on the pebbly shore, where I am not happy he should venture; the poor "fox" hunter cannot quite fathom, there are no foxes in this lonely place for him to hunt & bring back in triumph to his master.

10 November 1848. I am late making this Diary entry, having slept poorly & withstood a curious floating cloud, or mist, bearing stinging locustlike insects from the mainland; thankfully, a sudden gale-force wind bore upon us, & swept these harpies away! I have worked out my ideal schedule, however, & record it here:

Waking, precisely at dawn
Ablutions, shaving, et cetera
Breakfast, while reading & note taking
Exercise/meditation/"exploration"
Diary entry
Midday meal, while reading & note taking
Further meditation/note-taking/exercise et cetera
Evening meal, while reading & note taking
Lighting of the lantern
Bed & sleep

Ah, you are shaking your head, are you! That this schedule appears to you confining as an *imprisonment*. But, I assure you, it is not so. I am not a creature like poor Mercury, roused to terrier exuberance & frustration by these balmy spring mornings (November in the southern hemisphere, recall, is April in the northern), as if seeking not merely prey but a mate; I am perfectly at ease with *aloneness*. As Pascal observed in the 139th Pensée:

> . . . all the unhappiness of men arises from one
> single fact, that they cannot stay quietly in their
> own chamber.

This Diary shall record whether a "truth" is universal; or applies merely to the weak.

15 November 1848. At midday, sighted a ship some miles to the east. Bound for the Strait of Magellan & very likely the great port at Buenos Aires. In the bland waters of day, this ship had no need for the Light-House at Viña del Mar & I felt for the briefest moment a strange sort of outrage. "Sail in these waters by night, my friends, & you will not so blithely ignore the Keeper of the Light."

19 November 1848. Waking at dawn, a night of interrupted sleep. While breakfasting (with little appetite, I know not why) continued my painstaking translation of *Die Schwarze Spinne*; then, in relief turning to *The Enneads* of Plotinus, I had strangely neglected in my previous old careless life. (Dr. Shaw has been so generous, allowing me countless books among my more practical provisions; some of these already in my possession but most of the volumes & journals his.) Plotinus is an ancient whose treatises on cosmology, numerals, the soul, eternal truth, & the One are wonderfully matched to me, a pilgrim at the Light-House at Viña del Mar. For I continue to marvel how at ease I am with *aloneness,* which I believe I have yet to explore, to its depth.

Plotinus is the very balm for grief, which I feel still, in times of repose, following the death of my darling V. (of a burst vein in her alabaster throat, suffered while singing the exquisite "Annie Laurie" as I, in a transport of delight, accompanied her on the pianoforte) when I vowed I would remain celibate, & penitent, for the remainder of my unhappy life. As V. dreaded the bestial, which permeates so much of human intercourse, within even the marital bed, I have a like aversion; tho' I take pleasure in fondling Mercury & stroking his pricked-up ears, I would be revulsed to so intimately touch another human being! For even handshaking, one gentleman with another, leaves me repelled. "Your hand is very cold, my boy," Dr. Shaw teased, at our parting in Philadelphia harbor, "which the ladies assure me is the sign of a *warm heart*. Yes?"

(Here is a strangeness: in this solitude where the only sounds are those of the infernal seabirds, & the dull admixture of waves & whining winds, lately I have been hearing *Dr. Shaw's unmistakable voice*; & in drifting clouds overhead, *I see Dr. Shaw's face*: stolid, bewhiskered, with glittering eyeglasses atop a sizable nose. *My boy* he has called me—tho' in my forty-second year I am scarcely a boy!— *what a role you are destined to play in advancing the cause of scientific knowledge*. My deep gratitude to this gentleman, who rescued me from a life of dissolution & self-harm, to engage me in this experiment into the effect of "extreme isolation" upon an "average male specimen of *Homo sapiens*." The irony being lost to Dr. Shaw, seemingly, that tho' I am quite a normal male specimen of Homo sapiens, I am hardly average!)

28 November 1848. Ships sighted, at a distance. Seabirds, noisy & tenacious, until routed by Mercury & his master. A sudden fierce gale swept upon us in the night, leaving the usual sea filth (some of it yet wriggling with the most repulsive life, tho' badly mauled & mutilated) washed up on the pebbly beach.

If I have not recorded in the Diary much of this "wriggling life," it is out of fastidious disdain & a lofty ignorance of such low species. Tho' I should note, I suppose, that the sloshing waves of the beach are within fifteen paces of this perch, in the Light-House doorway. Fortunately, the wind blows in the other direction; my nostrils need not contract with foul smells!

Nights are not so peaceful as I might wish. Mercury whimpers & bites at himself, beset by bloodlust dreams as by fleas.

1 December 1848. How breathless I am! Not from climbing the damnable stairs, but from quite another sort of exertion.

After days of rain, dull & without nuance as the idiot hammerings of a coffin maker, at midafternoon there came a sudden sunburst through dense banks of cloud: Mercury began to bark excitedly, rousing his master as he dozed over Plotinus, & the two rushed outside to lark about quite like children. How V. would stare in amazement at such antics!

And yet: our domain is so very small: smaller than it had seemed, when the cutter brought us to the Light-House (how many weeks ago?); less than a hundred feet in diameter, I have estimated, & much of this solid unyielding rock. Directly outside the Light-House doorway, there are layered rocks that give the impression of crude stairs, leading into the ocean: no doubt, this is why the Light-House was constructed where it is, confronting these rocks. Directly to the left of the Light-House entrance is a grouping of immense boulders, buttressing the sea, I have called the Pantheon: for there is a crude nobility in the features of these great rocks, as in primitive faces; as if a sculptor of antiquity had been interrupted in his task of chiseling the "human" out of mere inert matter. (Tho' these great rocks are covered in the most foul bird droppings, as you may imagine. & where there are bird droppings, you may be sure there are greedy buzzing insects.)

More lurid yet, to the left of the Light-House entrance is the rank pebbly beach I have mentioned in passing, beyond a small field of rocks & boulders; this region, loathsome even to speak of, I have called the Charnel House, tho' more than merely the rotting corpses of sea life is to be found there. (Both Mercury & his master produce "waste" that must be disposed of; but, there being no sewers in so primitive an environment, still less servants to bear chamber pots away, this task is not so easily accomplished. Dr.

Shaw had not thought to mention it, being a gentleman of means & accustomed to the amenities of civilization, no more than Plotinus, Gotthelf, Pascal & Rousseau would have thought of alluding to such, in their writings.)

Well! 'Round & 'round the Light-House, tho' constrained by the Pantheon to one side & the Charnel House to the other, Mercury & his master clambered, basking in the sun of early summer as if sensing how such a happy conjunction of sunshine, mild winds & temperature, was not into the midst of gulls, sandpipers & terns, sending them shrieking & flapping their wings in terror of us; more boldly, we confronted a giant albatross, of the yellow-nose species: as I clapped my hands & shouted, & Mercury barked wildly, this singular creature erupted into the air & beat his seven-foot saberlike wings above our heads for some suspenseful seconds, as if preparing to attack, before he flew off. "We have routed the enemy, Mercury!" I cried, laughing, for of course it was purely play.

Even now, I am restless with thinking of the encounter, & my heart beats strangely. Tho' knowing that if I had managed to seize the beautiful bird's slender leg, I would not have done injury to him, but would have immediately released him, of course. Like my beloved V., I am a friend to all living creatures, & wish none harm. (As for Mercury, bred to aid his master in the hunting of foxes & similar game, with the reward of bloody spoils, I dare not speak!)

5 December 1848. I am most unhappy with Mercury, I will record in this Diary, tho' it is hardly of import to posterity.

Vexing dog! Refusing to obey me where I stand in the Light-House doorway calling, "Mercury! Come here! I am commanding you: *come here.*" At last the abashed-looking terrier appears, from the region of the Charnel House littered with every species of filth, in which a mutinous dog might roll himself in ecstasy, tho' forbidden by Master.

The Charnel House: what is its appeal? These are hardly foxes for the terrier to pursue, but the most disgusting "prey" as may have washed up overnight: dead & dying fish of all sizes & monstrous faces, small octopi & jellyfish, spineless pale creatures oozing out of their broken shells, & a particularly loathsome slimy seaweed that writhes like living snakes in the shallow water, as I have stared at it for long fascinated minutes in wonderment. At last, Mercury returns to me, quivering tail between his legs. "Mercury, come! Good dog." It is not my nature to punish, except I know dogs must be trained: if Master does not behave rightly, Dog will become confused & demoralized & in time turn against Master. So I am stern with Mercury, lifting my fist as if to strike his trembling head: seeing in his amber eyes, usually brimming with love for me, the glisten of animal fear; yet I do not strike, but only chide; withdrawing then to the Light-House, I am followed by the repentant creature, & soon we are companions again, devouring our evening meal before sinking, not long after sunset, into the swoon of sleep.

(Ah, sleep! How sweet it has become, when it comes! Tho' it seems that I am always in my bed, no sooner have I roused myself from my stuporous perspiring slumber, well after sunrise these days, than I discover that I am overcome by fatigue, & prepared to lie down again; tho' my lumpy bed smells frankly of my body, & my predecessors' bodies; for it has proved tedious to be always "airing out" bedclothes & mattress, as it is tedious to be always "undressing" & "dressing." For who is to observe me here, if my linen is not of the freshest, & my jaw not quite so clean-shaven as the ladies wish? Mercury does not mind if Master neglects some niceties of grooming, indeed!)

11 December 1848. Very warm day. "Airless"—"torpor"—"dead calm." Some miles to the east, a becalmed ship sighted through the telescope, at too great a distance to be identified: whether an American or an English ship, or another, I had no way of knowing. Tho' as always, without fail, for I will never fail in my duty, Mercury &

I climbed the damnable stairs to the great lantern, at sundown; to light the wick soaked in foul-smelling kerosene, that stings our nostrils even after weeks.

How many steps to the lantern? I have ascertained 196.

12 December 1848. Very warm day. "Airless"—"torpor"—"dead calm." Climbing the stairs, & lighting the wick, & a blood-tinged mist drifted across the sky, at dusk, & obscured all vision. & I did not know, *Is there any human out there, to observe this feeble light? To perceive me, a fellow spirit, drowning in solitude?*

17 December 1848. Very warm day. "Airless"—"torpor"—"dead calm." Then, at midday, interrupted by a furious squabble of the order of the battling angels of Milton's great epic, amongst a vast crowd of seabirds of numerous species, that anxious Mercury was eager to allow me to know had nothing to do with him: but the fact that a gigantic sea creature was washed ashore, to be pecked & stabbed by shrieking birds until its remarkable skeleton emerged through shreds of flesh. Ah, what a horror! & now, what a stench! So sickened, I cannot complete a single page of the difficult High German of Gotthelf.

Yet, I defend these belligerent fowls: for they are scavengers, & are needed to devour dead & putrefying flesh, that would soon overtake the living at Viña del Mar, & destroy us utterly.

19 December 1848. Today, a rude shock! I am not sure whether to record it in the Diary, I am so shaken.

Having set temporarily aside my Plotinus, & my Gotthelf, I turned to a stack of monographs of the Philadelphia Society of Naturalists that had been included with books from Dr. Shaw's library; & came upon a stunning revelation, in an article by one Bertram Shaw, Ph.D., M.D., for 1846, titled "The Effects of Extreme Isolation upon Certain Mammalian Specimens." To wit, a rat; a guinea pig; a monkey; a dog; a cat; a "young horse in good health." These luckless creatures were imprisoned in small pens, in Dr. Shaw's laboratory, provided as much food & water as they wished to consume, but kept from any sight of their fellows, & never spoken to or touched. Initially, the animals devoured food in a frenzy of appetite, then by degrees lost all appetite, as they lost energy & strength; slept fitfully, & finally lapsed into a stupor. Death came in "diverse ways" for each of the specimens, but far sooner than normal. Dr. Shaw concluded in triumph, *Death is but the systematic disengagement of the sentient being, on the cellular level*.

For it seemed that the creatures, trapped in isolation, were thus trapped in their own beings, & "smothered" of boredom; their vital spirits, a kind of living electricity, ceased by degrees to flow. With a pounding heart I read this monograph several times, forced to admire the scientific rigor of its argument; yet, finally, the monograph (which has become worm-eaten in the humidity of the Light-House) slipped from my fingers to the floor.

"Shaw's miscalculation is, his 'boy' is hardly an average speci-men of *Homo sapiens*." So gleefully I laughed, Mercury came bound-ing into the Light-House panting & barking & fixing me with an expression of hope: do I laugh because I am unhappy? Ah, *why?*

25–29 December 1848. Lost days, & thus lost entries in this Diary. I know not why.

1 January 1849. It is the New Year & yet: all that is "new" on the Light-House is the degree of my anger at the mutinous terrier.

Calling him through the afternoon, & now it is dusk. I will begin my evening meal alone, my sole companion the murky text *Das Spinne* . . . tho' I am having difficulty concentrating, my eye-lids swollen with fatigue, or with fleabites; my numbed fingers unable to grip the damned pen. I have lost "sight" of myself since an accident of the other morning when my shaving mirror, the sole mirror in the Light-House, slipped from my lathered fingers to shatter stupidly on the stone floor. "Mercury! Come here, I command you!"—& there is no response, but a jeering of the seabirds, & a drunken murmurous laughter of waves.

Mercury was so named by V., who brought him into our household as a foundling, very small & near death by starvation. Originally he was V.'s dog exclusively; then he came to be beloved by me, as well; tho' I am not easy with animals, & distrust the fanatic "loyalty" of canines, that looks to me like the toothy grin of hypocrisy. But Mercury was special, I believe: a most "corky" (that is, alert & lively) fox terrier; not purebred but boasting a well-shaped head, chest & legs; the agility & intelligence common to the breed; a zeal for digging, rooting, & seeking out burrows in which prey may be hiding; & much nervous energy. Named "Mercury" for his antic ways by V., from puppyhood he has been unusually affectionate; as stunned by V.'s death as I have been, & sick with grief. Tho' lately, embarked upon our South Pacific adventure, Mercury would appear to be making a recovery.

His coat is the usual terrier mixture of colors: curly white fur splotched with shades of fair brown, dark brown, & red; this fur has become shamefully coarsened & matted of late, for I have not had time to groom Mercury as he requires, as often I have not had time to groom myself. (It is strange how little time there is for such tasks, when time seems to yawn before us, vast as the great sea in which we might drown.)

I concede, perhaps I am partly to blame: for Mercury has had little appetite for the dry, dun-colored biscuits, sometimes crawling with grubs, which I provide him. It had not occurred to me to bring a different sort of food, meat in tins; & perhaps there would not have been space for such. My diet is purely vegetarian—tinned & dried fruits, vegetables, & such grain products as biscuits & rice cakes, & bottled springwater, assured by Dr. Shaw to be "copiously rich" in nutrients. My asceticism, as it was V.'s, has broadened to include an aversion to flesh of all types, including fish & seafood, of all organisms most repulsive to me. & yet, I understand that a terrier is a very different sort of creature, born to hunt; & it is pathetic, from the evidence of his muzzle & increasingly fetid breath, that Mercury has resorted to eating the flesh of dead things, as I have tried to forbid him to do, fearing he will be poisoned.

"Mercury! Come, it is suppertime. *I implore you.*" & yet no terrier, only just the sickly twilight & sloshing of waves, & a dread sound beneath as of the tearing of flesh, gristle & bone & mastication & obscene noises both guttural & ecstatic, *I am loath to interpret.*

18 January 1849. My birthday eve. Yet, I have forgotten my age!

19 January 1849. Today's surprise: an investigation of weevils in my supply of rice cakes I tried to pick out with my fingers; then gave up, overcome by nausea & vomiting.

23 January 1849. Today I discovered that the rocky firmament upon which the Light-House is built is ovoid, in the way of a misshapen egg. It is smaller than I had originally believed, less than ninety feet in diameter; as the Light-House appears to be a taller structure, each evening requiring greater strength & breadth to climb, to light the lantern in discharge of my duties as Keeper of the Light. (On misty nights, I might wonder if the lantern's flame penetrates such gloom; & to what avail my effort. For I see nothing, & hear nothing, that might be designated as "human"; & have come to wonder at the futility of my enterprise.)

Also, the Light-House descends more deeply into the chalky interior of the earth than I had believed. Almost, one might fancy that the hollow at the bottom is a species of burrow. (Most repugnant to consider: for what would dwell in such a burrow, descending far below the waterline? Mercury has whined & whimpered, when I urged him to explore this hellish space, & so convulsed beneath my hands, I laughed & released him.)

1 February 1849. This dusk, I did not climb the damnable stairs, & I did not light the damnable wick. Why?

I had sighted a flotilla of Spanish galleons. Whether mist ships, or visions stimulated by my swollen eyelids, or actual ships, I do not know & *I do not care.* These bold ships were sailing toward the Strait of Magellan, & beyond; & a low cunning came to me (yet "patriotic"!—let the Diary duly record) that I would not light the lantern to guide the Spanish enemy but would allow them to make their own way through treacherous waters. "Let the Captain pray to his Popish god, to guide him to the Strait."

4 February 1849. Heat. Torpor. Fetid exhaled breath of creation. Tho' it is but February, & more extreme temperatures to come in March & April.

An altercation with Mercury I fear has alienated him from me. & yet, I had no choice, for he had misbehaved, venturing into the Charnel House & feeding there, & reveling in filth, & daring then to return to me, his master, with a bloodied muzzle, & teeth sticky with torn guts, & the once silky coat V. had brushed, matted in blood & unspeakable filth. "Dog! You disgust me." As I raised my fist to strike, he cowered only more slightly, the pupils of his bloodshot eyes narrowed to slits; this time, I did not restrain my blow, but struck the bony head; nor did I restrain myself from kicking the cur in his skinny withers; when his hackles rose against me, & his stained teeth were bared in snarl, I reached for my driftwood cudgel, & smote the beast over the head so decisively, he fell at once to the ground, & lay whimpering & twitching. "So, you see who is the master, eh? Not a debased specimen of *Canis familiaris,* but an exemplary specimen of *Homo sapiens.*"

For it is a matter of species, I begin to see. Plotinus had not the slightest idea, nor even Aristotle; & not even Gotthelf, tho' living into this, the century of Darwin.

17 February 1849. & now, Mercury has died. I have covered the pitiful remains with rocks, to discourage scavengers.

20 February 1849. Life is stuporous, in the heat haze. I cannot grieve for my lost companion; by day I am too exhausted & by night I am too bestirred by rage. My Diary entries I make by lamplight, in a hand so shaky, you would believe the earth shook beneath me. For in a dream it came to me, all of Homo sapiens has perished in a fiery debacle, with a single exception: the Keeper of the Light-House at Viña del Mar.

1 March 1849. Cyclophagus, I have named it. A most original & striking creature, that would have astonished Homer, as my Gothic forebears to a man. Initially, I did not comprehend that *Cyclophagus* was an amphibian, & have now discovered that this species dwells, by day at least, in watery burrows at the edge of the pebbled beach: to emerge, in the way of the Trojan invaders, by nightfall, & clamber about devouring what flesh its claws, snout, & tearing teeth can locate. & in this way, Mercury died.

Primarily, *Cyclophagus* is yet another scavenger; tho' the larger specimens, clearly males, & magnificent tyrants of the beach they are, reaching the size of a wild boar, will attack & devour—living, & shrieking!—such creatures as very large spider crabs (themselves a terror to contemplate) & a great-headed fish, or reptile, with astonishing phosphorescent scales, I have named *Hydrocephalagus*, & the usual roosting seabirds, gulls, & hawks, lapsed into unwary sleep amongst the boulders; &, as it happened the other night, poor Mercury, who in a terrier bloodlust had unwisely blundered into the domain of one of these nightmare beasts. I can scarcely record it in this Diary—I had once hoped to express only the loftiest sentiments of humankind—how, wakened from sleep, I heard my companion's piteous cries, for it seemed to me that he cried "Master! Master!" & that my beloved V. cried with him, that I might save him. & so, casting aside my disgust for the Charnel House, I stumbled to Mercury's side, as the doomed fox terrier struggled frantically for his life, trapped in the masticating jaws of a *Cyclophagus* male intent upon devouring him alive. Desperate, I struck at the monstrous predator with rocks, & tugged at Mercury, shouting & crying, until at last I managed to "free" Mercury of those terrible serrated teeth—

ah, too late! For by now the poor creature was part dismembered, copiously bleeding & whimpering as with a final convulsion he died in my arms. . . .

I cannot write more of this. I am sickened, I am overcome with disgust. The shadowy regions of Usher are no more; *Cyclophagus* has invaded. Not the Gothic spider fancies of Jeremias Gotthelf himself could withstand such hellish creatures! In a nightmare vision my beloved V. came to chastise me, that I have abandoned our "firstborn" to such a fate. My astonished eyes saw V. as I had not seen her since our wedding day, when she was but fourteen years old, ethereal & virginal as the driven snow; & I heard her weeping voice as I had never heard it in life, in this curse:

"I shall not see you again, husband. Neither in this world nor in Hades."

Unnumbered Day 1849. (?) Damn! to take up this pen & attempt inky scratches of parchment paper! & the pen falls from my talon fingers, & much of my ink supply has dried up that my patron (whose name I have misplaced tho' I hear his jeering voice *My boy! my boy!* in the gulls' shrieks & see his damned face glaring at me, from out the clouds). As my precious "library" of books et cetera is worm- & weevil-riddled, & unreadable; & my tinned foods, contaminated by maggots. How all of Philadelphia might shudder at me now, beholding such a vision: "Who is that? *That* savage?"— recoiling in horror & then with great peals of laughter including even the ladies. ECCO HOMO!

Unnumbered Day 1849. (?) I must remember, Philadelphia has perished. & all of humankind. & "only I have escaped, to tell thee."

Unnumbered Day. The perplexity of stairs winding & twisting above my head, I have ceased to climb. Vaguely I recall a "lantern"—a "light." & vaguely, a Keeper of the Light. If Mercury were here, we would laugh together at such folly. For all that matters is feeding,

& feeding well, that this storm of mouths be kept at bay, from devouring *me*.

Unnumbered Day. In despair & disgust I have thrown the last of the contaminated tins into the sea. I have drunk the last of the tepid springwater in which, as I discerned with naked eye, translucent, tissuelike creatures swam & cavorted. So very hungry, my hunger cannot be quenched. & yet, it has only begun. The heat of the summer has only begun.

Unnumbered Day. Not quickly but yes, I have learned: where Mercury blundered, digging into the watery burrows of *Cyclophagus* before the tide fully retreated, impatient to feed on the succulent young that cling whimpering & mewing to the teats of the female *Cyclophagus*, I know to wait & bide my time amidst the rocks.

So strangely, the stench has faded. By night when I emerge from my burrow.

Where initially I shielded my eyes from my "prey"—even as my jaws ravenously devoured—now I have no time for such niceties, as the bolder of the sea hawks might swoop upon me & take advantage of my distraction. No more! I am quite shameless now, as my hunger mounts. Even temporarily sated I lie amongst the bones & gristle of my repast, in the stifling heat haze of Viña del Mar, & perversely dream of yet more feeding; for I have become, in this infernal place, a coil of gust with teeth at one end, & an anus for excretion at the other. If I am not dazed with hunger, I will take time to skin/defeather/declaw/gut/debone/cook over a fire prepared of driftwood, before consuming: more often, I have not time for such, for my hunger is too urgent & I must feed as the others feed, tearing flesh from bone with my teeth. Ah, I have no mystery for the flailing protestations & shrieks of the doomed:

—every species of seabird including even the smaller of the yellow-nosed albatross, that fly unwarily near my hiding place among the boulders, to be plucked out of the air by my talons

—great jellyfish, sea turtles, & octopi, whose flesh is leathery, & must be masticated for long minutes

—*Hydrocephalagus* young (delicate as quail, while the meat of the mature is stringy & provokes diarrhea)

—*Cyclophagus* young (of which I am particularly fond, an exquisite subtlety of taste like sea scallops)

—every species of egg (like all predators, I am thrilled by the prospect of an egg, that cannot escape from one's grasping claws, & offers not a twitch of resistance; awash with nutrients to be sucked through the skull—ah! I mean to say the shell)

A rueful fact, not to be shared with V., or the habitués of my old Philadelphia haunts, that I, descendant of a noble clan of the Teutonic race, must share his kingdom with any number of lowly animal, bird, & insect species! Of these, only *Cyclophagus* is a worthy rival, the most fascinating as it is the most developed & intelligent of the species, tho' far inferior to *Homo sapiens*. I have found it a most curious amphibian, ingeniously equipped with both gills & nostrils, as with fins & legs; no less ungainly in water as on land, yet it moves with startling agility when it wishes, & even the females are very strong. Its head is large as a man's, & its snout pointed, with rows of sharklike teeth; its upright, translucent ears humanoid; its tail of moderate length, to be picked up like a dog's, or to trail off at half-mast, defiled with filth. Its most striking feature is its single eye—thus, I have named it *Cyclophagus*!—which emerges out of its forehead, twice the size of a human eye, & with the liquid expressiveness of a human eye. The novelty of this organ is its capacity to turn rapidly from side to side, & to protrude from the bony ridge of the face when required. The *Cyclophagus* is covered in a velvety hide, wonderfully soft to stroke; it is of a purplish-silver hue that rapidly darkens after death. When cooked over a fire, the flesh of the *Cyclophagus* is uncommonly tender, as I have noted; tho' in the more mature males, there is a bloody-gamey undertaste repellent initially, but by degrees quite intriguing.

To think of *Cyclophagus* is to feel, ah!—the most powerful &

perverse yearning. I am moved to let drop this tiresome pen, & prowl in the shallows off the pebbly beach, tho' it is not yet dusk. Lately I have learned to go on all fours, that my jaws skim the frolicsome surf, & we shall see what swims to greet me.

Unnumbered Day. La Medusa. Jellyfish while living, the many transparent tendrils, so faintly red as to suggest the exposed network of veins, of a human being, offer quite a sting! dead, the tendrils are fibrous & oddly delicious, like spaghetti & to be devoured with a chewy, snaky-briny green like seaweed *Vurrgh*: a species of mammalian lizard of about three feet in length with short, poignant limbs & a feline tail, deeply creased skin, like fabric much folded coarse whiskers springing from the muzzle of the female an expression in repose both translucent & contemplative in the way of Socrates   these creatures I have named *Vurrghs* for in communicating with one another they emit a sequence of low musical grunts: "Vurrgh-Vurrgh-Vurrgh" in their death agonies they shriek like human females, sopranos whose voices have gone sharp the meat of the *Vurrgh* is chewy & sensually arousing like the meat of oysters their golden eggs slimy & gleaming By chance I discovered that the *Vurrgh* female lays her eggs in wet sand & offal, at the north side of the island the *Vurrgh* male then seems to saunter by, as if by chance (yet, in cunning nature, can there be *chance?*) & fertilizes these eggs through a tubular sex organ, sadly comical to observe

yet effective, & in nature that is all that matters the *Vurrgh* male then agitatedly gathers the eggs into a sac attached to his belly, like that of the Australian kangaroo it is the *Vurrgh* male that nourishes the eggs until they hatch into a slithering multiplicity of *Vurrgh* young slick & very pale, the females speckled, measuring about four inches at birth, delicious if devoured raw

Cyclophagus is my prime rival here, for the cunning creature employs its singular eye to see in the dark   & its snouted nose is far more sensitive than my "Roman" nose *Cyclophagus* has an insatiable appetite for *Vurrgh* young & would seem almost to be cultivating colonies of *Vurrgh* in the shallow waters just offshore very like *Homo sapiens* might do

These discoveries I am making, I might report to the Society of Naturalists except all that is vanished in a fiery apocalypse, that effete civilization!

Succubus: a sea delicacy a giant clam I would classify it often found spilling from its opalescent shell amid the rocks as a lady's bosom from a whalebone corset pink-fleshed boneless creature that is purely tissue & faceless yet on its quivering surface you may detect the traces of a very faintly humanoid face *Succubus* I have designated this clam for the way in which, forced into the mouth, it begins to pulse most lewdly in agitation for its life its protestations are uncommonly arousing its sweet flesh so dense, a single *Succubus* can require an hour's hearty mastication & quite sates the appetite for hours afterward & again, the damnable *Cyclophagus* is my rival for *Succubus* with this unfair advantage: *Cyclophagus* can swim in the sea with its serrated teeth bared in its mouth agape & trusting to brainless instinct as *Homo sapiens* has not (yet) mastered!

Hela I have named her my darling

Hela who has come under my protection Hela of the luminous eye Hela my soul mate in this infernal region ah, unexpected!

Hela, named for that fabled Helen of Troy for whom a thousand ships were launched & the Trojan War waged & so many valiant heroes lost to Hades & yet, what glory in such deaths, for BEAUTY! My Hela quivers with gratitude in my embrace never has she seen an individual of my species before! a shock to her, & a revelation my vow to her is eternal my love unquestioning having fled breathless & whimpering to me, a virginal *Cyclophagus* female pursued by an aroused *Cyclophagus* male out of the frothy surf of the pebbled beach as at twilight I prowled restless & alert, hunched over & with my cudgel at the ready Hela emerging as Venus from the sea to be rescued in my arms, from a most licentious & repulsive brute so large, he appeared to be a mutant

Cyclophagus rearing on stubby hind legs in imitation of man terrible teeth flashing as if he would tear out my throat with his teeth ah! could he but catch me! as he *could not* & in triumph I bore my Hela away, that none of her brute kind might claim her ever again!

This has been some time ago in the old way of reckoning

I am never certain what "time" it might "be" I have forgotten why these pages have seemed important There is "month" there is "year" it is still very hot, for the sun has stalled overhead

How terrified my darling was, when invaders came noisily ashore to the Light-House of my "kind" it was clear! in a small rowboat & the mother ship anchored some distance away calling for the Keeper of the Light & finding no human inhabitant, searching amidst my abandoned things my former bed & thwarted in their search, in bafflement departed in our snug burrow we were safe from all detection & in this chalky bedchamber Hela has given birth eight small hairless & mewing babies whose eyes have not yet opened sucking fiercely at her velvety teats Tho' these young are but single-eyed like their mother (& that eye so luminous, I swoon to gaze into its depths) yet each of the young is unmistakably imprinted with its father's patrician brow my nose that has been called "noble" in its Roman cast the babies weigh perhaps two pounds, & fit wonderfully in the palm of my uplifted hand Ah, a doting father holding them aloft! into the light where it falls upon the upper shafts of the burrow (when the dear ones are sated from sucking, that is! for otherwise they mew shrilly & their baby teeth flash with infant ire) I like it that their tails are less pronounced than the tails of most newborn *Cyclophagi* their snouts far less pointed the "Roman" nose will develop, I believe the nostrils more decisively than the gills for Hela cares not for the old, amphibian life & her young will not know of it, we have vowed these precious young will thrive in the sanctuary of the Light-House this structure erected for our habitation, & none other for there can be no purpose to it otherwise it is our Kingdom by the Sea our nest here, & none will invade for I have fortified it, & I am very strong Yet gentle with my beloved: for her skin is so very soft, its purplish-silver hue that of the most delicate petals of the calla lily her soulful eye so intense, in devotion to her hunter-husband together we will dwell in this place & we shall be the progenitors of a bold & shining new race of Immortals

Hela my darling forevermore

"The Fabled Light-House at Viña del Mar" has been suggested by the one-page manuscript fragment "The Light-House," found among the papers of Edgar Allan Poe after his death in 1849.

MR. AICKMAN'S AIR RIFLE

by PETER STRAUB

I

ON THE TWENTY-FIRST, or "Concierge," floor of New York's Governor General Hospital, located just south of midtown on Seventh Avenue, a glow of recessed lighting and a rank of framed, eye-level graphics (Twombly, Shapiro, Marden, Warhol) escort visitors from a brace of express elevators to the reassuring spectacle of a graceful cherry-wood desk occupied by a red-jacketed gatekeeper named Mr. Singh. Like a hand cupped beneath a waiting elbow, this gentleman's inquiring yet deferential appraisal and his stupendous display of fresh flowers nudge the visitor over hushed beige carpeting and into the wood-paneled realm of Floor 21 itself.

First to appear is the nursing station, where in a flattering chiaroscuro efficient women occupy themselves with charts, telephones, and the ever-changing patterns traversing their computer monitors; directly ahead lies the first of the great, half-open doors of the residents' rooms or suites, each with its brass numeral and discreet nameplate. The great hallway extends some sixty yards, passing seven named and numbered doors on its way to a bright window with an uptown view. To the left, the hallway passes the front of the nurses' station and the four doors directly opposite, then divides. The shorter portion continues on to a large, south-facing window with a good prospect of the Hudson River; the longer defines the southern boundary of the station. Hung with an Elizabeth Murray lithograph and a Robert Mapplethorpe calla lily, an ocher wall then rises up to guide the hallway over another carpeted fifty feet to a long, narrow room. The small brass sign beside its wide, pebble-glass doors reads salon.

The Salon is not a salon but a lounge, and a rather makeshift lounge at that. At one end sits a good-sized television set; at the other, a green fabric sofa with two matching chairs. Midpoint in the room, which was intended for the comfort of stricken relatives and other visitors but has always been patronized chiefly by Floor 21's more ambulatory patients, stands a white-draped table equipped with coffee dispensers, stacks of cups and saucers, and cut-glass containers for sugar and artificial sweeteners. In the hours from four to six in the afternoon, platters laden with pastries and chocolates from the neighborhood's gourmet specialty shops appear, as if delivered by unseen hands, upon the table.

On an afternoon early in April, when during the hours in question the long window behind the table of goodies registered swift, unpredictable alternations of light and dark, the male patients who constituted four-fifths of the residents of Floor 21, all of them recent victims of atrial fibrillation or atrial flutter, which is to say sufferers from that dire annoyance in the life of a busy American male, nonfatal heart failure, the youngest a man of fifty-eight and the most senior twenty-two years older, found themselves once again partaking of the cream cakes and petit fours and reminding themselves that they had not, after all, undergone heart attacks. Their recent adventures had aroused in them an indulgent fatalism. After all, should the worst happen, which of course it would not, they were already at the epicenter of a swarm of cardiologists!

To varying degrees, these were men of accomplishment and achievement in their common profession, that of letters.

In descending order of age, the four men enjoying the amenities of the Salon were Max Baccarat, the much-respected former president of Gladstone Books, the acquisition of which by a German conglomerate had lately precipitated his retirement; Anthony Flax, a self-described "critic" who had spent the past twenty years as a full-time book reviewer for a variety of periodicals and journals, a leisurely occupation he could afford due to his having been the husband, now for three years the widower, of a sugar-substitute heiress; William Messinger, a writer whose lengthy backlist of horror/mystery/suspense novels had been kept continuously in print for twenty-five years by the biannual appearance of yet another new astonishment; and Charles Chipp Traynor, child of a wealthy New England family, Harvard graduate, self-declared veteran of the Vietnam conflict, and author of four nonfiction books, also (alas) a notorious plagiarist.

The connections between these four men, no less complex and multilayered than one would gather from their professional circumstances, had inspired some initial awkwardness on their first few encounters in the Salon, but a shared desire for the treats on offer had encouraged these gentlemen to reach the accommodation displayed on the afternoon in question. By silent agreement, Max Baccarat arrived first, a few minutes after opening, to avail himself of the greatest possible range of selection and the most comfortable seating position, which was on that end side of the sofa nearest the pebble-glass doors, where the cushion was a touch more yielding than its mate. Once the great publisher had installed himself to his satisfaction, Bill Messinger and Tony Flax happened in to browse over the day's bounty before seating themselves at a comfortable distance from each other. Invariably the last to arrive, Traynor edged around the door sometime around 4:15, his manner suggesting that he had wandered in by accident, probably in search of another room altogether. The loose, patterned hospital gown he wore fastened at neck and backside added to his air of inoffensiveness, and his round glasses and stooped shoulders gave him a generic resemblance to a creature from *The Wind in the Willows*.

Of the four, the plagiarist alone had surrendered to the hospital's tacit wishes concerning patients' in-house mode of dress. Over silk pajamas of a glaring, Greek-village white, Max Baccarat wore a dark, dashing navy-blue dressing gown, reputedly a Christmas present from Graham Greene, which fell nearly to the tops of his velvet fox-head slippers. Over his own pajamas, of fine-combed baby-blue cotton instead of white silk, Tony Flax had buttoned a lightweight tan trench coat, complete with epaulettes and grenade rings. Wth his extra chins and florid complexion, it made him look like a correspondent from a war conducted well within striking distance of hotel bars. Bill Messinger had taken one look at the flimsy shift offered him by the hospital staff and decided to stick, for as long as he could get away with it, to the pin-striped Armani suit and black loafers he had worn into the ER. His favorite men's stores delivered fresh shirts, socks, and underwear.

When Messinger's early, less successful books had been published by Max's firm, Tony Flax had given him consistently positive reviews; after Bill's defection to a better house and larger advances for more ambitious books, Tony's increasingly bored and dismissive reviews accused him of hubris, then ceased altogether. Messinger's last three novels had not been reviewed anywhere in the *Times*, an insult he attributed to Tony's malign influence over its current editors. Likewise, Max had published Chippie Traynor's first two anecdotal histories of World War I, the second of which had been considered for a Pulitzer prize, then lost him to a more prominent publisher whose shrewd publicists had placed him on NPR, the *Today* show, and—after the film deal for his third book—*Charlie Rose*. Bill had given blurbs to Traynor's first two books, and Tony Flax had hailed him as a great vernacular historian. Then, two decades later, a stunned graduate student in Texas discovered lengthy, painstakingly altered parallels between Traynor's books and the contents of several Ph.D. dissertations containing oral histories taken in the 1930s. Beyond that, the student found that perhaps a third of the personal histories had been invented, simply made up, like fiction.

Within days, the graduate student had detonated Chippie's reputation. One week after the detonation, his university placed him "on leave," a status assumed to be permanent. He had vanished into his family's Lincoln Log compound in Maine, not to be seen or heard from until the moment when Bill Messinger and Tony Flax, who had left open the Salon's doors the better to avoid conversation, had witnessed his sorry, supine figure being wheeled past. Max Baccarat was immediately informed of the scoundrel's arrival, and before the end of the day the legendary dressing gown, the trench coat, and the pin-striped suit had overcome their mutual resentments to form an alliance against the disgraced newcomer. There was nothing, they found, like a common enemy to smooth over complicated, even difficult relationships.

Chippie Traynor had not found his way to the lounge until the following day, and he had been accompanied by a tremulous elderly woman who with equal plausibility could have passed for either his mother or his wife. Sidling around the door at 4:15, he had taken in the trio watching him from the green sofa and chairs, blinked in disbelief and recognition, ducked his head even closer to his chest, and permitted his companion to lead him to a chair located a few feet from the television set. It was clear that he was struggling with the impulse to scuttle out of the room, never to reappear. Once deposited in the chair, he tilted his head upward and whispered a few words into the woman's ear. She moved toward the pastries, and at last he eyed his former compatriots.

"Well, well," he said. "Max, Tony, and Bill. What are you in for, anyway? Me, I passed out on the street in Boothbay Harbor and had to be airlifted in. Medevaced, like back in the day."

"These days, a lot of things must remind you of Vietnam, Chippie," Max said. "We're heart failure. You?"

"Atrial fib. Shortness of breath. Weaker than a baby. Fell down right in the street, boom. As soon as I get regulated, I'm supposed to have some sort of echo scan."

"Heart failure, all right," Max said. "Go ahead, have a cream cake. You're among friends."

"Somehow, I doubt that," Traynor said. He was breathing hard, and he gulped air as he waved the old woman farther down the table, toward the chocolate slabs and puffs. He watched carefully as she selected a number of the little cakes. "Don't forget the decaf, will you, sweetie?"

The others waited for him to introduce his companion, but he sat in silence as she placed a plate of cakes and a cup of coffee on a stand next to the television set, then faded backward into a chair that seemed to have materialized, just for her, from the ether. Traynor lifted a forkful of shiny brown goo to his mouth, sucked it off the fork, and gulped coffee. Because of his long, thick nose and recessed chin, first the fork, then the cup seemed to disappear into the lower half of his face. He twisted his head in the general direction of his companion and said, "Health food, yum, yum."

She smiled vaguely at the ceiling. Traynor turned back to face the other three men, who were staring open-eyed, as if at a performance of some kind.

"Thanks for all the cards and letters, guys. I loved getting your phone calls, too. Really meant a lot to me. Oh, sorry, I'm not being very polite, am I?"

"There's no need to be sarcastic," Max said.

"I suppose not. We were never friends, were we?"

"You were looking for a publisher, not a friend," Max said. "And we did quite well together, or so I thought, before you decided you needed greener pastures. Bill did the same thing to me, come to think of it. Of course, Bill actually wrote the books that came out under his name. For a publisher, that's quite a significant difference." (Several descendants of the Ph.D.s from whom Traynor had stolen material had initiated suits against his publishing houses, Gladstone Books among them.)

"Do we have to talk about this?" asked Tony Flax. He rammed his hands into the pockets of his trench coat and glanced from side to side. "Ancient history, hmmm?"

"You're just embarrassed by the reviews you gave him," Bill said. "But everybody did the same thing, including me. What did I say about *The Middle of the Trenches*? 'The . . .' The what? 'The most truthful, in a way the most visionary book ever written about trench warfare.'"

"Jesus, you remember your *blurbs*?" Tony asked. He laughed and tried to draw the others in.

"I remember everything," said Bill Messinger. "Curse of being a novelist—great memory, lousy sense of direction."

"You always remembered how to get to the bank," Tony said.

"Lucky me, I didn't have to marry it," Bill said.

"Are you accusing me of marrying for money?" Tony said, defending himself by the usual tactic of pretending that what was commonly accepted was altogether unthinkable. "Not that I have any reason to defend myself against you, Messinger. As that famous memory of yours should recall, I was one of the first people to support your work."

From nowhere, a reedy English female voice said, "I did enjoy reading your reviews of Mr. Messinger's early novels, Mr. Flax. I'm sure that's why I went round to our little bookshop and purchased them. They weren't at all my usual sort of *thing*, you know, but you made them sound . . . I think the word would be *imperative*."

Max, Tony, and Bill peered past Charles Chipp Traynor to get a good look at his companion. For the first time, they took in that she was wearing a long, loose collection of elements that suggested feminine literary garb of the nineteen twenties: a hazy, rather shimmery woolen cardigan over a white, high-buttoned blouse, pearls, an ankle-length heather skirt, and low-heeled black shoes with laces. Her long, sensitive nose pointed up, exposing the clean line of her jaw; her lips twitched in what might have been amusement. Two things struck the men staring at her: that this woman looked a bit familiar, and that in spite of her age and general odd-ness, she would have to be described as beautiful.

"Well, yes," Tony said. "Thank you. I believe I was trying to express something of the sort. They were books . . . well. Bill, you never understood this, I think, but I felt they were books that deserved to be read. For their workmanship, their modesty, what I thought was their actual decency."

"You mean they did what you expected them to do," Bill said.

"Decency is an uncommon literary virtue," said Traynor's companion.

"Thank you, yes," Tony said.

"But not a very interesting one, really," Bill said. "Which prob-ably explains why it isn't all that common."

"I think you are correct, Mr. Messinger, to imply that decency is more valuable in the realm of personal relations. And for the record, I do feel your work since then has undergone a general improvement. Perhaps Mr. Flax's limitations do not permit him to appreciate your progress." She paused. There was a dangerous smile on her face. "Of course, you can hardly be said to have improved to the extent claimed in your latest round of inter-views."

In the moment of silence that followed, Max Baccarat looked from one of his new allies to the other and found them in a state too reflective for commentary. He cleared his throat. "Might we have the honor of an introduction, madam? Chippie seems to have forgotten his manners."

"My name is of no importance," she said, only barely favoring him with the flicker of a glance. "And Mr. Traynor has a thorough knowledge of my feelings on the matter."

"There's two sides to every story," Chippie said. "It may not be grammar, but it's the truth."

"Oh, there are many more than that," said his companion, smiling again.

"Darling, would you help me return to my room?"

Chippie extended an arm, and the Englishwoman floated to her feet, cradled his rootlike fist against the side of her chest, nodded to the gaping men, and gracefully conducted her charge from the room.

"So who the fuck was *that?*" said Max Baccarat.

II

Certain rituals structured the nighttime hours on Floor 21. At 8:30 p.m., blood pressure was taken and evening medications administered by Tess Corrigan, an Irish softie with a saggy gut, an alcoholic, angina-ridden husband, and an understandable tolerance for misbehavior. Tess herself sometimes appeared to be mildly intoxicated. Class resentment caused her to treat Max a touch brusquely, but Tony's trench coat amused her to wheezy laughter. After Bill Messinger had signed two books for her niece, a devoted fan, Tess had allowed him to do anything he cared to, including taking illicit journeys downstairs to the gift shop. "Oh, Mr. Messinger," she had said, "a fella with your gifts, the books you could write about this place." Three hours after Tess's departure, a big, heavily dreadlocked nurse with an island accent surged into the patients' rooms to awaken them for the purpose of distributing tranquilizers and knockout pills. Because she resembled a greatly inflated, ever-simmering Whoopi Goldberg, Max, Tony, and Bill referred to this terrifying and implacable figure as "Molly." (Molly's real name, printed on the ID card attached to a sash used as a waistband, was permanently concealed behind beaded swags and little hanging pouches.) At six in the morning, Molly swept in again, wielding the blood-pressure mechanism like an angry deity maintaining a good grip on a sinner. At the end of her shift, she came wrapped in a strong, dark scent, suggestive of forest fires in underground crypts. The three literary gentlemen found this aroma disturbingly erotic.

On the morning after the appearance within the Salon of Charles Chipp Traynor and his disconcerting muse, Molly raked

Bill with a look of pity and scorn as she trussed his upper arm and strangled it by pumping a rubber bulb. Her crypt-fire odor seemed particularly smoky.

"What?" he asked.

Molly shook her massive head. "Toddle, toddle, toddle, you must believe you're the new postman in this beautiful neighborhood of ours."

Terror seized his gut. "I don't think I know what you're talking about."

Molly chuckled and gave the bulb a final squeeze, causing his arm to go numb from bicep to his fingertips. "Of course not. But you do know that we have no limitations on visiting hours up here in our paradise, don't you?"

"Um," he said.

"Then let me tell you something you do not know, Mr. Postman. Miz LaValley in 21R-12 passed away last night. I do not imagine you ever took it upon yourself to pay the poor woman a social call. And *that*, Mr. Postman, means that you, Mr. Baccarat, Mr. Flax, and our new addition, Mr. Traynor, are now the only patients on Floor 21."

"Ah," he said.

As soon as she left his room, he showered and dressed in the previous day's clothing, eager to get out into the corridor and check on the conditions in 21R-14, Chippie Traynor's room, for it was what he had seen there in the hours between Tess Corrigan's florid departure and Molly Goldberg's first drive-by shooting that had led to his becoming the floor's postman.

It had been just before nine in the evening, and something had urged him to take a final turn around the floor before surrendering himself to the hateful "gown" and turning off his lights. His route took him past the command center, where the Night Visitor, scowling over a desk too small for her, made grim notations on a chart, and down the corridor toward the window looking out toward the Hudson River and the great harbor. Along the way he passed 21R-14, where muffled noises had caused him to look in.

From the corridor, he could see the bottom third of the plagiarist's bed, on which the sheets and blanket appeared to be writhing, or at least shifting about in a conspicuous manner. Messinger noticed a pair of black, lace-up women's shoes on the floor near the bottom of the bed. An untidy heap of clothing lay beside the in-turned shoes. For a few seconds, ripe with shock and envy, he had listened to the soft noises coming from the room. Then he whirled around and rushed toward his allies' chambers.

"Who *is* that dame?" Max Baccarat had asked, essentially repeating the question he had asked earlier that day. "*What* is she? That miserable Traynor, God damn him to hell, may he have a heart attack and die. A woman like that, who cares how old she is?"

Tony Flax had groaned in disbelief and said, "I swear, that woman is either the ghost of Virginia Woolf or her direct descendant. All my life, I had the hots for Virginia Woolf, and now she turns up with that ugly crook, Chippie Traynor? Get out of here, Bill; I have to strategize."

III

At 4:15, the three conspirators pretended not to notice the plagiarist's furtive, animal-like entrance to the Salon. Max Baccarat's silvery hair, cleansed, stroked, clipped, buffed, and shaped during an emergency session with a hair therapist named Mr. Keith, seemed to glow with a virile inner light as he settled into the comfortable part of the sofa and organized his decaf cup and plate of chocolates and little cakes as if preparing soldiers for battle. Tony Flax's rubber chins shone a twice-shaved red, and his glasses sparkled. Beneath the hem of the trench coat, which appeared to have been ironed, colorful argyle socks descended from just below his lumpy knees to what seemed to be a pair of nifty two-tone shoes. Beneath the jacket of his pin-striped suit, Bill Messinger sported a brand-new, high-collared black silk T-shirt delivered by courier that morning from Sixty-fifth and Madison. Thus attired, the longer-term residents of Floor 21 seemed lost as much in self-admiration as in the political discussion under way when at last they allowed themselves to acknowledge Chippie's presence. Max's eye skipped over Traynor and wandered toward the door.

"Will your lady friend be joining us?" he asked. "I thought she made some really very valid points yesterday, and I'd enjoy hearing what she has to say about our situation in Iraq. My two friends here are simpleminded liberals; you can never get anything sensible out of them."

"You wouldn't like what she'd have to say about Iraq," Traynor said. "And neither would they."

"Know her well, do you?" Tony asked.

"You could say that." Traynor's gown slipped as he bent over the table to pump coffee into his cup from the dispenser, and the three other men hastily turned their glances elsewhere.

"Tie that up, Chippie, would you?" Bill asked. "It's like a view of the Euganean Hills."

"Then look somewhere else. I'm getting some coffee, and then I have to pick out a couple of these yum-yums."

"You're alone today, then?" Tony asked.

"Looks like it."

"By the way," Bill said, "you were entirely right to point out that nothing is really as simple as it seems. There *are* more than two sides to every issue. I mean, wasn't that the point of what we were saying about Iraq?"

"To you, maybe," Max said. "You'd accept two sides as long as they were both printed in *The Nation*."

"Anyhow," Bill said, "please tell your friend that the next time she cares to visit this hospital, we'll try to remember what she said about decency."

"What makes you think she's going to come here again?"

"She seemed very fond of you," Tony said.

"The lady mentioned your limitations." Chippie finished assembling his assortment of treats and at last refastened his gaping robe. "I'm surprised you have any interest in seeing her again."

Tony's cheeks turned a deeper red. "All of us have limitations, I'm sure. In fact, I was just remembering . . ."

"Oh?" Chippie lifted his snout and peered through his little lenses. "Were you? What, specifically?"

"Nothing," said Tony. "I shouldn't have said anything. Sorry."

"Did any of you know Mrs. LaValley, the lady in 21R-12?" Bill asked. "She died last night. Apart from us, she was the only other person on the floor."

"I knew Edie LaValley," Chippie said. "In fact, my friend and I dropped in and had a nice little chat with her just before dinnertime last night. I'm glad I had a chance to say good-bye to the old girl."

"Edie LaValley?" Max said. "Hold on. I seem to remember . . ."

"Wait, I do, too," Bill said. "Only . . ."

"I know, she was that girl who worked for Nick Wheadle over at Viking, thirty years ago, back when Wheadle was everybody's golden boy," Tony said. "Stupendous girl. She got married to him and was Edith Wheadle for a while, but after the divorce she went back to her old name. We went out for a couple of months in 1983, '84. What happened to her after that?"

"She spent six years doing research for me," Traynor said. "She wasn't my *only* researcher, because I generally had three of them on the payroll, not to mention a couple of graduate students. Edie was very good at the job, though. Extremely conscientious."

"And knockout, drop-dead gorgeous," Tony said. "At least before she fell into Nick Wheadle's clutches."

"I didn't know you used so many researchers," Max said. "Could that be how you wound up quoting all those . . . ?"

"Deliberately misquoting, I suppose you mean," Chippie said. "But the answer is no." A fat, sugar-coated square of sponge cake disappeared beneath his nose.

"But Edie Wheadle," Max said in a reflective voice. "By God, I think I—"

"Think nothing of it," Traynor said. "That's what she did."

"Edie must have looked very different toward the end," said

Tony. He sounded almost hopeful. "Twenty years, illness, all of that."

"My friend and I thought she looked much the same." Chippie's mild, creaturely face swung toward Tony Flax. "Weren't you about to tell us something?"

Tony flushed again. "No, not really."

"Perhaps an old memory resurfaced. That often happens on a night when someone in the vicinity dies—the death seems to awaken something."

"Edie's death certainly seemed to have awakened you," Bill said. "Didn't you ever hear of closing your door?"

"The nurses waltz right in anyhow, and there are no locks," Traynor said. "Better to be frank about matters, especially on Floor 21. It looks as though Max has something on his mind."

"Yes," Max said. "If Tony doesn't feel like talking, I will. Last night, an old memory of mine resurfaced, as Chippie puts it, and I'd like to get it off my chest, if that's the appropriate term."

"Good man," Traynor said. "Have another of those delicious little yummies and tell us all about it."

"This happened back when I was a little boy," Max said, wiping his lips with a crisp linen handkerchief.

Bill Messinger and Tony Flax seemed to go very still.

"I was raised in Pennsylvania, up in the Susquehanna Valley area. It's strange country, a little wilder and more backward than you'd expect, a little hillbillyish, especially once you get back in the Endless Mountains. My folks had a little store that sold everything under the sun, it seemed to me, and we lived in the building next door, close to the edge of town. Our town was called Manship, not that you can find it on any map. We had a one-room schoolhouse, an Episcopalian church and a Unitarian church, a feed and grain store, a place called the Lunch Counter, a tract house, and a tavern called the Rusty Dusty, where, I'm sad to say, my father spent far too much of his time.

"When he came home loaded, as happened just about every

other night, he was in a foul mood. It was mainly guilt, d'you see, because my mother had been slaving away in the store for hours, plus making dinner, and she was in a rage, which only made him feel worse. All he really wanted to do was to beat himself up, but I was an easy target, so he beat me up instead. Nowadays, we'd call it child abuse, but back then, in a place like Manship, it was just normal parenting, at least for a drunk. I wish I could tell you fellows that everything turned out well, and that my father sobered up, and we reconciled, and I forgave him, but none of that happened. Instead, he got meaner and meaner, and we got poorer and poorer. I learned to hate the old bastard, and I still hated him when a traveling junk wagon ran over him, right there in front of the Rusty Dusty, when I was eleven years old. 1935, the height of the Great Depression. He was lying passed out in the street, and the junkman never saw him.

"Now, I was determined to get out of that godforsaken little town, and out of the Susquehanna Valley and the Endless Mountains, and obviously I did, because here I am today, with an excellent place in the world, if I might pat myself on the back a little bit. What I did was, I managed to keep the store going even while I went to the high school in the next town, and then I got a scholarship to U. Penn., where I waited on tables and tended bar and sent money back to my mother. Two days after I graduated, she died of a heart attack. That was her reward.

"I bought a bus ticket to New York. Even though I was never a great reader, I liked the idea of getting into the book business. Everything that happened after that you could read about in old copies of *Publisher's Weekly*. Maybe one day I'll write a book about it all.

"If I do, I'll never put in what I'm about to tell you now. It slipped my mind completely—the whole thing. You'll realize how bizarre that is after I'm done. I forgot all about it! Until about three this morning, that is, when I woke up too scared to breathe, my heart going *bump, bump*, and the sweat pouring out of me.

Every little bit of this business just came *back* to me, I mean everything, ever goddamned little tiny detail. . . ."

He looked at Bill and Tony. "What? You two guys look like you should be back in the ER."

"Every detail?" Tony said. "It's . . ."

"You woke up then, too?" Bill asked him.

"Are you two knotheads going to let me talk, or do you intend to keep interrupting?"

"I just wanted to ask this one thing, but I changed my mind," Tony said. "Sorry, Max. I shouldn't have said anything. It was a crazy idea. Sorry."

"Was your dad an alcoholic, too?" Bill asked Tony Flax.

Tony squeezed up his face, said, "Aaaah," and waggled one hand in the air. "I don't like the word 'alcoholic.'"

"Yeah," Bill said. "All right."

"I guess the answer is, you're going to keep interrupting."

"No, please, Max, go on," Bill said.

Max frowned at both of them, then gave a dubious glance to Chippie Traynor, who stuffed another tiny cream cake into his maw and smiled around it.

"Fine. I don't know why I want to tell you about this anyhow. It's not like I actually *understand* it, as you'll see, and it's kind of ugly and kind of scary—I guess what amazes me is that I just remembered it all, or that I managed to put it out of my mind for nearly seventy years, one or the other. But you know? It's like, it's real even if it never happened, or even if I dreamed the whole thing."

"This story wouldn't happen to involve a house, would it?" Tony asked.

"Most goddamned stories involve houses," Max said. "Even a lousy book critic ought to know that."

"Tony knows that," Chippie said. "See his ridiculous coat? That's a house. Isn't it, Tony?"

"You know what this is," Tony said. "It's a *trench coat*, a real one. Only from World War II, not World War I. It used to belong to my father. He was a hero in the war."

"As I was about to say," Max said, looking around and continuing only when the other three were paying attention, "when I woke up in the middle of the night I could remember the feel of the old blanket on my bed, the feel of pebbles and earth on my bare feet when I ran to the outhouse, I could remember the way my mother's scrambled eggs tasted. The whole anxious thing I had going on inside me while my mother was making breakfast.

"I was going to go off by myself in the woods. That was all right with my mother. At least it got rid of me for the day. But what she didn't know was that I had decided to steal one of the guns in the case at the back of the store.

"And you know what? She didn't pay any attention to the guns. About half of them belonged to people who swapped them for food because guns were all they had left to barter with. My mother hated the whole idea. And my father was in a fog until he could get to the tavern, and after that he couldn't think straight enough to remember how many guns were supposed to be back in that case. Anyhow, for the past few days, I'd had my eye on an over-under shotgun that used to belong to a farmer called Hakewell, and while my mother wasn't watching I nipped in back and took it out of the case. Then I stuffed my pockets with shells, ten of them. There was something going on way back in the woods, and while I wanted to keep my eye on it, I wanted to be able to protect myself, too, in case anything got out of hand."

Bill Messinger jumped to his feet and for a moment seemed preoccupied with brushing what might have been pastry crumbs off the bottom of his suit jacket. Max Baccarat frowned at him, then glanced down at the skirts of his dressing gown in a brief inspection. Bill continued to brush off imaginary particles of food, slowly turning in a circle as he did so.

"There is something you wish to communicate," Max said. "The odd thing, you know, is that for the moment, you see, I thought communication was in my hands."

Bill stopped fiddling with his jacket and regarded the old publisher with his eyebrows tugged toward the bridge of his nose and his mouth a thin, downturned line. He placed his hands on his hips. "I don't know what you're doing, Max, and I don't know where you're getting this. But I certainly wish you'd stop."

"What are you talking about?"

"He's right, Max," said Tony Flax.

"You jumped-up little fop," Max said, ignoring Tony. "You damned little show pony. What's your problem? You haven't told a good story in the past ten years, so listen to mine, you might learn something."

"You know what you are?" Bill asked him. "Twenty years ago, you used to be a decent second-rate publisher. Unfortunately, it's been all downhill from there. Now you're not even a third-rate publisher, you're a sellout. You took the money and went on the lam. Morally, you don't exist at all. You're a fancy dressing gown. And by the way, Graham Greene didn't give it to you, because Graham Greene wouldn't have given you a glass of water on a hot day."

Both of them were panting a bit and trying not to show it. Like a dog trying to choose between masters, Tony Flax swung his head from one to the other. In the end, he settled on Max Baccarat. "I don't really get it either, you know, but I think you should stop, too."

"Nobody cares what you think," Max told him. "Your brain dropped dead the day you swapped your integrity for a mountain of coffee sweetener."

"You did marry for money, Flax," Bill Messinger said. "Let's try being honest, all right? You sure as hell didn't fall in love with her beautiful face."

"And how about you, Traynor?" Max shouted. "I suppose you think I should stop, too."

"Nobody cares what I think," Chippie said. "I'm the lowest of the low. People despise me."

"First of all," Bill said, "if you want to talk about details, Max, you ought to get them *right*. It wasn't an 'over-under shotgun,' whatever the hell that is; it was a—"

"His name wasn't Hakewell," Tony said. "It was Hackman, like the actor."

"It wasn't Hakewell or Hackman," Bill said. "It started with an A."

"But there was a *house*," Tony said. "You know, I think my father probably was an alcoholic. His personality never changed, though. He was always a mean son of a bitch, drunk or sober."

"Mine, too," said Bill. "Where are you from, anyhow, Tony?"

"A little town in Oregon, called Milton. How about you?"

"Rhinelander, Wisconsin. My dad was the chief of police. I suppose there were lots of woods around Milton."

"We might as well have been in a forest. You?"

"The same."

"I'm from Boston, but we spent the summers in Maine," Chippie said. "You know what Maine is? Eighty percent woods. There are places in Maine, the roads don't even have names."

"There was a *house*," Tony Flax insisted. "Back in the woods, and it didn't belong there. Nobody builds houses in the middle of the woods, miles away from everything, without even a road to use, not even a road without a name."

"This can't be real," Bill said. "I had a house, you had a house, and I bet Max had a house, even though he's so long-winded he hasn't gotten to it yet. I had an air rifle, Max had a shotgun, what did you have?"

"My Dad's .22," Tony said. "Just a little thing—around us, nobody took a .22 all that seriously."

Max was looking seriously disgruntled. "What, we all had the same *dream*?"

"You said it wasn't a dream," said Chippie Traynor. "You said it was a memory."

"It felt like a memory, all right," Tony said. "Just the way Max described it—the way the ground felt under my feet, the smell of my mother's cooking."

"I wish your lady friend were here now, Traynor," Max said. "She'd be able to explain what's going on, wouldn't she?"

"I have a number of lady friends," Chippie said, calmly stuffing a little glazed cake into his mouth.

"All right, Max," Bill said. "Let's explore this. You come across this big house, right? And there's someone in it?"

"Eventually, there is," Max said, and Tony Flax nodded.

"Right. And you can't even tell what age he is—or even if it *is* a he, right?"

"It was hiding in the back of a room," Tony says. "When I thought it was a girl, it really scared me. I didn't want it to be a girl."

"I didn't, either," Max said. "Oh—imagine how that would feel, a girl hiding in the shadows at the back of a room."

"Only this never happened," Bill said. "If we all seem to remember this bizarre story, then none of us is really remembering it."

"Okay, but it was a boy," Tony said. "And he got older."

"Right there in that house," said Max. "I thought it was like watching my damnable father grow up right in front of my eyes. In what, six weeks?"

"About that," Tony said.

"And him in there all alone," said Bill. "Without so much as a stick of furniture. I thought that was one of the things that made it so frightening."

"Scared the shit out of me," Tony said. "When my dad came back from the war, sometimes he put on his uniform and tied us to the chairs. Tied us to the chairs!"

"I didn't think it was really going to injure him," Bill said.

"I didn't even think I'd hit him," Tony said.

"I knew damn well I'd hit him," Max said. "I wanted to blow his head off. But my dad lived another three years, and then the junkman finally ran him over."

"Max," Tony said, "you mentioned there was a tract house in Manship. What's a tract house?"

"It was where they printed the religious tracts, you ignoramus. You could go in there and pick them up for free. All of this was like child abuse, I'm telling you. Spare-the-rod stuff."

"It was like his eye exploded," Bill said. Absentmindedly, he took one of the untouched pastries from Max's plate and bit into it.

Max stared at him.

"They didn't change the goodies this morning," Bill said. "This thing is a little stale."

"I prefer my pastries stale," said Chippie Traynor.

"I prefer to keep mine for myself, and not have them lifted off my plate," said Max, sounding as though something were caught in his throat.

"The bullet went straight through the left lens of his glasses and right into his head," said Tony. "And when he raised his head, his eye was full of blood."

"Would you look out that window?" Max said in a loud voice.

Bill Messinger and Tony Flax turned to the window, saw nothing special—perhaps a bit more haze in the air than they expected—and looked back at the old publisher.

"Sorry," Max said. He passed a trembling hand over his face. "I think I'll go back to my room."

IV

"Nobody visits me," Bill Messinger said to Tess Corrigan. She was taking his blood pressure, and appeared to be having a little trouble getting accurate numbers. "I don't even really remember how long I've been here, but I haven't had a single visitor."

"Haven't you now?" Tess squinted at the blood-pressure tube, sighed, and once again pumped the ball and tightened the band around his arm. Her breath contained a pure, razor-sharp whiff of alcohol.

"It makes me wonder, do I have any friends?"

Toss grunted with satisfaction and scribbled numbers on his chart. "Writers lead lonely lives," she told him. "Most of them aren't fit for human company, anyhow." She patted his wrist. "You're a lovely specimen, though."

"Tess, how long have I been here?"

"Oh, it was only a little while ago," she said. "And I believe it was raining at the time."

After she left, Bill watched television for a little while, but television, a frequent and dependable companion in his earlier life, seemed to have become intolerably stupid. He turned it off and for a time flipped through the pages of the latest book by a highly regarded contemporary novelist several decades younger than himself. He had bought the book before going into the hospital, thinking that during his stay he would have enough uninterrupted time to dig into the experience so many others had described as rich, complex, and marvelously nuanced, but he was having problems getting through it. The book bored him. The people were loathsome and the style was gelid. He kept wishing he had brought along some uncomplicated and professional trash he could use as a palate cleanser. By 10:00, he was asleep.

At 11:30, a figure wrapped in cold air appeared in his room, and he woke up as she approached. The woman coming nearer in the darkness must have been Molly, the Jamaican nurse who always charged in at this hour, but she did not give off Molly's arousing scent of fires in underground crypts. She smelled of damp weeds and muddy riverbanks. Bill did not want this version of Molly to get any closer to him than the end of his bed, and with his heart beating so violently that he could feel the limping rhythm of his heart, he commanded her to stop. She instantly obeyed.

He pushed the button to raise the head of his bed and tried to make her out as his body folded upright. The river-smell had intensified, and cold air streamed toward him. He had no desire at all to turn on any of the three lights at his disposal. Dimly, he could make out a thin, tallish figure with dead hair plastered to her face, wearing what seemed to be a long cardigan sweater, soaked through and (he thought) dripping onto the floor. In this figure's hands was a fat, unjacketed book stained dark by her wet fingers.

"I don't want you here," he said. "And I don't want to read that book, either. I've already read everything you ever wrote, but that was a long time ago."

The drenched figure glided forward and deposited the book between his feet. Terrified that he might recognize her face, Bill clamped his eyes shut and kept them shut until the odors of river water and mud had vanished from the air.

When Molly burst into the room to gather the new day's information the next morning, Bill Messinger realized that his night's visitation could have occurred only in a dream. Here was the well-known, predictable world around him, and every inch of it was a profound relief to him. Bill took in his bed, the little nest of monitors ready to be called upon should an emergency take place, his television and its remote-control device, the door to his spacious bathroom, the door to the hallway, as ever half-open. On the other side of his room lay the long window, now curtained for the sake of the night's sleep. And here, above all, was Molly, a one-woman Reality Principle, exuding the rich odor of burning graves as she tried to cut off his circulation with a blood-pressure machine. The bulk and massivity of her upper arms suggested that Molly's own blood pressure would have to be read by means of some other technology, perhaps steam gauge. The whites of her eyes shone with a faint trace of pink, leading Bill to speculate for a moment of wild improbability whether the ferocious night nurse indulged in marijuana.

"You're doing well, Mr. Postman," she said. "Making good progress."

"I'm glad to hear it," he said. "When do you think I'll be able to go home?"

"That is for the doctors to decide, not me. You'll have to bring it up with them." From a pocket hidden beneath her swags and pouches, she produced a white paper cup half-filled with pills and capsules of varying sizes and colors. She thrust it at him. "Morning meds. Gulp them down like a good boy, now." Her other hand held out a small plastic bottle of Poland Spring water, the provenance of which reminded Messinger of what Chippie Traynor had said about Maine. Deep woods, roads without names . . .

He upended the cup over his mouth, opened the bottle of water, and managed to get all his pills down at the first try.

Molly whirled around to leave with her usual sense of having had more than enough of her time wasted by the likes of him, and was halfway to the door before he remembered something that had been on his mind for the past few days.

"I haven't seen the *Times* since I don't remember when," he said. "Could you please get me a copy? I wouldn't even mind one that's a couple of days old."

Molly gave him a long, measuring look, then nodded her head. "Because many of our people find them so upsetting, we tend not to get the newspapers up here. But I'll see if I can locate one for you." She moved ponderously to the door and paused to look back at him again just before she walked out. "By the way, from now on you and your friends will have to get along without Mr. Traynor's company."

"Why?" Bill asked. "What happened to him?"

"Mr. Traynor is . . . gone, sir."

"Chippie died, you mean? When did that happen?" With a shudder, he remembered the figure from his dream. The smell of rotting weeds and wet riverbank awakened within him, and he felt as if she were once again standing before him.

"Did I say he was dead? What I said was, he is . . . *gone*."

For reasons he could not identify, Bill Messinger did not go through the morning's rituals with his usual impatience. He felt slow-moving, reluctant to engage the day. In the shower, he seemed barely able to raise his arms. The water seemed brackish, and his soap all but refused to lather. The towels were stiff and thin, like the cheap towels he remembered from his youth. After he had succeeded in drying off at least most of the easily reachable parts of his body, he sat on his bed and listened to the breath laboring in and out of his body. Without his noticing, the handsome pin-striped suit had become as wrinkled and tired as he felt himself to be, and besides that he seemed to be out of clean shirts. He pulled a dirty one from the closet. His swollen feet took some time to ram into his black loafers.

Armored at last in the costume of great worldly success, Bill stepped out into the great corridor with a good measure of his old dispatch. He wished Max Baccarat had not called him a "jumped-up little fop" and a "damned little show pony" the other day, for he genuinely enjoyed good clothing, and it hurt him to think that others might take this simple pleasure, which after all did contain a moral element, as a sign of vanity. On the other hand, he should have thought twice before telling Max that he was a third-rate publisher and a sellout. Everybody knew that robe hadn't been a gift from Graham Greene, though. That myth represented nothing more than Max Baccarat's habit of portraying and presenting himself as an old-line publishing grandee, like Alfred Knopf.

The nursing station—what he liked to think of as "the command center"—was oddly understaffed this morning. In a landscape of empty desks and unattended computer monitors, Molly sat on a pair of stools she had placed side by side, frowning as ever down at some form she was obliged to work through. Bill nodded at her and received the nonresponse he had anticipated. Instead of turning left toward the Salon as he usually did, Bill decided to stroll over to the elevators and the cherry-wood desk where diplomatic, red-jacketed Mr. Singh guided newcomers past his display of Casablanca lilies, tea roses, and lupines. On his perambulations through the halls, he often passed through Mr. Singh's tiny realm, and he found the man a kindly, reassuring presence.

Today, though, Mr. Singh seemed not to be on duty, and the great glass vase had been removed from his desk. out of order signs had been taped to the elevators.

Feeling a vague sense of disquiet, Bill retraced his steps and walked past the side of the nursing station to embark upon the long corridor that led to the north-facing window. Max Baccarat's room lay down this corridor, and Bill thought he might pay a call on the old gent. He could apologize for the insults he had given him, and perhaps receive an apology in return. Twice, Baccarat had thrown the word "little" at him, and Bill's cheeks stung as if he had been slapped. About the story, or the memory, or whatever it had been, however, Bill intended to say nothing. He did not believe that he, Max, and Tony Flax had dreamed of the same bizarre set of events, nor that they had experienced these decidedly dreamlike events in youth. The illusion that they had done so had been inspired by proximity and daily contact. The world of Floor 21 was as hermetic as a prison.

He came to Max's room and knocked at the half-open door. There was no reply. "Max?" he called out. "Feel like having a visitor?"

In the absence of a reply, he thought that Max might be asleep. It would do no harm to check on his old acquaintance. How odd, it occurred to him, to think that he and Max had both had relations with little Edie Wheadle. And Tony Flax, too. And that she should have died on this floor, unknown to them! *There* was someone to whom he rightly could have apologized—at the end, he had treated her quite badly. She had been the sort of girl, he thought, who almost expected to be treated badly. But far from being an excuse, that was the opposite, an indictment.

Putting inconvenient Edie Wheadle out of his mind, Bill moved past the bathroom and the "reception" area into the room proper, there to find Max Baccarat not in bed as he had expected, but beyond it and seated in one of the low, slightly cantilevered chairs, which he had turned to face the window.

"Max?"

The old man did not acknowledge his presence in any way. Bill noticed that he was not wearing the splendid blue robe, only his white pajamas, and his feet were bare. Unless he had fallen asleep, he was staring at the window and appeared to have been doing so for some time. His silvery hair was mussed and stringy. As Bill approached, he took in the rigidity of Max's head and neck, the stiff tension in his shoulders. He came around the foot of the bed and at last saw the whole of the old man's body, stationed sideways to him as it faced the window. Max was gripping the arms of the chair and leaning forward. His mouth hung open, and his lips had been drawn back. His eyes, too, were open, hugely, as they stared straight ahead.

With a little thrill of anticipatory fear, Bill glanced at the window. What he saw, haze shot through with streaks of light, could hardly have brought Max Baccarat to this pitch. His face seemed rigid with terror. Then Bill realized that this had nothing to do with terror, and Max had suffered a great, paralyzing stroke. That was the explanation for the pathetic scene before him. He jumped to the side of the bed and pushed the call button for the nurse. When he did not get an immediate response, he pushed it again, twice, and held the button down for several seconds. Still no soft footsteps came from the corridor.

A folded copy of the *Times* lay on Max's bed, and with a sharp, almost painful sense of hunger for the million vast and minuscule dramas taking place outside Governor General, he realized that what he had said to Molly was no more than the literal truth: it seemed weeks since he had seen a newspaper. With the justification that Max would have no use for it, Bill snatched up the paper and felt, deep in the core of his being, a real greed for its contents—devouring the columns of print would be akin to gobbling up great bits of the world. He tucked the neat, folded package of the *Times* under his arm and left the room.

"Nurse," he called. It came to him that he had never learned the real name of the woman they called Molly Goldberg. "Hello? There's a man in trouble down here!"

He walked quickly down the hallway in what he perceived as a deep, unsettling silence. "Hello, nurse!" he called, at least in part to hear the sound of his own voice.

When Bill reached the deserted nurses' station, he rejected the impulse to say, "Where is everybody?" The Night Visitor no longer occupied her pair of stools, and the usual chiaroscuro had deepened into a murky darkness. It was though they had pulled the plugs and stolen away.

"I don't get this," Bill said. "*Doctors* might bail, but nurses don't."

He looked up and down the corridor and saw only a gray carpet and a row of half-open doors. Behind one of those doors sat Max Baccarat, who had once been something of a friend. Max was destroyed, Bill thought; damage so severe could not be repaired. Like a film of greasy dust, the sense descended upon him that he was wasting his time. If the doctors and nurses were elsewhere, as seemed the case, nothing could be done for Max until their return. Even after that, in all likelihood very little could be done for poor old Max. His heart failure had been a symptom of a wider systemic problem.

But still. He could not just walk away and ignore Max's plight. Messinger turned around and paced down the corridor to the door where the nameplate read ANTHONY FLAX. "Tony," he said. "Are you in there? I think Max had a stroke."

He rapped on the door and pushed it all the way open. Dreading what he might find, he walked into the room. "Tony?" He already knew the room was empty, and when he was able to see the bed, all was as he had expected: an empty bed, an empty chair, a blank television screen, and blinds pulled down to keep the day from entering.

Bill left Tony's room, turned left, then took the hallway that led past the Salon. A man in an unclean janitor's uniform, his back to Bill, was removing the Mapplethorpe photographs from the wall and loading them facedown onto a wheeled cart.

"What are you doing?" he asked.

The man in the janitor uniform looked over his shoulder and said, "I'm doing my job, that's what I'm doing." He had greasy hair, a low forehead, and an acne-scarred face with deep furrows in the cheeks.

"But why are you taking down those pictures?"

The man turned around to face him. He was strikingly ugly, and his ugliness seemed part of his intention, as if he had chosen it. "Gee, buddy, why do you suppose I'd do something like that? To upset *you*? Well, I'm sorry if you're upset, but you had nothing to do with this. They tell me to do stuff like this, I do it. End of story." He pushed his face forward, ready for the next step.

"Sorry," Bill said. "I understand completely. Have you seen a doctor or a nurse up here in the past few minutes? A man on the other side of the floor just had a stroke. He needs medical attention."

"Too bad, but I don't have anything to do with doctors. The man I deal with is my supervisor, and supervisors don't wear white coats, and they don't carry stethoscopes. Now if you'll excuse me, I'll be on my way."

"But I need a doctor!"

"You look okay to me," the man said, turning away. He took the last photograph from the wall and pushed his cart through the metal doors that marked the boundary of the realm ruled by Tess Corrigan, Molly Goldberg, and their colleagues. Bill followed him through, and instantly found himself in a functional, green-painted corridor lit by fluorescent lighting and lined with locked doors. The janitor pushed his trolley around a corner and disappeared.

"Is anybody here?" Bill's voice carried through the empty hallways. "A man here needs a doctor!"

The corridor he was in led to another, which led to another, which went past a small, deserted nurses' station and ended at a huge, flat door with a sign that said medical personnel only. Bill pushed at the door, but it was locked. He had the feeling that he could wander through these corridors for hours and find nothing but blank walls and locked doors. When he returned to the metal doors and pushed through to the private wing, relief flooded through him, making him feel light-headed.

The Salon invited him in—he wanted to sit down, he wanted to catch his breath and see if any of the little cakes had been set out yet. He had forgotten to order breakfast, and hunger was making him weak. Bill put his hand on one of the pebble-glass doors and saw an indistinct figure seated near the table. For a moment, his heart felt cold, and he hesitated before he opened the door.

Tony Flax was bent over in his chair, and what Bill Messinger noticed first was that the critic was wearing one of the thin hospital gowns that tied at the neck and the back. His trench coat lay puddled on the floor. Then he saw that Flax appeared to be weeping. His hands were clasped to his face, and his back rose and fell with jerky, uncontrolled movements.

"Tony?" he said. "What happened to you?"

Flax continued to weep silently, with the concentration and selfishness of a small child.

"Can I help you, Tony?" Bill asked.

When Flax did not respond, Bill looked around the room for the source of his distress. Half-filled coffee cups stood on the little tables, and petits fours lay jumbled and scattered over the plates and the white table. As he watched, a cockroach nearly two inches long burrowed out of a little square of white chocolate and disappeared around the back of a Battenburg cake. The cockroach looked as shiny and polished as a new pair of black shoes.

Something was moving on the other side of the window, but Bill Messinger wanted nothing to do with it. "Tony," he said, "I'll be in my room."

Down the corridor he went, the tails of his suit jacket flapping behind him. A heavy, liquid pressure built up in his chest, and the lights seemed to darken, then grow brighter again. He remembered Max, his mind gone, staring openmouthed at his window: what had he seen?

Bill thought of Chippie Traynor, one of his molelike eyes bloodied behind the shattered lens of his glasses.

At the entrance to his room, he hesitated once again as he had outside the Salon, fearing that if he went in, he might not be alone. But of course he would be alone, for apart from the janitor no one else on Floor 21 was capable of movement. Slowly, making as little noise as possible, he slipped around his door and entered his room. It looked exactly as it had when he had awakened that morning. The younger author's book lay discarded on his bed, the monitors awaited an emergency, the blinds covered the long window. Bill thought the wildly alternating pattern of light and dark that moved across the blinds proved nothing. Freaky New York weather, you never knew what it was going to do. He did not hear odd noises, like half-remembered voices, calling to him from the other side of the glass.

As he moved nearer to the foot of the bed, he saw on the floor the bright jacket of the book he had decided not to read, and knew that in the night it had fallen from his movable tray. The book on his bed had no jacket, and at first he had no idea where it came from. When he remembered the circumstances under which he had seen this book—or one a great deal like it—he felt revulsion, as though it were a great slug.

Bill turned his back on the bed, swung his chair around, and plucked the newspaper from under his arm. After he had scanned the headlines without making much effort to take them in, habit led him to the obituaries on the last two pages of the financial section. As soon as he had folded the pages back, a photograph of a sly, mild face with a recessed chin and tiny spectacles lurking above an overgrown nose levitated up from the columns of newsprint. The header announced charles chipp traynor, popular war historian, tarred by scandal.

Helplessly, Bill read the first paragraph of Chippie's obituary. Four days past, this once-renowned historian whose career had been destroyed by charges of plagiarism and fraud had committed suicide by leaping from the window of his fifteenth-story apartment on the Upper West Side.

Four days ago? Bill thought. It seemed to him that was when Chippie Traynor had first appeared in the Salon. He dropped the paper, with the effect that Traynor's fleshy nose and mild eyes peered up at him from the floor. The terrible little man seemed to be everywhere, despite having *gone*. He could sense Chippie Traynor floating outside his window like a small, inoffensive balloon from Macy's Thanksgiving Day Parade. Children would say, "Who's that?" and their parents would look up, shield their eyes, shrug, and say, "I don't know, hon. Wasn't he in a Disney cartoon?" Only he was not in a Disney cartoon, and the children and their parents could not see him, and he wasn't at all cute. One of his eyes had been injured. This Chippie Traynor, not the one that had given them a view of his backside in the Salon, hovered outside Bill Messinger's window, whispering the wretched and insinuating secrets of the despised, the contemptible, the rejected and fallen from grace.

Bill turned from the window and took a single step into the nowhere that awaited him. He had nowhere to go, he knew, so nowhere had to be where he was going. It was probably going to be a lot like this place, only less comfortable. Much, *much* less comfortable. With nowhere to go, he reached out his hand and picked up the dull brown book lying at the foot of his bed. Bringing it toward his body felt like reeling in some monstrous fish that struggled against the line. There were faint watermarks on the front cover, and it bore a faint, familiar smell. When he had it within reading distance, Bill turned the spine up and read the title and author's name: *In the Middle of the Trenches*, by Charles Chipp Traynor. It was the book he had blurbed. Max Baccarat had published it, and Tony Flax had rhapsodized over it in the Sunday *Times* book review section. About a hundred pages from the end, a bookmark in the shape of a thin silver cord with a hook at one end protruded from the top of the book.

Bill opened the book at the place indicated, and the slender bookmark slithered downward like a living thing. Then the hook caught the top of the pages, and its length hung shining and swaying over the bottom edge. No longer able to resist, Bill read some random sentences, then two long paragraphs. This section undoubtedly had been lifted from the oral histories, and it recounted an odd event in the life of a young man who, years before his induction into the armed forces, had come upon a strange house deep in the piney woods of East Texas and been so unsettled by what he had seen through its windows that he brought a rifle with him on his next visit. Bill realized that he had never read this part of the book. In fact, he had written his blurb after merely skimming through the first two chapters. He thought Max had read even less of the book than he had. In a hurry to meet his deadline, Tony Flax had probably read the first half.

At the end of his account, the former soldier said, "In the many times over the years when I thought about this incident, it always seemed to me that the man I shot was myself. It seemed my own eye I had destroyed, my own socket that bled."

ABOUT THE CONTRIBUTORS

Among **MARGARET ATWOOD'S** novels are *The Handmaid's Tale*, *Alias Grace*, *The Blind Assassin*, and *Oryx and Crake*. She lives in Toronto.

POPPY Z. BRITE is the author of seven novels and three short-story collections. Early in her career she was known for her horror fiction, but at present she is working on a series of novels and short stories set in the New Orleans restaurant world. These also involve the Stubbs family characters who appear in "The Devil of Delery Street." Her novel *Liquor* was recently published by Three Rivers Press, and her follow-up, *Prime*, will be released in 2005. She lives in New Orleans with her husband, Chris, a chef.

MICHAEL CHABON lives in Berkeley. He served as guest editor for the tenth issue of *McSweeney's*.

CHARLES D'AMBROSIO is the author of *The Point and Other Stories* and *The Dead Fish Museum*, forthcoming from Knopf. His recent plotless stories have appeared in *The New Yorker*, usually without any moment of truth, although he's still trying. He lives in Portland, Oregon.

RODDY DOYLE lives and works in Dublin. His books include *Paddy Clarke Ha Ha Ha*, *The Woman Who Walked into Doors*, *A Star Called Henry*, and, most recently, *Oh, Play That Thing*.

STEVE ERICKSON is the author of *Our Ecstatic Days*, which will be published in February 2005 by Simon & Schuster, and six previous novels, including *Days Between Stations* and *Tours of the Black Clock*. Erickson is the film critic for *Los Angeles* magazine and the editor of *Black Clock*, which is published semiannually by CalArts, where he teaches writing.

DANIEL HANDLER is the author of two novels under his own name, and (allegedly) twelve books under the name Lemony Snicket.

HEIDI JULAVITS is the author of two novels, *The Effect of Living Backwards* and *The Mineral Palace* (Putnam), as well as *Hotel Andromeda* (Artspace), a collaborative book with the artist Jenny Gage. She is a founding coeditor of *The Believer*.

STEPHEN KING was born in 1947 and grew up in rural Maine. For the last thirty years he has written novels, beginning with *Carrie* (1974) and ending with *Song of Susannah* and *The Dark Tower* (both 2004), the concluding novels of his Dark Tower cycle. He has promised to retire, but "Lisey and the Madman" is from what may eventually be a new novel called *Lisey's Story*. In his own defense, King points out that all novelists lie—sometimes to others, almost constantly to themselves.

JONATHAN LETHEM is the author of *The Fortress of Solitude* and five other novels. He lives in Brooklyn and Maine.

CHINA MIÉVILLE'S novels include *Perdido Street Station, The Scar*, and, most recently, *Iron Council*. He is a winner of the Arthur C. Clarke and British Fantasy Awards. He lives and works in London.

Although he began working as a professional comic book artist in the early 1980s, **MIKE MIGNOLA** is best known as the award-winning creator/writer/artist of *Hellboy*. He was also a production designer on the Disney film *Atlantis: The Lost Empire* and visual consultant to Guillermo del Toro on both *Blade 2* and the film version of *Hellboy*. Mignola lives in New York City with his wife and daughter.

DAVID MITCHELL'S first novel, *Ghostwritten*, appeared in 1999 and was awarded the John Llewellyn-Rhys Prize. His second novel, *Number9dream*, was shortlisted for the Booker Prize in 2001, and his third, *Cloud Atlas*, was published in 2004. He spent eight years in Hiroshima, Japan, and currently lives with his wife and daughter in West Cork, Ireland.

JOYCE CAROL OATES is the author of numerous works of gothic fiction, including the novels *Bellefleur* and *Mysteries of Winterthrun* and the story collections *Haunted: Tales of the Grotesque* and *The Collector of Hearts*. She recently edited *Tales of H. P. Lovecraft* (Ecco).

JASON ROBERTS lives in northern California. He is the author of the forthcoming *The Gentleman in the Distance* (Fourth Estate/HarperCollins), an examination of the life of James Holman (1786–1857), the blind man who became history's greatest traveler. Mr. Roberts's previous publications include three books on technology and one that was, at least in part, about shaving and campfires.

PETER STRAUB is the author of sixteen novels, which have been translated into more than twenty languages. They include *Ghost Story, Koko, Mr. X*, two collaborations with Stephen King, *The Tal-*

isman and *Black House*, and his most recent *lost boy lost girl*. He has written two volumes of poetry and two collections of short fiction. He has won the British Fantasy Award, four Bram Stoker Awards, two International Horror Guild Awards, and two World Fantasy Awards. In 1998, he was named grand master at the World Horror Convention. He is currently at work on his seventeenth novel, *In the Night Room*.

AYELET WALDMAN is the author of *Daughter's Keeper* and of a series of murder mysteries. She lives in Berkeley.

THIS BOOK BENEFITS
826 VALENCIA

Open since April of 2002, 826 Valencia is a writing lab disguised as a pirate-supply store, dedicated to helping students with their writing skills. It's our belief that students can benefit greatly from one-on-one assistance, and we've had more than five hundred volunteers devote themselves to the students, from grades K through 12, who come in every day. With rising class sizes, overburdened schools sometimes struggle to give all of their students the individualized attention they need. Under the supervision of Bay Area teachers, the tutors at 826 Valencia help bridge the gap.

Our volunteers include published authors, magazine founders, SAT course instructors, documentary filmmakers, graduate students, and all kinds of professionals who do everything from after-school homework help to evening and weekend workshops—covering everything from SAT prep to playwriting to digital filmmaking to broadcast journalism. And given that many public schools have had to cut their school-publication budgets, 826 Valencia helps schools and young authors design, edit, print, bind, and self-publish their own newspapers, literary magazines, and books. This spring, in collaboration with the Isabel Allende Foundation, we published *Waiting to Be Heard*, an amazing collection of essays by students at Thurgood Marshall High School.

Two or three times a week, we welcome entire classes in for field trips, a morning of storytelling or bookmaking, or a custom-designed curriculum on a subject a class has been studying. And because our own space is small and the need for tutors is great, we work with thousands of students in their own classrooms by sending tutors, platoons of them, into public schools, to assist teachers for as long as needed.

To this end—engaging students in their classrooms—last fall we established a permanent space at Everett Middle School, a Writers' Room where students can receive one-on-one feedback on their work from our trained tutors; this year, we'll open another, at Horace Mann Middle School. In 2003, we worked with over 6,000 students—more than 10 percent of the San Francisco Unified School District.

We also grant two scholarships a year, of $10,000 each, to graduating seniors from public schools. In addition, each month we present the 826 Valencia Teacher of the Month Award, a $1,500 prize honoring an exceptional local teacher. And, of course, we run a storefront selling nautical brigandage supplies—lard, hooks, mops—to full-time pirates and aspiring buccaneers.

Though *McSweeney's* takes care of most of the costs of running 826, we can always use more help, and this collection, co-published with Vintage Books, is providing a needed boost. For more information, please visit www.826Valencia.org, or come see us in San Francisco, on Valencia Street, between 19th and 20th—or, by the time you read this, at our new center in Brooklyn, 826NYC (www.826NYC.org) at 372 5th Avenue in Park Slope.

McSWEENEY'S MAMMOTH TREASURY
OF THRILLING TALES

Edited and with an Introduction by Michael Chabon

From Pulitzer prize winner Michael Chabon and the editors of the iconoclastic magazine *McSweeney's* comes a wildly entertaining collection of never-before-published stories.

McSweeney's Mammoth Treasury of Thrilling Tales offers an original and modern take on an old tradition of storytelling. From Nick Hornby's "Otherwise Pandemonium," a science fiction foray into the *Twilight Zone*, to Michael Crichton's "Blood Doesn't Come Out," written in the style of hard-boiled detective fiction, here are America's most popular and innovative writers reinventing the genres they love. This collection also includes stories by Elmore Leonard, Jim Shepard, Glen David Gold, Dan Chaon, Kelly Link, Carol Emshwiller, Neil Gaiman, Stephen King, Laurie King, Chris Offutt, Dave Eggers, Michael Moorcock, Aimee Bender, Sherman Alexie, Harlan Ellison, Karen Joy Fowler, Rick Moody, and Michael Chabon.

Fiction/Anthology/1-4000-3339-X